OVERWHELMING FORCE

BOOK 5 IN THE WAR PLANNERS SERIES

ANDREW WATTS

POINT WHISKEY PUBLISHING

ALSO BY ANDREW WATTS

The War Planners Series

The War Planners

The War Stage

Pawns of the Pacific

The Elephant Game

Overwhelming Force

Max Fend Series

Glidepath

The Oshkosh Connection

Books available for Kindle, print, and audiobook. To find out more about the books or Andrew Watts, go to andrewwattsauthor.com.

Shall we expect some transatlantic military giant, to step the Ocean, and crush us at a blow? Never! All the armies of Europe, Asia and Africa combined, with all the treasure of the earth (our own excepted) in their military chest; with a Buonaparte for a commander, could not by force, take a drink from the Ohio, or make a track on the Blue Ridge, in a trial of a thousand years.

— ABRAHAM LINCOLN

There are not enough Indians in the world to defeat the Seventh Cavalry.

— GEORGE ARMSTRONG CUSTER

1

"When did this happen?" The president's eyes twitched with fatigue as he read the update on his secure tablet. He frowned and handed it back to his chief of staff.

"Twenty minutes ago, Mr. President."

They walked quickly through the second-floor hallway of the West Wing. It was late. Past midnight. But no one would be getting any sleep tonight.

"And we're sure about this? There's no way this is a mistake? A military drill? Communications mix-up? Anything?"

"I'm afraid not, sir."

"North Korea invading the south. Son of a bitch, I can't believe they actually did it. Why now?"

Two Secret Service agents escorted them into an elevator. They plunged down several levels below the earth's surface. President Griffin arrived in PEOC a few moments later.

The Presidential Emergency Operations Center was alive and bustling. Filled with senior national security staff who had for weeks been warning him of an impending crisis in Asia. The military officers and career defense officials looked like the president felt: tired.

And worried.

"What's the latest?"

"Sir, in the past few minutes we've received word that US military assets near Japan have been attacked by air strike. Various reports of satellite and electronics outages. We're attempting to get updates, but most communications are disrupted."

"Japan?" President Griffin frowned. "Why would...?"

One of the military officers in the room looked up from his laptop. "General, Thule is down."

"Thule?"

The officer nodded. "Just happened. STRATCOM is trying tertiary methods of comms now, but...they say their satellite-based detection systems aren't responding either. This information is about two minutes time-late."

The president's chief of staff whispered, "They're referring to ICBM early-warning systems. The Air Force has a base in Greenland—Thule. Between that base, a few others, and the satellite sensors, it's how we would know of a nuclear missile launch."

President Griffin watched the general who had been receiving this information. His eyes widened a bit. He stood up, checked his watch, and then nodded to the Secret Service agent standing in the corner of the room. The general cleared his throat and said, "SUNSET."

The president was trying to shake the cobwebs off, wondering what the hell SUNSET meant, when the already-active room spun into overdrive. The Secret Service agents nearest the president each left their statuesque position near the wall and rapidly walked towards him.

"Mr. President, we need to evacuate you from the White House immediately." One of the Secret Service agents physically pulled the president from his seat and stood him up, walking him towards the door.

The president said, "The First Lady—"

"She'll be evacuated as well, sir. We're at SUNSET."

The president was rushed out of the room and up through a maze of stairs and hallways, with Secret Service agents spaced out along the way.

"Let's go!" one of them called, eyes wide with adrenaline.

The next thing the president knew, he was heading towards the underground parking garage where the Secret Service kept its vehicles. The military officer who carried "the Football" had appeared and was now walking just behind him, looking tense.

The Football.

SUNSET.

SUNSET was the code word for one of the doomsday evacuation scenarios. While they had made him train for these situations, the president honestly couldn't remember which one SUNSET referred to. It hadn't seemed important at the time. Those national security drills were just a part of the job. Like a fire drill. An annoyance to be minimized in duration so that he could get back to the real meat of running the country.

"Which one is SUNSET?" the president asked the military man.

"Strategic attack on the continental United States. Missiles inbound." The colonel's voice was without fear or judgment. The latter would come from God, it seemed. The president suddenly felt dizzy. The thought occurred to him that he should not have had that third scotch this evening. He wasn't supposed to drink with the blood pressure meds he was taking. Another thing that hadn't seemed important until now.

"Who's firing on us?" The president breathed heavily as he spoke. If a missile didn't kill him, trying to keep up with these young Secret Service agents might.

The military aide responded, "I don't have that information, sir."

"And they're firing at Washington?"

"We don't know yet, sir. STRATCOM will give us an update soon."

The president, his security detail, and the national security entourage made their way to the end of a long well-lit tunnel. President Griffin had transited several of the secret tunnels underneath Washington, but he'd never been in this particular one. A set of double doors swung open ahead of them at the end of the tunnel. They walked through the doors and into an underground parking garage.

A column of dark SUVs stood with their engines humming, doors open. Two dozen Secret Service agents, weapons at the ready, stood at various locations along the garage driveway, scanning for threats and listening carefully for any commands coming from their earpieces.

President Griffin ducked into The Beast, the armored presidential limousine. The doors slammed shut and the train of vehicles accelerated forward.

"You're sure my wife will be evacuated?" he asked the agent in the passenger seat.

"She's being taken out of the area now, Mr. President."

Wheels squealed through the sharp turns. The cars made their way up the ramp and onto the street in seconds. The president noted the face of one of the agents at the entrance as his car zoomed past. He had the oddest expression on his face: relief. *My God, if there really are missiles inbound...*they were leaving all of these men behind. The thought didn't fit with the expression the agent wore.

SUNSET. Each of the agents would have heard the term in their earpiece and known what it meant. Doomsday. A high probability of nuclear-tipped missiles headed inbound towards their location. How long would they have? Thirty minutes? Yet this agent was relieved. For a moment, President Griffin couldn't understand why. Then it occurred to him. The agent was relieved that his part of the job had been accomplished. Whether he lived or not.

"We'll be at Air Force One within two minutes, Mr. President. The rest of your national security team will meet us there. We'll evacuate to a secure location, away from any...from any potential target zones."

"The vice president?"

"He's being moved to a secure location."

"What are DNI and State saying about this?"

"Sir, this just happened. We haven't yet had time..."

There were two military men in the SUV. One monitored communications equipment. The other officer was the carrier of the Football—the bulky black apocalypse suitcase resting comfortably on his lap.

The officer manning the communications equipment was now wearing a headset, relaying information in a monotonous voice as if he were a computer program. "Nightwatch is airborne." Pause. "We're now at DEFCON 2." Pause. "Confirmation that Guam is under attack." Pause. He looked up at the president. "Mr. President, a National Event Conference has been activated and the National Military Command Center will be in communication with you shortly." The NMCC was the Pentagon's command and communication center for the National Command Authority. They were the ones that generated emergency action messages to the nuclear triad and to commanders in the field.

The president felt like he was in the middle of taking a test that he hadn't studied for. He kept hearing terms that he didn't recognize. And this damn kid in a uniform was talking so fast. *What the hell is Nightwatch?*

The military officer manning the communications console said, "Pentagon is up on secure UHF. The deputy director for operations' ETA is sixty seconds."

Their vehicle continued to bounce and swerve along the empty streets of D.C., racing east, the leader of the free world feeling clueless as he fled to safety.

For a brief moment, everything was quiet, and the president was alone with his thoughts. President Griffin was glad for this momentary reprieve. His pulse still raced from the physical exertions of his evacuation. He glanced out the tinted window, rubbing his eyes. Damn, he was tired. Floodlights lit up the Washington Monument, the clear night sky a dark backdrop. Would there be missiles streaking through that sky soon? Was he cut out to be a wartime president?

War.

War on an unimaginable scale. War that could begin and end with the flash of thousands of nuclear detonations. Or a conventional war that dragged on, transforming the entire globe into a muddy and bloody battlefield, ruining economies, and decimating a generation of lives.

God, let this madness come to an end.

The last time the world had been this close to a world war had been the Cuban Missile Crisis. Cooler heads had prevailed then. The president tried to convince himself that they would again.

But for this madman in China.

Cheng Jinshan. The newly installed Chinese president. Self-made billionaire and former Chinese intelligence official.

During President Griffin's daily briefing a few months ago, the CIA's analysts had painted a formidable yet frightening portrait of the man. A brilliant businessman. A master spy. A cunning strategist. He was an enigma. Unpredictable, and harboring a ruthless ambition.

It was only a few weeks ago that Cheng Jinshan had been in a Chinese prison for crimes against the state. He, along with a cadre of Chinese military, intelligence, and political leaders, had conspired to overthrow their government and, soon after, attack the United States. But the CIA had discovered the plot, resulting in a small naval battle in the Eastern Pacific Ocean.

Until then, Jinshan had kept the plans hidden from the former Chinese president and any leaders who were not in his inner circle. His rebellion had yet to be executed, and American intervention had exposed the plot to the former Chinese leader. The coup had been stopped, and for a brief time, with Jinshan behind bars, the world was once again at peace.

Then the former Chinese president had been assassinated. Chinese state media claimed it was a religiously motivated attack. The masked men had executed the Chinese leader, along with his wife and daughter, and live-streamed it over the internet.

The Chinese president and his wife's cause of death was hard to determine. It was either asphyxiation from hanging, or burning to death *while* hanging. Then, with billions of people watching around the world, their teenage daughter had been shot in the head.

The event had occurred on the rooftop garden of their Beijing penthouse. Cameras from nearby skyscrapers and news helicopters had caught the whole thing. The executioners had worn masks while on camera and had supposedly been killed by Chinese police immediately after the assassination.

One of the attackers had been ID'd as an American citizen. Some lunatic religious extremist. One of those guys with a loudspeaker and a sign around his neck, standing at the street corner. Chinese state media released videos the man had made, calling for the death of Chinese political leadership.

A horrific killing of the Chinese president and his family, on live TV, blamed on a US religious fanatic. But the Chinese populace wasn't being told he was a *fanatic*. They were led to believe that this was the new normal in the United States. That Americans' views were becoming radically anti-Chinese, inspired by religion. President Griffin knew that was untrue. But fighting a government-sponsored propaganda machine in a state like China was impossible.

The CIA believed the assassination to be a ruse, carefully orchestrated to maximize the emotional impact to the Chinese populace. The deaths themselves weren't faked. They were very real. But there was no way some aged Midwestern religious fanatic who spoke no Chinese and had no military training had been able to fly to China, get past the Chinese president's security detail, and do what he had supposedly done.

So who *had* done it?

According to US intelligence, Cheng Jinshan and his allies.

After the Chinese president had been killed, Cheng Jinshan had pulled off a political resurrection. He had vanquished his rivals and consolidated power within a matter of days. Anti-American policies had been enacted, and Chinese military readiness had never been so high.

State-sponsored media fanned the flames of civil unrest. Hate and angst directed at countries that promoted religious freedom, and at America specifically. The CIA analysts guessed that the religious angle was just a convenient fuel for the fire. Jinshan was not motivated by religion or hatred of it. But he needed an excuse to create anti-American loathing among the Chinese people. Propaganda soon began flooding onto Chinese social media and TV, all carefully curated by 3PLA. Jinshan's cyberwarriors.

And now, it seemed, Jinshan was finally able to execute his plans.

"Mr. President, you're on the line with the National Military Command Center. The Pentagon's deputy director of operations, General Rice, is speaking."

"Mr. President, this is General Rice, can you hear me?"

"Yes, General. What's happened?"

"Sir, we now have reports of large-scale attacks on multiple US bases in Korea and Japan, as well as Naval and Air Force assets in the Western Pacific region." President Griffin thought the general sounded shaken. "Mr. President, an ICBM launch alert was also just issued by NORAD."

"What does that mean, General? Are we under nuclear attack?"

Another voice over the speakerphone. "Mr. President, this is General Sprague at STRATCOM. I'm on board *Nightwatch*."

The president remembered what *Nightwatch* was now. It was the other Boeing 747 that the Air Force operated in conjunction with Air Force One, as a second mobile command center. The doomsday machine, there to pick up the reins in a flash in case Air Force One became "unavailable" in a different type of flash. President Griffin remembered smiling at the idea of such a plane when he'd first heard it. The term *doomsday machine* had sounded darkly comical then. Certainly unnecessary. Some silly holdover from the Cold War, never to be used.

How his mind had changed this evening.

General Sprague said, "Sir, our ability to detect and track nuclear threats has been diminished. We've lost our entire Space-Based Infrared System and eighty percent of our DSP birds. They were hit simultaneously during the past thirty minutes."

The president felt his face flush. "Now hold on just a second. I thought we didn't even have satellite capability, after last month's cyberattacks? How can we be so sure of all of this?"

The national security advisor said, "NRO and the Air Force have relaunched several reconnaissance birds to get our Defense Support Program back up since then. The new satellites have updated software. It's been a top priority. Our detection systems were in place today."

"Who fired, General?"

"We received initial indications of ballistic missile launches in the vicinity of North Hamgyong and Chagang provinces—"

The president said, "Where the hell is that? Can somebody please—"

"North Korea, sir," replied General Rice.

"So the North Koreans are attacking us?"

"We don't know for certain. The data is still coming in. It was shortly after the North Korean missile launch indications that our ballistic missile detection systems came under attack. For a short period, we were still able to get partial launch detection data. It was at this time that we saw several additional launch indications. That second set of missile launches did *not*, I repeat, *not* originate from North Korea."

"More missiles? Then where—"

"The second wave of missile launches originated from the Russo-Chinese border. Where the North Korean missile launches were small in number, the second wave of launches was more substantial."

"Where are those missiles headed?"

"We don't know, sir. We're attempting to get more data now."

The national security advisor swore. "This is completely unsatisfactory! Those missiles could be headed this way. We need to consider launching our own strike."

The president motioned for him to calm down. "Easy, now. We need to know who our enemy is first."

A voice on the phone said, "Sir, this is the CIA director. The North Koreans are incapable of pulling off the level of military activity we're seeing in the Western Pacific right now. These attacks are occurring over a very large geography, consistent with PLA and PLA Navy asset locations. Mr. President, I think we should consider this a Chinese military action. Possibly done in collaboration with the North Koreans."

General Rice said, "The Russians could be involved as well. We can't rule that out, based on where the second set of missile launches was detected."

General Sprague said, "It's possible that the second set of missiles was launched at North Korea, or a variety of other targets, sir. We simply don't know."

The national security advisor said, "But we're being attacked by conventional means at locations throughout the Pacific! Surely we have to take that into consideration here. For God's sake, let's use our heads."

Several voices began talking all at once, both in the presidential vehicle and over the phone.

The president quieted them with a question. "General Sprague, why don't we have a better picture of what's happening right now?"

General Sprague said, "Mr. President, less than thirty minutes ago, all of our data and communications with Thule and Pine Gap went offline. I don't want to speculate, Mr. President, but they may have been attacked. At about the same time, several antisatellite weapons began destroying the majority of our early-warning birds circulating the globe."

The president blew out a slow breath, then said quietly, "How is that possible?"

"They used different techniques, Mr. President. We believe the attacks were primarily space-based. They must have pre-positioned their own satellites near ours, in the same orbital plane. They likely used models that act like motherships, filled with smaller satellite craft. Those smaller satellites are sent out to attack ours, and most explode like mines when they come into contact with our satellites. Some of their weapons have lasers or mechanisms that will impair or destroy our sensors. These antisatellite weapons are very hard to detect, until it's too late."

"And you're telling me that the Chinese have destroyed all of the satellites—"

"Mr. President, without more evidence, I can't tell you with certainty that it *was* the Chinese."

"Now what the hell is that supposed to mean? You just said—"

"Sir, the Russians also have this capability. We should also not rule out the possibility that China and Russia have made an alliance and are both acting against us. Or that one is spoofing us into thinking that the other is acting. Until we know more..."

President Griffin felt his throat constrict. He closed his eyes, a searing migraine starting to form.

His chief of staff said, "Are you alright, Mr. President?"

He opened his eyes. "Yes. Yes, I'm fine."

The president's body jerked as the vehicle turned sharply. They were now turning into Joint Base Andrews.

The general said, "Some communications lines are being restored. The updates are coming in pretty fast now. We now have confirmation from Pacific Command. US military units are engaged in combat operations with Chinese and North Korean personnel, on multiple fronts. We have just received reports of attacks on US bases...uh...wait one..." The general sounded like he was reading the reports in his hands. "There seems to be some confusion here, sir. These bases are INCONUS. Sir, I'll need to reverify that. This says that Dover has been hit. That can't be right." The general's voice became muffled as he spoke to one of his subordinates off the phone. The president heard him say, "You're sure?" Then the general's voice became clear. "Mr. President, I stand corrected. The information on the domestic base attack appears to be accurate. And we now have a report of a second domestic military base being attacked in Texas."

The president and his chief of staff looked at each other in shock.

"Define *attacked*, General. What the hell is going on? Who the hell is attacking us *inside* the US?"

"Sir..." There was a delay as he spoke to someone next to him. "Sir, we're still evaluating the information that's coming to us, but it appears that a ground force, strength unknown, is attacking US Air Force bases inside the continental US."

"A *ground* force? *Inside* the US? This is in addition to attacks on our Pacific military bases?"

"That's correct. Yes, sir. I'm now being told that these attacks were by small groups of soldiers. Again, Mr. President, this is all very early. Preliminary information—"

"I understand. What do you know?"

"Stand by."

There was a momentary silence, followed by General Rice saying, "Mr. President, we have reports of several...as far as we can tell, *Chinese* special operations teams have attacked some of our INCONUS Air Force bases."

"When did this happen?"

"All in the past half hour, sir."

"My God..."

"Yes, sir. I think we should consider this a full-scale attack on the United States. This isn't limited to the Pacific Theater."

"Sir, I'm being told that they hit a specific group of Air Force bases throughout the country. We think they're trying to target our aerial refueling aircraft."

"Why?"

The national security advisor answered. "Mr. President, if they can disrupt our ability to refuel aircraft in flight, they greatly reduce our ability to wage long-range aerial warfare."

The president said, "Are these attacks ongoing?"

"No, sir, they appear to be put down. It's too early to say with any confidence, but initial reports are that dozens of Air Force tankers were damaged or destroyed. Possibly more than one hundred."

"Is that a lot?"

"It's a lot, sir."

General Sprague said, "Sir, I need to interrupt. We have another developing situation on the US Pacific coast. In the past thirty minutes, we have rerouted all commercial aircraft to land at non-US divert fields. But some of those commercial aircraft are still headed into the US, and they are unresponsive to communications. NORAD has informed us of some irregularities among these commercial aircraft—"

"What irregularities?"

"Sir, we now believe some of them may actually be Chinese military transports. It looks like they are over Canadian airspace right now."

The president opened his eyes, his face white. "What?"

The national security advisor said, "Sir, we've seen intelligence reports that this type of thing was included in Chinese war plans. Our interceptors will challenge them. If they don't respond correctly, they will be shot down. General, please keep us apprised."

"Yes, sir."

The national security advisor's voice came over the phone. "Let's focus on the bigger picture. If we have ballistic missiles inbound, we will need to consider a strike on the attacking nation's strategic missile sites, as well as any known nuclear ballistic missile submarines."

The president's chief of staff, sitting beside him in the car, frowned, shaking his head. "What kind of a strike? Tell me you aren't proposing what I think you are."

"We need our own nuclear response. That's what is called for in these situations."

"In *these* situations? How many of *these situations* have you seen? *None of us* has ever seen this before."

"Which is exactly why we have protocol. We have preplanned responses for—"

"Oh, don't give me that bullshit, Tom. Are you insane? Unless I'm mistaken, we know very little with any certainty right now. So you want to fire nuclear weapons? At *who*, precisely? China? North Korea? *Russia*? We don't even know for sure which side of the border that second launch came from. We don't know how many missiles are in the air. And if there are any, we don't know where the hell they're headed."

The president watched as his chief of staff fumed into the car's speakerphone. He made a good point, the president thought.

The comms was silent for a moment. Then STRATCOM's General Sprague said, "We do have some solid data. And we're getting more in every minute. I'm reading now that from our infrared cameras on the DSP satellites, before they were destroyed, Cheyenne Mountain observed a total of twenty-four objects in the first wave of launches. These were likely launched from North Korea, and the objects had an initial projected trajectory and speed consistent with ICBMs, heading over the Arctic circle. Exact target undetermined. Per our preplanned response, we activated our own ballistic missile defense units in Asia as soon as they launched."

The president nearly shouted. "What do you mean? Are you

saying that we fired back? We fired nuclear weapons already? Without my authorization?"

General Sprague said, "No, sir. *Defensive* measures only. This was ballistic missile defense. Surface-to-air missiles, if you will, launched from Korea and Japan."

The president grumbled. "I see." He felt like he was trapped in a nightmare, unable to control his destiny, and knowing that it was getting worse.

The national security advisor said, "What were the results of the defensive measures, General Sprague?"

"We believe at least a dozen of the objects were shot down, although it could be as many as twenty. We believe that at least four are still airborne. It's hard to say without all of our sensors operational, sir."

"So it's only four?" said the chief of staff, sitting in the car next to the president. "That doesn't sound so bad."

The president shook his head, dumbfounded. "What the hell does that mean? Four are airborne? We didn't get them all? What, did we miss or something?"

The general sounded frustrated. "Sir, those numbers are spectacular compared to our tests. Ballistic missile defense is not perfect."

"Well, excuse me, General, but I would think that's precisely the kind of thing that *should* be perfect."

"Mr. President, this means several ballistic missiles have headed north over the Arctic, but their exact targets are unknown. As we said, our ballistic detection network has been attacked. We don't know exactly how many missiles are up there, or where they're going."

"Well, where the hell do you *think* they will hit?"

Another barrage of voices, speaking over each other.

The secretary of defense said, "Sir, we need to activate our response."

"But if North Korea fired that many missiles, that means they expended everything they had. Hell, those things are likely not even going to work."

"...could hit California or somewhere on the West Coast..."

"...some of the Chinese models could reach as far as the eastern sector of the United States."

The Secret Service agent in the front of the vehicle called out, "One minute until arrival." They were almost at Air Force One.

General Rice said, "Sir, I don't see a nuclear strike on North Korea as beneficial to us. They likely expended their entire nuclear arsenal. But this second wave of missiles worries me. If China and North Korea are acting in concert, the North Korean missiles could have been meant as a diversion tactic. Perhaps to get us to delay long enough for Chinese antisatellite weapons to be used, masking the real attack."

"Couldn't Russia have done that too?"

The CIA director's voice came on the phone. "Sir, ties between Russia and North Korea aren't as strong. And the geopolitical climate doesn't suggest Russia would do something like this. China, on the other hand, has been quite belligerent of late."

The national security advisor said, "I agree. This is Jinshan. Mr. President, we know this."

The president said, "Gentlemen, we can't be wrong."

The national security advisor said, "Sir, respectfully, we also can't delay. Our military is now engaged in conventional combat operations throughout the Western Pacific, with China. We must assume that China launched ICBMs in that second wave of missile launches. Even if we discount the fact that we are already fighting the Chinese in the Pacific, there are only two countries that have the capability to attack our nuclear attack detection mechanisms. Again, Russia and China. But Jinshan is a known threat. He has made moves to harm our country already. This isn't hard. Sir, the facts support the case that this is China. We need to strike at them before it's too late."

The president leaned back into the cushion of his seat. He was exhausted and not thinking clearly. "General Rice? Do you agree?"

The general said, "They have taken out our early-warning sensors, and our ability to track the ballistic objects. This is the type of thing you would do if you were about to attack with ICBMs. Yes, sir. I agree. It's China, and the NMCC recommends that we execute our own nuclear response."

The CIA director said, "We are in the process of confirming a few things on our end. But I also agree. We just received further intelligence that suggests the second wave of missile launches came from the Chinese side of the border, not the Russian side."

The president said, "What is the intelligence?"

"HUMINT, sir. We feel very strongly that it is accurate."

The president couldn't tell who spoke next. But the voice said, "Well, that settles it, then. We need to strike China."

The car slowed. The president's chief of staff said, "Gentlemen, we're about to go offline for a moment."

The president said, "I'll make my final decision when I'm on board the plane."

The Secret Service SUVs came to a quick stop on the tarmac, forming an outward-facing shield, while the president and his party marched onto Air Force One. The behemoth frame of the jet loomed above them, looking menacing with most of its lights off. The VC-25A (the Air Force's designation for the presidential 747) already had its engines running. The president stepped out onto the concrete flight line, the whine of jet engines spinning up. Dozens of security personnel surrounded him, looking more tense than usual. The outside air had a cool bite to it.

"Why the hell are the lights off?"

"I believe they're trying to be covert, sir."

Almost nothing was lit up save for the stairway up to the cabin. "Son of a bitch. Is someone really going to shoot at me on my way onto the plane? I should be so lucky."

They hurried the president up the stairs. He snuck a glance out over the D.C. skyline, wondering if it would be the last time he saw the white monuments in the distance. Then he was inside the aircraft, the cabin door closed behind him, and the sounds of the world grew muffled. The president and his staff were shown into the Air Force One conference room.

The train of cabinet members and senior staff crammed in. There were only eight seats at the table. Thick, cushiony leather. A single flat-screen on the far wall, and multiple speakerphone devices on the table. A communications compartment in the next room was filled with technology and experts who worked feverishly to connect Air Force One with those who could provide accurate information.

Senior staffers who normally would be competing for the president's time were white-faced and silent. And these were the "lucky" ones. Most had been left behind. Getting the president evacuated even a few seconds sooner was worth more than the life of some staffers. Choices had to be made. Missiles were airborne.

President Griffin rubbed his temples. He looked at the Air Force steward standing in the room. "Cup of coffee, please." The enlisted woman nodded and headed to the coffeemaker.

Around the conference table were several of the men he had just been speaking to on the phone. The Pentagon's deputy director for operations, General Rice, the national security advisor, and the secretary of defense. They conversed in short, tense sentences filled with acronyms and military lingo.

"...but we still can't rule out a Russian response..."

"...a handful of the Chinese air transports may have landed in Canada or the US..."

"...more cyberattacks too—bad ones. Utilities, water purification systems, and transportation servers have all been affected. We just received an alert that several undersea cables have been disrupted."

"Undersea cables?" the president asked.

"Undersea fiberoptic cables connecting North American communications and data networks with Europe and Asia. Sir, this appears to be a full-scale coordinated attack, originating from the Pacific Theater."

The room went silent. The president stared at the general. "What's the status of our military response in the Pacific?"

"In Korea, Japan, and Guam, commanders have informed us that combat operations have begun. Chinese Air Force and Naval forces, as well as North Korean military forces, have commenced military operations directed against the United States and its allies. We have begun fighting back with our forces in theater. However, communications with most assets have been disrupted, and we're not completely clear on what the current status is."

A voice emanating from the speaker in the middle of the table said, "Mr. President, STRATCOM has just received indications of multiple nuclear detonations in North Korea..."

A few gasps around the room.

The president leaned forward in his seat. "In North Korea? Who fired the nuclear weapons, General?"

"We don't know the answer to that, sir."

"Well, find out! Were those the Chinese missiles that launched? Maybe we misread the Chinese missile launch intentions. Maybe they aren't working in concert with North Korea. Maybe they—"

From the speakerphone, a voice said, "Mr. President, this is

Homeland Security. Uh, sir, the emergency alert message just went out nationally."

"Fine. Thank you—"

"Yes, sir. But it seems that there were some *abnormalities…*"

"What abnormalities?"

"You see, sir, Homeland Security never issued the EAM."

Heads turned toward the president. Confused looks.

"What the hell are you saying?"

"We were about to send one out, sir. But…it just went out automatically right before we were going to send it. And, well, considering that we are under cyberattack, we wondered if—"

General Rice said, "Mr. Secretary, what did the message say?"

"It was a standard EAM for this scenario. It read, 'Remain indoors and stand by for further instructions.'"

General Rice narrowed his eyes. "Why would someone—"

The president said, "Fine. Fine. Whatever. What's the update on the missile threat? I want to…"

The president's voice trailed off. His eyes were fixated on the TV screen on the wall.

"What the hell am I looking at?" All eyes turned to the president and then followed his finger to the TV.

It was a live cable news broadcast. They were showing video feed of the Oval Office. The banner underneath said, "Live emergency address from the president expected soon."

The national security advisor said, "Cyberattacks didn't affect the TV broadcast?"

"This is part of the emergency broadcast."

"How could—"

"Everyone be quiet. Someone turn the volume up."

One of the military aides standing against the wall grabbed a remote control and increased the volume.

"This is live?" the president's chief of staff asked.

"Yes, it is," someone answered.

The president felt his body shift as the aircraft began taxiing.

He was looking at himself, on the TV screen.

"But that's *not me*. I'm here."

Yet there he was. Sitting at his desk in the Oval Office. About to make an address to the country on national TV.

"What in the Sam Hill is going on?"

2

The end of the world was announced just like everything else these days. With a mobile phone notification.

It was just after 2 a.m. when the phones started their screeching. The Emergency Alert System. Those terrifying dashes of ugly noise that every American who lived during the Cold War remembers.

David Manning shot up in bed. Groggy and confused, he peered into the dark, looking for the source of the noise.

"What *is* that?" his wife, Lindsay, asked. David fumbled for his phone on the nightstand, silencing it. But his wife's phone continued making the same terrible noise from the kitchen.

Lindsay put her pillow over her head, her muffled voice saying, "Turn it off."

Then the baby began crying from down the hall, and Lindsay let out the curse of a tired mother. "Oh, good Lord, you've got to be effing kidding me." She threw on her robe and headed to the nursery.

David got up and headed to the kitchen to silence his wife's phone. He squinted, trying to read the alert message as he walked, the text on the bright screen still blurry while his eyes were adjusting.

He reached the kitchen counter, silenced the alert noise on Lindsay's phone and turned on the light by the sink. David could see the display on his phone clearly now. There was a red outline surrounding a white triangle, with a black exclamation point inside. The message read:

Emergency Alert

Remain indoors. DO NOT DRIVE. Call 9-1-1 for emergencies only. Stand by for further instructions.

What the hell?

"*David*," his wife called from the living room. She had turned on the TV and was rocking their newborn while she watched the news.

"David, come here. Look at this."

The tone of her voice told him that something was wrong. She had been an anxious person before David had been taken to the island as part of a Chinese espionage operation. It had only gotten worse after.

Lindsay was hypersensitive to the news now. Truth be told, so was everyone else. In the past few months, the US had been engaged in combat operations against Iran and had been involved in skirmishes with the Chinese military in the eastern Pacific. Until very recently, David had felt like Chicken Little trying to convince members of the government that they needed to take Cheng Jinshan more seriously. Especially after his credibility was ruined following the Red Cell incident. But after

Jinshan had seized control of China's government, David's warnings were seen as prescient. He had soon found himself placed in the CIA's SILVERSMITH program, set up to counter Chinese aggression.

David entered the dark living room, the bright glow of the TV forcing him to squint. The baby was falling back asleep, whimpering on Lindsay's shoulder.

"What is it?" David asked.

"Look."

She had CNN on. A young black newscaster that David didn't recognize was talking to the camera, wide-eyed and looking nervous as he spoke.

The banner on the bottom of the screen read *BREAKING: Homeland Security Issues Nationwide Emergency Broadcast Alert After Explosions Rock Hawaii.*

Lindsay turned up the volume.

"*...so it was only moments ago that we received this alert from the Department of Homeland Security. No confirmation yet on whether that is related to the reports coming out of Hawaii. We can tell you that this is a nationwide bulletin. Our station is in the process of verifying its authenticity, as we are required to do. Our producer has told me that this is the first time since the creation of the Emergency Alert System that a national alert has been issued. We are required by the FCC to read you the message, and I'll do so now: 'This is the Emergency Alert System. The United States has been attacked by...'*"

The newscaster's voice cracked, and he looked to someone off camera. He regained his composure and continued.

"*...The United States has been attacked by nuclear weapons. Communications have been disrupted, and severe casualties are expected. Further details are unavailable at this time. All residents are urged to stay in their homes until further notice. Staying indoors will provide the best protection from potential blast or radiation hazards.*"

Tune in to local TV and radio stations to receive warnings and instructions applicable for your geographic area."

The newscaster looked off screen. He said, "Is this right?"

Lindsay plummeted to the couch, her hand covering her mouth, the baby squirming at her shoulder. "Oh my God. David?"

David's eyes were narrowed. His mind began racing, thinking about the latest intelligence reports he had read. Thinking about where the rest of his family was.

He brought up the contacts list on his phone and dialed his office at Langley. Nothing happened. He looked at the cellular signal. No bars. He accessed a news application, but the latest update was from yesterday. He tried to refresh but got an error message. He checked a few major news websites in the phone's internet browser. Nothing. Internet was down.

Lindsay sounded frantic. "Should we turn to the local station? It said to turn to the local station. David—"

"Hold on..."

The newscaster held his finger to his ear.

"Ladies and gentlemen, I've just been told that the president of the United States will be delivering a message. We're going to cut to the White House now..."

The screen switched to the United States presidential crest, then to the president himself, sitting behind his desk in the Oval Office, looking every bit the old man that he was. In the background, a picture of his family sat to one side, the American flag to the other.

"My fellow Americans, our nation has come under attack. NORAD has detected signs consistent with multiple ballistic missile launches, originating from North Korea. The United States has responded. Our ballistic missile defense was able to destroy most, but not all of these missiles.

"Moments ago, after conferring with the national security advisor,

the director of national intelligence, and the chairman of the Joint Chiefs of Staff, I have ordered a swift and proportionate response. The United States of America will not stand idly by while madmen plot treachery upon our free and peace-loving nation.

"The United States, under my orders, has launched a limited nuclear strike on North Korea. We are now engaged in combat operations on the Korean peninsula. If the United States is attacked, we will strike back. This includes the use of nuclear weapons against our enemies. I implore all nations to heed this warning.

"Americans should remain calm but alert. I assure you that we are taking every possible step to ensure the safety and security of the American people. We—"

Two men raced onto the screen. The president yelled something that sounded like a question. The screen was a blur of large men in suits rushing the president away. Then the presidential seal appeared once again.

Lindsay said, "What just happened?" Her eyes were moist, her free hand covering her mouth.

"I don't know...I don't know. They looked like they rushed him off."

"What *the hell* just happened?"

"Maybe—"

The next moment seemed like it went by in slow motion.

Through the cracks in the window shades, night turned to day. A bright light, white as winter and intense as daylight, lit up the outside world. The white light lasted for a few seconds, and then...darkness.

The TV turned off on its own. So did the kitchen counter lights. And the HVAC unit, the refrigerator fan, and the dishwasher.

The house became dark and silent.

Lindsay whispered, "Was that a bomb? David, oh my God,

tell me that wasn't a nuclear bomb." The baby had woken up and was crying again.

David grabbed the remote control and tried turning the TV back on, even though he knew that it was a waste of time.

He walked over to the curtain. "Everyone else's lights are out, too. No streetlights on, either."

"What was that light outside, David? The president said there were nuclear missiles. Can you see anything out there? Do you see...do you see a mushroom cloud?"

He peered through the shades. "Everything just looks dark." The wheels in his head began turning. He looked at his watch, then his phone. Neither was working. The electronics seemed fried. They were now paperweights.

"Honey, I think that bright flash was an EMP. An electromagnetic pulse weapon." A sickening feeling overcame him as he tried to figure out what their options were. "I'm going to go check the cars."

Lindsay shook her head. "They said to stay indoors."

David grabbed his keys off the kitchen counter. "I just want to go check. It might not be safe here, this close to D.C. We might need to go somewhere else."

"What the hell is *that* supposed to mean? Where would we go?"

He didn't answer. He walked into the garage, hitting the button to open the doors, but nothing happened. He swore to himself, walked over to the garage door and pulled the disconnect, then manually raised the door. He could hear voices in the neighborhood.

"...just lit up the whole sky..."

It sounded like Mrs. Barslosky across the street.

The minivan started up without incident. The sedan was a different story. He tried four times, but the engine wouldn't turn. He went back into the minivan and turned the ignition switch to the first indent so that the radio came on. He scanned through the channels but only heard static.

Lindsay stuck her head into the garage. "Did they start?"

"The Honda did."

"What should we do now?"

David looked at her. "I don't know."

3

The president slammed his fist down on the table. "That wasn't me on the TV!"

"Sir, I believe we just witnessed what is known as a deep fake. That was information warfare. Someone designed that video to make it look like an official presidential communication."

"What do you mean? It was computer-generated?"

"Possibly, Mr. President. There are a variety of techniques."

"And they can really do that?" The president swore. "How many people did that broadcast go out to?"

The DHS secretary's voice on the speakerphone said, "Sir... all of them. That was put out on every TV network. It was also live-streamed over many websites and news services, and relayed on social media."

The national security advisor said, "Sir, I think the more important thing to look at is what their intentions were within that particular communication. Why would the Chinese want to say that we fired our missiles? And why would they want to alert our nation that they have ballistic missiles inbound from—"

The conversation came to a halt as a daylight-bright flash ignited the sky, coming in through the cabin windows.

The Secret Service agents rushed to the president, making sure his seat strap was secure and telling him to crouch down into the crash position. The others present in the room followed suit, convinced of the worst, waiting for a nuclear shockwave that never came. After a moment, they stopped ducking, and the Secret Service men went back to their original sentry positions.

The aircraft had come to a halt on the runway numbers. Both of the pilots had been blinded by looking directly at the flash. They were replaced by a backup crew and sent to the medical bay. Furthering the delay was the need for some of the aircraft systems to be reset. There would be an additional two minutes before takeoff, the president was told.

Inside the presidential conference room, the TV and many of the electronics had ceased working. But many of the systems on Air Force One had been hardened to resist just such an attack. This included the majority of the communications devices on board, allowing the Pentagon and STRATCOM to remain on the line.

New information arrived in spurts. General Rice was getting updates from a phone at his ear. He said, "Sir, we have indications of multiple nuclear detonations over the continental United States. Very high altitude. There are also incoming reports of communications and electronics outages over the same area. Sir, this is consistent with an electromagnetic pulse weapon."

From the speakerphone, "Mr. President, STRATCOM recommends setting DEFCON 1. We now have high confidence that China is responsible for this strike. We should be prepared for a follow-on attack. Sir, we need to execute an immediate response."

The officer with the nuclear football laid the black leather satchel on the conference table and began unsnapping the straps. He removed a metal briefcase. The president watched his mechanical motions. He had asked the officer about the case during one of their training sessions. The metal case was made by Zero Halliburton, a Japanese luggage manufacturer. Ironic, considering the history of nuclear warfare. Now the officer flipped open the metal briefcase to reveal a computer screen and keyboard. He extended a single antenna, and then his fingers danced over the keypad as the computer screen came to life. From a cutout in the suitcase, he removed a laminated card with a series of challenge codes.

"Mr. President, if you're ready—"

The president frowned. "Everyone weigh in, quickly." He looked around the table.

The national security advisor, sitting across the conference table, said, "Mr. President, I have to agree with the NMCC here."

"General Rice?"

General Rice had a phone to his ear, speaking with his team at the Pentagon. "Mr. President, if we launch our missiles, we risk escalating the situation. China could then launch more missiles at us—"

General Sprague said over the speakerphone, "Which is precisely why we need to launch. We need to neutralize their ability to escalate, Mr. President. They're attacking our military bases throughout the Pacific. They've launched EMP weapons at us. Hell, our sensors are down right now. For all we know, there could be more incoming nuclear weapons headed this way right now. Sir, this is our job right now. We have to execute."

The president leaned forward, resting his elbows on the polished wood of the table. He massaged his own scalp and temples, trying to think clearly. The late hour and his raging headache made that almost impossible.

The officer manning the Football said, "Sir, do you have the

Biscuit?" The Biscuit was the laminated card that the president had on his person at all times—his ID verification for just this very moment.

The president looked up at the officer. He dug his hand into his breast pocket, pulling out the card holder. He held it in his hands, studying the men in the room.

The president looked at the speakerphone in the middle of the table. "General Sprague, are you one hundred percent certain that it was China who fired this latest group of ballistic missiles?"

"Mr. President, we can't be one hundred percent certain of anything, sir. Both Russia and China have this capability. But from looking at the real-time intel we've seen coming in, it appears that there is now a kinetic environment in the Pacific. Guam, Japan, Korea. At least one aircraft carrier has been attacked by Chinese conventional missiles. There's fighting near Hawaii—"

"Hawaii?"

General Rice said, "Yes, Mr. President. We are at war with China. Looking at the macro picture, I believe we should operate under the assumption that the Chinese have launched nuclear weapons at us."

The president could feel the sweat in his armpits and on his forehead. He didn't want to make the decision. Tonight was the culmination of a career of military studies and training for these men in uniform. A part of him suspected they almost enjoyed this moment. That it was some sort of glorious climax to end their military careers. The president was annoyed by their eagerness, and by the ease with which they navigated through the heavy jargon and complicated subjects. It was all so unfamiliar to him. But at the same time, he needed their expertise.

"What's your recommendation, General?"

General Rice said, "A limited strike on their strategic capability. We need to make sure the Chinese can't escalate. We need to neutralize their ability to launch further nuclear attacks on the US."

The president shot a glance to his chief of staff. He knew him better than these other men and trusted his judgment.

"Paul?"

"The missiles headed this way could be more EMPs."

"Unlikely, sir," said the STRATCOM general on the phone.

The national security advisor said, "Mr. President, EMPs *are* nuclear weapons. We would be within our rights to respond with our own nukes. Not only that, but EMP weapons are considered *first strike* weapons. They are meant to mask further strategic attacks."

The president looked at the NSA with annoyance. "I know that much, for God's sake."

The national security advisor said, "Mr. President, I disagree with the general. We need a full-throated response. You could end the war today. We now have information that our military is under attack by Chinese forces in the Pacific, our homeland has been attacked via cyber and EMPs, and there are Chinese military attacks going on within the boundaries of the US. I recommend a full-scale nuclear strike on the Chinese military. No restrictions."

General Rice shook his head. "Sir, I vehemently disagree. It is critical that we be measured. The use of nuclear weapons must be proportional and targeted appropriately."

The national security advisor frowned. "Think of the long-term ramifications. We have an advantage now. That could be gone tomorrow. We have the justification we need. This would be a defensive measure—"

General Rice said, "What do you propose? That we wipe out their entire military? Do you know where their military bases are? Do you know how many hundreds of millions of people would be killed? Their population centers are dense and coastal. And a strike of that size would have global implications. Nuclear winter."

"There were nuclear detonations in Korea!"

"North Korea isn't the US."

"Does it matter?"

"Mr. President, we don't have much more time..."

The voices broke out into arguments.

"...The Russians have thousands of nukes. If they see us launch..."

"...limited strike options. We can attack only Chinese strategic nuclear targets..."

"...simultaneously use backchannel communications with the Russians..."

"I don't recommend that, sir..."

"...but if we're trying to reduce risk..."

The president put up his hand, and the room went silent. "If I was to go with the limited nuclear response, what are my options?"

General Rice looked up at the colonel, who held the Football.

The colonel removed three large plastic cards. "Sir, based on the conversation with the National Event Conference, I understand that you wish to pursue a retaliatory strike on the Chinese military using assets from the nuclear triad. Am I correct in that assessment?"

The president nodded. "I'm giving the order. A limited strike." He removed the ID card from its case, holding it up.

The colonel read a challenge code. He looked up the code on his Biscuit card and responded appropriately.

The colonel looked at General Rice. "Sir, please verify that—"

"I verify that the order came from the president."

The colonel then nodded and typed the code into the hardened communications device within the suitcase. The message was coded, encrypted, and transmitted around the world via ELF radio transmitters.

The United States had just activated the nuclear triad.

Seconds later, the four General Electric GF-6 engines of Air Force One roared to life as it began making its takeoff from the runway.

4

Lieutenant Ping's team of Chinese commandos had been specially trained for this mission. They were the elite of the elite. Young and less experienced than their US special operations counterparts, but skilled and determined nonetheless.

Ping's team had been waiting in a rural section of Maryland for the past week. Twelve shoulder-mounted surface-to-air missiles, the latest generation of Chinese technology, were loaded into the back of two pickup trucks and driven to the top of a hill on the farm property. Ping had received the radio signal to prepare for the EMP detonation. He had quickly instructed his men to wait in their vehicles, eyes trained on the floor, until the event was over.

The flash lasted almost two full seconds. It made no audible sound, over one hundred miles up. But Lieutenant Ping watched as the bright white light of the EMP painted his knees while he sat in the passenger seat of the lead vehicle. When the world went dark again, he began issuing orders.

"Power up the weapons and radar. Check that everything is working." He hoped that the engineers who had planned for this mission had performed their calculations correctly. It would be a shame if the EMP had wiped out his ability to detect and target air contacts.

"Radar functioning normally. Op checks passed with no flags."

Ping nodded.

"We are in the window," the senior enlisted man told Ping.

Ping looked at his watch. Timing was everything. It was possible that they wouldn't get the opportunity to use their training. But if they did, it could change the war.

A decapitation on day one would send a powerful message. It could throw America into further chaos. He would be a hero.

"Contact!" one of his men shouted. The soldier was monitoring the returns from a hardened laptop computer, connected by wire to a set of six radar dishes, each aimed at the horizon. Together they formed a miniature phased-array. Again, the latest Chinese technology. No expense had been spared for this assignment. Still, it would require a bit of luck. Their mission required Ping's team to remain undetected. This meant that limited-range shoulder-mounted weapons had to be used.

Would their target venture into the range of these weapons? If the aircraft turned out to sea before acquisition or stayed low and traveled south...they would not get a shot off. But based on the threat, the intelligence experts from Beijing had expected the flight pattern to be to the northwest. Hence their current location in rural Maryland.

Two of his men were kneeling, aiming the shoulder-mounted weapons at the correct angle, and finished with their preparations.

"Stand by," called out the soldier monitoring the radar. They were each wearing hearing protection, so his voice was muffled.

The officer in charge walked over and stood behind him. He was nervous, double-checking his men's work even though he knew they almost never made mistakes.

"Target confirmed," one of the other men said, looking at a satellite phone in his hand. One of their men was sitting in a parking lot only a few miles from the runway where Air Force One had just taken off. "Turning to the north." Excitement in his voice.

"Coming in range. Almost there...in range."

"Fire at will," the officer shouted, louder than he had intended. Nerves.

The night sky lit up, and his ears, even over the hearing protection he wore, were filled with the thunderous sounds of the surface-to-air missiles firing off into the distance.

* * *

The president and his men stared silently at each other for a moment. Now that the nuclear launch order had been given, they sat in numb shock. The SecDef looked ashamed. General Rice was scribbling notes on a piece of paper, a phone to his ear, his eyes shifting between the president and the others in the room. The national security advisor looked pleased and strong. The president's chief of staff left the room in a rush, his face green.

"What's next?" the president asked.

"We'll continue to get updates as our order is executed, sir. The first volley will be from our land-based missiles near Cheyenne Mountain..."

A panicked voice came over the speakerphone. "General Rice! Sir...we have an important status update. Our ballistic missile data has been updated with new sensor information. Sir, the four missiles that we had been tracking have all fallen into the sea. There are no inbound missiles headed towards the US mainland. Repeat, no inbound missiles headed towards the US."

The president stood and leaned forward, hands on the desk.

"What does that mean? What about the Chinese missiles? The second set of—"

"Sir, we have a few active systems coming online. As a result, NORAD has a full picture. There are no Chinese missiles inbound. We don't know what happened to them. But we can now confirm that there are no further ICBMs headed to the US."

A stunned silence filled the room.

The president had just ordered a nuclear attack on China, but now he was hearing that they had not fired first. This was no longer a proportional response, even if China had launched the EMP attack.

He felt a sickening feeling enter his chest. "Can we turn off the attack order?"

STRATCOM answered over the phone. "Sir, the system is designed so that—"

"Yes or no, General?"

"Yes, sir. But—"

The colonel who kept the Football said, "Sir, the order may not be received in time."

The president looked around the room, his heart beating in his chest.

The national security advisor said, "Mr. President, I advise against changing course. Regardless of whether the Chinese have nukes headed this way, you have made the right call, sir. We need to—"

General Rice looked horrified. "I disagree. I think we should try to terminate the order. Regardless of Chinese actions, our strategic response should be proportional in nature. If—"

The president nodded. "Agreed. Terminate the order. *Now*."

Two of the officers in the room sprang into action. One began calling for *Nightwatch* on the radio and relaying a set of coded instructions. A frantic back-and-forth ensued. The president could barely understand the language the men were using, with many of the words heavy jargon, code words, or military acronyms.

After sixty seconds of this, the colonel who manned the Football once again turned to the president. "Sir, we'll need you to provide your challenge code again."

The president nodded and began to speak but was interrupted by a warning alarm that began blaring over the overhead speaker system.

The Air Force pilot's voice was loud, clear, and professional. "This is the pilot. Surface-to-air missile warning. Secure passengers and brace for impact."

The president's personal security detail jumped to their feet and began treating him like an emergency room patient. Their hands raced over him, once again making sure that he was secured and in the crash position.

The aircraft banked sharply to the left, and the president felt his head grow heavy and his body pressed down into his seat as increased G-forces came over the aircraft. The Secret Service agents were tossed back into the opposite wall and then rose off the floor towards the ceiling as Air Force One dove.

The president saw one of the Secret Service men, now unconscious on the floor after bumping his head. Then the president noticed the officer in charge of the Football sitting next to him, pounding on the surface of the table. The man's mouth was moving, but the president couldn't understand what he was saying.

The officer had one hand on the Football computer and was pointing at the president's chest. General Rice was also now yelling something.

The sound of the world was coming back. An Air Force steward was pointing at the president. "Sir, your head is bleeding…"

Everyone at the table was yelling for his attention.

"...pass code!" General Rice said.

Pass code.

The president touched his head and felt something wet. He removed his hand and saw blood. Something must have struck him when the aircraft had maneuvered.

The overhead speakers announced, *"All personnel, brace for impact!"*

* * *

The first two surface-to-air missiles were tricked by countermeasures released from Air Force One, sailing harmlessly past and landing in the Chesapeake Bay. The third missile drove itself right into the innermost engine on the left wing, exploding and sending metallic fragments throughout the aircraft. Less than one second later, a fourth missile exploded after impacting an engine on the opposite wing, the detonation igniting one of the aircraft's fuel cells. The subsequent explosion of jet fuel was catastrophic.

The blast killed everyone on board and was clearly visible five miles away on the ground, at a hilly farm property in rural Maryland.

Lieutenant Ping allowed his men a moment of quiet celebration and then ordered them to stow all gear in the trucks and move out. The war had just begun. And with any luck, their contributions would be many.

5

First Lieutenant Lucy Esposito hated the feeling she always got at the beginning of her shift. She sat in the passenger seat of a US Air Force pickup truck. The vehicle bounced and jolted as it made its way down the gravel farm road in the middle of the night. This meant that she was near her destination. The nuclear missile silos were spread out over acres and acres of Nebraska farmland.

Flight Golf was hers. Ironic, since she'd been a golfer at the Academy. But there was no golfing out here. Golf was part of the phonetic alphabet—the letter G identified this section of the US Air Force's missile field. One hundred and fifty nuclear-tipped intercontinental ballistic missiles, stuffed five stories below the earth, awaiting the moment they were needed to end the world.

Which was like, *never*. It was a bullshit job, thought up decades ago by a bunch of men who were all dead now. Yet here she was, wasting her life away underground.

God help her.

Three years ago, Lucy had been a senior at the US Air Force Academy in Colorado Springs. Her hopes had been high. Like most Air Force Academy cadets, she had wanted to become a pilot after graduation. But the Air Force was minting more drone pilots than manned aircraft pilots nowadays. And Lucy didn't have the class rank to get her first choice...or her fourth choice, for that matter. Never in a million years had she expected to spend her career in a missile silo. But that was sure as shit where she'd ended up.

It had started out a little rough, but she was at least proud of the progress she'd made. Now she was a twenty-five-year-old commander of a two-person missile squadron combat crew. There were ten missile silos in her flight, with a single missile alert facility centrally located.

Lucy was stationed at F.E. Warren Air Force Base near Cheyenne, Wyoming. Her life was spent standing duty, studying for her qualifications, and working on her military education credits.

It was dead out in this part of the country. She missed the city. Lucy had made her way home to Brooklyn on Christmas leave back in December. It had been good to see them, but hard to leave. Her older brothers couldn't believe it when she'd described her job. They'd taken her out drinking, and she had proudly told them that she was now a steely-eyed missile man.

She sighed, bouncing around in the truck. She missed her family.

The driver made a call over the radio as the truck continued down the dark road.

"Golf Control, Trip 14 on your axis, request entry Lieutenant Esposito plus one."

The voice over the radio responded, "Roger, entry granted."

She watched as the gate opened in front of them.

The rectangular missile alert area in front of her was not large—only two acres. Dim lights flickered on overhead as they arrived. The land had been purchased by the government from a local farmer several decades ago. It had easy access to the main road—you could see it from where they were. And it was surrounded by chain metal fencing and barbed wire. Towering poles mounted with flood lights overhead, each with tiny security cameras that monitored the barren area around the missile silo.

A few minutes later, the pickup truck had dropped off Lieutenant Esposito and parked next to the lone building inside the fence. It would wait here until she was done with her watch turnover, then it would bring the man she was relieving back to F.E. Warren Air Force Base, a little over an hour away.

"Have fun, Ma'am."

"Oh yeah." She gave him a thumbs-up and threw her duffle bag over her shoulder, shutting the passenger door behind her.

Inside, she went through more security. ID checks and signing the log. Security personnel behind glass windows, ensuring that even though they knew her, she wasn't able to get past the first room of the building without passing muster.

A few minutes later, she was opening the metal-grated double doors of the elevator. The outside of the elevator had a big sticker with a picture of a red devil on it. A bubble quote coming from his mouth said, "See you down there!" Lucy loved the dark humor.

She closed the two metal grate doors behind her and pressed the button for the elevator to bring her fifty feet down to where two other officers were waiting, one of whom she was relieving.

The watch turnover took about twenty minutes. They went over schedules of topside transportation, maintenance and training. There were a few items that needed repair, but nothing mission-critical.

"Make sure you read the geopolitical intel brief. The CO said the stuff with North Korea is getting hairy."

"Same old thing."

"Maybe." He shrugged. But Lucy noticed a funny look in his eye. They finished turnover, and he was heading up the elevator the second they were done.

Lucy stuffed her bag in her locker and sat down at the computer terminal where she would spend most of her time for the next twenty-four hours. She looked ten feet away, where another first lieutenant sat. He was about a year greener than her.

"Hello, Johnny."

"Hello, Lucy."

"You dump your girlfriend yet?"

"Nah."

"You still trying to figure out the best way to do that?"

"Yup." He grinned as he looked back down at the three-inch-thick binder on his lap. It was filled with highly classified procedures and maintenance information. "I figure that my not calling her anymore, not returning her emails, and blocking her from all of my social networks will do the trick."

"Dude. Just sack up and tell her." Lucy scanned the panels in front of her, checking the readouts and system status of the missiles under her control. "I mean, come on already. Be a man."

Johnny laughed. "Says my female missile combat crew commander."

Their conversation stopped as a loud two-toned alarm sounded throughout the room.

The two junior officers sprang upright in their chairs, Johnny practically throwing the binder onto the floor.

Lucy's eyes scanned the information coming in to her on her screen. She yelled, "Stand by to copy the message."

Over the encrypted communications channel in front of Johnny came the fast-talking voice of a senior enlisted Air Force man who was on base at Warren. *"Alpha...Seven... Charlie...Foxtrot..."*

Both Lucy and Johnny wrote down the verbally transmitted authentication code with rapid precision. When the transmission was finished, they both stood up and proceeded to unlock their separate locks on the safe. Inside was the launch key.

The next several minutes were spent communicating back and forth with two other officers in a separate launch facility, verifying the codes' authenticity and the accuracy of their transcription.

Then Lucy heard the words she had never expected to hear.

Lucy made the man on the radio repeat it. "Say again, this is *not* an exercise."

"Affirmative, this is *not* an exercise. This is real-world."

Lucy and Johnny looked at each other, their faces confused. Lucy could feel her heart pounding in her chest.

"Come on, let's go, Johnny," she said.

"They said this was real-world..."

"We'll talk in a second. Let's enable the missiles."

He nodded quickly, his face white.

They each inserted their separate keys into the large metallic sections on the wall where they were needed. Lucy had done this so many times she thought she could do it blindfolded. But now her arm turned to mush, and her body moved like it was weighed down with sandbags.

She began reciting the verbiage that would start the launch of her missiles, reading from the long checklist on the binder in front of her. "Unlock code inserted."

"Stand by...unlock code is inserted," replied Johnny. He glanced at her. "How is this real? Lucy, this can't really be real? Who are we...?"

She ignored him. The red digital clock on the wall was ticking away. Closing in on ten minutes. They would need to hurry. "Enable switch to Enable."

Johnny moved his hands over the knobs and dials. "Enabled..."

Almost there, Lucy thought. *Almost there. Follow your training, Lucy. You're a steely-eyed missile man.*

* * *

Five stories above and one mile to the west, a farmer drove his Ford pickup truck along the outskirts of his property. He watched as the floodlights near the missile silo up on the hill came on. *Well, that's weird*, he thought.

He stopped his vehicle and got out of the cab, squinting, trying to make out what he was seeing.

"Now what in hell is that?"

Steam or smoke of some type was coming out of the silo.

"Government fools...probably leaking radiation everywhere..."

It was a clear night, and the air was crisp. A beautiful canvas of twinkling stars overhead. The farmer turned to head back into his truck when the noise began.

A low rumble and a grating alarm, barely audible in the distance. He looked again at the hill. Now more smoke was coming out of the silo. Billowing white smoke. Then flame. Huge tongues of yellow-and-orange flame, shooting out of the exhaust openings.

The first missile launched upward in a rage of bright fire, its thick smoke trail following it into space. The farmer caught sight of another missile launching out of the corner of his right eye. The rumbles grew more intense and he could feel them in his feet. Or was that his knees shaking?

"God have mercy."

He turned around in place, seeing a third missile take off on the horizon, several miles to the north. He continued turning round and round, scanning the sky. There must have been a dozen of them, all arcing upward and away. Giant white vessels of death, traveling to a distant land.

6

USS Farragut
75 nautical miles north of Guam

The war had only just begun, and Victoria Manning had already experienced the rush of combat. With the assistance of a P-8, she had scored a confirmed kill on an enemy submarine. It was likely one of the submarines that had attacked Guam with cruise missiles an hour earlier. Now it was cracked open, on the bottom of the ocean.

She had almost sortied again, right after landing. One of the young sonar technicians thought he got a sniff of a second Chinese sub. Instead, they had told her to shut down while the P-8 covered the area with buoys. It had turned out to be a false alarm, but she didn't mind. There was going to be a lot of that, she realized. And she would rather launch on a false alarm than be on board when a submarine targeted their ship.

The battle of Guam had awakened the crew from any remaining vestiges of peacetime lethargy. Now every blip on the radar scope could be an enemy aircraft. Every odd noise heard through the sonar technician's headphones might be a Chinese fast-attack submarine opening up its torpedo doors. Everyone was now high-strung. Lives were at stake. And there was no pressure on earth like the desire to keep her fellow members of the pack protected. No one wanted to let their shipmates down by missing something. But Victoria knew that this optempo would cause burnout.

As officer in charge of a helicopter detachment on the USS *Farragut*, steaming in the eastern Pacific on the opening day of war with China, Victoria would need to manage her men's mental state as much as their workload. She needed her men to be at peak effectiveness.

She herself was not immune to these conditions. She knew that she would need to get rest, food, sleep, and exercise whenever she could. But that was easier said than done.

She had missed dinner, but when the young CS on duty in the wardroom found that out, he had rushed down the nearest ladder to the galley to get her something to eat. It was just a little gesture of kindness, but many on board had begun treating Victoria differently over the past few weeks. There was an increased sense of pride among the crew. They were a family, and family took care of each other. All at the same time, Victoria was like a parent, a sibling, and a boss. The crew treated her with a special reverence. She had shown the wisdom and capability to lead the ship to victory, and out of harm's way, when the storm was darkest. She had earned a reputation for competence, and as someone who placed her men above all else.

So she understood the cook's gesture of kindness but was nonetheless touched. She had smiled and thanked the CS before he had left her alone in the wardroom. She was glad he did, because she had eaten no more than three bites before her hands started shaking and she doubled over, trying not to cry.

Victoria got up quickly and went back into kitchenette, which was connected to the wardroom, throwing her food in the trash, careful to cover the uneaten morsels with a paper plate so she wouldn't insult her cooks. She stood in the kitchen area, sweating and gritting her teeth, willing herself to calm the fuck down. Beads of sweat ran down her forehead.

She breathed in deeply and blew air out her mouth. Through the porthole in the wardroom galley, she could see the blue horizon moving up, pausing, and then moving back down, the rhythm of the waves never-ending. She breathed to that rhythm now, forcing herself to relax by thinking of something that made her feel safe and happy. She thought of her father. She wished she could see him again. Then she began wondering if he, as the admiral in charge of America's newest carrier strike group, was being hunted by a Chinese submarine this very moment.

She slammed her open palm into the steel refrigerator door, trying to get ahold of herself. Flashes of today's flight entered her mind's eye. Gripping the stick and adjusting the heading even though she wasn't technically flying the aircraft because she didn't trust her 2P not to screw up the weapons run. Eyes scanning back and forth between the multipurpose display that showed the submarine track and the switches and buttons and her tactical checklist. The whitewater shooting up into the air on her left side when the submarine detonated below. The wave of relief and guilt and pride she'd felt when she'd seen it. The cheers and smiles of the men in the hangar when she'd landed. And the fear that she knew had been in all of their hearts.

Victoria knew she should be pleased. Proud, even. She had succeeded in her mission. She had been the acting CO of her ship a few weeks ago when they had fired missiles at a group of Chinese warships. She had given the order then. But tonight had been the first time she'd actually pushed the button. Victoria had once again been tested. And once again, she had answered with skill and courage.

So why now, after the fact, couldn't she stop thinking about those silent killers in the deep blue? How many more subs were out there? For every one they found and killed, how many more were now leaving port? Or already hunting them, getting closer to ending the lives of everyone aboard that she had worked so hard to lead?

It was her duty to hunt down and kill every Chinese attack submarine that might be a threat to the USS *Farragut* and the rest of the warships in company, before they sent a torpedo into her ship's hull.

Logically, she knew that she shouldn't take all of this responsibility on herself. There were hundreds of people who were fighting this fight. But as the senior helicopter pilot on board, and one of the top ASW experts in her surface action group— the group of destroyers and warships she was with—she felt a unique burden.

She couldn't get herself to stop thinking about the Chinese sailors that were now dead on the ocean floor. Or perhaps they were trapped in some compartment, freezing to death as they ran out of air? Victoria knew that the Chinese were her enemy, and that they were trying to kill her. But try as she might, she couldn't prevent these thoughts from coming to her now.

Alone in the small galley, praying no one would walk in on her, she used meditation techniques to calm down. Focusing on her breath. Letting the unpleasant thoughts pass her by. After a minute, her pulse and breathing began to slow.

It helped to think about her father. While she worried about him, her love for him calmed her. She would see him again soon, she told herself. His carrier was near Hawaii. With any luck, they would meet there. Maybe they could get a few days off. Have dinner. Have a conversation. Anything would suffice. She just wanted to spend time with him.

For years she had lived her life trying to prove herself to him and telling herself that she didn't care. Then she'd harbored a deep anger towards him after the death of her mother. There were a lot of little reasons for the way she had felt, none of them any good.

But over the past few months, their relationship had finally gotten to a better place. Now it wasn't their strong-willed personalities keeping them from talking, but time and distance. Fate and war.

A ray of setting sun shone through the sole porthole in the space. A whistle signaled the top of the hour, along with some mumbled announcement that she couldn't quite make out.

"Okay. Let's go, Victoria," she whispered to herself, closing her eyes and forcing her way out the door.

She walked down the darkened passageway of the destroyer, balancing herself as the ship rolled with the waves. She could smell the start of dinner being cooked in the galley below decks, heard the sounds of the ship alive around her. The high pitch of running engines. The white noise of radios and electronics being cooled by fan motors, of fluid running through pipes in the walls and the sound of many steel-toed boots walking through the passageways. The banging of maintenance and the blood-curdling screech of needle guns. Dozens heading the opposite direction greeted her as she walked through the passageway.

"Afternoon, Airboss."

"Good afternoon."

"Afternoon, ma'am."

"Afternoon."

Victoria made her way aft and into the maintenance shop in the hangar and began doing her paperwork for postflight. She chatted up her lead maintenance petty officer and then decided to check on some of the other men doing work on the bird.

It was a quiet afternoon, the bright orange sun just above the horizon. She stood near the edge of the flight deck, arms folded across her chest, staring into the distance. Trying not to over-think her flight and trying not to worry about her father. She was drunk with fatigue. Her eyes burned with a combination of sweat and oil, and she tried to rub them clean with the dry sleeve of her flight suit.

"Boss, they wanna know if they can wash the bird. Flight schedule says we're not flying for the next eight hours when we pick up the alert again. You still good with that?"

She looked up and saw LTJG Juan "Spike" Volonte standing over her, the dim light of the open hangar outlining his flight suit and jet-black hair.

Normally this wasn't something that Spike would ask. The maintenance crew would just do it according to the schedule. But the US Navy was now in open combat with the only other superpower in the world. Even now, a Chinese submarine officer might be looking at them through his periscope. Spike was making sure that any change to their ability to fly and fight was communicated effectively.

The freshwater washdowns weren't for looks. Well, maybe a little. But mostly they were to keep the saltwater from corroding the aircraft. Keeping equipment clean and working was an essential part of being a warfighter.

"Yes, go ahead with the wash. We need it. I told the captain we were done flying for the next eight hours."

"Roger." He walked away and spoke to the maintenance senior chief and gave him the thumbs-up. Then he walked back to Victoria.

Spike didn't speak. He just stood next to his boss as they both looked out over the sea. The sun cast an orange light around the other ships in their group, each of those ships heaving and rolling as they steamed forward. She realized that Spike was the one other person on the ship who had launched a torpedo and sunk a submarine in combat. Yesterday, she would have also realized that he was the only other person in the Navy that could say that. But yesterday had been a different world. Now that the Chinese fleet had attacked the US Navy near Korea, Japan, Guam, Australia, and Hawaii...who knew how many other submarine killers there were?

"There goes five-one-two," Victoria said. She was referring to the side number of the helicopter taking off next to their ship.

On the flight deck of the USS *Michael Monsoor*, an MH-60R helicopter lifted off the deck and nosed forward, gaining speed and altitude. It would patrol the skies for the next two and a half hours, using its radar and FLIR to detect and identify enemy ships, carrying sonobuoys, torpedoes, and a dipping sonar in case they needed to react to enemy submarines.

"How long they up for?"

"They've got three bags planned. *James E. Williams'* crew takes the baton from them at zero two hundred, then we pick it up again at zero four thirty."

There were three ships in the group with embarked helicopter detachments. Each day they worked out a flight schedule so that someone was always flying, and another was on alert. The helicopters were used, along with a few drones, to identify the unknown radar contacts and respond to any number of other issues that might come up. Logistics. Search and rescue. An enemy submarine.

"How's the team holding up?" Victoria was asking Spike about the enlisted maintenance men who he was now in charge of. They made up the majority of the thirty sailors in her air detachment.

"They're alright, boss. AE2 is worried about his pregnant wife. Everyone's worried about their families. But overall, everyone's holding up fine. Senior Chief has been good about making sure people were sticking to the training and maintenance schedule."

Victoria said, "Routine is our friend right now. Everyone has a job. The routine gives us something to focus on. Let's plan to get everyone together tomorrow before the flight schedule starts. We got anybody you want to recognize?"

"We have a few awards we can give out."

"Good. Let's do that, and I'll speak to folks about—"

On the fantail, there was a young enlisted girl standing aft lookout. She wore a sound-powered headset. It was bulky and uncomfortable, and she kept shifting it around. It worked like a homemade walkie-talkie. The girl spoke frantically into it now, pointing at the horizon as she yelled.

Spike and Victoria turned in the direction she was pointing. "What the hell?"

To their north, a cloud of white-gray smoke had formed over the distant surface of the water, and a missile was arcing up into the sky above it. The smoke trail was very thick, reminding Victoria of space shuttle launch footage. A moment later, a second missile launched in the same direction. It was so far away they couldn't hear the noise.

Bells and sirens rang throughout the ship, and the 1MC blared: "*General quarters, general quarters. All hands, man your battle stations...*" Men began running on the flight deck, quickly stowing their gear and heading towards their stations.

Victoria tensed up but didn't move. She just kept staring out at the horizon, studying the distant smoke trail. "Those missiles aren't headed towards us."

She could feel Spike's eyes on her. "*Boss*, come on, we're going to GQ. We gotta go."

The enlisted girl manning the rear of the ship now ran past them, headed inside the skin of the ship.

"That smoke trail was thick," said Victoria.

Spike nodded for her to follow him inside. He probably thought she was losing her mind. "*Boss...come on.*"

Another missile launched from the same area of white smoke on the horizon.

Victoria said, "The missiles are headed away from us. That's an ICBM, and it's headed west." Her mind began racing through ranges and distances. She swore softly under her breath. "I think we just launched nuclear missiles at China."

7

Khingan Mountain HQ
China

Cheng Jinshan walked slowly down the corridor, heading towards the central planning center. The bunker network was a unique construction. One wall of the hallway was the actual bare rockface of the mountain. The other wall and the floor were concrete. Along the ceiling ran pipes and ventilation ducts, fiberoptic cables and power lines. Should there be a power outage, backup systems would provide the nearly one thousand inhabitants with electricity and ventilation for months. Food and water stores would last much longer.

The Chinese had built several of these mountain bunkers, each located approximately one hundred kilometers from one another within the Greater Khingan mountain range. Jinshan and his staff were well protected here, along with his seniormost military officers and Central Committee members. The mountain range was hundreds of miles from Beijing, and the bunkers were connected by a system of subterranean high-speed rail lines. This allowed them to frequently change location, reducing the risk of American attack.

As Jinshan entered the planning center, he scanned the room.

The multilevel space had a dozen manned stations towards the far end, which was on a lower elevation plane. Each person manning the stations monitored several computer screens and wore a headset with a boom mike. These men and women, Jinshan knew, were getting the raw data from multiple battlefronts. Sitting at the table in the elevated rear portion of the room, overlooking the computer terminals, were the seniormost military and intelligence leaders in all of China. These men were receiving the most crucial elements from the front section of the room and inserting their decision-making authority into active war plans when needed.

The process had been reviewed and refined by the late Natesh Chaudrey, a brilliant entrepreneur and operations manager, but one with a conscience and stomach far too weak for wartime leadership.

Jinshan had dispatched Lena Chou to eliminate Natesh. She had disposed of him earlier that day in Tokyo. Jinshan didn't like risking Lena like that. Americans were still in Japan. But Natesh knew too much and was a counterespionage risk. Jinshan needed to get rid of him, and for Jinshan's most important work, he only trusted Lena.

The lead team stood up from their seats as Jinshan entered. He nodded a greeting and they all sat. A PLA colonel standing to the side of the table clicked a handheld device and the large flatscreen directly in front of Jinshan changed to a digital map of the Pacific Theater.

"Chairman Jinshan, before we begin, our most important update is that we have just received indications of American ICBM launches from near their base at Cheyenne. Initial trajectory puts their target in China. Likely our northern missile fields. We also have received infrared indications of an ICBM launch one hundred miles north of Guam. There is no trajectory data on those missiles yet, as American antisatellite and cyberattacks have now degraded our capability."

Jinshan nodded, his face calm. "I understand."

To Jinshan's immediate right sat General Chen, the man he had recently installed as the senior-most commander in all of China's military, second only to Jinshan himself. General Chen was also the estranged father of Jinshan's protégé, Lena Chou.

General Chen said, "We must fire our submarine-based nuclear weapons at their American targets as soon as possible. I also recommend using our land-based strategic nuclear weapons to hit American targets along the West Coast of the United States."

Jinshan turned to meet the gaze of General Chen, a flicker of distaste in his eye. "We shall not respond with our nuclear weapons. That would be against our strategy."

General Chen clenched his jaw but showed uncharacteristic restraint in his silence.

Jinshan then looked to the colonel and said, "Proceed with your report."

The colonel's eyes darted from the general to Jinshan, and then he continued with his update. As Jinshan listened, he studied the faces around the table. Most seemed only slightly less nervous than General Chen. Had they not been mentally prepared for this moment? Perhaps they had misjudged the United States, believing that the Americans didn't have the fortitude to use their great atomic stockpile? General Chen at least had the excuse of being newly introduced to many of the war plans. The others had been privy to the plans for months.

Cheng Jinshan was not surprised by the Americans launching their nuclear missiles. He knew the American military, intelligence, and political decision makers. He had operated in the US and knew the people and procedures. He had set loose spies in the government that no one else in China had access to. Operatives who gave him the very best intelligence. No one save the American military would be ready for this moment, and the military would follow their doctrine.

He fully expected a limited nuclear strike on a very specific set of Chinese targets. Jinshan had made sure that the Americans received exactly the right recipe of intelligence to give those orders. His question was how the rest of the war was developing.

"What of the battle in the Pacific?"

Admiral Zhang, head of the PLA Navy, said, "Both American carriers in the Western Pacific have been sunk."

Jinshan nodded. "This is very good news. Well done, Admiral."

"While we are pleased at the progress our air attacks have made, I remain concerned with the American undersea threat. They have more than one dozen fast-attack submarines in the area, with our signals intelligence suggesting that more are on the way."

Jinshan said, "This was expected."

"Yes, sir. But because our war planning timetable was moved forward so much, the Jiaolong has not yet gotten underway. Without the Jiaolong technology, it will be very difficult for us to get our convoy through."

"Especially considering Guam was not taken...which you said would be done by now," said General Chen.

The admiral frowned at General Chen but held his tongue.

General Chen showed no such restraint. "Perhaps Admiral Song was not up to the challenge."

The admiral frowned. "I do not believe it was a leadership failure. The island was fortified with an unexpected surface group. Their air defense wreaked havoc on our attack jets."

One of the men monitoring the screens in the front of the room spoke into his headset, his voice transmitted overhead. "Update on the American ICBM status. Estimated time on target is fifteen minutes."

General Chen sighed. "Do we have an update on the trajectories?"

"We will work on it, sir."

Jinshan shook his head. "No. Just continue the brief, please."

The colonel nodded and continued the update. Jinshan could hear General Chen's sigh of frustration. He was worried about those incoming missiles. Everyone was, except for Jinshan.

Jinshan listened to the brief. The initial Chinese attacks on Hawaii and Guam were both failures. Still, those were high-risk, high-reward attempts, and Jinshan hadn't expected both of them to succeed. But he was pleased to hear enough had gone well over the past few hours that China had the advantage.

After a few minutes, General Chen rose from his seat and began pacing the room. He walked over to one of the men at the computer monitors and asked him for an update on the missiles.

Jinshan turned to Admiral Zhang. "What is your recommended course of action, now that Guam remains in the hands of the Americans?"

"Chairman, you are familiar with our previous plan, which used the Jiaolong to guard our convoy across the Pacific. But we don't yet know how well she will perform in combat operations."

"The testing looked very promising."

"Indeed, sir. Still, I worry about the Americans launching air attacks from Guam. With your permission, I would like us to consolidate our Southern Fleet with the Jiaolong. Japan has signaled that they will surrender. Korea is quickly becoming irrelevant militarily. But I do not believe we can support operations in the Western Pacific without destroying America's air power on Guam."

Jinshan raised an eyebrow. "Agreed. Proceed as requested."

One of the Central Committee members said, "What of South Korea?"

General Chen said, "The American response to North Korea's initial attack was swift, but our participation in the attack was unexpected. As a result, we have severely crippled the American air defense and air attack capability based in South Korea. Now, chemical weapons are providing the North Korean troops an advantage. Artillery and missile strikes are bombarding the south with nerve agent. The North Korean leader is asking for our assistance. He claims the Americans have hit his missile silos with nuclear weapons."

A few of the men around the table exchanged glances at that. Not everyone here knew it was a Chinese false flag operation that was responsible for sending submarine-launched nuclear missiles at North Korean targets. But the ones who weren't in on the plans could sense something was afoot, and their political instincts kept them quiet.

Jinshan cleared his throat. "Do not send our ground forces there, General. Continue to provide assistance by air, if it serves China."

"Yes, sir."

An analyst came running up to the elevated platform where the lead team was seated. He headed to the colonel who was leading the brief, whispering something to him. The color drained from the colonel's face.

General Chen stood feet away, one hand in a balled fist, rubbing the palm of his other. "Well?"

The colonel nodded, and the young analyst said, "We have just received trajectory updates. Sir, we are tracking ten launches from the American land-based missile fields. Our first estimates appear correct. We are confident those missiles are targeting our northern missile sites, near our Russian border."

General Chen stood menacingly over the young man. "The other missiles—what of those?"

"Sir, we are less confident about the target of the missile launches that originated from the southern Pacific Ocean. We believe there were four ICBMs—each from a submarine. They could be targeting Beijing military targets. Or Beijing itself. Or..."

"Or what?" General Chen fumed.

"Or the Khingan mountain bunkers, General," Jinshan finished the thought. His voice was calm. Fearless.

The table fell quiet, save General Chen, who was looking at the analyst. "When will they hit?"

"Between five and ten minutes, sir."

General Chen cast a panicked glance back at Jinshan, which he ignored.

Jinshan was now the leader of the largest nation in the world, with the largest military in the world. But even he was powerless now. The only thing to do now was wait until these missiles hit their targets.

Jinshan waved the colonel on. "You may continue with your update, Colonel."

General Chen looked as if Jinshan were ignoring a charging tiger, his eyes wide.

The colonel began speaking again. His voice shaky. He went over the cyber and EMP attacks on the United States. He touched on some of the special operations missions inside the US, and the failed mission to strike Hawaii.

Finally General Chen interrupted, "Chairman Jinshan," he began, "I must urge you to respond to America's aggression with our nuclear weapons. We cannot wait any longer. If their missiles are inbound as reported, we have only moments left to order the strike."

Jinshan cocked his head. "Why, General?"

"Excuse me, sir?"

"*Why* would you have me do it?"

A bead of sweat had formed on the general's forehead. He turned to the map. There was now a series of circles over the northern strategic missile locations, as well as the Beijing military region, which included the network of mountain bunkers they were in.

The general shook his head, speechless.

Jinshan said, "If this were a full-capability nuclear strike, there would have been many more missiles fired. Therefore, we may assume that only a limited strike was ordered. This was my expectation. No, General, this was my *hope*."

"Hope? Sir?"

Jinshan forced himself to be patient. This was the penalty for installing a puppet. Jinshan didn't want to worry about a second coup. While he could have picked a more capable man for General Chen's billet, Jinshan valued the predictability of the ambitious dullard over any strategic thinking that alternate selections might have provided.

With the recent political upheaval and changing of the guard in military leadership, Jinshan worried about the loyalty of his leadership team. Every odd glance from a flag officer was suspect. Every time he turned his back, he worried about knives coming out. Already he had removed several high-ranking officers from their posts at the mere whisper of them questioning his legitimacy.

Jinshan's expression remained impassive as he stared at his nervous general. Chen owed everything to Jinshan. The only reason he had made it past colonel was because he had agreed to

Jinshan's offer for his daughter decades earlier. That had been a wise investment for both of them. Jinshan had obtained his greatest operative, the ultra-talented sleeper agent, Lena Chou. In return, General Chen had been able to resurrect his lifeless career, even now reaping the rewards as he obtained the highest military post in all of China. The trade for his daughter had long since been repaid, of course. But Jinshan preferred to live with the devils he knew. It would not do to have a thoughtful military man in that position. Someone who might second-guess Jinshan's decisions. Let the thinkers come later, when the war was won.

Jinshan didn't have much longer anyway. He just needed to get through this year. Two at the most. He looked down at the liver spots on his hands. His skin was yellow from jaundice. The cancer treatment was slowing his inevitable end, but nothing could stop it.

He sighed. The others knew his health was failing. Jinshan needed to project enough strength to ward off ambitious would-be replacements. Or inspire enough fear that they wouldn't dare whisper the thought that must be in their heads.

Even General Chen wasn't really loyal to him. He was just a less-thoughtful attack dog. Chen recognized that his master held meat in one hand and a club in the other. The moment Jinshan was unable to provide either of those was the moment Chen would betray him too. General Chen served his purpose for now. But seeing his reaction to the pressure of war caused Jinshan to question whether his predictability was worth the complete lack of value added in moments like these.

"General, please take your seat."

The general's face was practically twitching with fear. The man's eyes were on the electronic display that was updating missile trajectories. Now only minutes until the first of the missiles hit their Chinese targets along the Russian border.

Jinshan's prewar brief gave estimates that ninety-eight percent of China's ICBM capability would be destroyed.

Chen looked to the colonel. "How long would it take us to launch—"

"Enough." Jinshan cut him off with a slightly elevated tone that was rare for him.

All eyes were on Jinshan now.

"Gentlemen, the American response is a limited strike. Their doctrine prescribes that any nuclear response be proportional, and that the targets be of appropriate type. Therefore, we have assumed that they would strike at our ICBM assets in the north. After that limited strike is complete, we can continue to fight the war with conventional assets."

General Chen leaned forward on his hands, his frame over the long conference table. "We can only respond if we *survive* their limited nuclear attack."

Behind Chen's eyes were waves of fear and uncertainty. Jinshan knew that until you saw someone perform under true pressure, you didn't really know how they would react. He had now seen enough of Chen to second-guess his appointment. If General Chen was unable to control his emotions and operate under pressure, Jinshan couldn't trust him in a position of this much power. Chen's weakness and need for control would eventually become a problem. Jinshan stored the thought in his mind for later.

General Chen continued, "And the submarine-launched weapons may be headed here, towards the—"

The Ministry of State Security representative at the table said, "Our intelligence suggests the Americans do not have our exact whereabouts. We believe that the Americans know there are bunkers in these mountains, but they don't know we have developed them as a wartime headquarters. And even if they do find out, our procedures have made it almost impossible for them to know which of the six bunkers we currently reside in."

"But there is at least a chance that they could hit us—"

Jinshan raised his voice, his face flushing. "And if that happens, General, someone will take over for us. It is not worth wasting time discussing the possibility of our own demise."

The table went quiet.

General Chen's eyes fell to his lap. Jinshan swallowed his disgust and then said, "In all likelihood, we will survive the next few hours and come out political winners. The Russians will issue their condemnation on the world stage, along with an ultimatum. Our strategy dictates that America be made to look villainous. In order to do that, we must keep our war efforts conventional."

One of the Central Committee members said, "But we have used EMP weapons. We have fired nuclear weapons into North Korea..."

Jinshan noticed a few of the other men around the table cast disapproving glances at the politician for his argument. Perhaps even their looks were for Jinshan's benefit, to communicate to their leader that they remained unwavering. So many games.

Like General Chen, this politician had not been involved in many of the planning stages of the war. Many of the military movements were a surprise to them.

Jinshan would indulge them momentarily. "You are mistaken." He gave a slight smile. "It was America who fired nuclear weapons at North Korea, not China. This is what is being put out on global media networks even as we speak. Our own military actions are in response to America encroaching on North Korea's sovereign territory. Our actions take place in the context of their continued religiously motivated attacks inside of China. The People's Republic of China is standing up for the freedom-loving people of the world. America shall be painted as a rogue state. One to be shunned."

"But Western news sources will surely refute our—"

"Western media are under attack. American media will be in chaos in the aftermath of the EMPs. And we have armies of cyberwarriors and intelligence organizations that are working to shape global opinion. No one wants to go to war, or to see their economies ruined. Japan has already agreed to surrender. The Europeans will follow suit after the Russian ultimatum. We must isolate the American military from their allies. Without the cooperation of other nations, and without the fuel and resources of other nations, we will prevail. This limited nuclear strike by the Americans plays into our hands. America has crossed an unfathomable line, which will not be tolerated by other peace-loving nations of the world."

Jinshan watched General Chen as his eyes moved rapidly back and forth over the table, taking in information that he should have already known, had he studied all of the documents that had been provided to him.

The colonel picked up a ringing phone and began speaking into it. He nodded and hung up, then turned to the table of senior leaders. "We have lost communications with our strategic missile force along the Russian border. We believe that the American ICBMs have struck their targets."

One of the other generals at the table said, "Please provide a damage assessment as soon as possible."

"Yes, sir."

Jinshan remained calm and turned to the admiral sitting at the table. "We need to discuss our naval plans. Those will be the most essential element of the next few weeks. Provide me with an update on the Jiaolong-class ships."

The admiral said, "Due to the shortened timeline of our attack plans, we were only able to outfit one ship with all the new weapon systems. It was slow progress, due to the need to keep the work covert."

Jinshan nodded. "I understand. This was a prudent decision to keep the ships hidden in port. Tell me, do we think the Americans are still unaware of the technology?"

The minister of state security said, "This is our belief, Chairman Jinshan. The Americans know we have ramped up construction on our new naval warships at this location, but we have been providing them false information as to the details of this particular weapon system. They believe that these ships are two new Type 055 guided-missile destroyers."

Jinshan nodded. "When will they be able to get to sea?"

The admiral said, "We expect the first to get underway within the week, sir. We have had to skip many of the maintenance tests new ships normally go through. But we have conducted simulations in port that should mitigate much of that risk. The second ship will take longer."

"Very well."

General Chen frowned. "If these ships are so important, why have we not used them in the opening attacks?"

The admiral said, "General, with respect, the essential nature of these weapons is precisely why we wanted to keep them out of harm's way. The Jiaolong weapons systems are the first of their kind. If their technology works, they could make any battle group impenetrable to enemy forces."

Jinshan felt a shudder and could see commotion in the pit of computer terminals below. The phone rang, and once again the colonel who was standing next to their table answered it. Keeping the phone to his ear, he said, "We have lost communications with Bunkers Four, Five, and Six."

General Chen said, "Bunker Four was located one hundred kilometers from here. If they were hit..."

The colonel said, "All American missiles have hit their

targets. There are no more ICBMs inbound. The base safety officer reports tunnels between all bunkers have been sealed and ventilation systems are operational. He recommends that we transfer via the tunnel train to Bunker Two at your earliest convenience, sir. Given the prevailing winds, this will minimize any radiation risk during future air transports."

General Chen let out a sigh, shoulders slumped, wiping sweat off his brow.

Jinshan nodded. "Very well. Give us the next two hours and then make the arrangements." He turned back to the admiral, unfazed by their new lease on life. "How does Admiral Song intend to use the Jiaolong?"

"He agrees with me, sir. He wants to finish off Guam."

General Chen was shaking his head, looking at the other men around the table. "What is the status of our strategic nuclear forces?"

The military officer standing near the computer terminal had a phone to his ear. He nodded to acknowledge the question and relayed it into the phone.

"We do not have full confirmation, General, but it appears that the Americans have struck direct hits on our missile fields and nuclear weapons storage depots."

General Chen cursed. "And the ballistic missile submarines?"

Admiral Zhang frowned. "We have not heard from them in the past hour. They may have been hit."

"Hit?"

"Sunk, General."

General Chen slammed his fist on the table. "This is exactly why we should have fired our nuclear weapons first." He looked between Jinshan and Admiral Zhang. "You should not send Song's fleet to Guam. Guam's base was hit. They will be nursing their wounds. We should send Admiral Song's carrier group with the others, towards Hawaii. If we conquer Hawaii, there shall be nothing else in our way."

Admiral Zhang said, "Respectfully, General, I recommend that we—"

General Chen said, "The Jiaolong is an unproven technology. You should have faith in your men, Admiral. We should sail east and land our forces on Hawaii while the Americans are in disarray."

The two flag officers began arguing, but Jinshan silenced them.

"You have sufficiently registered your disapproval, General." Jinshan stood, his leathery face wrinkling into a frown. The room went quiet, and General Chen lowered his eyes. "Now, if anyone has further questions on our strategy, you may take them up with me in private."

Jinshan left the room, coughing into his fist.

8

David and Lindsay had gone back and forth as to whether they should get in their one working car and get the hell away from D.C., or whether they should stay put. With no electricity or cellular connectivity, there simply wasn't any way to get information about what was happening out there. A few of the neighbors had come outside and David had spoken with them briefly. At least two families on their street had packed up and left. One father had a holstered pistol on his hip as he got into his minivan. He didn't say where they were headed.

David and Lindsay decided to stay put. They were at war now, and he felt the call of duty. David was needed at his work. A part of him wondered if he should try to go to Langley right now, in the middle of the night. But without direction, he decided against it. He would be more capable after a few hours of rest.

Lindsay put their youngest back down. Their older child—a toddler—had, as David had always expected, slept through World War Three. Lindsay and he had lain back in bed but hadn't been able to sleep.

"It feels wrong, going to bed right now," David said. "But I mean, what the hell are we supposed to do?"

"There are a lot of sirens out there," said Lindsay.

"Yeah." David was happy that law enforcement and emergency services were functional, at least. There was a debate among men like him on how bad an EMP attack would really be, with worst-case predictions that no vehicles whatsoever would work after the strike.

"We should try to go to the grocery store first thing in the morning."

David sighed. "I'll need to work."

"I know."

"Don't go to the store alone. People will be scared."

"You're probably right." Lindsay lay on his shoulder. "Should we go somewhere...I don't know...more rural? I feel like it would maybe be safer there. My mother can go to her sister's place out in Purceville. Do you think there's enough room for us all there?"

"I'm not sure that the apocalypse is enough to get me to live with your mother."

Lindsay didn't laugh. Nothing seemed funny right now. They stayed that way in bed for a while. Unable to sleep. Minutes of silence interrupted by bits of worried conversation. David didn't know how long it went on. Nothing that told time was still functional.

But eventually, headlights appeared through his bedroom window.

"Is that in our driveway?" He threw a robe on and headed towards the knocking at his front door. Two polite but nervous-looking enlisted Army men stood there.

"Good evening, sir, is your name David Manning?"

"That's right."

"Sir, everyone working on SILVERSMITH has been recalled. I'm to drive you and your dependents in as soon as possible."

"My dependents?"

"Yes, sir. Anyone who might need to accompany you in the event of a location transfer."

"Transfer to where?"

"Out of the D.C. area, sir. That's all I know."

"Now?"

The two men didn't answer. The looks on their faces said it all. One couldn't have been much more than twenty years old, by the look of it. Both looked tired.

David thought he understood. Given the speech he had seen on TV, the emergency alert message, and the EMP detonation, the CIA and the Pentagon needed to respond immediately. The Pentagon must have had plans ready for an event like this. A "break glass in the case of disaster" plan. This was going to be a different type of war than the United States had faced before.

David waved them in. "Come inside, guys. You can sit on the couch while I rustle the troops." The two Army men exchanged glances, the bright flashlight illuminating their shrugs. Then they followed David in.

Lindsay already had sweats and sneakers on when David was back in the bedroom. She had heard the conversation. Lindsay wasn't happy that they needed to grab the kids and leave their home in the middle of the night. But she didn't complain either. Her motherly instinct intermingled with her own sense of national duty. She knew the type of work her husband did. Whatever Uncle Sam needed David to do, they would do it.

They packed fast and were soon riding in the back of the white government van, the kids sleeping and the parents wondering what the hell was in store for them. The drive was shorter than David expected. They must have still been in Vienna, Virginia.

"We're not going to Langley?"

"They told us to take you here, sir."

There were mobile generators connected to floodlights in the parking lot of a four-story building, dark glass windows and beige stone. Identical to most other office buildings in the area, except that their vehicle had to go through a checkpoint with multiple armed guards to get past the barbed-wire fence. If David could have seen the roof of the building, he would've seen the surplus of satellite dishes and antennae on the roof.

There were dozens of similar white government vans dropping off other families. They shuffled through the doors through multiple ID checks and then gathered in a conference room that clearly wasn't meant to hold this many people.

A man wearing a track suit ushered people. "Families over here, please. SILVERSMITH personnel down the hall."

"You gonna be all right?" David squeezed his wife's shoulder.

"We'll be fine," Lindsay said.

Maddie, their three-year-old, was now awake, courageously walking while holding her mom's hand. Their infant still slept in a Babybjörn on Lindsay's chest. Lindsay looked exhausted, but resolute.

"I'll find you after," David said. He kissed her on the cheek and walked away.

The SILVERSMITH personnel funneled into a meeting room one floor above where the civilians were being tended to. General Schwartz and Susan Collinsworth, the CIA operations officer in charge of the group, stood at the front of the room.

"Close the door, please," said Schwartz.

Susan said, "We'll be quick, because we need to get moving. Within the past few hours, the Chinese military has begun attacking the US, both overseas and domestically."

Murmurs from around the room.

"At least one EMP was detonated over the mid-Atlantic, which has caused massive power and electronics outages throughout the eastern seaboard. We're receiving intel reports that describe at least three electromagnetic pulse detonations over the US in the past hour. But the information we've been getting has been incomplete and, in some cases, contradictory."

She glanced at General Schwartz, who took it from there. "Ladies and gentlemen, we've been ordered to decentralize and relocate the entire US military and intelligence apparatus. SILVERSMITH will be transported together, with dependents, and a security detail provided to ensure our safety. We expect that tomorrow will bring widespread chaos to the civilian population."

More whispers from around the room.

"Transportation will be difficult. In many cases, infrastructure will temporarily cease to function. Our intention is to start our relocation process immediately."

"Where are we headed?" someone asked.

"We won't be making that known, for security reasons."

"What does immediately mean? Like, now?"

"The buses are gassing up. Ours should be here within the hour."

"What about our houses? Shit, I got a cat, man. What about my cat?"

A few swears. Some people shaking their heads.

"Ladies and gentlemen, we just witnessed the beginning of the third world war. This day will be in the history books. Each of you read the Red Cell threat analysis report. You know what to expect. EMP attacks coupled with cyber and special operations assaults. Attacks on American infrastructure and utilities, transportation hubs, political leadership. We need to assume that all of this will be attempted. As part of team SILVER-SMITH, you hold a critical knowledge and ability to help manage our defensive strategy and tactics. We need to ensure that the government continues to function, and this is one of the ways in which we'll do that."

A knock at the door. An Air Force officer handed a piece of paper to the general, who read it and gritted his teeth.

He looked up. "The president is confirmed dead."

Mouths dropped open. Someone said, "*Holy shit...*"

"The vice president has been sworn in as the new commander in chief, and the executive branch has declared martial law until further notice." General Schwartz paused and looked up at the faces in the room. "We'll be departing soon. Please help your families get aboard the buses."

There were two buses and two escort vehicles. The SILVER-SMITH workers and their families piled on, and the buses departed shortly after, taking the Beltway and then heading south on I-95. David guessed it was still before five a.m. when they got on the highway. Normally the southbound traffic wouldn't be so bad at this time. But not today. There were already a lot of vehicles traveling the highway.

By dawn, they passed Richmond, Virginia. That was when the signs of panic became visible.

Lindsay pointed out the tinted bus window. "What's that? What *is* that?"

A huge bonfire had been lit atop one of the highway over-passes. The SILVERSMITH convoy of defense and intelligence workers and their families passed underneath. A sedan was ablaze. A limp body rested a few feet from the flaming vehicle, limbs hanging through the chain-link fence of the overpass. The person had been shot in the head. There were no police or emergency services in sight.

The escort vehicles had blue lights flashing at this point. They traveled in the left-hand lane, and most vehicles quickly got out of the way. But as the morning went on, the highway became much more crowded. Their escort vehicle began sounding the sirens and honking horns, and people in the left lane became slow to move out of the way.

Susan caught David's eye from the front of the bus, gesturing him to come up. David checked that his wife and kids were asleep, then headed up the aisle and sat across from his boss.

"Morning, David. Join us, please. I'd like you to hear the latest." General Schwartz and several of David's colleagues were in the seats adjacent to her. The seat directly in back of the bus driver was filled with two men David knew were with Cybercommand. They had military-grade laptops that were connected to a large black communications device.

"STRATCOM's online. PACFLEET. CENTCOM. Homeland Security's up. Okay, we're getting real-time data now. It's slow, but it's coming."

David offered Susan a puzzled look. She whispered, "They've set up a drone-based network over the US to provide coverage until we can get our replacement satellite networks up. It will be spotty, but it's better than nothing, and we're relatively confident it hasn't been hacked."

David nodded.

After a few moments, the group began going over updates from various sources around the globe. The situation was dire. It was now less than twelve hours since the war had begun, and there was no electricity or internet for the vast majority of the United States. The effects of the EMPs weren't as bad as the sci-fi movies would have you believe. But the collective result of cyber, EMP, and whatever the Chinese special operations teams were doing was quite potent.

"We have several nuclear power plants that came very close to having a meltdown. One hasn't reported in yet. Cyberattacks have wiped out a lot of data centers. It looks like the companies that handle logistics and transportation were the worst hit."

"Is that really a big deal?"

David said, "Yes, it is. It means they won't be able to plan the trucks or tell how many packages to fill. Everything is digital now. Some warehouses will have surpluses while others go barren. The end result is that people won't be able to get food and water, or soap and toothpaste, within a few days. Although with the panic and riots, that will probably be a matter of hours."

General Schwartz said, "What do you see on the Chinese ground forces in the US?"

The communications specialist said, "Eight bases were attacked. All were Air Force heavy bases—aerial refueling aircraft appear to have been the targets. Most attackers were killed or captured, but not all. There are reports of some larger numbers of Chinese ground forces in the northern plains states. But those are unconfirmed. Lots of people are calling into the police stations on landlines and saying they saw Chinese people after the emergency broadcast. A lot of stuff like that. We don't know how true any of it is, but local authorities have been told to keep an eye out. Problem is the normal means of communication are shot for the most part."

Susan said, "Any diplomatic communications between China and POTUS?"

David heard the squeal of the bus's brakes as it came to a halt. The highway was now a sea of red brake lights, the traffic on I-95 south having come to a complete stop.

"The State Department has been directed to start an open dialogue with the People's Republic of China and an immediate deescalation of hostilities."

David said, "Not sure how that's going to go over, I don't—"

The rapid-fire siren of the lead security vehicle came on and then off as their convoy of two buses and two security vehicles moved over to the shoulder lane and began traveling forward at a slow pace.

"Hold on—just got this—both the UN and China have just put out a statement via official channels. They are calling for an immediate cease-fire of all hostilities between the PRC and the United Sates."

"Are you effing kidding me?"

David said, "What else is in the Chinese statement?"

The communications specialist scanned the message with his finger. "China denies any wrongdoing. They deny accusations of instigating hostilities. They are calling the cyberattacks and blackouts the US has experienced another religiously motivated terrorist attack. They condemn the US for their nuclear response—"

"Nuclear? What the hell are they talking about?"

"—and demand the rest of the world condemn those actions as well. Something about American radical religious antagonism. I don't know what that is...some sort of propaganda speak, I guess. They're calling for a one-week cease-fire to remove civilians from each other's territory and are encouraged that the United Nations is willing to manage the truce."

David said, "They just put that out?"

"Yup."

"And they're already citing the UN's statement."

Susan said, "Seems scripted, doesn't it?"

General Schwartz said, "Agreed."

David said, "What the hell are they talking about with the nuclear response?"

Susan shot the general a look. He nodded. Susan whispered, "The US fired a small number of strategic nuclear weapons on Chinese nuclear missile sites, as well as one military installation in northern China."

David sat back in his seat, his hand over his mouth. "Son of a bitch..."

Susan glanced around the bus. They were out of earshot of any of the other passengers. "Keep that to yourself."

* * *

The trip lasted another twenty-two hours. They made a few stops, and a boxed lunch was handed out about halfway through. After that, it was water-only until their destination. The convoy gained a more substantial military escort in North Carolina. Three Humvees and an MRAP. By then, the left lane of all major highways had been cleared, designated for military and official government vehicles only. Every highway ramp had either a police or military vehicle posted.

David was called up to the front of the bus several times to hear updates and provide his opinion on global developments. The more he understood about the scope of the Chinese attack, the more worried he was about his sister, brother, and father. His sister Victoria's ship had been involved in a sea and air battle near Guam. His brother Chase had been in Korea when the attacks had begun, but David learned that he was unharmed and now in Japan. David didn't know the status of his father, who was on board the USS *Ford* near Hawaii, but he assumed that Admiral Manning was safe for now.

By the time they arrived at Eglin Air Force Base, they were all ready for the trip to be over. The families on the bus needed space, and more than a single bathroom.

There was a woman in an Air Force uniform waiting for them as they got off the bus. She wrote down all of their names on a notepad and began directing them to temporary housing. David and his family ended up in the bachelor officers' quarters. It was basically a two-room hotel suite, with a queen bed and a pull-out couch. Lindsay changed their youngest while Maddie sat coloring on the couch.

"I need to get over to the office. Susan said we have an orientation briefing at eleven. Are you okay?"

Lindsay nodded. She had bags under her eyes. "We'll be fine. I'll see you later."

David left the BOQ and walked down the road towards the building he would be working in. A convoy of troop transports and Humvees drove by, and in the distance he could hear the roar of jet engines.

It was early morning the day after the war began. David wasn't so sure things would ever get back to normal.

9

Chinese aircraft carrier Liaoning
Philippine Sea
Day 3

Admiral Song stood behind the expansive plexiglass windows of his personal bridge, looking out over his fleet. The carrier steamed west into the wind as she recovered another replacement squadron of attack aircraft.

The aircraft carrier's captain watched with him. "These pilots will be less experienced."

The admiral said, "And what are we? Veterans of a three-day-old war? At least they are alive. The same cannot be said for the men whom they replace."

In other company, Admiral Song wouldn't dare suggest his men were anything less than invincible. But the two senior officers had known each other for decades. The carrier captain had been a junior officer when the admiral was himself a ship captain. Now he was one of the admiral's few confidants.

The captain said, "We will be finished recovering our new air wing by evening's end."

The admiral kept his eyes on the jet that was coming in on its final approach. Its tailhook sent sparks flying as it skimmed the surface of the carrier's flight deck and clutched one of the arresting gear wires, which slowed it to a full stop. The admiral could see the pilot's head jerk forward at the rapid deceleration. Then the aircraft taxied forward, directed by the flight deck crew to its parking spot on the bow.

Admiral Song said, "We will travel north this evening."

"The American submarine presence is stronger there."

"The Americans have accepted our cease-fire agreement. We have a reprieve."

"Do you think it is wise for us to trust such an agreement?"

Admiral Song shrugged. "We have our orders. We shall head north and meet up with the Jiaolong. The first of its class."

The captain arched his brow. "The Jiaolong-class ships are ready for sea?"

"Only one. But it will be underway tomorrow."

"Has it been tested?"

"I have been assured that they will meet our operational requirements."

The two old colleagues exchanged knowing glances. Usually new technology didn't work so well at first. This was especially true for complex new military equipment. "If this is true, it is excellent news."

The admiral turned back to the flight deck, extending his hands on the rail. The jet that had just landed was being taken towards the elevator. Its wings had been folded up, and a trolley cart was pulling it along the starboard side of the flight deck. It would be taken below into the hangar deck, alongside dozens of other new arrivals. Maintenance crews were turning wrenches and checking oil levels. Ordnance men were filling ammunition pods and attaching missiles.

"We cannot have another loss like we suffered at the war's opening. We will join up with the Jiaolong and several troop carriers. Then we will head back to Guam."

"General Chen's daily message indicated that his priority was Hawaii. He directed us to draw up plans to accomplish this. Are we not going to follow his orders?"

Admiral Song felt strongly that General Chen was an imbecile. He should have never been promoted past major, let alone become the highest-ranking military member in all of China. Admiral Song had an immense level of respect for Cheng Jinshan, but he failed to see the wisdom of Chen's appointment to his current position.

"We do not work for General Chen."

"He is the highest-ranking—"

"We work for Admiral Zhang."

"Who works for Chen."

"And they both report to Chairman Jinshan."

The captain waited patiently for an explanation. Admiral Song watched the next jet land and then turned back to the captain. "I received counsel from Chairman Jinshan himself. Admiral Zhang was present. General Chen was not. We do not require General Chen's approval to reattack Guam."

Admiral Song could see the surprise on the face of his subordinate.

"General Chen will be displeased that he was cut out of the process. He strikes me as the type of man that may take retributive action against those who are not in a position to avoid it."

"I believe that you are correct in your assessment of the general's response. I fear for the day when China's fate rests on the judgment of such a man."

"Why do men like that play such games?"

Admiral Song smiled. "That you would ask such a question

tells me you are not such a man. And that is a good thing. It is why I have chosen you for this position."

A series of bells and a voice on the ship's overhead speaker announced that it was time for evening meal.

They ate in the admiral's wardroom. Real silverware and ornate china plates. The admiral announced their orders to the eight senior-most officers in the battle group. These were loyal and capable men. He had handpicked them and trained them himself. Their faces held the eagerness and intensity of a warrior headed into battle.

"The Jiaolong-class ship will give us a definitive tactical advantage. We must do everything in our power to protect them and keep their capability a secret for as long as possible."

The aircraft carrier captain said, "This means that any American submarines or aircraft that come into range will need to be engaged."

One of the officers said, "Sir, we have a cease-fire. What will our rules of engagement be if we come across an American asset while we have the Jiaolong in company?"

Admiral Song said, "Then we must engage them. Peace treaty or not."

When the dinner was over, Admiral Song and the aircraft carrier captain were left alone at the table. They sipped tea and discussed their plans in detail.

A sailor from the communications department entered the room and handed the admiral a folder. He put on his glasses and read the message, then handed the folder back to the sailor, who left them.

Admiral Song said, "General Chen has given his approval for the change in plans that was discussed with Chairman Jinshan."

The captain looked puzzled. "Did you ask his permission?"

The admiral smiled. "I did not. The man is posturing."

The captain smirked.

Admiral Song shook his head. "If General Chen had half of his daughter's ability, this war would be over in a week."

"I do not know of his daughter."

"Probably safer for you that way."

10

Japan

Lena Chou had arrived in Tokyo on the day the war began. Her plane had landed just as the first wave of Chinese missiles had begun striking American and Japanese military targets on the mainland.

She had been sent to kill Natesh Chaudrey. Natesh had aided the Chinese espionage operation to extract war plans from two dozen American experts. But he had become a liability. Now Lena was lying low, trying to stay hidden from the Americans in Japan until they all left. She expected that American agents were still looking for her.

One in particular.

She felt mixed emotions when she thought of Chase Manning. She admired him for what he was. A water walker like her. Someone who had the mental fortitude and physical gifts to do anything in life. But their stars were crossed. He would never see the world the way she did. She had been enlightened by Jinshan's teachings, and lucky enough to be selected for her special assignment at a young age.

A part of her wished that she never had been thrust into this life of espionage and violence. Especially when she thought about the things she had to do. The flash of that young girl's face entered her mind. But as quickly as it came, she forced it out.

Lena had killed many in the name of her country. Especially lately, as her cover had been blown and her talents had been used in a different way. But nothing had been like killing the former president of China and his wife and daughter.

That experienced had changed her.

A knock at the door.

"Enter."

One of the Ministry of State Security (MSS) operatives came in and left a tray of food on the room's lone table. The table was only a foot off the floor, as was customary in traditional Japanese homes. On the tray lay a simple meal and a glass of water. The MSS was China's equivalent of the CIA. It was the organization Lena had worked for, in one way or another, since she was a teenager.

"Do you require anything else?"

"No."

The young man bowed and then exited the way he had come.

Lena sipped from the cup of hot soup, staring out through the sliding glass door. A small garden lay on the other side of the glass. High stone walls and a single leafless tree. Lena finished the soup, its broth warm and soothing. Then she used chopsticks to finish off the rest of the food, a bowl of sticky rice and raw fish.

She finished eating and stepped outside. Her breath was visible in the cool air, and she held her arms close to her chest. The booming explosions in the distance had ceased. Finally. She was beginning to worry that things had not gone according to plan.

When her hands began to numb, she opened the sliding door and reentered her room. She did some calisthenics and yoga but felt sluggish. With all the travel and the medical rest after suffering serious burns, she hadn't been able to keep up her usual vigorous exercise routine. She frowned as she looked in the mirror, not liking the extra pound or two she saw.

She flipped on a small TV and kept the volume on low. There were only two stations still broadcasting. One was the national news, which Lena knew was being heavily influenced by Chinese psychological warfare specialists. The other was Skynews, which had also been infiltrated by Jinshan's network, but not as thoroughly. The Chinese Ministry of State Security had been laying the groundwork for years, inserting their agents into global news networks as production executives, directors, and video editors. Each one of them was carefully trained as to how to influence the minds of the masses to be receptive to Chinese political goals.

During Lena's time as an agent living in America, she had always been amused when the news would report shifts in public opinion. A change in consumer confidence in the economy, or in support for a given policy. Public perception was driven directly by the information people received, which was in turn shaped by a select few gatekeepers. In each news room, producers and executives chose which stories to run, and how they would be portrayed. People didn't have their own opinions. Not really. They were told what to think, and how to think it. Jinshan saw this phenomenon as the single greatest structural flaw within democratic nations. The leaders of nations should know better than to allow media conglomerate owners and executives to shape opinions that would affect them. For progress to be made, Jinshan himself had to shape those opinions.

On the TV screen, the newscaster was giving a summary of the UN summit that had taken place yesterday in Geneva.

They kept showing the same footage. The person at the head of the podium was a Russian diplomat. Lena watched the man's lips move and heard a British-accented English translation being broadcast with a few seconds' delay.

"The Russian Federation is appalled and dismayed at the recent aggression the United States has shown on the world stage. The United States has violated international humanitarian law by using nuclear weapons in a first strike against North Korea and the People's Republic of China. In light of these transgressions, the Russian Federation has chosen to issue the following ultimatum. If the United States uses any additional weapons of mass destruction, including chemical, biological, or nuclear weapons, then the Russian Federation will have no choice but to enter the war in defense of China. However, we demand that all other UN member-nations also remain neutral. We also demand that the United Nations immediately ratify international economic sanctions against the United States, including the embargo of foreign petroleum products and any supplies that may be used to make war."

The newscaster came back on the screen. "In the aftermath of the Russian ultimatum, several members of NATO have disavowed any allegiance to the United States and left the organization. Japan has agreed to a peaceful settlement with the People's Republic of China and has called for the expedited departure of all American troops currently stationed there. This brings us to the most important development of the day, which is the Chinese-US cease-fire agreement. The US president has agreed to the Chinese terms, which surprised many."

An analyst said, "Indeed. Inside the US, political parties are fighting over which direction to take while their nation will wake up tomorrow facing its fourth day without electricity.

Many in the US are clamoring for a more aggressive response, especially in light of the death of the former US president. While the official cause of the Air Force One crash is still under investigation, leaked preliminary reports point to a surface-to-air missile attack."

The newscaster shook his head. "Horrifying."

"Indeed. While the Chinese deny any such action, that doesn't stop the anger welling up among many of the American people. So, it is quite shocking to see the new US president accept this peace treaty. But what we are hearing from US diplomats and military experts that the US president felt there was a need to deescalate. He wanted to get any Americans in the Asia-Pacific theater out of harm's way. And the Americans were afraid that further use of nuclear, biological, or chemical weapons could damage their nation beyond repair."

The TV screen showed a still image of the former vice president of the United States as he was sworn in as president. A recording played his voice. "My fellow Americans, our most important responsibility is to the safety and security of our citizens, including the hundreds of thousands who are now located in Asia. While we strenuously object to the military action China has taken, we must make peace to ensure the stability of our great nation."

The analyst said, "Many Americans are not happy with the president's decision to accept the Chinese peace treaty. Some in the president's own party are calling on him to resign."

The news host held his hand to his earpiece. "Now, can you go into the details of the peace treaty? Explain what the two nations have agreed to exactly."

The camera switched to a third man. "Of course. China has demanded that the United States remove its troops from its bases in the Western Pacific, and it seems that the US has acceded to that demand. Now I'm told that all US forces must move east of a certain longitude line within a certain timeline..."

"And is the US in fact complying with China's wishes, then?"

"It seems that yes, they are. Japanese and American commercial airliners have been commandeered to begin transporting any US civilians and troops back to the United States, and US military forces are—well, they aren't officially calling it a retreat, but that is what I've heard several military experts refer to it as."

"Fascinating. And how will this play out globally? Are any other countries bound by the agreement? We've seen some very steadfast declarations of American backing from Australia, Canada, and of course the United Kingdom. But no members of the European Union have committed to supporting the US? Or even other members of NATO?"

"Well, a few NATO members have said that they would respond with military action if the United States and China restart hostilities. Or if Russia—"

"Yes, now this Russian ultimatum...that seems to have thrown a wrench into everything, hasn't it? Are they really saying what I think they are saying? That Russia would actually start a thermonuclear war with the United States if the Americans were to use any additional nuclear weapons?"

"Well, I just want to make one correction to your statement there. We don't know for sure that the United States *has* actually used nuclear weapons."

"How can you say that? There are reports of nuclear detonations in North Korea and China."

"I understand that. However, until we get confirmation from the United States government, I would urge us to take all of the information we're hearing with a healthy dose of skepticism. I'm hearing from my sources that China and North Korea were the aggressors here. That they launched a surprise attack on US forces in the Pacific."

"Even if that were true, it does not refute the fact that the United States launched nuclear weapons in retaliation. How can you dispute that?"

"I'm not disputing it. I'm saying that I don't know that it's true."

The newscasters began talking over each other heatedly. Then the host said, "Well, tell me this—do you think that the United States will take Russia's threat seriously?"

"I do. And here's why: the Russian Federation simply has too large an inventory of nuclear weapons for their threat *not* to be taken seriously. No one wants further bloodshed. And I'm shocked that it has come to this between United States and China. But if there is to be fighting, I think the entire world has a shared interest in the fighting being done with conventional weapons. Your reporting states that there were at least ten nuclear explosions on the day the war began. That alone is very dangerous. The loss of life, the radiation, and the potential environmental effects are devastatingly real. I hope with all my heart that if anything good comes out of it, it is that world leaders will take a breath and settle down—perhaps work out their differences peacefully. I realize that's a lot to ask after what we've seen in the past few days."

Lena heard another knock at the door and shut off the television.

"Enter."

The same MSS man who had brought her food came into the room again. "Miss Chou, we have received a cable. Your transportation to the mainland will arrive tomorrow."

Lena was surprised. "Oh? I thought that I was to wait here for the next week."

"You have been summoned, Miss Chou."

"I see."

She didn't have to ask who had summoned her.

11

Chase Manning sat in the back of a Toyota sedan, parked outside the premier business terminal at Narita Airport near Tokyo. The driver, a young CIA operative who worked for Tetsuo, was inside making sure all of Chase's paperwork was in order and that there would be no trouble as he made his way onto the US government plane. There were stories of US intelligence agents being apprehended and hauled away by Tokyo-based Chinese intelligence operatives.

"See the red armbands?" Tetsuo handed his binoculars to Chase, nodding over towards the commercial terminal arrival area. Busloads of American troops and their dependents were being dropped off outside the airport. This was the American mass exodus of the country, set in motion by the peace agreement.

"I see them."

"The red armbands are pro-Chinese. Those are Japanese citizens that are eager for the Chinese to come take over."

"You gotta be kidding me. What the hell are they thinking?"

"Look a little to the right. You'll see a gray sedan parked

behind them. Diplomatic plates. That's from the Chinese consulate. I recognize the driver. Chinese intelligence."

"What's the angle?"

"Looks like they're firing up the locals. Probably been recruiting these guys for a while. But they want it to appear like the Japanese all want us out of the country. Someone will get video of the scene on their phone and then circulate it online. It'll get picked up by influencers and maybe even major media outlets, and then that'll become the narrative. *Japanese kick out American oppressors*. That's what they want people saying at the dinner table."

"But we're not—"

"You're preaching to the choir, brother. Trust me. I know." Tetsuo reached out his hand and Chase gave back the binoculars.

The Chinese intelligence officers were being aggressive. The cease-fire was only a few hours old, yet there they were, staking out their territory. A Chinese occupation would come soon. The PLA wasn't here yet, but it was only a matter of time. Then this country would really change.

A 747 jumbo jet had just taken off, its landing gear collapsing into its giant belly, filled with American families and service-members headed to Hawaii or San Diego. The evacuation was in full swing. The Japanese government had made it clear that American servicemen and government employees were to depart the country immediately in fulfillment of the cease-fire agreement. Japan saw this as their only option to avoid disaster. Neither Chase nor Tetsuo had seen it coming.

Tetsuo was a CIA operations officer stationed at the American embassy in Tokyo. Chase Manning was with the CIA's special operations group. He had been on a special assignment to help uncover covert Chinese war plans. A week ago, he had been embedded with an Army Delta team performing reconnaissance on a Chinese military base. He had just left China and arrived in South Korea when the war had begun. He had barely escaped Korea, flying to Japan on a military transport as North Korean rockets had pummeled the country. But Chase's mission had been helpful. He had supplied the CIA with vital information, allowing the American military to prepare for attacks on Hawaii and Guam.

When Chase had arrived in Japan, he had been ordered to move Natesh Chaudrey—a Chinese agent the Americans had managed to turn—to safety. Things hadn't gone according to plan.

"You thinking about her again?"

Chase shot him a look but didn't answer.

Tetsuo gave a slight smile. "Brother, if you survive this war, they're going to sit you down on some shrink's couch and go deep inside your head, and Lena Chou is gonna be waiting for you there. Trust me. I can tell."

Chase chewed on his lower lip, bouncing his knee. "She's probably still here, you know. In Tokyo."

"I'll keep my eyes peeled." He didn't look too concerned.

"I got good eyes too."

Tetsuo shot Chase a skeptical look. "Don't be a dumbass. You have orders now."

Images of Lena flashed through his mind. He imagined her as she had been in Dubai. They had been lovers there for a time, while she had still been working for the CIA, before anyone had been aware of her true allegiance. Memories of their bodies intertwined on fresh linens in fancy hotels. Open windows and waves crashing outside. Her flowing jet-black hair running down her luscious body and tickling his bare chest. Silk-skinned and wildly passionate. Her eyes, stoic yet seductive.

Chase knew that his mental vision of her was no longer accurate. She had burn scars along her left side now. Burn scars that *he* had created. Perhaps he'd deluded himself into believing she was anything but an enemy.

He told himself not to harbor any sympathies. Lena Chou was a monster. A traitor. *Was she a traitor?* She had been loyal to her own cause. She had been a sleeper agent, implanted into the US years ago. Chase tried to wrap his mind around it. How long had she been living that lie? A part of him almost admired her for the dedication and discipline it must have taken.

Chase had seen her do horrible things. But he knew what he was capable of doing to his fellow man, in the name of his country. While he suffered the inner demons of a warrior, he was mostly able to wash it away with the belief that he served honorably and on the side of justice. Was it possible that Lena was abiding by that same warrior code?

He shook the thought away, not trusting his own mind to behave rationally towards her. This was sympathy for the devil. Chase needed to convince himself that Lena wasn't the woman he'd been with all of those nights in Dubai. It must have been a charade for her. She had used him to gain information and access, just as she had everyone else she'd worked with at the CIA. How many others had she taken into her bed? He wasn't special. He shouldn't be so naïve. Lena had betrayed the United States, a country that had been her home for many years. He should want to kill her for that betrayal. He should be filled with disgust and rage.

But he wasn't.

He was conflicted. Whether it was remnants of love or lust, or some strange kindred spirit warrior-spy understanding, Chase had an intense desire to find her. What he would do if he found her, he wasn't sure.

Chase turned to Tetsuo. "Just give me twenty-four hours."

"No."

"The planes are leaving nonstop. We still have a few days."

"*Hell* no."

"Let's at least discuss it…"

Tetsuo looked at him sideways. "Listen, white boy. In case you haven't noticed, this is *Tokyo*. See those guys wearing the red flags? They don't like you. You won't be able to operate here anymore. Chase. Let it go. You ain't gonna find her. Get on the plane. Follow your orders. Don't let your emotions cloud your judgment."

Chase let out a slow breath through his nostrils. Another jumbo jet took off from the runway.

"Here comes my boy." Tetsuo's fellow CIA officer exited the private aviation terminal and headed towards their car. Tetsuo rolled down the window as he walked up. "Everything good?"

"Sort of."

"Sort of isn't good."

"I know the guy at the desk. We should be alright. Plane lands in a few minutes. Wheels up another thirty after that. We'll have five of our VIPs from the embassy on board. Chase here makes six. No empty seats. Pilots are American, and both check out. I'll go to the other car and brief the State Department folks."

"So what gives?"

"They say people have been calling around. Government folks asking for passenger manifests."

Tetsuo looked at Chase.

"What?"

Tetsuo nodded in the direction of the Chinese intelligence operatives over by the commercial terminal. "Those MSS guys are probably looking for some high-value targets to snatch and grab, if they can get away with it. I'm sure you're on their list."

In the distance, another gray sedan parked in back of the first one. An Asian man exited the rear vehicle, walked up to the lead vehicle and began speaking to the driver.

Tetsuo said, "As long as they stay over there, we should be good. There's plenty of official security over there. They probably don't realize that we're getting special transports for our VIPs at the business terminal."

Tetsuo's CIA colleague standing outside the car said, "Alright, I'll be back momentarily. Chase, good luck."

Tetsuo rolled up the window.

Chase shook his head. "This whole situation is just wrong. Tucking our tails and leaving like this. You know how much military equipment we're leaving behind?"

"They're loading most of the important stuff onto ships now."

"They really aren't, though. It would take months to do it right. No, we're going to be forced to leave a ton of supplies, ordnance, and data behind at all of those bases. They'll destroy what they can, but that takes time, and they have very little time. So what will happen is the Chinese are going to take it all."

Tetsuo shrugged. "Shock and awe, man. And the will of the people. We lost the opening battle, and the international community isn't behind us."

"Fuck them."

"Yeah, well, our new president thought differently."

"Him too, then."

"You find out where they're going to send you yet?"

Chase said, "Some task force. The orders didn't say much about what I'll be doing. All I know is I'm supposed to meet with someone in San Diego once I get off the plane."

"Agency?"

"I don't think so. The cable gave a name and location and said to await further instructions." Chase sighed. "What about you?"

"We'll go dark. Start running agents and sending info back however we can. It's going to be a whole new ballgame once

Japan becomes Chinese-occupied Japan. The world has changed, my friend. The world has changed."

Chase swore softly. A Gulfstream taxied up near the terminal in front of them, the high-pitched whine of its engines loud enough that Tetsuo rolled up his window.

"Looks like this is it."

Chase held out his hand. Tetsuo took it and shook firmly. "Be safe."

Ten minutes later, Chase was on the aircraft. Everyone was buckled in and the door had been shut.

The pilot's voice came over the speaker. "Just a few moments, ladies and gentlemen, and we'll be off the ground."

Out Chase's cabin window, he could see Tetsuo and his CIA companion sitting in their Toyota. Two gray sedans pulled up behind them, cutting off their ability to move. Chase gripped his seat belt and moved closer to the window. For a brief moment, he contemplated running out of the aircraft and going to help.

Several men wearing red-and-yellow armbands got out of the car. Two of them were pointing weapons at the CIA men. Shit. Chase tried to think of something he could do.

Then he spotted Tetsuo. He was looking right at the plane. Right at Chase. Their eyes met. Tetsuo had an almost imperceptible smile and shook his head ever so slightly.

A flash of gunfire and spiderweb cracks in the glass, blood on the pavement.

The two armed men who had been standing outside Tetsuo's vehicle were on the ground, unmoving. Tetsuo's car door opened and he stepped out, towering over the bodies. His movements were deliberate, calm, and swift. He raised his pistol and began firing into the driver's side of one of the sedans. Tetsuo's colleague was also out of the vehicle, firing into the other sedan.

The other passengers on the plane were now watching. Chase heard a few gasps of breath, but no one spoke or cried out. They just watched in tense silence. Outside their window, the violent spasms of a fresh new war played out.

The plane jolted forward and began taxiing, faster than normal. Just before Chase lost sight of Tetsuo, he saw him fire at a man running away on the street. The running man took three bullets in the back and collapsed onto the pavement.

Tetsuo was right. The world had changed.

12

USS Ford
1000 nautical miles west-northwest of Hawaii

Admiral Manning stood behind his polished wood desk, thumbing through blue folders filled with documents. An ornately decorated chestnut inbox was filled to the brim with stacks of the blue folders. Orders, status reports, and approvals. Everyone seemed to need his signature. The cover page of each folder was signed off in rank order by the appropriate chain of command. He would never get through the pile. Eventually the strike group's chief of staff, a Navy captain, would sign most of them and bring the admiral only the most important documents.

Like the message that was now resting on his leather desk pad.

FROM: USPACCOM
TO: FORDCSG

SUBJ: OPERATION DILIGENT PROTECTOR

US-CHINA CEASE-FIRE IN EFFECT. ALL US MILITARY AND
CIVILIAN DEPENDENTS STATIONED IN JAPAN AND
KOREA UNDER MANDATORY EVACUATION, ESTIMATED
TIME OF COMPLETION TWO WEEKS. FORD CSG WILL
PROVIDE SECURITY AND ESCORT AS NEEDED FOR ALL
US-BOUND WARSHIPS AND SEA TRANSPORTS, AS WELL
AS ALL MILITARY AND COMMERCIAL AIR TRAFFIC IN
PACIFIC THEATER.

"They're ready for you, sir."

Admiral Manning looked up at Lieutenant Kevin Suggs, the
tall African-American Navy fighter pilot standing across from
him. Suggs was the admiral's personal aide, or Loop.

"Okay, thanks. Any news from the SAG?" Surface action
group—the group of Navy ships that had been sent along the
southern half of the Pacific.

The admiral's Loop said, "Minimal damage, sir. USS
Farragut's crew is all present and accounted for."

Admiral Manning nodded, trying not to show the wave of
relief that flooded over him. The admiral's daughter, Victoria
Manning, was on board the USS Farragut, serving as the officer
in charge of the ship's helicopter detachment.

The Farragut had entered combat near Guam several days
earlier, when the war had begun. Admiral Manning had been
thinking about each of his children, but especially his only
daughter, Victoria. Technically, the admiral had TACON, or
tactical control of her ship. This was an extremely rare situation,
and one that in peacetime would likely have been avoided

administratively. While he felt an enormous responsibility to each of those he served, the question of Victoria's well-being had been weighing on him.

"Thank you, Mr. Suggs." The admiral made brief eye contact. Suggs was sharp. He knew what the admiral was really asking for, and why he was embarrassed to ask. He nodded towards the door on the side of his office.

Suggs opened it and held the door, standing at attention and calling, "Attention on deck!"

The *Ford* Strike Group conference room, known as the War Room, was once again filled with the senior officers and planners in the strike group. Representatives from all of the clans stood silently at attention as the admiral made his way in: the CAG, leader of the air wing; the commodore, in charge of DESRON; the information warfare commander; and the commanding officer of the aircraft carrier. Each of these men was an O-6, a Navy captain. Several O-5s had been deemed important enough that they also had seats at the center table. The long conference table was then surrounded by two dozen other seats. In front of each of those surrounding chairs stood the midlevel officers: the lieutenants and lieutenant commanders who ran the strike group's day-to-day operations. These men and women had a variety of different functions. They provided intelligence, planned ship and aircraft movements, wrote the flight schedule, launched and recovered aircraft, and flew the aircraft. They knew everything that was going on in the strike group and communicated with all of the other assets that supported them, like drones, submarines, and special forces units.

"Seats, please."

The group sat, and the chief of staff, sitting to the admiral's right, spoke. "Admiral, good afternoon. First up, we have the geopolitical update. Events have been unfolding fast, so we felt it would be good to re-base everyone here on the latest." The COS nodded towards a Navy intel officer in the front of the room, who went through a few slides with summarized information on the state of the United States and the world three days after the war began.

There were a million names for this brief. Here on the USS *Ford*, it began every day at zero eight hundred sharp. Military units around the world held the same periodic ritual. Many referred to it as the "ops-intel" brief. Operations and intelligence. This was the meeting where all of the folks running the show heard what was coming and allowed the bosses to hash out any decisions that needed to be made.

Like any military meeting, it was supposed to be quick, efficient, and emotionless. Those qualities were becoming harder to achieve.

"...We are now approximately one hundred and fifty miles south of Midway Island. Our current tasking has us escorting commercial aircraft and ships that are evacuating American families from Japan and Korea."

Admiral Manning turned to the carrier CO and his CAG. "How many lines today?" The flight schedule operated on a set structure in order to maximize efficiency. Launches and recoveries were conducted in groups, or lines.

"Sir, we have eight planned. A section of fighters on each launch. Alert swing load aircraft on deck if needed."

"ASW support?"

"We'll have a P-8 and a P-3 overhead at all times, and three lines of helo coverage."

Since this brief was classified only at the secret level, the admiral didn't ask about where the submarines were located, but he knew that there were several fast-attack subs in the water space beneath them.

"VPU has a special projects plane tasked to monitor the US convoys headed out of Japan."

"All ships and aircraft understand our maneuvering restrictions?" Under the terms of the US-China cease-fire agreement, US military assets were not permitted to travel west of the 144th east longitude line.

"Yes, sir. It's been put out and is being closely monitored by all warfare commanders and watch teams."

Admiral Manning nodded and looked at the intel officer standing by the projector screen. "Continue."

The young officer summarized the situation. The *Ford* Strike Group, now over twenty ships strong, was moving its warships west to better provide security for the troop transports and cruise liners filled with American civilians fleeing Asia. China was allowing this tactical retreat to go unchallenged by their military, after the new US president had agreed to China's temporary cease-fire.

The Chinese president, Cheng Jinshan, had proposed the temporary truce. US intelligence believed that Jinshan saw the cease-fire as a way to gain political favor globally. It also gave his forces the ability to maneuver into strategically advantageous positions while the Americans ceded valuable territory: Japan and Korea.

The negotiated cease-fire gave the Americans two weeks to move their forces east of the 144th east longitude line.

"What is the progress of the evacuation in Japan?"

"They expect to meet the timeline, sir. Civilians should be completely transferred by next week. Most of our critical military assets have been either moved or destroyed."

"Destroyed?"

"Yes, sir. Several of the aircraft were damaged badly enough that they didn't expect to be able to fly them out. Demo teams destroyed them so the Chinese couldn't get any use out of it. At

Kadina, the runways were demolished. PACCOM decided to cut our losses and destroy what was left on the ground there."

"I see."

The chief of staff said, "What about Korea?"

One of the officers sitting at the central table, the information war commander, spoke up. "Our intelligence reports show that the Korean peninsula has sustained heavy damage from shelling, rocket, and chemical attacks."

Someone from the outer seats mumbled something. The only word the admiral heard was "...wasteland."

"The number of US casualties—civilian included—is estimated to be in the tens of thousands. When the Koreans are factored in, some estimates put the death toll into the seven-figure range. It's bad, sir. There are bodies lining the streets in many places. The North Koreans aren't adhering to the cease-fire as of yet. They've moved their troops into Seoul, and there's heavy fighting still going on."

Silence filled the room. Admiral Manning knew from his top-secret-level briefs that the reason the North Koreans had been so effective in their initial attack was because they'd had Chinese military assistance. He also knew that Chinese diplomats and children of Chinese VIPs were being flown out of the US as part of the cease-fire deal. This was done without public knowledge, which wasn't hard, since most electronics were down. But the fact that this information was being kept from the public was interesting.

"What about INCONUS?"

Most in the room held their breath as they watched the young intel officer bring up new slides. Everyone was worried about what was going on back home. The hardest part of this war wasn't the fear of what might happen to you; it was knowing there wasn't a damn thing you could do to protect your family back home as the US faced a postapocalyptic nightmare.

"Sir, the US is on day four since the EMP and infrastructure attacks. In some places, especially population centers, there are reports of riots and social unrest. Martial law had been declared, and the information I have suggests that the overall situation is gradually stabilizing."

Admiral Manning knew that the cities were the worst hit. The population centers were reliant on a constant high volume of food and supplies. When the transportation of goods ground to a halt, the cities would begin to starve. And burn, in many cases, as rioters and looters took to the streets.

The brief ended, and once again the room stood at attention. Normally the admiral gave a little pep talk. Today he only said, "Thank you, all." Then Admiral Manning walked out with his chief of staff and warfare commanders in tow.

The CAG, the commodore, and several other senior leaders were soon seated in his office. The admiral stood behind his desk, arms folded across his chest.

"The US plan is to hold Guam and Hawaii at all costs. With those, they can maintain control of the Pacific."

"I've heard that there's a Chinese special forces unit inside the US. There are even rumors of a brigade-size force that flew in from Canada. Is that true?"

"Scuttlebutt."

Admiral Manning interrupted the gossip of his senior commanders. "Gentlemen, I suggest that we worry about the things that we can control."

"Yes, sir."

"Our concern is the mission of this strike group. Right now, that is for us to ensure as many Americans as possible get from Asia to US soil."

The CAG said, "Sir, the Chinese are using this as part of the strategy. They've gotten us to give up our positions..."

Admiral Manning met his eye. "And we will do the same."

The CAG raised his eyebrow.

Admiral Manning nodded to his chief of staff, who said in a low tone, "The US is also using the cease-fire to reinforce its strongholds. As we speak, the Air Force is readying for a massive deployment to Guam."

Admiral Manning said, "The Chinese didn't attack us to make peace. We'll be ready if and when the fighting resumes."

The chief of staff continued. "East Coast naval assets are en route to the Pacific through the Panama Canal. As many of you know, CENTCOM has opened up as a hot spot in the Arabian Gulf. Russia is deploying more of its troops to Syria, and the moment our carrier in the gulf headed east towards the Pacific, Iran launched missiles on Saudi Arabia. We believe Iran is being prodded along by China. China wants us to play zone defense. We're being stretched thin around the globe. Our CENTCOM assets will be taken out of the war if we choose to keep them in the region. But if we don't, we risk cutting off our long-term fuel supply."

"That fuel will be crucial down the road."

"We're already seeing signs of supply issues..."

"Where is the carrier headed? The one that was in the gulf."

"*Truman*. The destination is a question for Big Navy. Diego Garcia has been demolished. Nothing can land there for now. Our Australian allies and US military assets in the country were attacked as well. The Pentagon is looking at options that would send the majority of our CENTCOM forces to Australia, but they're examining the details of the peace treaty to find out if that would be in violation. China's invasion of Taiwan is all but complete, and the Philippines will be a hot zone once the fighting begins. Australia was hit by the Chinese, but not hard. And assuming we can put our forces there, it'll be far enough away to provide a defensive buffer, but close enough that we can access the region quickly."

The CAG said, "So if and when hostilities resume at the end of the cease-fire, where will *Ford* be located?"

"That's what I want to discuss with you," Admiral Manning said. "PACFLEET has asked us to evaluate land-based landing sites. They want our take on whether we could use World War Two–era island airstrips as bases, if need be."

Someone laughed.

"You're kidding?"

Admiral Manning shook his head. "I'm not. They're calling them unsinkable carriers."

"Unsinkable doesn't mean indestructible."

Admiral Manning said, "There are only a handful of islands that fit our criteria. Ones that are big enough to fit a runway and face into the prevailing winds. We can use helicopters or tiltrotor, but PACFLEET prefers not to station anything at an island we can't get larger air transport into, for efficiency. The Air Force likes the idea too. They want to send two to four fighters and a C-17 filled with gas and maintenance equipment to each island."

"So we're going to be deploying to...where, exactly? Midway?"

The chief of staff nodded. "We have the contracts all drawn up. The Navy Seabees are being flown out in waves. Contractors will arrive via boat to most locations within a few weeks. These new US bases will be our virtual pillboxes in the Pacific. With the reduction of our aerial refueling capability, our strike range has been diminished. This plan helps restore our reach. If the Chinese attempt to bring over a large force, we'll have multiple Pacific bases from which to strike."

"How many are we talking about?"

"The exact number is still being discussed. But they've brought up Midway, Wake Island, the Johnston Atoll, Palmyra Atoll, and Samoa."

A knock at the door interrupted the conversation. The information warfare commander poked his head in.

"Please, come in."

The carrier's navigator followed him in. A commander and an aviator, the navigator didn't normally have much interaction with the strike group's IWC. Admiral Manning's mind raced ahead, looking for the problem that would connect the two men.

The IWC said, "Sir, I'm afraid we have some bad news."

The navigator looked sheepishly at the aircraft carrier captain, who was sitting on the admiral's couch. The aircraft carrier captain was the navigator's boss.

The IWC said, "About an hour ago, just before the morning brief, the navigator came to see me about a few anomalies he had discovered…"

The navigator continued. "Sir, we've been plotting out our course using the ship's navigational software. We have a RAS tomorrow, and I wanted to double-check something…" The RAS stood for replenishment at sea, the periodic evolution where warships would go alongside the supply ships to replenish fuel, food, stores, and ordnance.

Admiral Manning said, "Spit it out, Commander."

"We're in deep water here and will be for the RAS. But that's not what the computer's navigational software was telling me."

The CAG shifted in his seat. "I don't understand. So go by the charts. Why is this—"

The navigator said, "CAG, I did that. That's not my concern. The problem is that I think these false shallow water zones were maliciously inserted into our software."

The room went quiet.

Admiral Manning looked at the IWC. "What have you found?"

The IWC said, "I have our experts looking at it now. But the preliminary results aren't good. Our cyber experts found a back door in our network that had recently been exploited. They've identified a logic bomb that had been implanted in our servers and managed to quarantine it, as well as the worm that had been manipulating the carrier's onboard navigational software."

The navigator said, "We're adjusting our procedures to make sure we cross-reference all of our software data with paper."

"Weren't we already doing that?"

"Yes, sir, but previously if the nav computer told us there was shallow water, we would have turned the ship's course."

Admiral Manning looked to the ceiling, reaching the conclusion first. "But if the software has been intentionally corrupted by Chinese hackers, then these false insertions of shallow water may be directing us to places they want us to be. Correct?"

"Herding us like sheep. That is a possibility, sir. If they can direct the strike group along a certain path, they could lead us into a trap. A minefield. A group of attack submarines. Anything."

The chief of staff muttered, "Christ. Their submarines wouldn't have to do anything. Just sit there quietly waiting while the targets came to him."

Admiral Manning nodded towards the navigator. "Good job finding this." He turned to the IWC. "We need your cyber teams to audit every server, computer, program on the ship. And be sure to pass this up the chain. The intelligence folks will want to know about this, for sure."

The phone rang on the admiral's desk. He picked it up and muffled the receiver with his hand. "We need to be sure that our decision-making process isn't being manipulated. All warfare commanders need to review their procedures and evaluate whether we need to cut off from networks that might be insecure." He held the phone to his ear. "Admiral Manning, go ahead." The admiral's face grew grim. "Understood." He hung up the phone.

"They just found a spy on one of our escort ships. Some E-5 is being flown over to be placed in the brig. They caught him trying to insert a thumb drive into a secret computer."

The carrier CO rose from his seat. "Sir, if you'll excuse me, I'm going to go discuss this with my XO. With five thousand people aboard, we need to be prepared in case the same thing happens here."

The chief of staff indicated the navigator. "Captain, I believe it already has."

The *Ford* CO nodded, frowning, and left the room. The navigator and IWC followed him out, and the hatch was shut behind them.

The intelligence officer began updating them on the top-secret-level plans for the US Navy's submarine fleet.

"The one bright spot in the WestPac battles were the complete domination of all US submarine battles. We believe that gave us some leverage in the cease-fire agreement. We estimate that US Navy submarines have sunk over twenty-five Chinese warships and eight submarines. We were able to deny large areas of water to the Chinese fleet."

The chief of staff, who wore the gold dolphins insignia of a submarine officer on his chest, smiled broadly. "If the fighting starts back up, it will all be over in a few weeks, gentlemen."

The admiral observed nods of approval at the rare bit of good news.

"Where are the Chinese carrier groups?"

The intelligence officer turned his laptop around and flipped to a specific slide. "Sir, the Chinese have divided their naval forces into two main groups. The first is a two-carrier group near the Sea of Japan. It has been hugging the territorial waters of coastal China. One of our LA-class boats was trailing them as of this morning. The second group is a single-carrier fleet located near the Philippines. The carrier is the *Liaoning*. This was the one that launched the failed air attack on Guam."

"Is she being trailed?"

"She just went through a delousing process, sir. They've set up a very large sonobuoys field with their maritime patrol aircraft as she travels west, back towards China."

"West?"

"Yes, sir. We believe the *Liaoning* is taking aboard new squadrons of aircraft. Our intelligence reports say she may be going into port. Although..." The intelligence officer demurred.

"What is it?"

"Well, there is some disagreement at ONI about whether or not the *Liaoning* is actually going into port. She's headed that way, but they don't seem to be making the normal preparations in port for her arrival."

The CAG said, "So we're not sure what her intentions are, and we don't have an exact position on the carrier. Is that right?"

The officer's eyes shifted around nervously. "Yes, sir."

The CAG rolled his eyes. "We need to know where the enemy is, and what they're up to."

"Yes, sir." The intelligence officer cleared his throat. "Separately, we have recent reports that a very large group of ships are about to depart their commercial shipping centers, and those groups may include some naval vessels that were docked there."

"Why would they do that?"

"We don't know."

Admiral Manning tapped his desk. "Thank you. You may leave." The intelligence officer scurried out of the admiral's stateroom.

"Gentlemen, we must be prepared for what comes next. We must be prepared to strike back."

The submariner chief of staff smiled again. "The element of

surprise is gone now. If the fighting starts up again, we'll crush them. It'll be over before you know it, sir."

Admiral Manning frowned. He had always thought his COS an intelligent man. How many wars had begun with otherwise intelligent men uttering those words?

13

Lena Chou traveled through Beijing in a convoy of government sedans. Her hair was in a tight bun, and she wore a hooded sweatshirt that kept her warm and hid the scars on the left side of her face.

She had been in the city just a few weeks ago, but already much had changed. The pattern of life was different. The looks on people's faces were different. The people themselves were different.

Digital billboard signs that had been advertising nail polish or dish soap now displayed a call to arms.

FIGHT FOR CHINA, read one of them. It showed a picture of a handsome young man holding a rifle aimed towards the sea, his family behind him, huddling together.

MAKE A DIFFERENCE. SERVE YOUR NATION, read another. This advertisement showed three women standing side-by-side. They were all very pretty. One was dressed in a flight suit, holding her helmet by her side. Another wore green camouflage. The third wore the white-and-black dress uniform of the Navy, complete with black tie and shoulder boards. The women looked determined and proud.

Lena's vehicle turned down a busy street. She saw that similar government propaganda had been plastered on every storefront. At the street corner, a line of young men waited outside a recruiting center. The line went around the block, with most of the boys looking at their phones.

She expected that they were reading carefully curated articles designed to enflame their spirits. The digital ads and articles, social media posts and images...they all blended together now, serving one purpose: transform China into a wartime state.

Their convoy slowed at a traffic jam, and the driver flipped a switch on the dash. An overhead light began shining red, and a siren sounded. The tone was different from what she'd grown accustomed to in America. The sea of cars parted, and Lena's convoy zoomed on through.

A few minutes later, she pulled into a small gated army base in the center of the city. A PLA helicopter was spinning on the pad. Lena was escorted into the cabin of the aircraft and the door slid shut. They took off, and she could see the contrast of different parts of the city. The wealthy and modern parts, with their bright LED screens and marvelous skyscrapers, and the impoverished working-class sections, with drab one-bedroom homes covered with sheet metal. But all of the neighborhoods were crowded with volunteers, headed to fulfill their national duty. Cheng Jinshan's dynasty was beating the drums of war.

For an hour, the aircraft traveled over mountainous terrain covered by an endless evergreen forest. The aircraft set down on a square concrete landing pad hidden among tall pines. The door slid open and one of the aircrewmen escorted her out of the spinning rotor arc.

A military escort led her into an army vehicle, which drove fifty meters before coming to a full stop at the base of a rock wall. Security guards inspected her and then went into their camouflaged guard house.

In front of the vehicle, the mountain moved.

What had appeared to be a dark stone facing was a carefully painted door. The door slid to one side, revealing a long, well-lit tunnel that dove into the earth at a steep grade. The drive took approximately five minutes, and then she was dropped off at a loading dock.

Her escort was female. A pretty young officer in the PLA. Probably one of the ones from the recruiting poster, Lena mused. The woman was all business. She didn't break the silence as they marched through several sterile hallways and up two flights of stairs. Lena wondered how the woman had ended up here. Would this have been her own path, had she not been recruited as a teenager by Jinshan?

They walked up another flight of stairs and through a maze of hallways, each busy with uniformed men and women scurrying about. Every face looked exhausted and intense.

Lena's escort stopped outside a door and knocked. A red nameplate on the door had five stars below a familiar name. Lena's eyes widened slightly as she read it. She looked at the woman escorting her, who nodded politely, but there was no hint of recognition at the significance.

Lena's escort was not aware that Lena's father's name was on the door. A man she hadn't seen in twenty years. A man who had agreed never to see his daughter again. To give her up to China, so that she could be used as a sleeper agent.

And that man had apparently risen to be the highest-ranking general in all of China. Quite a step up from where he had been when she had left her home without so much as a goodbye.

The door cracked open. A balding colonel showed his face. "She may enter," he said, looking at Lena. The escort bowed and departed, never uttering a word.

Lena had many natural gifts. These capabilities, both physical and mental, had given her an enormous sense of confidence. She had always been so sure of herself.

But her knees felt weak as she walked into General Chen's office and saw him sitting behind his desk. The general looked proud as he watched her enter.

"Have a seat."

The general indicated one of the chairs across from his desk. His aides left the room, leaving father and daughter alone in silence.

"Would you care for some tea?" He gestured to a tray that had been set out next to his desk.

Lena hesitated, and the general said, "Make us both a cup."

"Yes, General." The first words spoken to her biological father in over twenty years.

Lena rose from her seat and began preparing two cups of tea. Her father studied her as she poured hot water over dried tea leaves. A woody aroma filled her nostrils as steam rose up from the cups.

General Chen said, "It must come as a surprise to you, being brought here like this after all of this time."

Lena interpreted the statement as an attempt to change the subject to her years spent in America. She was about to answer when the general continued. "Seeing me like this, I mean. In charge of the entire People's Liberation Army."

She paused, studying him. Then she nodded and continued stirring the tea. "You honor me with your accomplishments, Father." She made sure to keep her tone respectful, despite the emotion she felt.

Long-forgotten memories of her childhood flooded her mind. She had served her father tea many times as a young woman. But she was a different person now.

"Inviting you here is my pleasure."

The tone he used suggested that he considered this meeting

something Lena should be grateful for. "After all, you are my daughter." She paused again, and their eyes met briefly. Then she continued stirring.

Lena remembered from her upbringing that there were many underlying meanings wrapped into Chinese tea culture. Serving tea to her father was a sign of respect. Serving tea could also be a way to refresh a family bond. Or to apologize.

No. This was none of those things.

Lena sensed that there was no regret or sorrow in this man's heart. His suggestion that she serve him should be interpreted as an assertion of dominance. As a reminder of his position. Why?

She set a cup down on his desk and then took her own cup from the tray. As she stepped away, Lena watched for the general to tap a few fingers on the table next to his cup. This was the traditional Cantonese gesture of gratitude. It never came.

He sipped his tea. "I understand you have served China well over the years."

"I have tried to serve honorably, General."

"The chairman speaks highly of you."

The chairman. Of course. He was the reason her father was interested in her. And the reason he feared her, even if he didn't realize it himself. She immediately felt her confidence return, her power over him evident in her mind.

"I am humbled that this is so."

"Do you have any questions for me? Anything you require?"

Lena thought for a moment and then said, "How is my mother?"

The general's face tightened. "She is well."

They continued to speak like this for a few moments more, in uncomfortable, forced bursts of conversation.

She kept her gaze low, observing her father only out of the corner of her eye. Lena was intentionally carrying herself with a manner of subservience. This was uncharacteristic of her personality, but she had a keen instinct for danger.

While the military battles might be raging thousands of miles from these mountain bunkers, this was not a safe place. It wasn't an American attack she should fear. Lena now resided in the lion's den. Each flag officer and each elder statesman would be posturing for future position. To them, Lena was either a pawn or an obstacle. Even to her father.

General Chen seemed much more comfortable when speaking about himself and his achievements, which, according to him, were many and great. He also seemed interested to hear what Lena had to say about Jinshan, which she kept to a minimum.

"Has he promised you anything?"

Lena cocked her head. "Promised me anything? Like what, General?"

"Title. Position?"

"Jinshan knows that these are things I do not seek."

The general's eyes narrowed. "Of course not."

A knock at the door. The general ignored it. He said, "Why has he summoned you here?"

Lena kept her mask on. "I have not yet been informed of the reason."

Another knock at the door.

"Come in!" the general shouted, a hint of frustration in his voice.

The woman who had escorted Lena to her father's office opened the door. She said, "Chairman Jinshan has requested your presence."

"Fine. I'll be there soon."

The woman said, "Yes, General. And so that I may not be misunderstood, he requests both of you be present." She bowed and left, the door closing behind her.

General Chen's face grew a shade redder. Lena forced her gaze to the floor, not wanting to challenge him. She realized that while she had changed, he was the same man from her youth. His flaws were more pronounced to her now. Lena's years of training kept her intelligence operative's mind humming away in the background as they spoke. Documenting every word, noting every reaction.

If General Chen were an American and Lena had come across him in the field, she would have written up a report on him later and sent it to her Chinese handlers. This hypothetical report would have said something like, *Top-level PLA flag officer over-indexes in characteristics of pride, ego, arrogance. Believe subject would be susceptible to appeals to his vanity and ambition. Due to his positional authority, subject has access to broad array of information and influence. Recommend immediate development into operational asset.*

General Chen frowned. "So Jinshan has summoned both of us. Well, I suppose we shall both learn why you are here."

* * *

Jinshan's quarters were much larger than General Chen's, but still sparse by his standards. Jinshan, through skill and government connections, had made himself into a multibillion-dollar businessman. This personal journey, Lena knew, had started as a simple cover occupation when he had been a low-level MSS operative. His superiors had had no idea what he was capable of back then.

Lena was pleased to see him. He greeted her warmly, clasping her hands in his own. "It is good to see you, Ms. Chou." She noted that he used the name she went by now. The cover name that she had taken in the United States. She wondered how the good general felt about that.

She offered Jinshan a respectful bow. "Thank you, Chairman Jinshan."

Aside from General Chen, there were two others in the room. A PLA Navy admiral by the name of Zhang, and a man that Lena knew was high up in the MSS. The group sat at a table while the MSS man updated them on the day's findings.

Lena observed the meeting in silence. Taking in everything. Studying the men around the table. What they said and how they said it. She guessed at their motives, and at their opinions of each other, updating and refining her views as more information came to light.

She had been correct in her assessment. Each man was posturing. Playing not to win a war, but to earn a title, to seize dominion over the others. Her father, General Chen, seemed obsessed with the invasion of Hawaii. Admiral Zhang, head of the PLA Navy, disagreed that this was their most pressing objective. He wanted to use a new type of ship to attack Guam first, and then move on to Hawaii. But the additional step could add weeks or even months to the timetable.

General Chen said, "The Americans will reinforce Hawaii during the next few weeks. We cannot afford to wait until—"

Admiral Zhang said, "Admiral Song is the fleet commander. We should respect his judgment in this. As he has stated, it is imperative that US air power in the western half of the Pacific Ocean be destroyed before bringing our fleet to Hawaii. Guam's runway has already been refurbished. If Guam is not destroyed—"

General Chen said, "Then we can split the fleet. We have enough ships."

The admiral shook his head. "This is not a good plan. Our sea combat strategy..."

"Don't talk to me about strategy, Admiral. I am an expert in military strategy."

Lena glanced at Jinshan, whose face remained impassive. Like her, he was a listener. She noticed how tired and frail he looked. There was a yellow tint to his skin. The cancer, she knew. The Central Committee members must realize that he was failing. If his health grew weak enough, they would begin thinking about what came next. When that happened, he would be in danger, if he wasn't already.

She now understood Jinshan's urgency. Why they had made some moves earlier than planned. Jinshan needed to see the war through. To be sure that no one else—like her bumbling father—screwed it up.

Admiral Zhang sighed. "We will need the Jiaolong-class ships to win any battles with American carrier groups."

General Chen scoffed. "The Chinese Navy should be fully capable of defeating our adversaries in battle. If you cannot lead us to victory, Admiral, perhaps we should find someone else—"

Jinshan smiled. "That will be enough, General. I suggest that we remember who our enemies are." He paused in thought and then turned to Lena. "Miss Chou, tell me, what would you have us do?"

Lena ignored the disapproving eyes of her father as she said, "We must assume the Americans are already reinforcing their military capabilities at both locations. Both locations are important to them, but Guam's proximity to China makes it unique. If Guam tumbles, our fleet will be able to traverse the Pacific towards Hawaii with impunity. But with the American airfields at Guam operational, they will be able to harass our convoys as they head west, and launch more effective attacks on our sea bases."

Jinshan allowed a thin smile to form on his lips. "I concur," he said. "We will support Admiral Zhang's recommendation to attack Guam before all else."

Lena could see the expression of contempt growing on her

father's face as he looked between her and Jinshan. *I have made myself an enemy to my own father*, she realized. *So be it.*

Lena met General Chen's gaze. This time she didn't break her stare. He did. And she could tell that he was fuming inside.

"General Chen..."

The silent battle of wills was disrupted as the head of the MSS asked General Chen for input on something. The men conversed a few minutes longer. After a few final details were agreed upon by Jinshan and his military council, he dismissed them.

"Lena, please remain," Jinshan said quietly.

He waited until the others left and then said, "I commend you on your accomplishments. You have succeeded beyond my highest expectations."

She smiled. "You honor me with your praise, Chairman Jinshan." She meant it.

Lena understood that logically, she should harbor ill will toward Jinshan. The man who had stolen her life away when he had recruited her into the MSS's program for illegal operatives. This world of black operations and espionage had transformed her into a vicious and violent woman. She knew that he was at least partly responsible for the mental and emotional damage she had suffered over the years. The occasional nightmares. Her inexplicable secret desire to commit violent acts, even when they were unrelated to her work. She had researched both of these symptoms. They were both indicative of a larger psychotic issue—one that was likely the result of her violent and some-times traumatic work.

But that same world of espionage was also filled with excite-ment, fulfillment, and passion. A life of highs unlike anything else. She had been taken as a know-nothing teenage girl and forged into one of China's greatest weapons. Jinshan was respon-sible for this growth. In that way, he was more of a father to her than General Chen had ever been. He had molded her into the woman she was today. He was proud of her achievements. The teenager he had recruited was gone. Li Chen had been a scared little girl. But Lena Chou, despite her scars, internal and external, was invincible.

It was Jinshan who showed signs of mortality.

"How is your health, Chairman?"

Jinshan shrugged. "All of us have limited time. I am confident I will remain able-bodied until we achieve our goal."

Lena wasn't so sure, but she let it be. "How may I serve you, then?"

Jinshan pointed to a digital map on his wall. It showed the Pacific Theater. "I wish you to join us here for the time being, as counselor to the chairman. You shall sit in on our leadership team conferences. Your insight will be a welcome addition."

"As you wish."

"You have unique insight into the hearts and minds of American intelligence. I wish you to work with the minister of state security. Already we have apprehended many of the American intelligence operatives within China. Soon we will be doing the same in Korea, Japan and any other territories as we expand. Some of the information that comes in will need..." He searched for the right word. "Vetting. I cannot be there to oversee these projects. We will need to evaluate the accuracy of the information we receive from our American agents. The Americans will attempt to deceive us. Your understanding of American intelligence, military, and politicians goes beyond many of our best analysts. Insert yourself into the program. Understand our top-level strategy, and whether the intelligence we receive supports our decisions."

Lena nodded. "I am at your service, Chairman."

14

Wisconsin, United States
Day 5

"You there! What are you doing?"

Lin Yu looked wide-eyed at his company sergeant. The chief sergeant second class was as new to combat as Lin Yu, but he was older and had been in the PLA much longer.

"Sergeant, I was just—"

"Never mind. Get in the vehicle."

The airfield where the Chinese had landed was a flurry of activity. The soldiers were packing up gear, taking down tents, and moving into the tree line, out of sight of any drones or aircraft that might be looking for them. Vans arrived every few minutes, and squads of men would scurry from the trees to get into them. The vans then ferried the Chinese troops away from the airfield. Lin Yu didn't know where they were going.

Two months ago, Lin Yu had worked in a small electronics shop in Guangzhou, the third-largest city in China. His job had been to sell bulk orders of secondhand cell phone parts to international manufacturers.

Then the Chinese president had been assassinated in a treacherous American plot. Lin Yu had read all about it on his social media feed. The Americans were religious zealots. They hated the Chinese because they didn't believe in their Christian God. Just like the Muslims and other religions. China was a peace-loving country, but it had to protect itself.

At least, that was what all of the Chinese media news articles said. These ideas were reinforced by the political awareness classes they all took during their two-week military basic training.

Lin Yu wasn't sure what to believe.

His presence here was an abnormality. He was by far the most junior of the group. But he had been selected for a special assignment due to his aptitude and English language skills. Someone in one of the more advanced PLA units had been injured at the last minute, just before the war had begun. Lin Yu had been chosen to replace him.

The flight across the Pacific had been strange at first, and then frightening. It was the first flight Lin Yu had ever taken. A commercial aircraft had picked them up from a military base. They had sweated while wearing their winter utility uniforms throughout the long flight. Two meals and eight hours of broken sleep later, things took a turn for the worse. The airplane's lights were purposely shut off. Their windows were shut. Lin Yu and his fellow passengers screamed when the plane began turning and diving wildly. The company sergeant said that someone had fired at them, and that they were over Canada.

They had landed on a darkened airfield in the middle of the night. Lin Yu and the troops had been offloaded and had begun setting up camp. A few gunshots in the distance had alarmed the men, but the company sergeant had told them that it was nothing to worry about. The company had scored their first kills, you see. Later, Lin Yu had learned that they were American policemen, come to see what was going on at an airfield that was supposed to be abandoned. Lin Yu had seen many American movies. The policemen never seemed like they were bad.

Lin Yu worked as an administrative assistant for the company operations officer, a young college graduate not much older than Lin Yu himself. The boy put on a brave face, but Lin Yu could tell that he was just as afraid of where they were. Behind enemy lines. In the Operations tent, Lin Yu learned that they were in North Dakota, one of the northernmost territories within the United States. Chinese attacks had successfully knocked out most of the American electrical grid and radars. The operation Lin Yu was a part of had landed almost two thousand PLA troops at the airfield.

They were met by a team of PLA commandos who had been waiting for them. The troops were sent out in companies and platoons, each unit given a different objective. Lin Yu's company was moved one hundred kilometers to the south. The men had to sit in the back of a large commercial truck. When they reached their destination, which wasn't much more than a farm and some trees, they set up their tents and camouflaged them with natural elements. Leaves, branches, pine needles. Lin Yu wasn't sure if this would matter, but the company sergeant kept barking orders, and the men obeyed.

They had been in America for five days now. Their company had been hiding here for the last four, waiting for orders. They were supposed to have moved on day one, but there had been a communications problem. Their rations were running low, and it was cold. Lin Yu hadn't done much other than stand guard duty up near the farmhouse and monitor the periodic radio reports from other PLA units.

But today was going to be different.

The company sergeant was smiling when the PLA commando team arrived. Two pickup trucks of Chinese men, each wearing American-made clothing for hunters or hikers. Black semiautomatic rifles slung over their shoulders. Experience and pride in their eyes.

"These men are the best of the best," the sergeant had whispered to his platoon. Someone asked him what made them so good. The sergeant replied, "They are the elite. South Sword naval commandos. All of the top missions go to these men. They were here weeks ago. They are killers." He said it with envy.

Lin Yu saw the company commander and operations officer greet the elite Chinese special forces team. They led them into the farmhouse and gave them food and a place to sleep.

After an hour, the company commander called over Lin Yu's sergeant. Two of the special forces team members were going to be sent out on an assignment with some of Lin Yu's company. They were to acquire transportation for the company at the nearest town.

"Lin Yu, you speak good English. You will come with us. We will take the second platoon and go into town."

Lin Yu's sergeant was again smiling. He wanted to kill Americans, Lin Yu knew. He wanted to taste war. Lin Yu wasn't so sure about how he felt. But he went along, because that was his duty and he was afraid.

"Yes, Sergeant."

They drove in a two-vehicle convoy. A pickup truck with four PLA special forces men, and the trailing sedan, which held Lin Yu, his sergeant, and two other company-mates. Their vehicles bounced along the gravel road that wound through rolling grass hills. A wide-open, clear sky. It was very cold here in America, but the natural beauty was striking compared to the swampy city Lin Yu had grown up in.

The vehicles left the dirt road and began traveling on a highway. They saw a pickup truck heading the opposite direction, and the passengers in Lin Yu's car grew tense at the mere sight of it. When they arrived on the outskirts of the small American town, Lin Yu heard the clicks and slaps of his comrades checking their weapons.

Lin Yu looked around at the faces of the others in the vehicle. He realized that he was the only one who hadn't been informed of the plan. Seeing his face, Lin Yu's sergeant said, "You stay in the car. We may need you as an interpreter. We will call for you if that is the case." Lin Yu nodded nervously, looking at the homes and storefronts as the two-vehicle caravan passed through town. Two old white men, bundled up in winter jackets, sat on the front walkway in front of one of the shops. Lin Yu read the name of the store. Barber Shop.

They pulled into a large parking lot filled with cars. A car dealership. The Chinese vehicles skidded to a halt and their doors opened. Lin Yu could see an American man looking through one of the glass panels that made up the walls of the central building.

His eyes went wide as he saw submachine guns being trained on him and realized what was happening. One of the PLA special forces soldiers was signaling him to come outside, but the American was frozen with fear. Two other soldiers ran into the building and dragged him outside. They began yelling and pointing. The man had his elbows bent, hands half-raised. He was shaking his head vigorously, saying something that Lin Yu couldn't make out.

A plump black woman was dragged outside next. She just kept her head down, looking at the ground.

Lin Yu turned his head to the street, looking for any sign of trouble. The town had seemed deserted on their way in. He wondered if there were any military or policemen nearby. But there were only eight of them. They wouldn't last very long if...

"Lin Yu! Get out here!"

"Yes, Sergeant." He flung open his door and jogged over.

Another white man was being walked out of the building at gunpoint. Two PLA soldiers behind him. "The rest of the building is clear," one of the soldiers said in Mandarin.

The sergeant said, "Lin Yu, tell them we need them to begin unlocking twenty-two of their vehicles, and providing us with the keys. We want four-wheel-drive vehicles and will need them to be fueled up."

Lin Yu nodded and translated into English.

The first man who had been taken outside listened and looked like he understood. He seemed to be the one in charge. He pointed towards the building. "I'll need to get my codes. They all have locks on the cars. I'll need to get the codes..."

Lin Yu explained this to his sergeant, who nodded. Two minutes later, the portly American was fumbling with the lock pad combination on the first vehicle. When the code didn't work, it made a beeping noise. He looked up. "I think the codes may have changed."

Lin Yu said, "What does this mean?"

"Headquarters might have changed them. They can do that. They must have changed the codes. So I can't unlock them anymore. The keys are in these little lockboxes. But if my codes don't work, we can't get them."

Lin Yu translated this to his sergeant, who frowned. "Tell him to try again."

Lin Yu relayed the order in English, and they got the same result. The American man was shivering in his button-down shirt, rubbing his hands together to keep warm. He said, "It's still not working. There's nothing I can do." Lin Yu translated this to his sergeant.

In the distance, a police siren began to wail.

One of the special forces soldiers came over. "What's the problem?" The sergeant explained. The special forces soldier called over the other two Americans. He raised his rifle and shot the black woman in the chest. The man next to her howled and began to rush them. The soldier fired two more shots into the approaching man and he went down. His head imploded.

Lin Yu felt bile coming up and turned away, trying to catch his breath. When he looked up again, he saw that the American man who had been claiming the locks wouldn't work had wet his pants. His fingers shaking, he typed in the code on the lock and it opened, revealing a key fob. The special forces soldier took it and unlocked the vehicle, checking that it would start without problem. He then checked the fuel and said, "This one is good. Twenty-one more."

Moments later, a single American police cruiser appeared on the lot. The Chinese special forces troops had been listening to the siren get closer, and they were ready. Two of the soldiers were positioned in an L-shape, ready to ambush the police. They fired into the police cruiser from less than ten meters away. As soon as the vehicle came onto the property, its windows were filled with bullet holes. Then they moved quickly through the wreckage, ensuring their targets were killed, and looking for any valuable communications equipment or weapons.

Fifteen minutes later, the Chinese had twenty-five vehicles fueled up and ready to go. They sent three of the vehicles with one driver each back to the PLA company campsite. They returned with a total of twenty men. Enough to drive all of the cars.

Lin Yu's sergeant shot the American man in the back of the head before they departed. The sight haunted Lin Yu as he sat in his sergeant's passenger seat on the way back to the company camp. The sergeant didn't say a word.

The company operations officer called Lin Yu into the farmhouse when they returned to help him mark up some of the paper charts before they left. As he worked, Lin Yu overheard the company commander, the operations officer, and the special forces team leader discussing what lay ahead.

"...we will move out within the hour..."

"...will the explosive ordnance experts be there when we arrive?"

"Yes, sir. Those teams have been pre-positioned and told what to expect."

"And we won't get any further aerial reinforcements? Is that what you are hearing?"

"That is correct, sir. We were able to deploy a single regiment. The other planes were not able to make it."

"What happened to them? Never mind. It doesn't matter. The Americans will be recovering from the EMP attacks. We must move quickly."

"Will the South Sword Team accompany us south?"

"For now."

Lin Yu finished rolling up the charts as the PLA special forces men left the farmhouse. Twenty minutes later, his entire company had stowed their gear in their recently acquired American vehicles and were headed south on the highway.

Lin Yu gazed out the window as they drove through the vast countryside. He tried to imagine a day where he could enjoy this beauty without seeing the faces of those he had just helped to kill.

15

San Diego, California

Chase landed at Naval Air Station North Island at just after 1300 local time. They had a short layover in Honolulu, but Chase wasn't allowed off the airport. He had gone into the FBO building and listened to people talk about the EMP attacks and the war. But accurate news and information were hard to come by. Everything was gossip. Now back on mainland USA, Chase wondered what he would find.

The government jet taxied up to base ops, where it came to a stop and shut down. The ladder was lowered, and two escorts awaited. One for the diplomats, the other for him.

"Chase Manning?"

"Yes, sir."

"Name's Pat. Hop in." Pat wore a desert nylon shirt with no name tags or patches, save an American flag on his shoulder.

Chase threw his bag in the back and sat in the passenger seat of a blue government sedan. Pat drove them off the flight line at base ops towards the buildings where the SEAL teams were located.

Chase said, "You know where they're putting me?"

"You'll be with SEAL Team Five. We leave tonight."

"For where?"

Pat looked over at him. "The Midwest. That's all we know so far."

"For what?"

"Hunting."

Chase was puzzled but figured that when he needed to know more, they'd tell him. Pat turned out to be a chief. He'd been with the Teams for nearly fifteen years. Deployed to both Afghanistan and Iraq more times than Chase. He seemed like a decent guy.

They entered the building Chase recognized from the early days of his training. He'd been stationed mostly on the East Coast, so he hadn't seen Coronado much after BUD/S. The culture was slightly different on each team. But they were all very tight crews. Hardened eyes studied him as he entered the unit's spaces.

"You can have this locker. Jake over there will get you geared up. The CO wants to see you now."

Chase dropped his bag in the locker room. He nodded politely to the other members of the team on his way out.

"Guy smells like officer. You an officer, man?"

Chase said, "Guilty."

"Great. Just what we need around here, another fucking officer."

Pat said, "Shut up, Jones." He looked at Chase. "You can ignore him. Everyone else does."

Chase shrugged, a mild-mannered smile on his face.

Pat marched him down the hall and entered an open area where two female secretaries were working behind desks. Behind them stood a closed wooden door.

"Afternoon, Mary. CO in?"

"He said for you to go on in with Mr. Manning when you arrived."

"Thanks."

Pat nodded for Chase to follow and knocked on the door, opening it as he did. Three men sat in the office. All were wearing green fatigues. Two were commanders, the other a master chief.

Pat said, "Sir, this is Chase Manning. I'm sorry, sir, is it Lieutenant or..."

Chase shrugged. "I guess it's technically Lieutenant Commander now. Reserves. But I haven't drilled in..."

The master chief stuck a thick hand out. "Glad to have you with us, Mr. Manning. I served under your father once at the Pentagon. Shit job. But your dad made it bearable."

"Thank you, Master Chief."

Chase shook hands with the CO and XO.

"Thanks, Pat. We got it from here," said the CO.

"Yes, sir." The chief left the room, closing the door behind him.

"Have a seat, Chase."

Chase sat on the couch next to the master chief.

"I understand you've been doing some work with the Agency. That correct?"

"Yes, sir."

"General Schwartz has assigned you to our unit for the foreseeable future."

Chase was pleased. "Sounds good, sir."

The SEAL team commanding officer said, "Less than a week ago, as the Chinese were detonating EMPs over the continental US and attacking our bases in the Pacific. They were also using cyber and electronic attack weapons to bring down many of NORAD's radars along the Canadian and Alaskan coastline. We estimate that as many as four dozen large commercial aircraft, each filled with specially trained Chinese infantry, flew into the area just after these attacks took place. We recognized what was going on eventually. Our fighters shot many of the aircraft down. Some turned around and we think probably ran out of fuel over the Pacific. But some got through."

Chase couldn't believe what he was hearing. "How many?"

"We don't know. Maybe one or two? Maybe a few dozen. The radar data is gone now, and the intel reports are going on interviews with radar controllers who were basically having the worst night of their lives. The high-end estimate is four thousand Chinese soldiers, now operating INCONUS. The low end is a few hundred Chinese troops. These soldiers will be joining what we believe are at least six remaining PLA special operations teams that had inserted themselves into the US *prior* to the attack. You may be aware that several US Air Force bases were hit on the day the war began. Those raids were conducted by these SOF teams, using mortars and other weapons."

Chase suspected that he had seen these exact Chinese SOF teams training in China.

The commander said, "Chase, SEAL Team Five will join a JSOC unit that is being tasked for an INCONUS assignment. We were about to rotate back to Korea when the balloon went up. Given the current status of the Korean Peninsula, this was deemed a better allocation of resources."

"Yes, sir."

"You have been detailed to us by General Schwartz. According to him, you're familiar with the teams we're to be hunting down. I'm told you saw them training. In *China*. Is that correct?"

"I have. Yes, sir."

"Well, that makes sense, then. You'll be a good asset to have in the hunt."

* * *

The next day, Chase sat in a high school classroom somewhere in Nebraska. The rest of the seats in the classroom were all occupied by a SEAL Team Five platoon. Other platoons were getting separate briefs in some of the other classrooms. Down the hall, similar briefs were being held for Green Beret teams and Ranger units. The school had been converted into a makeshift base of operations for the hunters. Sandbag bunkers and ID checks. Guard dogs, security towers with snipers, communications antennae and radar. Each of those had become part of the high school's transformation.

Chase heard the thumping of rotorcraft landing and taking off outside. The sports fields had become the LZs for Blackhawks, Chinooks, and the Little Birds of the 160th SOAR.

A man dressed in jeans and a pullover sweater walked into the front of the class. He had two-day-old stubble, and the rings around his eyes made it look like he had been without sleep for the past week. Chase was sure he was a spook.

The INCONUS intelligence streams were still coming online. Drones were being flown over the US. The datalink networks had to have new encryption software installed. In some cases, even the hardware was corrupted. Chinese cyber operators had infiltrated so many US systems that many US drones were labeled as hard down while they underwent audits. With all but a few satellites out of commission and the global demand for intelligence, surveillance, and reconnaisance (ISR) through the roof, manned aircraft were supplementing the shortage inside the continental US.

The targeting brief lasted thirty minutes. The helicopter crews and SOF teams had gone over plans extensively earlier that morning. There were minimal questions now. Just final updates on the situation and objectives.

When the brief ended, Chase's platoon headed to the football field, where spinning helicopters awaited them. They split into two Blackhawks and two MH-6 Little Birds. Two SEALs sat on the outboard platforms of the MH-6s, one SEAL per side. The tiny helicopters were designed for quick precision assaults. An additional pair of AH-6 Little Birds provided extra fire support. These carried no SEAL passengers. Instead, the extra weight was used to carry miniguns and rocket pods.

The Little Birds took off first, their rotors sounding like an angry hornet compared to the heavier, full-throated thumping of the Blackhawks. The Little Birds used the length of the football field to take off, keeping their skids low until they picked up speed, then nosing upward near the end zone. The Blackhawks took off from their spots in unison. A tight formation, noses pointed towards the ground as they built up speed. The six aircraft sped northwest, dark green wraiths traveling into battle, skimming treetops and suburban roofs alike.

Chase sat in the cabin of the rear Blackhawk. Each door had three SEALs sitting shoulder to shoulder, feet dangling out. They wore green utilities and various styles of tactical boots. Wraparound sunglasses and green protective headgear. Dark gloves would help protect their hands if and when they fast-roped. Forward of the Blackhawk's cabin door on each side, a 160th SOAR aircrewman manned an M134 Minigun.

From his seat, Chase could see a neighborhood zooming by below them. He had flown low over the US a few times when he was with the Teams. Normally people waved and smiled. Chase caught a glimpse of a few civilians down there, looking up at them. He could tell from their expressions that things were different now. Scared wasn't the right word for the looks on their faces. They were serious. Determined. It was like a switch had flipped in the American psyche. We were once again a nation at war, the warrior tribe mentality in our DNA seeping to the surface. These civilians looking up at the formation of Army helicopters racing through the sky weren't observers in this war. They were *participants*.

Chase held his seat as the aircraft banked sharply and dove over a ridgeline.

"Two mikes out. Contact. Strength fifty. Ten vehicles in convoy. Little Birds inbound first."

Chase saw nods and thumbs-ups from the other SEALs in the aircraft. Game faces on. The men sitting at the doors had the fast ropes ready to go. Those sitting on the inside cabin seats had their knees bouncing. Most looked at the deck, waiting for it to begin. Some were reinspecting their gear. One was chewing gum, singing to himself. Everyone had their own style of pregame.

The two H-60s and two MH-6s peeled off to the right and began holding in a racetrack pattern as the tiny AH-6 attack helicopters made their assault run.

Chase could just make out the convoy of ten pickup trucks and sedans on the horizon, traveling along a narrow single-lane highway. The highway was a narrow cutout in a sea of pine trees.

The targets had been spotted by specially modified King Air surveillance aircraft. A DIA fusion team had evaluated the imagery with the help of an NSA-owned facial recognition program. They'd only gotten one hit, but it was confirmed with over ninety-eight percent confidence to be a company officer in a PLA infantry unit.

Now the two AH-6 helicopters traveled at just over one hundred and twenty knots. The tree line cutout surrounding the road formed a canyon-like shape on either side of the highway. The nimble aircraft used it to their advantage, masking their position low over the trees and then diving below the treetops, only feet above the road, tailing the convoy as they lined up for their attack run.

The miniguns fired first.

An eighteen-inch tongue of flame shot out of the six-barrel machine gun as it rotated, firing 7.62mm rounds at a rate of over two thousand per minute. The high-pitched whine of the minigun filled the cockpit as empty shell casings dropped to the road below.

Bullets riddled the vehicles and ripped open several rooftops. The lead aircraft traced his fire along the line of trucks, firing rockets from the M260 FFAR rocket pods when he reached the lead vehicle. The high-explosive rockets killed everyone aboard the lead vehicle and ignited its fuel tank, causing it to leave the pavement as it exploded. Two of the ten vehicles ran off the road, and one crashed into a tree.

The first AH-6 peeled off as the remaining cars began scattering from their convoy, still traveling in the same direction. As personnel from the surviving vehicles began firing at the lead helicopter, the second AH-6 made its attack run, its minigun streaming metallic death into the convoy. Rockets fired into the replacement lead vehicle, causing more devastating explosions.

The MH-6s and Blackhawks circled around the slowing convoy in a tight formation. Miniguns from these aircraft fired towards anyone who returned fire. The convoy was completely stopped now, smoke and flames and dead Chinese soldiers strewn about along a mile of highway. The Blackhawks and MH-6s each landed along an open stretch of road, and Chase and the SEALs jumped out, splitting up evenly to kill anyone who resisted, and take prisoner anyone who surrendered.

Chase and two of the SEALs moved quickly towards one SUV that had run into a tree. His SCAR stock held firm against his shoulder, he trained the weapon on the vehicle as the SEALs searched for survivors.

Movement in the trees.

A target. Chinese soldier, aiming his weapon. Chase

depressed the trigger twice. Crack. Crack. Two shots center mass. More rifle fire to his left. Chase kept his weapon trained along the threat axis he was responsible for, trusting the others in his team to do their jobs.

A minor firefight erupted to the north but quickly ended with the resistors killed in their pickup truck. There were seven remaining Chinese soldiers, and everyone who was medically able to indicate their surrender did so. Five were injured, two of them badly. The SEALs' medics immediately began stabilizing the injured Chinese soldiers. The others were restrained with zip ties and blindfolds.

"One minute until pickup."

"Roger."

The platoon of SEALs had formed a perimeter around the central part of the convoy, weapons trained away from the group in a defensive posture as others gathered Chinese communications gear or data storage that might be used for intelligence. In a few more minutes, a Chinook would arrive with a joint military-FBI forensics team to conduct a more thorough search. But Chase and his unit were now complete with their objective. Their skill was needed elsewhere.

"Here we go."

The helicopters had been circling overhead, close enough to provide support if needed, but far enough away not to make themselves a target. Now they made their approach and landed on the highway. The SEALs ran onto the helicopters, stuffing their recently acquired prisoners and intel into the cabins of the H-60s.

Later that night, Chase sat with the SEAL Team Five platoon commander, a lieutenant, and its senior chief, a grizzled veteran of two decades of fighting. They ate together in the cafeteria, where Army mess cooks had taken over and rustled up a reasonably good meal of rice, chicken, and vegetables.

Chase filled them in on what he had learned from the intel debrief he'd just attended. "That Chinese unit had been headed towards a water purification plant twenty miles from here. They were supposed to sabotage it and then work their way down a list of other targets."

"So they're just here to screw with us?"

"I don't think so. The intel folks think it's more to create a diversion."

"A diversion from what?" asked the senior chief.

"We don't know the answer to that yet."

16

USS Ford
Day 8

Lieutenant Bruce "Plug" McGuire was approaching his sixth and final hour of standing watch as the Zulu tactical action officer for the *Ford* Carrier Strike Group. At the computer terminals to his right sat a lieutenant junior grade and a chief. They were Plug's assistant watch standers and, like him, both assigned to the Destroyer Squadron. Their boss, the commodore, was the sea combat commander of the *Ford* Strike Group and reported directly to Admiral Manning.

As the commodore's air operations officer, Plug had to stand six hours of watch every day as part of his collateral duties. Here, he monitored the network's tactical displays to make sure the ships and aircraft under their control were doing what they were supposed to be doing, which seemed never to be the case.

"What the hell are those numbnuts on *Stockdale* doing? Oh my God. She literally has one job right now. One job." He leaned closer to the large monitor that showed the location of each ship and aircraft. He whispered to the monitor, "*Stay in your box.*"

The monitor did not reply.

Plug shook his head. "Her screen is freaking fifty miles across. Someone tell me, how is it that she cannot stay in her zone? What are they doing over there?"

"Do you really want to know, sir?"

Plug frowned at the tactical display, ignoring the question. The chief had been kind enough to place their now twenty-five ships in a meticulously detailed screen. It had taken Plug two hours to get approval for it. The screen was a giant circular set of layers that surrounded the aircraft carrier. Each layer was carved into sections like pieces of a pie. The ships in company— destroyers, cruisers, supply ships and littoral combat ships— each had a specific zone to stay in. As the carrier raced around to make wind for jet launches and recoveries, each ship was supposed to stay in its specific quadrant. This kept all of the escorts surrounding the carrier in the right defensive position, but it required the people driving those ships to pay attention and keep up as the carrier moved. And the carrier waited for no one.

"Tell the freaking *Stockdale* that if she doesn't get back in her box, she won't be able to get her mail." The LTJG began typing over the classified chat messenger system. Using Chat, as it was known, was supposed to be secondary to the radios. But for millennial sailors like him, instant messenger was so much more efficient. Not to mention second nature. The network had been down for the first few days of the war, thanks to the crippling Chinese cyberattack. But the information warfare specialists had changed out much of the crypto and software, and Plug was back to the surface warrior's addiction that was ship-to-ship instant messenger.

"*Stockdale* says they have flight quarters set to have the helo deliver their mail in one hour."

"Not if they don't stay in their box, they don't. I'll call up the

HSC guys and tell them not to bother going out there. That helicopter can't get to them and back to the carrier in time for the next cycle if *Stockdale* doesn't stay in their freaking screen position." The Helicopter Sea Combat (HSC) squadron on the carrier flew MH-60S variants of the Seahawk helicopter. They were tasked with many of the logistics missions due to their impressive storage capacity.

As part of Plug's job, he helped to write the flight schedule for all of the helicopters in the strike group. It was easier when there were three or four ships. Now that there were twenty-five, with all of the potential landing spots moving locations, it was like trying to solve one constantly changing mathematical equation. Since he had influence over the position the ships were kept in screen, he used that to help him with his collateral job, planning the helicopter schedule. If he kept the ships in certain places, he could plan to have the helicopters move people and parts around the strike group in an efficient manner. But the moment one domino fell, the whole thing came crashing down. Then you had fuel emergencies and missing parts and broken radars and unknown surface contacts and the *yelling*. Oh God, the yelling. Mostly from the O-5s and O-6s who were pissed off they'd gotten passed over for promotion. Why had he ever agreed to leave his aviation billet? Oh yeah, he hadn't. The geniuses at the Bureau of Naval Personnel had decided he should be put here. He hoped to God those same guys weren't working at St. Peter's gate someday.

"*Stockdale* says 'roger out.'"

Plug mumbled under his breath. "They better freaking say roger out..."

The lieutenant junior grade typing at the station next to him said, "You know, Plug, I think you're getting the hang of this. You've got that disgruntled SWO junior officer look down pat. You should consider getting your officer of the deck quals while you're here. I'm sure the *Ford* guys would be able to help you out..."

Plug sighed. "You're probably right. I'm pretty sure that my brain is slowly transforming to full SWO. It's been slowing down since I got here. And my eyes are becoming overly sensitive to daylight. I'm like a vampire now. I can't even go topside. Soon I'll start eating more donuts. Then my flight suits won't fit."

"Alright now, easy there, flyboy," the chief said. "I'd like to see you do a PRT at my age."

"Chief, I mean no disrespect. I only jest."

The chief smiled.

Plug sipped the last drop of coffee in his mug. It was cold and bitter, like his almost-SWO soul.

Plug stared intensely at the USS *Stockdale*'s little blue symbol on the large digital display in the front of the room. He didn't allow himself to blink until he saw the Arleigh Burke–class destroyer change its course and speed. A blue line extended out of the *Stockdale*'s ship symbol and changed direction to where he wanted it to go. Satisfied, Plug turned his attention to the monitor above him. It showed a live video feed of the aircraft carrier flight deck. Two helicopters were spinning, the aircrews changing out while they refueled.

Plug felt a hand on his shoulder. "Missing your past life? Don't tell me you want to go back."

He looked up to see Subs, the DESRON's submarine officer. Subs was his roommate, friend, and most importantly, his watch replacement.

"And give up all this glamour?" Plug waved his hand around the room. Two of the four computer workstations had their screens turned off. Post-it notes read "IT repairs in progress." The static hiss of multiple radios filled the space.

The chief and JG that Plug was in charge of during his duty stared back at him, smiles on their tired faces. Chief said, "I think this place is growing on him, sir." Then their own watch replacements appeared at the door and they began their turnover briefs.

"Yeah, I guess you're right," Subs said. He held out his fist, which Plug bumped. Then he rose from his swivel chair and stretched out. Subs had shown Plug the ropes down here, teaching him a lot in a short period of time.

"Hey, Commodore asked you to represent us at a meeting at zero nine thirty. In the War Room. Both the commodore and the deputy commodore are going on ship visits during that time."

As if on cue, a series of bells rang on the 1MC overhead speaker. "DESRON, departing."

The room looked up at the TV monitor in the corner as one of the helicopters lifted off the carrier's flight deck. A distant rumble of spinning rotors could be heard, even down here.

Someone said, "Oh thank God," joking that they were happy their boss was gone for a while.

Subs turned back to Plug. "Okay, *technically* they asked me to go, but I figure you'd rather attend a meeting than stand more watch. The meeting is supposed to be important, and they want somebody familiar with submarines to go."

"And you're sending *me*?"

"Familiar is a relative term."

Plug sighed. He was on four hours of sleep for the fifth day in a row and really needed a nap. From 0930 to 1000 was his only free time today. He would give anything for thirty minutes in the rack.

Instead, he found himself saying, "I'll be there. And thank you for this extra opportunity to serve my country. I'm really looking forward to it."

"Attaboy." Subs looked around the room. "Damn, man, what the hell is *Stockdale* doing out of screen? The battlewatch captain's gonna have my butt. Alright, I'll clean up the mess you left me. What else do you got?"

Plug ran through the status of all ships, the relevant parts of the flight schedule, and several other hot items.

Beneath the surface of their routine conversation and light-hearted jokes was a tension that hadn't been there two weeks earlier. Everyone was on edge, trying that much harder to be perfect at their jobs, and worrying that at any time, an attack might come on their carrier, which was one of the most valuable targets in the entire US Navy.

Plug said, "As you know, the subsurface threat remains high. We have ASW flights going around the clock now. Two maritime patrol aircraft will be on station during the day. One is a P-3, one is a P-8. Do me a favor, Subs. When those guys are up, just let them do their thing. Pass along any contact info you have, but don't micromanage them. They know what they're doing. Please. For my sake."

Plug found that if left to their own devices, the tactical action officers on ships would treat the aircraft like they were part of a video game, forgetting that they had highly trained and capable aircrews that were fully autonomous. As a pilot, nothing pissed Plug off more than when he was about to prosecute a sub contact and the geniuses in charge ordered him to fly twenty miles away without reason.

Subs said, "Got it. Any more condescending advice?"

"Nope, that about covers it."

"Good. Then go get yourself some coffee so you can have a bright smile for the zero nine thirty meeting."

"I stand relieved." Plug mock-saluted.

Another set of bells rang on the 1MC. This time they were followed with, "Captain, United States Navy, arriving."

All eyes in the room went up to the flight deck camera

image. A C-2 Greyhound had just landed on the carrier. The start of today's fixed-wing flight schedule.

"Who's that?"

Subs said, "I think it's the PACFLEET intel officer. He's here for the meeting too."

* * *

Ninety minutes later, Plug entered the carrier's War Room with his trusty mug of coffee. Suggs, the admiral's Loop, was sitting on one of the outer chairs that surrounded the conference table. Suggs was an F-18 pilot. Like Plug, he was a lieutenant who had done multiple deployments and was on the cusp of making O-4. Plug took a seat next to his friend.

"So what's the deal here, man?"

"Hey, Plug. Not sure. I wasn't in with the old man just now. I'm on the flight schedule again." Due to the shortage in pilots, strings had been pulled that allowed Suggs to get in a few flights per week, even though his job was technically a nonflying billet.

"Oh. Nice."

The hatch that lead to the admiral's stateroom swung open, and the *Ford* Strike Group's chief of staff entered the space. The Navy captain stood to the side of the doorway, calling, "Attention on deck."

Everyone stood at attention in silence as Admiral Manning, now a two-star, entered the space. Another Navy captain—one Plug didn't recognize—followed him in. Admiral Manning sat at the head of the table while the Navy captain walked towards the opposite end of the long conference table, looking ready to give a presentation.

Admiral Manning said, "Ladies and gentlemen, due to the sensitive nature of what we're about to hear, the PACFLEET thought it would be best to deliver this information in person. The Pacific Fleet intelligence officer will be giving the brief."

The Navy captain standing next to the presentation screen began. "As you all know, we're five days into the cease-fire agreement with China."

The screen flipped to a map of the Western Pacific. The briefer clicked a button, and the map was filled with red and blue symbols.

"Here's where Chinese and Allied forces were located prior to the start of combat operations."

He clicked the button again, and most of the blue symbols either disappeared or moved to the far-right side of the map.

"And here's where we are now. You'll notice that we don't have any ships in the vicinity of the South China Sea or the East China Sea. Per the agreement, the last remaining ships in the Philippine Sea should be on our side of the hundred and forty-fourth east longitude line within forty-eight hours. Evacuation of American civilians from Korea is estimated to be fifty percent complete, with the North Koreans recently agreeing to a temporary cease-fire at the behest of China. We are now over eighty percent complete with US civilian evac from Japan and Okinawa. Military movements from these zones are more complex but are generally following these trends."

The PACFLEET intelligence officer looked up at the room. Plug could tell from his expression that something important was coming.

"Now...here you can see where two of our fast-attack submarines in the Western Pacific were recently located."

Plug noticed that everyone in the room had the good sense not to point out that this was in violation of the cease-fire agreement.

"We obviously have other submarines in the region, but these two are the ones relevant to our discussion."

Plug saw all of the symbols on the map disappear except for two blue submarines. One was located approximately one hundred miles south of Hong Kong. The other was near the Luzon Strait.

"This was their location at the start of the cease-fire. Their orders were to maintain position, and to observe and report on enemy naval movements."

The screen changed to show dozens of red symbols. "These were the last known positions of Chinese surface and subsurface tracks prior to the start of the war. As you can see, the PLA Navy is formed up into a scattering of assets located predominantly in the South China Sea and East China Sea."

The screen changed again. This time the two American subs in the South China Sea disappeared and the red tracks were more concentrated into the two separate strike groups.

"This is as of forty-eight hours ago. You notice that the Chinese have consolidated into two strike groups. The southernmost Chinese strike group was the one that attacked Guam. The high-value unit of this group is the Chinese aircraft carrier *Liaoning*. After its failed attack on Guam, the *Liaoning* Strike Group transited west towards China and joined up with another group of ships that just recently put to sea. The northernmost Chinese strike group contains the other two Chinese aircraft carriers and dozens of warships. The northern group has moved to the south of Tokyo and seems to be monitoring the US exfiltration there."

Plug noted that the captain didn't use the word *retreat*.

"We don't have an exact estimate on the order of battle of these carrier groups. But our sources tell us that many of these ships left port after the cease-fire began, and that number is well over fifty ships sortied in each group."

Someone whistled.

"As for the two American subs..."

The screen changed again. Both blue submarine symbols disappeared. Two X symbols were there instead, each with the words "last known posit" next to it.

"As of yesterday, the southernmost Chinese strike group is believed to have transited the Luzon Strait. We have lost communications with both of those submarines."

The room was filled with an uncomfortable silence. Brothers in arms recognizing both the loss of fellow sailors and a significant threat on the horizon.

The map changed to a presentation screen with bullet points. The briefer read from it, almost verbatim.

"Both of the US fast-attack submarines had reported coming into contact with a large group of Chinese warships. At contact minus two hours, the submarines checked in. In each instance, after that time, the fast-attack boats went dark."

The *Ford* CO, the aircraft carrier's captain, said, "Define dark."

"No further communication whatsoever. All attempts to reach the subs in question have failed."

The *Ford* CO said, "Well, is it possible that they are there and just having communications problems? Hell, we've got one of the most advanced communication suites on the planet and we're having a hell of a time right now. If they're damaged or sunk, they're supposed to send up a beacon, right?"

The PACFLEET intelligence officer said, "Assuming that the beacon wasn't damaged, yes. If the submarines were hit by enemy weapons, the emergency positioning locator beacon should have been released in all three cases. During normal operation, these radio signals would be picked up by our satellites. We could locate the distressed submarine immediately and begin rescue ops. However, seeing as our GPS and satellite capability has been knocked out of play, we've been relegated to using alternative communications networks for our submarines.

The Chinese are now heavily jamming all radio transmissions in these areas. We just aren't able to confirm what happened."

Admiral Manning said, "But we can assume the worst."

"Yes, sir. I'm afraid that is the logical conclusion."

The *Ford* CO said, "So the Chinese are already breaking their peace treaty. Is that what you've come here to tell us?"

Plug listened eagerly for a response. Most of them figured that the peace treaty between the US and China was going to be temporary. The American diplomats would try to make it permanent. But if anyone really believed they would succeed, they were fools, as far as Plug was concerned. The big question was, how long would peace last? Or had the presumed sinking of these two submarines already ended it?

Admiral Manning said, "Please describe what you were telling me before the brief, Captain."

The PACFLEET intelligence officer nodded. "Both of these submarines provided similar information during their last reports. This included a description of abnormal acoustic signatures and strange tactics being employed by the approaching group of Chinese ships. Based on their location, we can assume that these approaching Chinese ships were the newly-sized-up *Liaoning* Strike Group, the southernmost Chinese carrier group. At the ranges our submarines were picking up these acoustics, it was impossible for them to identify exactly what they were hearing. But the onboard computers weren't able to classify it as anything we've seen before."

One of the helicopter squadron commanding officers sat a few seats down from Plug. The commander raised his hand and asked a few questions about the acoustic signals. The tactics and technical details of antisubmarine warfare were quite complex, and many in the room were unable to follow.

Their conversation went back and forth for a moment before the CAG interrupted, saying, "Alright, guys. Dumb it down for the old jet jock, please. You must have some thoughts on what these noises were."

The briefer said, "In short, CAG, we think it's some new type of ASW platform. A completely new technology. These fast-attack boats should be practically invisible to the Chinese until they're right on top of them. But apparently, that's not what happened. We don't know how the Chinese are doing it, but they've found a way to detect our submarines at long ranges from their surface units and prosecute them with deadly efficiency."

More uneasy silence in the room.

Admiral Manning said, "If true, this changes the balance of power significantly."

"Yes, sir."

"What are the latest locations of each Chinese fleet now?"

The PACFLEET intelligence officer shifted his weight around. "We're working on getting an update, sir. But it's been more than twenty-four hours, and it's hard to comply with the cease-fire agreement and gain an exact location. These submarines were able to do it covertly. But—"

"But that's not an option anymore."

"Correct, Admiral."

Admiral Manning said, "And we can't get ISR in there?"

"Sending aircraft that far west would violate the cease-fire agreement."

"That's assuming the Chinese fleets are abiding by that agreement. What if they're moving east of the one-forty-four?"

"Sir, we're working on a solution. Even if hostilities resume, without satellite coverage, and with the denied area expanding, ISR will be challenging. Prior to the cease-fire, surface-to-air missiles took out many of our drones and reconnaissance aircraft. The Chinese surface-to-air range has proven to be much greater than originally thought. The Air Force is working on getting more recon satellites up, but we don't have confirmation on when that will be."

The CAG said, "Cease-fire my ass. They're reloading and taking territory."

Admiral Manning said, "Has the US made any complaints to the Chinese about violating the cease-fire?"

"Sir, that's been discussed, but it's a hard point to make given their location. In both cases, our submarines were in violation of the cease-fire agreement since they were west of the hundred and forty-fourth longitude line."

Admiral Manning frowned. "I suppose as long as we pretend that we weren't there, the Chinese will pretend they didn't sink them."

The PACFLEET intel officer opened his mouth to speak but decided against it. People began talking heatedly around the room.

Admiral Manning said, "Alright, let's settle down and wrap up."

"Thank you, sir." He looked around the room. "Many of you are probably wondering why I've flown out here to tell you this, with the *Ford* Strike Group being so far away."

Plug certainly was.

"Our China analysts believe that if the war heats up again, the PLA Navy will continue pushing east, challenging our Pacific Fleet for dominance. If that happens, we expect that Hawaii and Guam will again both be prime targets. We'll need the *Ford* Strike Group to be prepared to face these Chinese fleets, and to assume that our submarines will need to stand off until we can counter this new ASW technology."

Admiral Manning frowned. "Thank you for the brief, Captain. Please relay my request up the chain. The warfighters need locations on the two Chinese strike groups. We need to know exactly what this new ASW technology is and how to defeat it. And we need both of these intelligence reports *yesterday*."

"Yes, sir."

"Ladies and gentlemen, there's an old saying in the Navy. I'm paraphrasing a bit, but it goes something like this: If you want to put a hole in a carrier, use a missile. If you want to sink a carrier, use a torpedo. If this Chinese ASW capability is as deadly as our analysts think it is, that takes away our submarine force's ability to sink those enemy carriers. That puts us at a significant disadvantage. Because they can still sink us."

17

Eglin AFB
Florida

The war was only a week old, but already David felt like the country had been transported back in time to the 1940s. Periodic radio and TV broadcasts had supplanted the internet. Fuel, meals, and clothing were being rationed. Patriotism was through the roof, and military recruitment centers had lines around the corner as able-bodied men and women tried to sign up for the armed forces. Yesterday David had even seen a report come across his desk that several US auto manufacturers were converting their factories to make military equipment.

The workers at those manufacturing plants would keep their jobs. Others weren't so lucky. Over the last twenty years, the global economy had been built upon global trade and had grown increasingly reliant on high-speed internet connectivity. With the Chinese EMP attack, that era had come to a halt.

Access to information, workers, resources, and money was made extremely difficult. With the internet inoperative, millions of jobs disappeared overnight. That alone was enough to cause panic and chaos. But when combined with electrical blackouts and food shortages, it was devastating.

Even if there was food in the grocery store, how were you supposed to pay for it? Most people didn't carry much cash around anymore. The little they had dried up fast. The world had grown completely reliant on technology to perform the simplest tasks. Now credit cards and smartphones were both worthless. The panic of survival instinct kicked in fast.

The bus ride down had been eye-opening. They saw firsthand what a fearful society could become. During those first few days, some scenes reminded David of a zombie apocalypse. Riots. Shootings. Fistfights over gas shortages and bare grocery stores. Everyone was scared, trying to protect their families and stay alive.

Within the first thirty-six hours, the new president had declared martial law. Together, the American military and law enforcement had taken to the streets and ensured order and discipline. The national guard and military reserves were fully activated. A week later, most utilities and electric grids were still down, but they were being restored, however slowly. While the internet and cell phone networks weren't going to be the same for a while, people were adapting.

Emergency centers were formed in every town. The trucking industry was nationalized. The military and government disaster response agencies worked with businesses to ration resources and allocate them the best they could. It was like a Cat 5 hurricane had hit every city in America overnight. There were many deaths. Estimates varied, but the low range was over one hundred thousand, and the counting had only now just begun. Dehydration or starvation. Accidents and sickness. Hospitals without electricity. Prisons where the guards had stopped showing up for work. Railroad accidents. Car pileups. Plane crashes.

But the worst events often bring out the best in people, and David was moved by the stories he heard of private businesses and citizens putting their own interests on hold in order to help their fellow Americans. In times of trouble, people come together. They turn to the brave. Rescue personnel. Soldiers. Nurses and doctors. And the untested often find that they are capable of more than they ever thought possible.

David thought of this as he looked out his front window, a blue-gray dawn illuminating his front yard. A few men and women walked to work on the base road. Driving was discouraged unless absolutely necessary. Gasoline had become sacred.

"There's cereal on the table." David's wife touched his arm, breaking his spell.

"Thanks." He kissed her on the forehead, pulling her close and feeling the softness of her bathrobe. "You sleep at all last night?" The baby had been crying enough that Lindsay had ended up staying in the other bedroom.

"A little."

David poured himself some cereal and milk. His wife had gone shopping at the commissary on base the day before. The shelves were sparse, but better stocked than the empty civilian grocery stores in town. And life on base was much better than the stories he'd heard about the emergency food distribution centers rationing bread and water around the nation's worst-hit areas.

They were lucky that David's job had put them on base housing at Eglin Air Force Base. A single-floor Florida-style home with two bedrooms and a quaint backyard. Running water and electricity were available upon arrival, which was more than much of the country could say right now.

David finished his breakfast, said goodbye to his wife, and walked a mile to his office building, arriving just after six a.m. He worked for an hour at his desk in the SILVERSMITH team's new operations center before jet noise overhead told him that it was almost time for the morning brief. The fighter squadrons took off at the same time each morning, when the field opened.

Susan tapped on the top of his gray cubicle. "You coming?" A throng of team members walked by her on the way to the morning meeting, most carrying folders and cups of coffee.

"Yeah. One sec." David grabbed his classified notebook. He had to check the notebook in and out of the document control office each day, but it helped if he could jot down important facts and figures at these meetings, all of which were classified.

David got up and walked with his boss.

"I saw in my inbox that we're now connected to the Raven Rock data stream."

"Yes. Most of the Pentagon leadership is working from there now."

"ONI put out a request to our group on that channel. Something about a new class of Chinese warship?"

Susan glanced at him, impressed. "They must have sent a thousand requests over this morning, yet you always manage to pick out the most relevant bits. We'll be working on that one. Our mission is evolving."

"Yes, I imagine it would."

"We'll need to provide an evaluation on that Chinese ship. And there's something else I'd like to bring you in on. A special project we've set up on the other side of the base."

"Oh?"

"We'll talk later." She held the door for him, and they entered a classroom that was being shared with some of the F-35 training squadrons on the base. Now that David's team was using the room, an NSA tech was doing a sweep for bugs every few hours. An Air Force Security Force sergeant checked IDs at the door. David held up his name tag, which the young man studied. The Air Force kid waved David through, and he took his seat.

General Schwartz and Susan sat up front. There were a lot of new faces around the room. With the China expertise on the team, SILVERSMITH was quickly becoming a premier resource for the brass. Whereas a few weeks ago, their job had been to prevent war, now SILVERSMITH was an analysis and idea factory. An information hub where top-level members of the intelligence community, military, and law enforcement shared what they knew and offered solutions up the chain of command.

The door shut, and everyone went silent.

The screen at the front of the room came on, showing a map of the US.

General Schwartz said, "Good morning, ladies and gents. Our INCONUS SOCOM task force is making solid progress. We now have over nine hundred Chinese INCONUS killed or captured, with an estimated five hundred remaining. Local law enforcement is sending tips to the regional military liaisons, which are forwarding their info to the SOCOM cell. Our hope is to destroy any remaining Chinese INCONUS units by the end of the week. Prisoners will be held in detention centers, where they will be interrogated."

General Schwartz shot Susan a look that David didn't understand. Did she have something to do with prisoner interrogations? It made sense that she would want to see any intelligence that was gleaned from Chinese prisoners.

A man sitting towards the front of the room raised his hand. "General, isn't this ongoing Chinese INCONUS activity evidence that they aren't abiding by the cease-fire agreement?"

"Obviously, yes. It is."

"So...are we going to do anything about it? I mean, diplomatically speaking?"

General Schwartz said, "The State Department has raised

objections through official channels on the continued presence and illegal activities of Chinese military units within the boundaries of the United States. The Chinese are denying the veracity of these claims. They say that they don't have anyone here. The international community is in disagreement, and somewhat useless to us in this matter."

Eye rolls and scoffs from around the room.

The man who asked the question said, "But if they're violating the cease-fire—"

Susan spoke up. "Excuse me. We don't *want* the cease-fire to end. The powers that be have decided that we've lost any realistic possibility of holding Korea or Japan, and negotiated a truce to remove our people from those nations. So, every day of this cease-fire is another day we can use to get Americans out of harm's way."

David knew she was right. Commercial aircraft and ships were packed with American servicemembers and their families leaving Japan and Korea.

Someone said, "Why would Cheng Jinshan agree to the cease-fire in the first place? I mean, if China is attacking the US..."

One of the CIA analysts said, "Two reasons. One, it allows him to get VIPs out of the US. Children of politicians and wealthy businessmen. That's important for him to do because it helps him to keep the power brokers in China happy. Which helps keep him on the throne."

"Why didn't he just do that before the war?"

"It would have telegraphed his intentions."

"What's the other reason?"

David said, "Because he gets to keep Korea and Japan. He just moved the football forward, big-time."

General Schwartz nodded. "Exactly."

David said, "Sir, if I may? Cheng Jinshan's ultimate goal isn't just to take control of Asia, or even the Pacific. His ultimate goal includes taking control of the United States. This would eradicate his only real opposition to power around the globe. His ultimate goal is a world dominated by China."

Someone said, "Russia know that?"

Susan narrowed her eyes. "What's your point, David?"

"We all know that there's a third reason for the cease-fire. Jinshan is using this lull in the fighting to his strategic advantage. He's an extremely detail-oriented individual. There must be some reason he needs us to abide by these specific terms."

General Schwartz said, "Well, Mr. Manning, that's why we're here. To identify enemy intentions and create ways to counter them."

The general pointed at the young military officer manning the computer. The screen changed to a view of the Pacific. "The Chinese Southern Fleet, as it has been dubbed by our friends at the Office of Naval Intelligence, has traveled beyond the Luzon Strait and is now in the Philippine Sea. We have lost communications with two submarines in the vicinity of this fleet over the past few days. We believe they were sunk by assets from the Chinese Southern Fleet. There's a high demand for ISR on this group. Right now, we have a rough idea of where they might be, but that circle of uncertainty is expanding."

David thought of the message he had read on the possible new Chinese antisubmarine warfare capability. He thought about his family members out there right now. Without the US submarine advantage, the Chinese would be much more formidable opponents in a naval war.

Susan stood up and the screen changed to an image of a very odd-looking container ship.

Susan said, "They call them the Jiaolong class. It's a battleship. Or the PLA Navy's take on what a modern battleship should be. This picture was taken several weeks ago, when the ship was under construction. It's the only one we have. It's big. It's secretive. And beyond that, we don't know much about it."

David studied the image. The container ship was painted haze gray, like a warship. A tall superstructure with a wide bridge on the aft end. Strange-looking platforms extended outward amidships, two on each side, and two tall towers protruded upward from the fore and aft section of the ship. Scaffolding surrounded the towers. It reminded David of the Washington Monument when it was being refurbished, although these towers appeared to be metallic, and functional components of the massive ship.

Someone asked, "What's with the towers?"

"We think it may be a new type of radar."

"And those are flight decks?"

"We don't know. But HUMINT sources in China reported that at least one of these ships has left port this week, under the cover of darkness. We believe it's now accompanying the aircraft carrier *Liaoning* as part of the Chinese Southern Fleet."

David looked up at the map on the screen. He could see a group of American Navy near Guam. Surface Action Group–121. David's sister Victoria was on one of those ships, the USS *Farragut*. The expanding circle showed where the Chinese Southern Fleet could be. It was approaching her ship. And in another week or two, that circle might extend closer to Midway Island, near the USS *Ford*. His father was there.

General Schwartz continued the brief. "The US military is reinforcing Guam. If hostilities resume next week, it will become a major hub for US air power. If the *Liaoning* Strike Group tries to reattack Guam, they'll have a surface action group and significant air power to deal with. We're already planning offensive operations if the Chinese Southern Fleet comes within range. The problem is still in locating them. We have the submarine USS *Columbia* located in between Guam and where the Chinese fleet might be, but that's past the one forty-fourth east longitude line, and we're very nervous about her getting too close without a full understanding of this new ASW technology. Satellite recon birds are still a week from launching, our UAVs have proven highly susceptible to electronic attack, and the U-2s would be sitting ducks against Chinese SAMs."

David frowned. "Sir, when I was with In-Q-Tel, I worked on a project that involved the..." He looked around the room, suddenly aware that he wasn't sure whether he was allowed to discuss the program.

Seeing this, General Schwartz said, "Spit it out, son. We don't have time for the normal bullshit."

"...the SR-72. The Air Force's future aerial reconnaissance aircraft, with the scramjet propulsion. It'll be high and fast, and able to get imagery well over the one forty-fourth without being impacted by electronic attack. And it's too fast for SAMs."

General Schwartz shook his head, "That program is several years away. They don't even have a full-scale prototype."

David smiled. "Sir, I beg to differ."

18

Tonopah Test Range Airport
Nevada
Day 11

Colonel Johnny "Flipper" Wojcik crept around the outside of his aircraft, examining every rivet. Each step he made was under the close watch of Air Force security services. This hangar had five armed guards at any given time, and it was only opened at night. Tonight was special, however. Three additional men were also watching Wojcik conduct his preflight. Two had recently traveled here. The third was a defense contractor, there to provide support on behalf of his company.

Colonel Wojcik had been a pilot for the last thirty years. A test pilot for the last twenty. The last eight years, though, had been spent in the arid Nevada desert, at Tonopah. This was where the fun stuff happened. The projects that didn't exist. The jets that no one knew about. Colonel Wojcik was one of the few active-duty military men that got to take part in all of this. The others were all former military, now contract test pilots. While they had more expertise, it was his active-duty military status that had made him the right choice for this particular assignment.

There were two identical-looking aircraft in the hangar. Dark metal, futuristic. Sleek aerodynamic angles rounding out the fuselage. Colonel Wojcik had spent a few hours a day for the past few years in this hangar, and he still thought the thing looked like a goddammed spaceship. The SR-72 had all the sex appeal that a top-secret reconnaissance aircraft should have, he thought to himself. The engineering design team had outdone themselves with this one.

He conducted tonight's preflight with love. Colonel Wojcik felt like a jockey brushing his prized racehorse before the Kentucky Derby. *Don't let me down now, baby. We'll win this together.*

The operational capabilities of the optionally manned prototype he was about to fly were known only to a few people in the world. Articles on the Air Force SR-72 program had been put out by his company, of course. That helped generate buzz around Capitol Hill, which helped ensure funding.

But only a few knew the specifics. One of those men happened to be David Manning, a former employee of In-Q-Tel, the CIA's private equity firm. David was now watching the colonel conduct his preflight inspection of the aircraft.

"So they made you come all the way out here to watch me take off?"

"Actually, sir, I won't see you take off. I leave for D.C. in about fifteen minutes. My new bosses wanted me to make sure we effectively communicated the mission requirements, since communications haven't been particularly good of late."

The colonel's hand paused on the smooth surface of the left wing. He turned to meet David's eye.

"What are you headed to D.C. for?"

David hesitated, and the colonel saw the look of discomfort

and held up his hand. "Don't worry. I've been doing this long enough. I know when I don't need to know. You have effectively communicated the mission requirements to me, Mr. Manning. I am to go fly halfway around the world and take some pictures of a Chinese super-fleet, then fly back and get those pictures to the thirty-pound brains so they can figure out what the hell is killing our submarines."

The thick-mustached test pilot looked up at David again and winked. "That about sum it up?"

David smiled. "That's about right, sir."

"Let me ask you a question, Mr. Manning. Those towers you showed me on the top of the ships—any chance that's why you're headed to D.C.?"

David smiled again, remaining silent.

"That's what I thought. Told you I been doing this awhile."

David and two other members of the SILVERSMITH team had been flown to Nevada once the Air Force and Lockheed had agreed to use the SR-72 prototype for this mission.

"Now, Johnny, you will need to be careful once you get her above Mach 4."

"I know, Al. I know."

"And we haven't tested any of the ISR pods they made us install. Those were meant for the U-2. We did the best we could to integrate the systems, but...well, it's possible that you'll fly out there and have nothing to show for it." The company guy was getting all worked up. "There's a big difference between operational capability and a prototype for reusable hypersonic aircraft! This was something we explained to In-Q-Tel when Mr. Manning was here last year."

David interrupted. "We understand the risks, sir. I expressed that your company was not to blame if anything goes wrong."

"Hey, I mean officially, Al, she's not even built yet, right?" said the colonel, grinning.

David and his colleague shook hands with the colonel.

"Godspeed, sir. Fly safe."

"Thank you, Mr. Manning. Good luck to you too."

David and his colleague left and were taken to the CIA's Gulfstream. They were airborne within minutes, headed to D.C.

Ninety minutes later, the SR-72 taxied to the approach end of the runway and took off into the night sky.

Most air defense systems didn't even spot it on their radar scopes. The ones that did were immediately informed that it was a friendly and instructed not to communicate anything about it on open channels.

Colonel Wojcik flew at subsonic speed until feet wet over the Pacific. The cockpit was dark and tightly enclosed. A very small window a few feet in front of him gave him glimpses of the outside world, which would be dark until he crossed into daylight over the Pacific. Then he ran through his checklist, ensured he was strapped in tight, and said a quick prayer. That never hurt.

His gloved thumb and forefinger hovered over the final switch in his checklist before turning on the scramjet engine. He both loved and hated this part.

Flick.

Up went the switch.

The sound was the first thing he heard. A rhythmic booming sound emanated from the rear of the aircraft, each noise jolting him deeper into his seat, the digital airspeed indicator jolting up and up and up along with the noises.

A decade earlier, aviation enthusiasts had caught sight of the scramjet engine prototype aircraft's contrail. Big puffs of cloud, separated thousands of feet from each other. That engine had been improved, and it was now getting warmed up behind him. The noises getting louder and louder.

WHOMP. WHOMP. WHOMP.

The scramjet engine continued to accelerate. The thick cockpit window in front of him began to lighten as he chased the setting sun into the previous day. His flight path would take him west almost six thousand miles, from Nevada to the Philippine Sea. At Mach 6, it would take him less than eighty minutes to get there. Then he would make a wide turn and tank near Hawaii before heading back to Nevada.

The rhythmic explosive noises coming from the engine continued, dulled by his hearing protection. But the speed had reached equilibrium. At an altitude of eighty-five thousand feet, the SR-72 was now traveling at forty-six hundred miles per hour.

Colonel Wojcik ran through his next checklist, reciting the steps out loud to himself out of habit as his fingers danced over an electronic keypad. The multipurpose display in front of him divided into three as the surveillance systems came online.

The SR-72's surveillance and reconnaissance payload was the most advanced equipment in the US Air Force's inventory. It included electro-optical and infrared cameras and synthetic aperture radar as well as a multispectral targeting system. Colonel Wojcik had to laugh at that name. He was traveling at Mach 6 with no weapons. What the hell was he supposed to target? There was also a signals intelligence payload that would collect a variety of data, which the NSA would pore over.

Wojcik looked at the left-most screen to make sure that the aircraft's autopilot was navigating them on his intended track.

Twenty minutes until he was over the 144th east longitude line.

The rightmost screen displayed the images being captured by the optical camera. While the camera would record everything in its field of view, Colonel Wojcik had the ability to adjust the zoom and focus of his display with software, so he could zoom in on a subsection of the larger picture but still allow the equipment to record the entire scene for later. Wojcik moved a trackball and tapped a few keys to zoom in on a white dot on the ocean's surface. Eventually the white dot increased in size until it transformed into a merchant vessel. Op check complete.

The aircraft started vibrating, and he checked the center panel. One of the scramjet engines' internal cooling systems was right on the operational limits.

Come on, baby. Just a few more minutes and we'll be able to slow you down.

The world sped by in a blur, and the rattle grew louder. Wojcik felt a twinge of fear in his chest. Or was that the vibrations of the aircraft? He checked the chart. They had just reached the checkpoint for the left turn. A slow one-thousand-mile arc over the Pacific. The turn would take them over the entire area of uncertainty where the southernmost Chinese fleet might be.

The engine noise grew louder. His eyes shifted to his instruments. *Shit.* Internal temperature was now out of limits in the scramjet engine.

He looked at the right-side screen. A large cluster of white dots was surrounded by a computer-generated red square. Wojcik tapped a key, and the image zoomed in and became clear. Dozens of white wakes.

It was the Chinese fleet.

A red flashing light came on, and a ringing tone sounded in his helmet earpiece.

WARNING: ENGINE TEMP

The master caution panel was telling him what he already knew. If he didn't dial back the airspeed, the cooling system wouldn't be able to keep up with the friction generated by the speed of air molecules entering the intake, and catastrophic engine failure could result.

Another flashing light, and a distinctly different tone in his earpiece.

WARNING: SAM RADAR DETECTED

The electronic sensors had detected the signature of Chinese surface-to-air missile radars.

His breaths came fast and heavy in his oxygen mask. Each WHOMP of the engine was like the flash of a moment in time. Colonel Wojcik's decades of training forced him to take action.

WHOMP. His eyes scanning the navigational chart, heading, and altitude.

WHOMP. His mind calculating the time it would take for the Chinese ships to launch an attack on his aircraft if he kept his speed versus if he slowed to below Mach 1, as the emergency procedure prescribed.

WHOMP. His eyes darting back to the image of the Chinese fleet, now showing...

What the hell are those? For a brief moment, everything else fell away. The alarms, the flashing lights, his mind focused on a new and interesting riddle. Trying to place the giant whitish-gray shapes he saw clustered around the aircraft carrier. *They almost look like...*

BOOM.

His master caution panel lit up like a Christmas tree.

EJECT.

EJECT.

EJECT.

Everything seemed to go in slow motion. The gyro showed

his aircraft was now banking hard to the left. His speed was bleeding down. Mach 4.2. Mach 3.8. The light sky and dark blue of the ocean began revolving in the tunnel of a window. Then everything went bright white as the aircraft disintegrated around him.

Colonel Wojcik felt his stomach flutter as negative Gs came on. He was being shoved downward, the aircraft's safety system initiating bailout procedures. His pressure suit inflated, which was good. The pressure suit would keep his blood from boiling at almost eighty-five thousand feet above sea level, and act like an escape pod...as long as it held. It also gave him oxygen. A small kick near his back told him that the tiny parachute behind his seat had been activated. It was designed to slow him down and prevent tumbling motions.

He hurtled towards the ocean, wondering if he would live through the next few minutes.

19

Victoria Manning heard the familiar sound of an ELT in her headset. The emergency locator transmitter was checked before every flight. Every aircraft had one. It broadcast a high-pitched audio sound on Guard, the emergency radio frequency that aircraft and ships monitored at all times.

"Control, Cutlass, you guys hearing that ELT?"

"Affirm, Cutlass, stand by."

Victoria sat in the right-side pilot's seat of her helicopter, rotors spinning over the deck, the horizon moving slowly up and down with the rolls of the ship.

She glanced down at her fuel. They were almost topped off. This was the second bag of her two-flight shift. Patrolling the ocean north of Guam, scanning the area with her radar and ESM, looking for any sign of the monstrous Chinese fleet everyone was talking about.

"Cutlass, Deck."

She looked at the glass window of the LSO shack, behind which stood her maintenance officer, Spike.

"Go ahead, Deck."

"Cutlass, Deck, I just got off the phone with OPS. Sounds

like this ELT is a real SAR scenario. I called up to the AW shack, and your second aircrewman is throwing his gear on now. He'll be out shortly."

Victoria clicked the trigger on her cyclic twice, which transmitted two rapid clicks over the UHF, acknowledging that she understood.

"Control, Cutlass, please put the TAO on secure."

"Roger, Boss."

They switched to the secure communications channel, and the ship's tactical action officer came on the radio.

"Boss, it's CSO. We have a rough position of where the survivor is located. It's about two hundred miles northwest of here...stand by..."

Victoria watched as the hangar door opened and her second aircrewman came out wearing a wet suit and carrying his rescue equipment.

"Two hundred miles? Boss, we aren't supposed to go that far out, right?"

Victoria glanced at her copilot. "Let's hear the scenario out first."

Another voice on the radio. Commander Boyle. "Airboss, this is the captain. We just got notified by Seventh Fleet that this is a top-priority rescue mission. Operational necessity has been declared by the admiral. We'll give you whatever support you need, but you're the closest air asset."

"Understood, sir. Please advise on the location."

"Passing lat-long now."

Victoria looked at the multipurpose display. An X popped up with the words "AF rescue" next to it.

"What's the distance?" Victoria said on the helicopter's internal comms.

Her copilot used the joystick to measure from their current position. They were having a hell of a time getting accurate navigation information without GPS, but since they'd just landed on the ship, it would be as accurate as they could make it.

"One ninety-seven nautical miles, Boss."

Victoria said over external comms, "Captain, how accurate is that location?"

"It's a bearing cut from us and the *Michael Monsoor*. There's a P-8 that just launched and will help with the search, but..." He paused. "But that location is about twenty miles west of the one forty-fourth."

Victoria looked back at the digital map on her display, flipping her visor up to see it better. "And they're letting us go?"

The captain said, "Seventh Fleet says this is highest priority. You have been granted approval to go over the line."

Victoria wondered who this crash survivor was, and if he was even going to be alive when they found him. "Roger," was all she said to the captain. "Your controls," she told her copilot.

"My controls."

Victoria released her hands from the cyclic and collective and slid out her pen from the metal spiral on her kneeboard. She began scratching out the math. It would take her about eighty minutes to get there at one hundred and fifty-five knots, but that would burn up half her fuel. They would need time on station to locate the survivor, then rescue the survivor, and both of those evolutions would burn fuel. Call it five hundred pounds.

"Boss, we're all set back here," her aircrewman called over the internal communications system.

"Copy." She switched to external. "Request green deck."

"Cutlass, Deck, you have yellow deck for breakdown, green deck for launch."

"Roger break, Captain, I'll be crunching the numbers in flight. Request you proceed towards the survivor at best speed as soon as we're airborne."

"Already in the works, Airboss. Good luck."

The flight deck team had removed the chocks and chains and held them up for Victoria and her copilot to inspect. She gave a thumbs-up and then turned back to her math. She decided to fly at their max range airspeed of one hundred and twenty knots. That would give her a little more fuel. If the ship traveled at twenty-eight knots...

"Ready, Boss?" her copilot said.

"You got it. Clear right. Gauges green."

"Coming up."

Victoria shoved her pen back into the metal spiral on her kneeboard and kept both hands hovering an inch away from the controls. Close enough that she could take them if her copilot made a mistake, but far enough away to let him do the flying. The aircraft sprang straight up and drifted aft. The feeling of the ship's constant rolling in the sea ceased as the helicopter freed itself from the deck.

"Clear right."

"Clear left, nose coming right."

The copilot used his foot pedals to yaw the aircraft right forty-five degrees.

"Gauges green and clean, pulling power. One, two, three positive rates of climb. Safe single-engine airspeed, nosing it over. Radalt on, please."

"Radalt on."

Victoria tapped the square button that placed the helicopter's computer-controlled radar altitude hold on. She inserted a fly-to point where the SAR survivor was supposed to be and observed with approval that her copilot had turned to that heading without her having to tell him to do so. Good aircrew chemistry like this saved time. At top levels, pilots, copilots, and aircrewmen practically read each other's minds, anticipating commands and maneuvers, shaving precious seconds off time-consuming procedures.

"I'll get the after-takeoff checks. Make your speed one hundred and twenty knots, please. AW2, please conduct the SAR checklist."

"In progress, Boss."

Twenty minutes later, the P-8 checked in with them. The P-8 Poseidon was the Navy's version of a Boeing 737, outfitted for maritime reconnaissance, antiship and antisubmarine warfare.

"Cutlass 471, Mad Fox 436."

"Mad Fox, Cutlass."

"Mad Fox is on station over the datum, beginning circle search."

"Roger, Mad Fox. Cutlass is twenty mikes out."

"Copy."

Victoria checked in with the ship again, verifying that the *Farragut* was indeed headed towards her helicopter at best speed. The entire scenario was one big math problem. Would they be able to find the survivor before Victoria's helicopter ran out of fuel? And even if they could, would she have time to conduct the rescue and still keep enough fuel to make it back to the ship? She looked down at her math. The final number she kept coming up with had a negative sign in front of it. She erased it and then changed her bingo fuel calculation—the quantity of fuel she would use to trigger the return to her ship. The new number got her back on deck, but it didn't give her much time to conduct a search.

"Cutlass, Max Fox, we have located the survivor. Stand by for coordinates."

Victoria felt a jolt of elation. "Send 'em."

The P-8 sent over the latitude and longitude of the survivor, which Victoria used to update their heading. The aircraft banked slightly to the left as her copilot made the adjustment.

She relayed the update to her ship and recalculated the fuel problem.

"We should have about ten minutes to spare. How quick can you guys be, Fetternut?"

"Boss, we'll be in and out," the first-class petty officer replied through the internal comms. "You just watch."

Victoria redid her fuel calculation for the third time in a row. Her voice went up an octave. "Good. Because we are *very* limited on fuel."

"Understood, Boss."

She knew that her rescue swimmers were good. She had conducted plenty of SAR training with them in the past. Enlisted aircrewmen were a unique breed of crazy. But when the game was on the line, there were no better men to be with. Navy helicopter aircrewmen prided themselves on being some of the best in the world at search-and-rescue operations. And her boys were no exception.

Victoria could see the signal smoke now. She repositioned herself in her seat, hunching forward and placing her left hand over the collective, right hand on the cyclic, and the balls of her feet on the pedals.

"My controls."

"You have the controls."

"I have the controls," Victoria replied. "Coming down to fifty feet. Smoke is at twelve o'clock."

Her copilot said, "Boss, we just crossed the one forty-four line."

"Copy."

The P-8 pilot said, "Cutlass, Mad Fox is at your three o'clock high. We'll be staying to the east of the line."

"Roger, Mad Fox."

"Boss, can you give us a fifteen and zero?" her aircrewman said.

"Fifteen and zero, roger. Survivor is at twelve o'clock, about one mile. Coming down to fifteen feet, zero knots."

Victoria pulled aft on the cyclic with her right hand and lowered the collective lever with her left. The nose of the aircraft pitched up slightly as they descended and decelerated. Her eyes rapidly scanned outside and inside the helicopter, back and forth.

"Winds are out of the southwest, Boss."

"Roger, I'm using the smoke. I'll make my approach into the winds."

Continuously updating her situational awareness. Feeding into her decision loop. Altitude, two hundred feet. Vertical speed indicator, five-hundred-foot-per-minute descent. The wisp of white smoke ahead of her began drifting to the left in her sight picture, so she moved the cyclic right for a beat to adjust her course. The aircraft responded by banking right. Then she leveled the nose to steady on her new heading and reevaluated her drift.

Now the survivor was visible. A floating white object under the smoke. No longer drifting, just growing larger in her windscreen. She checked the chop of the waves.

"Fifty feet," said her copilot. "Radalt off?"

"Yes, please."

He reached over and pressed the button. "Radalt is off. Setting the pipper for ten feet."

"Roger."

"We're all set back here, Boss."

"Roger."

The survivor was just in front of the helicopter now. He wore what looked like some type of white space suit, with a futuristic-looking helmet. It must have been watertight and pressurized, because it looked inflated. An orange-and-white parachute dragged in the water behind the guy, eight-foot waves lifting him up and down every few seconds.

"Twenty-five feet. Seas are a little rough."

"Roger." Victoria began pulling in more power, slowing their descent. A vortex of white sea spray circled into the air around them as the rotor wash hit the ocean's surface.

"Fifteen feet."

Another smidgen of collective. Her head was turning left and right, scanning the horizon, then rechecking her instruments. The sea spray coated the cockpit windscreen now.

"Wipers on."

Her copilot's gloved hand shot up and flipped the switch that powered on the windshield wipers.

Victoria leaned her head to the right, looking out her side window and through the chin bubble at her feet. The survivor was just ahead of them, and with the waves, this was as low as she wanted to get. "Fetternut, how's this look?"

"Looks good, Boss."

"Roger, Jump. Jump. Jump."

* * *

In the rear of the aircraft, AWR1 Fetternut signaled the rescue swimmer that they were ready.

Wearing a black wet suit, gloves, mask and snorkel, the rescue swimmer shimmied his butt along the gray cabin deck of the helicopter, adrenaline pumping as he kept his legs forward and pulled himself towards the edge of the door. He tried not to think about the size of the waves as they crested mere feet below the wheels of the helicopter. The survivor was at his two o'clock position, floating face-up, arms and legs extended outward, his astronaut-style helmet closed.

Two hard taps on his back, and AWR2 Jones pushed himself

over the edge. He dropped towards the blue-and-white ocean surface, flexing his legs together, holding his fins pointed straight down, arms across his chest.

The drop was deceptively far. He must have fallen a full twenty-five feet by the time he hit the water. The loud engines and rotor noise disappeared into dark silence as he went under. Greenish blue light above. Then his head bobbed above the waterline and the noise came back. Jones quickly threw his mask on. An imaginary timer ticked along in his head as he kicked his powerful legs and swam towards the pilot.

When he reached the survivor, Jones began to worry that the guy wasn't alive. The helmet visor was reflective, and Jones couldn't see his face. But then the man gave a slight movement with one of his hands.

A wave washed over them, causing momentary disorientation. When Jones regained his position aside the survivor, he saw Fetternut signaling him from the cabin of the helicopter and pointing at his watch. *Hurry up.*

Fighting the spray from the helicopter and the rolls of the waves, Jones used a sidestroke to pull the downed pilot towards the helicopter's hovering position. Fetternut was already sending the large metal rescue basket down the rescue hoist. Jones quickly but carefully placed the survivor in it and gave a thumbs-up. He stabilized the basket as Fetternut reeled it up. A moment later, the rescue hoist came down again, sans basket. The powerful rotor wash kicked up sea spray all around them, like a hurricane, the waves sending him up and down towards the aircraft. Finally, Jones hooked himself to the hoist and was reeled up.

The second he was in the bird, he saw Fetternut yelling something into his helmet microphone and felt the aircraft nose forward.

The man in the space suit was sitting upright, helmet off

now. Fetternut was tending to him. The pilot was older. Probably at least fifty, by the look of him, Jones thought. What the hell was that old guy doing out here?

* * *

Victoria had just washed up and put on a clean flight suit when the phone in her stateroom rang.

"Airboss."

"Ma'am, the captain requests your presence in Medical."

"I'm on my way."

Victoria walked through officer's country and through the wardroom. Dinner was being served. The sounds of plates being scraped bare and loud conversation. An old action movie playing on the TV in the corner of the room.

"Boss, you gonna join us?"

"I have to see the captain."

"Jones said he wants a medal. He hasn't stopped talking about his rescue. Thinks he saved an astronaut and won the war."

Despite the seriousness of the situation, Victoria couldn't help smiling. "Astronaut, huh? Well, tell him to put that in the write-up."

One of the cooks asked, "Airboss, you want us to save you a plate?"

"That would be great, CS2."

"What do you want?"

"Anything is fine. I could eat a horse."

One of her pilots whispered, "Good, that's what they made."

She left and walked down the p-way and then down the ladder, heading towards the ship's medical compartment. There was a master-at-arms standing outside the door, an M-9 holstered on his hip.

"Ma'am."

"Guard duty, huh?"

"XO's orders, ma'am."

She spotted the captain through the open doorway. "Please come in, Victoria."

She entered and saw the captain and XO standing next to the man they'd rescued, who sat on the blue examination table. He had a bruised left eye and a bandage on his neck. A thick gray mustache and an exhausted look on his face. Someone had given him a set of Navy coveralls to wear, with the crows of an O-6 collar device pinned on.

"This is Colonel Wojcik. He's just flown in," the captain said as if it was nothing remarkable.

Victoria held out her hand. "How are you feeling, sir?"

"You'll excuse me if I don't get up. I'm still a bit sore." They shook hands. "I understand that you were the one who rescued me?"

"One of my rescue swimmers did, sir. I was flying the aircraft, though."

"Well, my most sincere gratitude to you and your men. Please know that if we're ever in the same bar, none of you will ever pay for another drink as far as I'm concerned."

"You might think differently about that if you knew my aircrewmen, sir."

The colonel laughed, then winced, holding his ribs.

"Sir, may I ask what happened? Were you shot down?"

"Actually, as far as I can remember, it was just an accident. Mechanical failure of the engine cooling system. We would have to retrieve the computers to know for sure. The aircraft is a prototype...was a prototype, I should say. They threw this mission together knowing that something like this might happen."

"It was a reconnaissance mission, sir?"

"It was."

Commander Boyle said, "Victoria, I'm afraid the colonel has some urgent news. I wanted you and the XO both to hear it. I'll brief the other department heads myself."

Victoria looked back and forth between them.

The colonel said, "Before my aircraft went down, I saw that the ISR pod was capturing data on the Chinese fleet movements. I only saw a few of the images up close, and it was hard to tell what I was looking at."

Commander Boyle said, "The data from the ISR pods was uploaded to a storage drive in the colonel's helmet. We have it in a safe."

"You won't be able to access the information on the ship," the colonel said. "But if we can get to Guam, they might have the equipment there. If not, they'll be able to get us back to the States."

Victoria said, "Of course. When do we launch?"

"Seventh Fleet is going to send one of their helicopters to pick up the colonel and his helmet," the captain said. "I've asked your maintenance officer to bring the bird into the barn to clear the flight deck."

"Yes sir." Victoria frowned. "Then...do you need anything from me?"

The colonel said, "I think your captain wanted you to hear the description of what I observed when I passed over the Chinese Southern Fleet."

20

Day 12

Admiral Song stood next to the PLA Marine Corps general. They stood on the admiral's bridge, enjoying the outdoor time in between briefings. The general was visiting for the afternoon, touring the aircraft carrier *Liaoning* and dining with the admiral.

"Your men are well taken care of, General?" asked Admiral Song.

"They are. Thank you." Waves crashed along the bow of the large ship positioned off their port beam. The general was examining the ship with interest. "So, this is the mighty Jiaolong-class?"

"Yes. A marvelous ship. More than a ship. An entire system of weapons."

"The ship looks like an oil tanker. Or a merchant. Except for those flight decks and towers, of course."

"The Jiaolong-class ships were not made for looks, General. But I assure you, they are quite lethal. I inspected this one myself when she was still under construction. You are correct in your observation, however. The Jiaolong class of ship uses the hull of a cargo tanker. They are much cheaper and more quickly produced than a warship. We can make many of them in the time it would take to complete a Type 055 destroyer hull. Even now, we are converting other tankers into this class of ship. The military modifications are all modular. Some of the modules are installed via premade shipping container. Again, very economical. But the technology is unmatched."

"How were you able to keep it a secret with those giant contraptions floating atop them?"

The admiral smiled. "They were kept in nearby hangars until the war began. They were moved at night, just before the Jiaolongs set sail."

"Incredible."

The Jiaolong-class ship heaved and rolled in the blue sea. Four elevated flight decks jutted out from amidships: two platforms on either side, one forward and one aft. But no one noticed the flight decks when they looked at these ships.

It was what was hovering *just above* the flight decks that was so jaw-dropping.

The general said, "They don't look like I thought they would."

Admiral Song nodded. "Everyone says that."

"Well, I don't care what they look like as long as they are able to provide safe passage for my marines."

"I am confident they shall, General. They have already proven effective against two American submarines."

A phone rang on the far side of the admiral's bridge. One of the staff officers picked it up, speaking rapidly. He looked up. "Admiral, they have detected another American submarine."

No sooner had the officer spoken than the sun was blocked out by a giant silent aircraft, slowly lifting from the Jiaolong-class ship and moving forward into the distance.

Admiral Song turned to face the messenger. "Very well. I will be down soon." He turned to the general. "Come join me in the combat operations center. You will see just how formidable the Jiaolong weapons system can be."

* * *

USS Columbia (SSN-771)
Los Angeles–class submarine
Philippine Sea

Commander Wallace, captain of the USS *Columbia*, walked into the bridge as the initial contact reports were called out.

"Conn, Sonar, new contact, designate Sierra-Two-Four bearing three-three-five, classification warship."

"Sonar, Conn, aye."

The conning officer quickly briefed the captain.

"How many?"

"At least fifty contacts now, sir."

"Warships?"

"Forty of them are warships, sir, various types."

"What are the others?"

"Classified as Group Three merchants or transports. But they're all part of the same convoy, sir. Never seen anything this big. This has got to be the Southern Fleet." He pointed at the display. "I think these contacts here are troop transports or supply ships for the convoy."

Commander Wallace looked at the display screen. Tiny electronic symbols were popping up at the far range of their sonar coverage, autopopulated by their submarine's sonar and computers. The surface tracks formed a column over twenty miles long, moving east.

"What's the speed?"

"Averaging fifteen knots, Captain."

"Anything more on Sierra-Two-Four?"

Sierra-Two-Four was a suspected Chinese submarine. Favorable acoustic conditions had allowed them to detect it from very far away the previous day.

"Nothing since last night, sir."

"Very well." The submarine captain let out a long breath, eyes moving back and forth over the different screens, taking in all of the information.

With the closing speed of the approaching Chinese convoy, they would have to be careful not to draw any attention to themselves, lest they become the hunted. If the approaching convoy's warships were farther away, Commander Wallace might take a risk and increase their speed while conducting a search for the Chinese submarine. In a perfect world, he would eliminate the Chinese submarine threat before making an attack on the enemy convoy. But it was not a perfect world, and his orders would not allow such an attack.

Wallace walked into the bridge and examined the space. His men looked tired, but intensely focused. But he knew that behind each dedicated face was a range of emotions. Husbands wondering if their wives were okay. Fathers wondering if they would see their children again. Young sailors wondering if they would live through the next twenty-four hours. There were those who wanted to perform bravely and those who just wanted to get home.

They had been operating at a crushing pace since the war had begun. Their submarine had been sortied out of Pearl Harbor within the first few days and told to seek out and destroy Chinese targets. Spirits had been high at first. The American submarine force was the best in the world. They were going to win the war and be home in a few months. They were going to be heroes.

Then word came of the American "strategic withdrawal"

from Japan, and the new ROE that came with the cease-fire agreement. The crew had been pissed and frustrated at the restrictions, but they were still hopeful that the USS *Columbia* would be given the chance to make an impact. For some, it was more personal. Commander Wallace knew that many of his men wanted revenge for the thousands of Americans who had been killed in the war's opening round.

When the USS *Columbia* had left port, the new orders had come. Per the cease-fire agreement, there were to be no US military movements beyond the 144th east longitude line. The only American forces west of that line were supposed to be retreating to US territory. But the US submarine force was adept at covert operations in hostile waters. The *Columbia*'s orders to monitor Chinese surface and subsurface movements took it well past the line. The officers and crew were revved up. Commander Wallace kept looking at their position on the digital chart, mentally willing his submarine to move into position faster. Everyone was eager to make an impact in the war.

Then came the news of missing submarines.

The first reports came from the Operations Department. One of the US fast-attack boats that had similar orders and was already in position in the South China Sea. Someone in Radio noticed that this submarine had missed its communications window. Twice. Then three times. Then a second submarine in the same vicinity, just after making contact with the Chinese fleet.

Somehow, the Chinese were sinking their attack boats with impunity. News spread through the crew like wildfire as confirmation had come forth in the emotionless text of Navy message traffic. COMSUBPAC sent a priority message informing the entire fleet that the Chinese had a new type of very effective antisubmarine warfare technology. Further details were being gathered.

No shit.

Yesterday the *Columbia* had gotten a message from the Office of Naval Intelligence providing a bit more information. Two submarines had sent out emergency burst communications just before entering combat. The communications included reports of unusual acoustic signatures surrounding the Chinese fleet.

Navy antisubmarine warfare experts at the Undersea Warfare Development Center believed the noises might have been air-dropped munitions or sonobuoys. Since satcom was down, limited-bandwidth communications were coming from stealth drones the US Air Force was flying over the Pacific—a temporary fix to a big problem. This meant that the *Columbia* didn't have the ability to download the actual sound files and include them in the ship's computer. So Commander Wallace's sonar experts didn't even know what they were listening for— just that it didn't sound like anything else in the US Navy's recognition training files.

Yesterday, as the USS *Columbia* had traveled west in the Philippine Sea, COMSUBPAC had sent them another round of updates to their orders. Not only were they to locate and track the submarine-killing Chinese fleet, now *Columbia* was to "gather as much visual, electronic, and acoustic information" as they could on the new ASW technology and send back the data using the submarine's own reconnaissance drone. Special navigational programming instructions had been sent for their drone.

Very few members of the crew were told of the new mission. Those who were understood the implications; those who weren't could read the writing on the wall. The cease-fire ROE meant that they couldn't attack the convoy. The convoy was killing every sub that got near it. And the *Columbia* was heading straight for them.

Commander Wallace was met by his XO as he entered the bridge. "Good morning, Captain."

"Morning, XO."

"We estimate about four hours until we are within scope range of the lead ship in the convoy."

The two men stood over her chart. The OOD joined them and said, "Sir, with your approval, this is where we'll hold station until they hit closest point of approach."

The lieutenant pointed to a spot ahead of and slightly offset to where the convoy would be. Commander Wallace examined the chart, nodding. The attack boat would wait silently for the convoy to come into range, collecting data, feeding into the hard drive on the drone, and launch it the moment they were fired upon. If they were lucky enough not to be fired upon, they would wait for the convoy to pass and begin trailing it, launching the drone when they were a safe distance away.

As had been the case since the dawn of submarine warfare, their chief strategic advantage was *stealth*. Submarines were able to get into hot zones and gather information, insert special forces, take on intelligence operatives, or quietly observe future targets. If Commander Wallace had it his way, the USS *Columbia* could stay far enough away to track the largest Chinese fleet ever to set sail.

If and when the cease-fire ended, *Columbia* would be ready. They would unleash their weapons and inflict maximum damage to the enemy with minimal risk to the sub. With luck and skill, Wallace would maneuver his submarine to remain undetected and reattack, picking off both warships and transports as they made their way east across the Pacific, a shark slowly eating away at a school of fish until there was nothing left.

There was a part of him that was revolted by the thought of firing on Chinese transport ships. Warships were one thing. But the transports, filled with soldiers and sailors with families at home and futures ahead of them, that gave him pause. An internal conversation that he wouldn't voice to his men. But he also knew that when the time came, any revulsion he felt would be set aside. The wheels of war were now turning, and anything other than ruthless efficiency allowed the enemy to have their way.

The same kill-or-be-killed instinct that applied to animals in nature had governed enemy tribes as long as man had formed them. As soon as this cease-fire ended, his duty, however cruel it might be, was to destroy the enemy before they had the opportunity to inflict death and destruction upon his brothers in arms. The Chinese were bringing cargo vessels across the Pacific. Those ships were filled with men and munitions that would be used to kill Americans. He would sink them.

Perhaps, with luck, he would never have to take such action. Perhaps the world leaders would come to their senses. For now, he would run silent and—

"Conn, Sonar. Multiple splashes in the water. Believe it to be air-dropped, sir."

Commander Wallace frowned. Sonar should be providing direction and distance.

The conning officer said, "Bearing and range, Sonar?"

"Twenty thousand yards is the closest. But, sir...they're saturating that area. There must be twenty splashes, and they keep coming. Building a big buoy field out there."

The conning officer walked towards the navigational chart in the center of the space.

"Sir, it looks like that buoy field is forming a barrier parallel to the course of the Chinese convoy. Gonna be hard for us to get anywhere near them."

The XO said, "Well, what the hell is spitting the buoys? Do we have aircraft noise?"

"Negative, sir. Might be a high-altitude maritime patrol aircraft?"

The captain rubbed his chin, looking at the chart. "How far away?"

The sonar tech called out a bearing and range to the nearest sonobuoy's drop. "I'm assuming it's a sonobuoy, sir. They're sure dropping a ton of them. P-3s don't even drop this many."

The XO gave the captain an uneasy look. They were standing close enough that no one could hear their conversation.

The captain whispered, "XO, if they want visuals, this might be our shot."

"Sir, the range to that buoy field—"

"Is only going to decrease as the convoy approaches. I sure as hell don't like it. But this might be our most conservative option for gathering ELINT and FLIR."

The XO looked between the captain and the data indicating where the latest sonobuoys had been laid and let out a breath.

The captain said, "Tell me what you're thinking."

The XO said, "If this was any other group of targets, I wouldn't hesitate to come up at this range. But the intel reports... there's something different about their ASW equipment." He paused. "Sir, I think we should take a look. But we'll need to be cautious."

The captain nodded. He turned to face the bridge team. "This is the captain, I have the conn. Lieutenant James retains the deck." He waited for his statement to be acknowledged, then said, "All stop. Take us up to PD. Let's get a look."

"Aye, sir."

* * *

Moments later, the camouflage-painted periscope was raised

mere inches above the wavetops. The cameras and sensors fixed to the periscope rotated around twice, then the periscope retracted back down beneath the sea.

The bridge was deathly quiet, the men rapt as images of the ocean's surface replayed on the screen. The video showed a white-gray sky with several dark silhouettes on the horizon to the northwest.

"Stop. There. Go back. Okay. Stop. Take it back to two-six-five." The video was rewound until the heading showed two-six-five on the magnetic compass.

The XO said, "At least a dozen masts on the horizon. Looks like a few Type 52s and Type 55s too. What's that one?"

"Frigate. Type 54. And there's the carrier." To the west, the silhouette of the large aircraft carrier was easily recognizable, the ramp on its flight deck protruding from the bow. The ships were very close together. Closer than most surface groups liked to operate.

The captain looked at the chart and then back at the video screen. "Where are they?"

"Where are what, sir?"

"The aircraft. What's dropping those buoys?"

All eyes studied the screen.

That captain narrowed his eyes. "Zoom in on the horizon. There. What is that?"

"What's what, sir?"

"Above the group three immediately aft of the carrier."

The officer of the deck said, "What...*the fuck*...is that?"

"Is that a blimp?"

"Thing looks like a floating battleship."

"Or a cloud. Sir, I think that's just a cloud."

"So the Chinese are dropping sonobuoys from blimps?"

"It's not a blimp. Don't be ridiculous."

"Sir, that doesn't look like any blimp I've ever seen."

The XO walked up and pointed at the screen. "You are talking about this? Looks like a cloud."

"I don't think so. It's angled too sharply. Looks man-made. Okay, back up the video and play it in real time."

The video rewound and then played again. It was hard to tell whether the object was moving or not due to the relative motion of the camera angle. The periscope camera had performed two spins, so everything they were watching was moving.

"Look, there's another one. At heading two-seven-five. Aft of the formation."

"Are you sure?"

The captain sighed. He wasn't. The image was grainy at that distance. His eyes might have been playing tricks on him. He walked over to the chart again. "Sonar, Conn, any more buoys hit the water?"

"Conn, Sonar, negative, sir. Nothing since the last field prior to the periscope, sir."

The captain said, "I want to take another look."

"Sir, I don't think we should push our luck," the XO said.

The captain gave his XO an uneasy look. "This is what we were sent here for." Then he said, "Up periscope."

This time, everyone on the bridge held their breath as the image came on the screen. The captain gripped the periscope and took it through one rotation.

"Down periscope!" the captain yelled. "Take us down! Make depth six hundred feet."

Echoes of the command and then the floor tilted forward beneath their feet, the men leaning back to keep their balance as the depth gauge ticked down.

On the monitor, the most recent periscope image had been frozen.

A giant dirigible was right on top of them.

* * *

Admiral Song watched the digital updates from the dark combat operations center on board his carrier. The three-hundred-foot-long dirigibles moved at speeds of up to one hundred knots—about the speed of a slow-moving single-engine airplane. That velocity, however, was more than enough to overcome headwinds and keep up with the ships in the battlegroup. More importantly, it could keep ahead of the submarines attempting to hunt them.

While the aircraft was optionally manned, their standard operating procedure used a line-of-sight datalink connection for control. Each dirigible was connected to the Jiaolong-class mother ship, which operated as their ground control station. Their payload was equivalent to a C-130 transport aircraft, which allowed them to carry a deadly antisubmarine warfare package: hundreds of sonobuoys, dozens of torpedoes, and even an advanced dipping sonar system. The whisper-quiet flight operations allowed for near-silent dips, a nightmare for their underwater prey.

The Jiaolong-class ships and their dirigibles had been designed to provide ASW for very large battlegroups. They were fitted with the most advanced sensors, including radar, electronic support measures, and FLIR. Using a line-of-sight datalink connection posed challenges at long distances from the motherships. To counter this challenge, new tactics had been developed, and the antisubmarine warfare drone operators had to stay vigilant in their quest to sanitize the fleet's path. Each ship in the battlegroup, as well as each dirigible, was fitted with a special datalink antenna that would receive and transmit the encrypted information at high speed between the dirigibles and the controllers on the mothership.

This system created a network of nodes from which the dirigibles could reliably operate far from their motherships. The datalink was so advanced that all eight drones could be simultaneously controlled from a single ship, sending video imagery and acoustic data through the node ships for processing.

The eight dirigibles of the fleet operated as pack hunters. At any given time, two of the monstrous airships flew well ahead of the fleet, using their near-silent dipping sonar as a passive sensor to detect American subs at long range. Meanwhile, two other dirigibles laid dense buoy fields along each side of the convoy. Two other dirigibles were used to cover the rear of the formation. The final two were either resupplying or having maintenance performed. The dirigibles used a rigid-shell variable-buoyancy design, with inner membranes that were filled with helium using pressurized tanks. Four stabilizers formed a giant angled tail section, allowing for directional control. Two side-mounted propellers and two rear props for extra thrust. They could stay airborne for days without refueling, constantly sweeping the ocean for enemy submarines. They were overly susceptible to the effects of foul weather, but the Chinese had created procedures to mitigate that risk.

The sonobuoys themselves were an advanced new design. Their battery life was short, but the smaller batteries allowed the engineers to use that saved weight for other purposes, such as computing power and more advanced acoustic sensors.

During antisubmarine prosecutions, the Jiaolong dirigible ASW drones used a sophisticated mesh network controlled by artificial intelligence computers. As the convoy of ships moved forward and the sonobuoys either ran out of battery life or became useless due to their lagging geographical position, one of the dirigibles would fly in, hover over the buoy at low altitude, and pick it up with a mechanical arm. The dirigible would store the used buoys in an onboard chamber and drop them off on one of the Jiaolong's unused flight deck platforms. Here, the buoys would be recharged and then reloaded onto a dirigible that was ready to go to work.

The Jiaolong received and processed the massive amount of acoustic information from the drones dipping sonar and many sonobuoys. The entire system had been developed in secret over the past fifteen years. During the Cold War, antisubmarine warfare had relied upon skilled operators to listen, analyze, interpret, and make decisions. Humans had to guess where a target might be based on small bits of acoustic data. Data that might or might not be accurate.

This new Chinese system completely transferred the analysis and decision making to computers. Machine learning allowed the dirigibles to identify the most likely positions where an enemy submarine might make its approach. The computers concentrated their sonobuoy and dipping sonar placements in these areas, covering wide swaths of ocean, far ahead of where submarine captains might expect them to be. And they were lethally efficient.

Inside Jiaolong, one of the ASW officers monitored the latest report from the drones.

"The American submarine is forty-five thousand meters to our east. The ASW drones are prosecuting the target."

"Very well," came the reply from the senior officer.

Another American submarine had fallen into their web.

USS Columbia

Commander Wallace had watched with horror as his periscope showed the Chinese aircraft right on top of their position. Soon his sonar room was reporting splashes all around them.

The captain said, "Conn, get us safely east of here. Whatever the hell they have up there, we don't want to be in this area."

The conning officer said, "Increase speed to all ahead two-thirds. Come right to zero-two-zero and make depth six hundred feet."

Commands repeated throughout the bridge, and the crew began leaning in unison as the submarine responded to new commands.

The navigator said, "Sir, shallow water to our east."

"Understood."

A high-pitched ping echoed throughout the submarine's metal hull. Whispered cursing from the crew.

"All ahead flank, come right to one-seven-zero," the captain called out, doing the conning officer's job for him.

"Conn, Sonar, another splash in the water one thousand yards, bearing one-eight-zero."

Commander Wallace took in the new information. They had put another buoy down in the water right in front of where he'd intended to take his submarine. At least, he hoped it was a buoy...

"Make new heading zero-nine-zero."

"Zero-nine-zero, aye."

How the hell were they putting buoys down in exactly the right spot? It was like the Chinese knew the command Wallace had given. He now realized why the other two submarines that had faced this convoy had not come back.

Another loud ping echoed throughout the hull. More cursing. Wallace noticed that one of his young officers, an ensign who had been aboard no more than a month, was no longer at his station. He was now walking around the compartment, muttering something to himself over and over, his eyes darting every which way. The kid looked like he was cracking up. Wallace made eye contact with the XO and nodded to the ensign. The XO quickly nodded back and had the chief of the boat escort him out of the space. The XO then took his station.

"Conn, Sonar, we have another splash."

"Bearing and range?"

The voice sounded deflated. "Right on top of us, sir."

"Conn, Sonar, transient! Torpedo in the water!"

The torpedo's pinging began. These pings sounded different than the previous ones, which had come from a sonobuoy or dipper, and they sounded painfully close.

The pings became more rapid.

"Sir, the torpedo has acquired us."

"Launch countermeasures! Left full rudder—"

But Commander Wallace knew that it was too late.

* * *

The dirigible launched its torpedo with targeting information that had been derived from a total of seventeen acoustic devices that held contact on the USS *Columbia*. The targeting information had been processed and refined, and the artificial intelligence computers calculated where the submarine would be when the torpedo was released, with ninety-eight percent probability.

The lightweight torpedo dropped from a height of one hundred feet, its parachute barely having time to open before making contact with the water. The seawater-activated motor kicked on, and it let out a few pings to acquire its target, then increased the frequency of its pings as it began homing.

On board the aircraft carrier *Liaoning*, Admiral Song received his report.

"The enemy submarine has been destroyed, sir."

21

Raven Rock Mountain Complex
Pennsylvania
Day 13

David Manning sat in a private conference room reading over the morning intelligence reports with Susan Collinsworth. She had flown up to Raven Rock to brief the new director of the CIA and military leadership. They wanted to know what the hell this new Chinese ship was capable of. Her brief would be based on the SILVERSMITH team's analysis of ISR imagery taken from Colonel Wojcik's reconnaissance aircraft, as well as the results of a conversation they were about to have with three experts.

Thousands of the US government's political, military, and intelligence leaders were being housed at Raven Rock and a series of other emergency complexes along the Appalachian Mountain Chain. Raven Rock was where the highest-level military plans were being made.

"We lost contact with another sub?" David asked, reading the daily brief.

Susan frowned, nodding slowly. "The *Columbia*."

"Why are we sending submarines anywhere near that Jiao-long-class ship? Shouldn't we keep them at a standoff distance until we have a way to fight the threat?"

"The Pentagon now agrees with that assessment."

"Wonderful. And it only took three sunken subs to get them there."

The door opened and in walked their three specialists. One wore a lab coat and rimmed glasses. David recognized him as the representative from DARPA, the Defense Advanced Research Project Agency. The second man was an air and missile defense expert. The third was the expert on naval warship technology.

David put the folder down and stood as introductions were made. Susan began the conversation with disclaimers on the classification level and stressed the obvious importance of their task. Then she opened a manila envelope and placed a series of images on the table.

She said, "Gentlemen, what you're looking at is known as the Jiaolong-class warship. The Chinese are referring to it as a battleship."

The three men took turns passing around the photographs, exchanging whistles and hums. They were intrigued.

"Looks like they're using merchants as a hull template. Smart. We've been looking into that. You can buy 'em much cheaper than the cost of making a destroyer."

David said, "So we've been told."

"What are these towers?"

Susan said, "That's what we're here to discuss."

"You have any images that are zoomed in...oh, here's one." The DARPA scientist reached for a picture of the tower on the Jiaolong-class ship.

The expert on naval warships said, "It's odd that they've positioned the flight decks off to the side. They plan on landing four helicopters at once?"

David said, "We believe that each one of those side-mounted flight decks is for an unmanned dirigible. The dirigibles are about three hundred feet long. You can see a close-up of one of those here." David slid over another image. "And while we don't have much data on them, we believe that they're extremely effective as ASW platforms."

The man arched his eyebrow at that. "No kidding. Dirigibles."

The DARPA representative said, "We had a project like that a few years back. Not for ASW, mind you. Ours was for cargo transport and logistics. You could carry twice the load of a C-130 at a much lower cost per mile."

David said, "Why did the program get shut down?"

"Well, that's what's so surprising about this. Dirigibles have obvious risks when used in a military environment."

"You mean they could get shot down easily."

"Of course. A three-hundred-foot target would be a sitting duck if it's in range of—well, just about any antiaircraft weapon."

David said, "So why would the Chinese take such a risk?"

One of the men said, "You said that it was very effective. How effective?"

"We've lost three US fast-attack boats in the past week. To our knowledge, our submarines weren't even able to make it into torpedo range before they were destroyed."

"During the cease-fire? Well, why the hell haven't we reattacked the Chinese?"

David and Susan looked at each other. Then David said, "That's not what we're here to discuss."

Seeing that they weren't satisfied with that answer, he continued, "There are still some battles being fought. Ones that we don't talk about. We have a hell of a lot of civilians and military personnel that are being allowed to leave Asia unharmed. But that's above our pay grade, I'm afraid."

"Sorry."

The air defense expert said, "What a minute. These towers... I think I know what they might be."

* * *

"Directed-energy weapons."

After speaking with the three experts for an hour, Susan and David now sat in the Raven Rock executive conference room with the national security advisor, several flag officers, and the director of the CIA.

"That's what these towers are?"

The room was focused on the projection screen, which displayed one of the images of the Jiaolong-class ship.

"That's our hypothesis, sir. We think they're being used as a new type of air defense weapon." Susan tapped a button, and the presentation screen changed to an infrared image of one of the Jiaolong-class ships. "Our analysts believe these Jiaolong-class ships have modular nuclear power systems installed solely for these weapons. If that's true, it would provide a nearly unlimited source of electric power."

An admiral at the end of the conference table looked skeptical. "We have our own directed-energy weapons. The list of canceled projects goes on and on. How have they solved the range and beam attenuation issues? These systems aren't yet viable air defense weapons. How do you even know that these things really work?"

David spoke up. "Sir, I've spoken with our experts who have seen the Chinese design. They're convinced that the Chinese are on to something. They're using billions of carbon nanotubes, stacked on top of each other throughout the towers. These nanotubes absorb the light and convert it to different types of energy."

Blank stares.

"What's the range?" asked an Army general sitting at the table.

"We don't know that, sir."

"Then why is this even something we're discussing?"

"Because the Chinese must believe them to be pretty damned effective to risk using dirigibles for ASW. A blimp is an easy target for surface-to-air weapons."

The general shot back, "Then maybe the Chinese are just stupid. They are communists, after all. Just send in an air strike and take out those dirigibles, then send in the submarines."

David shook his head.

General Schwartz cleared his throat. "Ladies and gentlemen, how many wars have been lost because rooms like this underestimated the effectiveness of a new technology?"

David looked around the room. Some of the men and women here still didn't seem convinced. He didn't care if he spoke out of turn. He needed to make them understand.

David stood, and all eyes were on him. "This Jiaolong-class ship contains two disruptive technologies: a leap in ASW capability, and a leap in air defense capability. If any ship were to hold just one of these new capabilities, it would still be susceptible to attack. The American military would still retain its advantage. For example, if a Chinese destroyer had this new directed-energy weapon but no new leap in ASW capability, we could still sink that destroyer with one of our submarines. But *together* they could make this Chinese fleet quite lethal."

"You're making a jump, son. The ability of these directed-energy weapons remains to be seen."

A Navy captain said, "The Chinese screen formation was

unusually tight. That would make sense if they were all trying to stay under one umbrella. Instead of the destroyers protecting the high-value unit in the center of the formation, it seems like the HVU is protecting the entire fleet. The closer they stick together, the greater the level of protection."

David nodded. "Exactly. If this directed-energy weapon works well, the Chinese fleet, with these Jiaolong-class ships, would be able to move with impunity throughout the Pacific."

The skeptical admiral at the end of the table said, "That's if this directed-energy weapon proves to be as effective as you're suggesting."

"Yes, sir." *But why else would they go out on a limb like this? Jinshan isn't stupid.*

A phone rang at the table, and one of the flag officers picked it up. "When? Very well. I'll let everyone know." He hung up the phone, then looked up at the group.

"The Chinese fleet has been picked up on radar, heading towards Guam. They just crossed the one forty-four."

USS Farragut
100 miles north of Guam

Victoria walked into the combat information center shortly after general quarters was called. The captain had ordered her air detachment to bring the bird into the barn, and she was hoping to lobby him against that decision.

Like any good athlete, she wanted to be on the field during the game. There might be a submarine threat, after all. Or they could provide over-the-horizon targeting or surveillance. Hell, it might take them a while, but she could even have her men throw on a few Hellfire missiles if it would help. But as she surveyed the room, her "put me in, coach" attitude diminished.

The basic concept of naval warfare hadn't changed much in the last few hundred years. Target and sink the enemy's ship before they sink you. But the complexity of modern tactics lay in the vast amount of information being streamed into the warfighter. Gigabytes of data were pumped into the ship via datalink, radio, sonar, radar, electronic and other sensors. Even the lookouts on the bridge fed information via sound-powered phone. Now all of these sensors reached out into the unseen distance, searching for their enemy, who was in turn searching for them. The same old game.

A dim blue overhead light illuminated the captain as he spoke to the tactical action officer. Together, they were studying the tactical picture. The USS *Michael Monsoor*, a brand-new Zumwalt-class destroyer, was five miles to their west. Their captain was in charge of the Farragut's surface action group.

"SAG is directing us to adjust the screen, sir."

The captain said, "Very well. Get it done."

Victoria watched the combat team as they prepared to fire antiship missiles at targets for which they still had no coordinates.

The captain, seeing Victoria, waved her over. "Sir, is there anything I can do to help?"

"I wanted to bring the helicopter inside the hangar in case we take any fire. I figured that would help the aircraft survive better so we can launch you when we get closer. Be ready to go."

"Yes, sir."

One of the operations specialists turned from his computer terminal and said, "TAO, Seventh Fleet just informed us that friendly aircraft will be transiting overhead for the next hour. They expect to give us targeting information soon."

* * *

Twelve B-52s launched in rapid succession from Anderson Air Force Base on Guam. The aircraft had deployed to Guam from two squadrons: the Twenty-Third Expeditionary Bomb Squadron and the Sixty-Ninth, both out of Minot AFB, North Dakota.

Dark trails of exhaust flowed from the engines as they climbed. Soon after, ten more aircraft launched. These were B-

1Bs from the Thirty-Fourth and Thirty-Seventh Bomb Squadrons. Within minutes of launch, the B-1s went supersonic, heading to a position southwest of the Chinese fleet. Once there, they slowed and spread their wings, loitering while the B-52s flew into position.

F-15 and F-22 interceptors flew combat air patrol, stationed in between the two groups of bombers. An E-3G AWACS aircraft, with its round radar dish fixed atop the large Boeing airframe, acted as the command-and-control platform.

On board the E-3, airmen watched as the Chinese fleet appeared on their screen. Radar and other sensors picked up over fifty ships, all headed towards Guam at twenty knots. The Air Force's electronic sensors matched the fleet's radar and other signals to their archives of Chinese military systems.

An Air Force major on board the E-3 spoke into his microphone. "Send the execute order to all aircraft."

Within seconds, the bomb bay doors of the B-1s and B-52s opened, revealing the blue ocean twenty thousand feet below. From the bomb bays fell dozens of the US military's new AGM-185 long-range antiship missiles (LRASM). These missiles had been specially transported to Guam the week before.

Thin wings and a small vertical fin extended from the sleek black missiles. The LRASMs used all of the data that had been shared between the attacking Air Force squadrons to chart their course, making continuous corrections as they dove towards the sea at just under the speed of sound. They skimmed low to the water to avoid radar detection and used their inertial navigation systems since the Chinese had destroyed GPS.

The missiles coordinated with each other autonomously, widening their formation to make it harder for the Chinese to defend. Their attack profile had been preprogrammed by Air Force experts prior to launch. Now they sped closer to the

Chinese fleet, setting themselves up to attack from three directions simultaneously.

On board the E-3G command-and-control aircraft, the mission commander stood in the tunnel, watching a digital display over the shoulder of one of his men as over two hundred missiles closed in on their targets.

"Everything look good?"

"Yes, sir. Fifty miles out. Any second now."

The mission commander knew that the weapons would be in their final phase of flight now, using onboard electronic sensors to home in on enemy radar to—

"What the hell? What just happened? Where did the missiles go?"

* * *

Victoria melted into the wall of Combat, unable to stop watching as the battle unfolded.

An operations specialist petty officer said, "Sir, we're losing contact on friendly air tracks."

"Are they hitting their targets?"

The OS said, "Not sure, sir."

"Is it a datalink issue?"

The petty officer shot a look to the OS chief standing nearby. The chief had his arms folded across his chest. "Sir, I don't think it's the link. I think our missiles got shot down."

"All of them?"

A sickening feeling formed in Victoria's stomach.

"Another dozen aircraft just launched from Guam, sir."

The captain said, "Do we have targeting coordinates yet?"

"Negative, sir."

Victoria could hear radio calls going to and from each of the ships in company. The ships were adjusting their formation for combat and acknowledging the change to the screen commander. The familiar sounds of young military voices over the radio, static noise, and electronic beeps.

The TAO's voice was subdued. "Captain..."

"What is it?"

"Seventh Fleet is saying that all twenty aircraft we launched from Guam have been shot down."

No one spoke for a moment. Then the captain said, "What's the expected range of the enemy fleet?"

"The data is time-late, sir..."

"I understand. What's the range?"

"One hundred twenty miles, sir."

Victoria could feel the tension in the room. The tacticians operating the ship's weapons systems needed targeting data if they were going to engage the enemy.

An electronic alarm emanated from the air-defense section of the space. A split second later, Victoria heard a voice over the net.

"VAMPIRE! VAMPIRE! Multiple missiles inbound!"

The room erupted in shouted commands and reflexive movements. Then a rumble in her chest and a roar from outside the skin of the ship as surface-to-air missiles fired off.

"What's the count?" asked the captain.

"Ninety-six, sir. Ninety-six missiles inbound."

Victoria watched as the ship's combat team coordinated with the other destroyers in their group. Much of it was done electronically over the datalink. Deciding who would target which inbound missile, how many to fire, and when. Every few seconds, she heard the roar of another SM-2 missile launching off the USS *Farragut*.

Her heart beat faster as she watched the tactical display, the incoming missiles growing closer by the second.

* * *

Chinese aircraft carrier Liaoning

Admiral Song sat in his elevated flag officer's chair in the expansive combat operations center. Until today, the Jiaolong's directed-energy air defense technology was untested.

But not anymore. Within the past few minutes, it had worked exactly as the engineers and scientists claimed it would, shooting down hundreds of targets without breaking a sweat. Admiral Song almost felt sorry for his opponents with how outmatched they now were. The Jiaolong technology was truly a step change in sea power. He was now one of the privileged few commanders in history to be the first to use a powerful new technology in combat. He found himself thinking of other examples. The first Gatling gun, or the tank, or—

"Admiral, we detect American surface-to-air missile launches."

"How do the numbers match up?" the admiral asked.

"The Americans are matching their surface-to-air missiles with our antiship missiles nearly one for one."

"Good." He wanted the Americans to use up their inventory.

"Range to American fleet is now two hundred kilometers, sir."

The admiral rose from his chair and walked to the massive chart table nearby. Two of his senior officers joined him.

He looked at the digital display that showed the progress of the Chinese antiship missiles. Most had been shot down at the midway point between the two fleets. The problem with launching their weapons was that, as with any emission, doing so gave away the approximate position of his ships. That gave the Americans updated targeting data.

The Americans were shooting down Admiral Song's first

volley of missiles. Now the Americans would be faced with a choice. Use this new data to reattack and give away their own position? Or close the distance, gather more information, and fire at a range that gave them an increased probability of a kill? Both paths came with their own set of risks and advantages. Which would the Americans choose?

An alarm sounded, and the admiral had his answer.

"Sir, the American fleet are firing their antiship missiles. Approximately forty missiles inbound. Bearing one-five-zero. Range one hundred fifty kilometers."

The admiral nodded. "Understood." He could see that the faces of his men were filled with fear. They were going into combat for only the second time, and taking action that was contradictory to all of their training. But they held firm. The admiral had trained them well.

No one asked to initiate surface-to-air missile launches in their defense.

* * *

The Chinese YJ-18 surface-to-surface missiles were almost all intercepted by the American Navy's surface-to-air missiles. Ten Chinese missiles broke through the American wave of SAM defense.

Those ten missiles continued to close the American destroyers at subsonic speed. The US Navy ships fired a second wave of interceptor missiles, destroying all but two.

Those final two Chinese missiles had just hit their late-stage supersonic kick, diving towards the water and then skimming the ocean's surface as they headed for their targets.

A thunderous WHRRRRRTT. WHRRRRTT. WHRRRRRT noise could be heard on the USS *Farragut* as the Phalanx Close-In Weapons System fired its revolving gun at the remaining two missiles. One was destroyed, its fragments landing harmlessly in the ocean. The final missile scored a hit on a nearby littoral combat ship, slamming into the superstructure and detonating its 660-pound warhead. A gray-white explosion erupted from the ship.

One hundred miles to the northwest, the American volley was arriving at the Americans' best guess of where the Chinese fleet was located. Dozens of SM-6 missiles fired from the Navy destroyers were about to enter their final phase of flight, where they would drop towards the water and skim the sea at a speed of Mach 3.

But that never happened.

* * *

Chinese aircraft carrier Liaoning

"Directed Energy System is synced to phased-array radar network, Admiral. All air tracks are targeted."

A few kilometers away, on both of the Jiaolong-class ships, the towers were being put to work. Thermonuclear reactors fed an enormous supply of energy into the system. The entire Chinese fleet of air defense radars was searching for the smallest air contact and feeding in that data to the Jiaolong-class ships. That was supplementary information, however. Within each tower, billions of micrometer-size antennae had been created by using carbon nanotubes. The towers were a new type of phased-array radar, able to overcome the plasma breakdown in the atmosphere that had hindered previous generations of directed-energy weapons.

Each incoming American missile was detected, tracked, and targeted within a fraction of a second. The towers directed lightning-quick pulses of concentrated energy at each of the incoming missiles.

One after the another, the inbound missiles came under attack, their onboard computers and guidance systems fried. There were a few explosions as some of the energy bursts triggered warhead detonations. But in most cases, the inbound missiles, now lobotomized, just continued on overhead, passing by their targets. Eventually the missiles ran out of fuel and fell harmlessly into the ocean.

The Chinese air defense team had already seen how well the directed-energy system worked when the US fighter-bomber aircraft had attempted to locate and attack the fleet earlier in the battle. But those aircraft were much larger and easier to detect. Enemy missiles were tiny. No one had known with certainty whether it would work. The destruction of the air-launched missiles gave them confidence. Now they were overjoyed.

"We are invincible, Admiral."

Admiral Song cast the officer who had uttered such nonsense a disapproving glance. "We have a momentary advantage, that is all. We had best use it. Send in the next slew of anti-ship missiles."

"Shall we launch our fighters, sir?"

It was the same young officer who had just claimed they were invincible. The admiral would need to remember to reassign that one. "No. We must continue launching our cruise missiles until the American ships have depleted their air defense capability. Only then will we launch our fighters."

* * *

USS Farragut

Another alarm sounded throughout the combat information center as more Chinese missiles were detected by the SPY radar.

Victoria watched in horror as the ship's number of surface-to-air missiles began dwindling.

She heard someone whisper, "What do we do when we run out of SM-2s?"

No one answered.

The blue friendly air tracks headed towards the red inbound missile tracks on the display screen at the front of the space. Just as before, the numbers were close to evenly matched. A few missiles got through, and the roar of rocket engines thundered outside the ship as more defensive missiles fired out of the Mk-41 vertical launch system.

Another Klaxon alarm sounded throughout the ship, and Victoria again heard the giant WHHRRRRT of the CWIS Gatling gun. The familiar noises of air defense. But this time, there was a new sound—a shaking boom that rattled her teeth —and then the room went dark.

They had been hit.

She was in pitch blackness. The white noise of computers and radios had gone silent, and now she heard the sickening sounds of secondary explosions somewhere in the distance. The air had a stale metallic taste, and she could hear cursing as someone tripped and fell to the floor in the darkness.

Victoria found herself holding on to the chart table next to her, feeling a slight panic as the floor moved underneath her. A wave? Or had they been hit that badly that they were already listing?

People regained their awareness and began shouting. Someone opened the hatch in the aft of the space. A faint ray of daylight flooded into the compartment, giving them the gift of sight, and then the door shut again, plunging them back into darkness. It was only temporary, however, as a dim yellowish light came on around the edges of the compartment. Backup electric power had kicked on. The computer screens fluttered to life as systems began to reboot.

The 1MC let out a loud series of bells followed by, "Fire, fire, fire...fire in engineering..." A description of the spaces and then, "Flooding, flooding, flooding..." and more announcements.

Bodies leapt into action throughout the USS *Farragut*. The men and women on the ship formed into preordained damage control parties. Years of training forcing them to overcome the fear of fire, drowning, darkness, and death. Sailors who might normally be cooks or helmsmen or sonar experts or rescue swimmers were now aligned to the same mission: save the ship.

Victoria departed the space and headed up to the bridge. On the bridge wing, she could see thick black plumes of smoke rising up from two of their ships in company. From the USS *Michael Monsoor*, more defensive missiles shot up from its vertical launch system, their white trails of smoke arcing off towards a distant threat.

"Captain on the bridge!"

The captain climbed up out of the ladder, standing in the center of the large space. The officer of the deck briefed him on the ongoing damage control team's progress.

"Where's CHENG?"

"Sir...I just got off the phone with AUXO. He said the CHENG was killed. We're still conducting an assessment of the damage."

Commander Boyle gritted his teeth. "Understood."

The operations officer appeared, climbing up the ladder and onto the bridge. "Captain, Seventh Fleet is directing us to move east, out of range of the Chinese warships. They want us to make best speed, sir."

"Did they give a destination?"

"Not yet, sir. They just said proceed east at best speed. Maintain safe separation from Chinese fleet."

"Son of a bitch." The captain shook his head. "OOD, who's in engineering now, AUXO?"

"Yes, sir."

The captain picked up one of the phones and dialed a four-digit number. After a brief conversation, he hung up the phone and turned back to the bridge team.

"Make speed sixteen knots. Contact *Michael Monsoor* and let them know that's the best we can do."

"Sir, the lookout says they can see survivors in the water."

Commander Boyle cursed again. Then his eyes met Victoria's. "Airboss, bring your helicopter out and try to rescue as many people as you can. We need to keep moving east. I don't know how many more missile volleys we can sustain."

Victoria nodded vigorously. "Yes, sir."

She raced down the ladder and headed to officer's country, telling her pilots the plan. Then she headed to the hangar, where the maintenance senior chief listened intently. Like Victoria, Senior was relieved to have something to do.

As they traversed the helicopter onto the flight deck, Victoria was on the phone with the tactical action officer in combat, getting a rough position of the sinking ships. When she hung up, she saw that several of her men were standing on the starboard side of the ship, craning their necks around the outer hull so that they could see something forward.

At first she thought they were looking at more incoming missiles, or perhaps men in the water. But as her curiosity got the better of her, she looked too. There was an eight-by-ten-foot hole in the steel hull, about thirty meters forward of the hangar and only about ten feet above the waterline.

"Alright, gentlemen, that's enough."

"Are we gonna sink, Boss?"

"No. Now let's get the blades extended, quick. We have ship-mates in the water, and they might not be there for much longer."

She didn't bother voicing another reason that she wanted to take off quickly: she wanted to get airborne before another missile arrived. It wasn't that she wanted to save herself. In an odd way, she felt guilty for reducing her risk. But she also felt protective of her aircraft. She didn't want anything to happen to it.

Fifteen minutes later, Victoria was flying search and rescue, picking up sailors from the sunken littoral combat ship and ferrying them back to her own. She was airborne when the next wave of missiles came.

"Cutlass, ASTAC, remain clear of Mom for next twenty mikes." The kid sounded sick with fear.

Victoria looked at her fuel. "Roger, ASTAC."

From her cockpit, Victoria and a cabin filled with rescued sailors watched as explosions and tracers filled the sky. Some of the ships emitted huge clouds of chaff, metallic confetti twinkling in the sky. Another ship in company —a destroyer this time—took a fatal set of missile hits. A giant white geyser of water erupting from its center. The explosions were so severe that the destroyer went under in less than a minute. Victoria would later learn that that ship had expended all of its surface-to-air missiles, and its CWIS had malfunctioned.

The rest of the day was a nightmare of nonstop search-and-rescues, missile attacks, and heading east. The surface action group was getting picked apart like a school of fish surrounded by sharks. Every once in a while, another ship would get taken under, and there was nothing the others could do.

Twelve hours later, they were almost two hundred miles to the east, and the attacks had finally subsided. Victoria had handed off SAR duties to crews out of Guam, now that they were in range of the base there.

She landed her helicopter and shut down. When the engine wash was complete and the postflight duties were over, she ate in silence on the rolling flight deck. All of the ship's lights had been turned off to avoid visual detection. The stars above were putting on a show. Victoria was drunk with fatigue from flying so long. She ate a dinner of dry cereal and water, hugging her knees, her ass sore from the rough nonskid deck.

Victoria thought about the implications of that day's battle, and their ship's course. They were retreating. The Chinese would soon attack Guam. The Chinese had a superior fleet. The American attacks hadn't been effective. Why? She didn't know. All she knew was that they had—inexplicably—lost.

She had seen too much death and destruction today. Now she just wanted comfort. Her family. Her father. The war's end.

As she looked up at the stars, her eyes twitching with tiredness, she thought of her childhood. Of the summers in Annapolis when her father had taught her and her brothers how to use a telescope. That had been the beginning of her love for astronomy and science and technology.

She wondered if her father was looking up at these same stars now. She hoped to God he was okay, and that she would someday be able to share this view with her brothers and him again.

23

Eglin AFB
Florida
Day 18

David knocked on the door to General Schwartz's office and cracked it open. Susan was sitting on the chair opposite the general's desk. General Schwartz waved him in. He was on a landline phone and held up his pointer finger to signify that the call was almost finished. The door clicked shut behind David as he entered the room. Susan pointed to the chair next to her and David sat. After a moment, General Schwartz hung up the phone.

David said, "You wanted to see me?"

"We did," said Susan.

They were both staring at him with funny looks on their faces.

Susan said, "David, how familiar are you with the Double-Cross System that MI5 used during World War Two?"

David searched his memory. "The Germans had spies inside

of England during the war. The Brits caught them and tried to turn them into double agents or something. Right?"

Susan tilted her head from side to side. "Eh. Sort of. It was a bit more complex than that."

General Schwartz said, "Let's get on with it. We have a busy morning, Susan."

Susan said, "David, the United States has identified a large number of suspected Chinese spies operating in our homeland."

"Okay."

"Almost all of them are being sent here."

David was taken aback. "Where? Eglin?"

Susan nodded.

"Why?"

"I told you the responsibilities of the SILVERSMITH program would shift. We've converted several old hangars on the other side of the base into temporary prisons and interrogation centers. Most of our top interrogation teams are already here, as well as our linguists and support personnel."

"So, what, are you in charge of the interrogations now, too?"

"No, no. That would be too much. But I work closely with the interrogation teams. One of my new responsibilities is managing the information that comes out of these interrogations."

"Why?"

General Schwartz said, "Because we want to control what information they're sending back to China."

David said, "Excuse me? What do you mean? How could they still be sending anything back if we've arrested them?"

Susan glanced at him. "Read up on the Double-Cross System, David. It's not in our best interests to just have them stop. That's the essence of the whole game. Once we identify someone as a legitimate Chinese spy, we want two things. One, we want to know everything they know, and two, we want them to keep providing information to their Chinese handlers via radio transmission, dead drops, and more. We're managing over sixty separate networks now."

David began to see. "You want to spread false information." He shook his head. "But wait. Don't the Chinese suspect that their spies have been compromised?"

"Of course they do. And we suspect that many of our intelligence streams from HUMINT sources in China are also compromised. Proper deception is an art form. We feed them some truths, some half-truths, and some outright lies. But the whoppers, we save for when it really counts."

David stared at her, amazed. "Why are you telling me this?"

"You're being brought in on the operation, David. General Schwartz and I discussed it. You're bright and at the heart of much of our planning. My belief is that organizations are best served when the cadre of planners and decision makers are all well aware of current and future operations. This allows them to realize the impact of their choices."

"I'm surprised to hear you say that, considering you're a CIA officer."

She smiled. "Don't get me wrong. I still value the importance of secrets. I just think it's damaging to keep secrets from the people who should know them."

David nodded. "Okay. What do I need to do?"

"We'll take you over to the other side of the base later today. You can see for yourself what we've got going on. You'll have full access if you need it. The three of us will meet once per day to go over new information and how it might impact other recommendations SILVERSMITH is making up the chain of command."

"Yes, ma'am."

General Schwartz leaned forward. "David, how's the progress with the Jiaolong-class ships?"

David had been placed in charge of a team of scientists and engineers looking for ways to defeat the new Chinese technology. There were two groups, one focused on the antisubmarine warfare threat, the other on the air-defense problem. David wasn't nearly as well versed in the details as the experts he had brought in, but his work at In-Q-Tel had made him somewhat of a jack-of-all-trades on future technologies and their military applications, so he at least knew enough to comprehend what the scientists and engineers came up with and could translate it to the decision makers, like General Schwartz and his bosses.

"Sir, we have a few ideas. But they could take a long time to test."

The general shook his head. "Time isn't available. The Chinese fleet at Guam is already resupplying. Our intelligence reports that they want to take Hawaii next."

"How long will it take them to get there?"

"We need to be prepared for an attack on Hawaii within two weeks' time. That's what the Office of Naval Intelligence is telling us. We need to make a recommendation to Pentagon leadership by tomorrow."

David swore.

Susan said, "David, I know it seems impossible. Just get us whatever you have."

* * *

David met with his technical experts later that afternoon. The same three men that had been at Raven Rock had relocated to Eglin, and they had each recommended several other leaders in their respective fields. Security was tight. Some of those individuals were denied access based on past actions and political views that might be seen as sympathetic to China. Others couldn't be located, which was a legitimate problem in a nation that was still facing food and water shortages from an EMP attack. Nevertheless, the group of a dozen men and women that David did have access to were top-notch.

David addressed them in one of the secure conference rooms. "Ladies and gentlemen, I've got food and coffee coming. We'll be pulling an all-nighter. We'll need to get a recommendation on General Schwartz's desk by tomorrow morning."

"Regarding what?"

"We expect the Chinese to attack Hawaii just like they did Guam. We need to find a way to defeat the Jiaolong technology."

"What's the timing?"

David told them, and they provided him with the expected response. "Calm down, please. Trust me, I feel the same way. But we've got to come up with something. We cannot cede the Pacific."

"Aren't there conventional ways of fighting the Chinese Navy?"

Someone said, "You read the papers, right? You see what happened in Guam? We're in a new arms race. He wouldn't be holding this meeting if there was another way."

David sighed. "I'm afraid he's right."

And with that, the group set to work, brainstorming new ideas and rehashing ones that had already been proposed in previous meetings. Until today, no one had given them a timetable.

In his mind, David was realistic. He knew that this was a near-impossible task. But he also knew that wars were the catalysts for technological breakthroughs.

Six hours later, they had gone over countless ideas, but each one had been poked full of holes by the group.

Someone had proposed copying the Chinese version of the

directed-energy weapons. "We're years behind them, by the sound of it. Nothing but a blueprint would be ready in time."

Using submarine-launched nuclear torpedoes. "Not an option. That would trigger Russia entering the war."

Another idea was to use a new type of electronic jamming device that could cause very-low-altitude aircraft to be completely hidden from radar.

David was excited at that one. "Can we place that on our LRASM missiles? That might get them through—"

"No way. This would need to go on an aircraft."

"What about fitting it on a fighter or bomber and having them attack—"

"They would guzzle fuel at that altitude. Plus, we're talking really low. Like twenty-five feet above the ocean's surface. As soon as the aircraft came up to get on an attack profile, they would be toast."

"What about helicopters?"

"We don't have anything that's outfitted for electronic attack right now, but maybe. But then you have the issue of ordnance not being suitable. Helicopters won't have a good antiship missile option like the LRASM."

The group shifted to other possible options. Finally, one scientist brought up some type of weapon system based on black hole energy waves.

David did a double take. "I'm sorry. Did you say *black hole*? That sounds like something out of a science fiction novel."

The scientist, a woman in her midforties, said, "When we say black hole, we're really just naming it for the radio frequency it operates at. It's not like we're actually making a black hole. That would be impossible."

"Sure. Sure."

The woman continued, "Black hole jets, or gamma ray

bursts. Black holes create huge amounts of power at very high frequencies—higher than anything we have in the US electronic warfare arsenal today. Theoretically, we could put out these bursts of energy from an antenna."

David shook his head. "And what would it do?"

She looked at him as if that was a stupid question. "Obviously it would fry whatever it came into contact with. Enemy electronics being our target."

"And the Jiaolong's air defense system—does that operate the same way?"

"No. Completely different technology. But the black hole weapon could do some serious damage to the Jiaolong's antenna system."

"And we have this capability?"

"Well...we've been doing some testing..." The scientist began arguing with two other physicists using terms that David couldn't understand.

David held up his hand. "Please. In English."

"Well...theoretically, we could build a prototype quickly. But it would be limited in range."

The other physicist said, "And maybe power, too! These are brand-new ideas. Very costly and—"

David said, "How limited would the range be?"

The female scientist said, "Depends on the height of the antenna. It would be line-of-sight, so you could theoretically mount it atop a two-thousand-foot radio tower."

"That sounds great. What's the problem?"

"The current idea for generating the weapon is unrefined."

One of the physicists said, "You'd have to be a madman to go near it, she means."

The woman frowned at him. "There's a reasonably high probability that it could set off a cascade event..."

David cocked his head. "Like a nuclear detonation?"

She clicked her tongue. "No, no. Nothing like that."

David let out a sigh of relief.

"More like a neutron-bomb blast, destroying all life within a certain radius."

David blinked.

The physicist she had been arguing with said, "Don't waste your time, Mr. Manning."

The woman said, "We have nothing else."

"Even if it worked, and even if you could build it quickly, the range is a real problem," the other physicist said. "This is because it would have to be land-based. It's too unstable and dangerous to place on a ship or aircraft. It would also need an enormous power supply. You sure as hell wouldn't want to place it on Hawaii with all the people there."

Another of the team members said, "You could place it on an island."

"An island with no one else on it, maybe."

David said, "But what would the point of that be?"

One of the experts in surface warfare spoke up. "David, maybe we're thinking about this the wrong way? What if we created a barrier around the Hawaiian Islands, but these black hole devices were used as gates?"

"What would the barrier be?"

"Mines."

"That's a shit ton of mines."

"Yes, it is. But you don't need the mines to be everywhere. Just the possibility is enough to deny a certain area."

David nodded. "So, we use the mines to form a denied area barrier around the Hawaiian Islands, and place this black hole energy device on an unmanned island to serve as a gateway in and out of the castle?"

"Yes, exactly."

"And it wouldn't harm friendly ships?"

"No, no. Of course not. Our operators on the gateway islands would know not to target friendly ships, just like with any other weapon system. Think of it like a drawbridge. All the Allied warships and merchants could enter near those drawbridge islands. But the Chinese fleet would either have to pass through a minefield or go within range of the black hole device islands in order to get to Hawaii."

David's face lit up. "Could this really work?"

The surface warfare expert said, "It really would take a huge number of mines. I assume that the Chinese will have minesweepers deployed within their fleets. But we could lay undetectable nonmetallic mines, slow them down and spread them out. That could be an opportunity to pick off the peripheral ships, or launch some type of attack."

The female scientist who had come up with the black hole idea said, "The islands would need to be chosen carefully. The black hole device would need a nuclear reactor or some other type of very large power supply. And the antenna and technology that goes with it would need to be built immediately."

The surface warfare expert said, "And we would need to check on our mine inventory. With the numbers that we are talking about, the factories might need to go into overdrive increasing production. And all current inventory would need to be pre-positioned on Hawaii and then pushed out to the proper locations."

"Don't forget you'll need to coordinate this with all of the ships coming and going in the Pacific right now."

David nodded. "Look, however we do this, it will be an enormous undertaking. But the full weight of our nation will be behind it. I'm sure of that."

A knock at the door. Susan and General Schwartz entered. "Mind if we sit in?" the general asked.

David tried not to be annoyed. Not only were they giving him an impossible task with an impossible deadline, but they were going to look over his shoulder while he made his attempt. At least now, he had a lead idea.

"Not at all. We were just discussing building black holes."

"Lovely," said Susan, sitting in the back of the room. General Schwartz sat next to her and began scribbling in a notebook. He stopped and raised his hand.

"Yes, sir?"

"Can you catch us up? Give me the two-minute version."

David and the group did their best to fill them both in.

General Schwartz said, "So it's low probability of success? Do we agree on that?"

Reluctant nods from around the room, including David.

The general said, "How quickly can we do it?"

All heads turned to the private sector representation, an executive from one of the largest American defense contractors. "I'll have to get an estimate on construction. As you can imagine, this isn't a typical project. Just shooting from the hip, I think most of our project managers would laugh at any timeline under six months. But that's with a very limited understanding of the technology. It could be longer."

Shouting and arguing commenced, ending when David gave a loud whistle. "Alright, thanks, everyone. Let's take a short break."

As people began getting up and heading towards the restrooms, David huddled with Susan and General Schwartz in the corner of the room. David found himself saying, "I realize it's a long shot, but I think this could be our best bet."

Susan said, "Keep fleshing out the details, then meet us later to finalize a plan of action."

David nodded. "Yes, ma'am."

Susan said, "There's something else you should know, however."

"What?"

"Both Chinese fleets have resupplied and begun moving again. Exact whereabouts and destination are unknown."

24

Raven Rock Mountain Complex
Pennsylvania
Day 21

Edward Luntz, one of the top-level civilians in the Office of Naval Intelligence, listened quietly as General Schwartz gave his recommended plan. Everything about it sounded crazy. The new technology. The timeline. The sheer number of mines that would need to be deployed. Apparently, the national security advisor agreed.

"General Schwartz, you're telling me that you want us to fill the ocean around the Hawaiian Islands with mines? That sounds pretty drastic."

"Normally I would agree with you, sir, but desperate times..."

The Pentagon's senior military officer representative said, "What's the distance from Midway to Johnston Atoll?"

"About nine hundred and thirty miles, sir."

"Is our mine inventory able to handle an operation of this size?"

"Sir, our mines are essentially just converted five-hundred-pound and one-thousand-pound bombs. We've talked to the manufacturers, and they're already converting over several production lines to help us out."

"So will we have the inventory available or not?"

"Yes, sir, we think so. It should be ready for deployment in about two weeks' time."

The senior military and intelligence leaders began discussing it among themselves. Luntz normally didn't butt into this kind of stuff, but he figured he should show that he was paying attention. That way, they would keep inviting him to these meetings.

"Can you describe why you chose the...uh...security gate islands that you chose?"

General Schwartz said, "Midway and Johnston Atoll both now have military facilities and runways established. They're located sufficiently far away from population centers in case of —er—any accidents."

The conversation went on for a few more moments before the national security advisor said, "Do we really think we have a chance of building these black hole devices and getting them to work before the Chinese get there?"

"We're going to do our best, sir."

* * *

After the meeting, Luntz typed up his report to the ONI's director, a rear admiral. It pissed Luntz off to no end that he'd been there for decades, and the Navy kept putting idiotic admirals in charge of him. He was smarter and more knowledgeable about the job than any of them. He should be in charge of ONI. But instead he was treated like some second-class citizen because he wasn't in the military. It was bullshit.

But the one thing that made his daily charade worth it was proving just how stupid they all really were.

He finished typing up his summary of the meeting and placed it into the top-secret message folder, where it would be reviewed and sent to his boss back in Suitland, Maryland.

He then folded up his computer and headed out of the office.

"Going to lunch, Luntz?" one of his nosy coworkers asked.

"Yup."

"Want some company?" The guy was CIA. The whole office was a hodge-podge of three-letter agencies and military, all supposed to work together like one big happy family. Fuck that.

"Oh, no, thanks. I need to run a few errands." *And send our plans to my Chinese handler.*

He left the building and drove into town. It was a quaint little place. The kind of old-town America that you could still find in rural areas. Places like these were great for dead drops or a covert rendezvous. There were fewer people who could be watching him, which meant that his surveillance detection routes could be much more efficient.

While he drove, he quietly recited what he had heard in the brief, as if he were talking to himself. "So they want to use Johnston Atoll and Midway as locations for a new technology that could neutralize the Jiaolong-class ship, and deny all other areas of water around Hawaii with large minefields. The minefields could be ready in a few weeks, but they don't know if the new weapon system on the islands will be ready in time, or if it will even work."

He made a turn and drove onto a curving road that would take him to the next town. There was a drugstore open there. A rarity, considering the supply-chain issues America was facing now. Before he went into the store, he removed a memory stick from the small audio-recording device under his steering wheel.

The device had automatically encrypted the memory stick contents.

Inside the drugstore, he picked up a small pack of ibuprofen. As he did, he fixed the memory stick to the underside of the product shelf, where it was hidden from passersby and wouldn't be touched by shelf stockers.

He purchased the ibuprofen and a bottle of water.

The guy at the register said, "Headache?"

"Yeah."

"Hope you feel better."

"Thanks." *Asshole.*

Luntz was glad to help Jinshan. Jinshan had certainly helped him. Two decades ago, in Thailand, the police had jailed Luntz for a full day after catching him in the act with an underage prostitute. His career would have been over if the US government had ever found out.

Enter Cheng Jinshan. Luntz knew that he was only doing it to get something in return. But Jinshan offered a lot. He'd not only gotten the Thai authorities to drop all charges, but he'd made sure that Luntz got even better girls that evening. Jinshan had no problem with Luntz's fondness for young Asian women. And Jinshan had even helped Luntz's career through various means. He doubted he would be a GS-15 today if not for some of Jinshan's string pulling. Jinshan still sent Luntz presents of women. The two men always coordinated meetings to coincide with Luntz's vacations. Jinshan and Luntz hadn't met in years; both men were too senior now. But the relationship had turned into something so much more than just a way to score hot girls. Now it was about the excitement of sticking it to the government assholes who didn't appreciate him.

As Luntz drove back to Raven Rock, he knew how happy Jinshan would be with him when he got today's message.

25

Khingan Mountain HQ
China
Day 22

General Chen sat behind his desk, sipping tea as his staffers briefed him on the day's events.

"Guam has been fully reinforced, General. Our long-range bombers have been placed on the island, along with several infantry divisions."

They rolled out a monitor. One of the staffers began flipping through different slides they had prepared. Maps displaying Chinese military positions. Images from key engagements. Twice a day, General Chen joined Chairman Jinshan's senior leadership team for updates on the status of the war.

Within the Chinese mountain bunker headquarters, thousands of intelligence analysts received reports from around the globe, dissecting and identifying the most important reports. Piping them up their chains of command. Editing what was to be shared and what was to be held back. Massaging the information. Formulating the best message.

The general's staff knew that he didn't like bad news. Therefore, they minimized any negative information in his briefs. He also detested facts, figures, or details in general. Instead, they packed his presentations with images. The general liked to select only the very best images to bring to Chairman Jinshan, like a cat presenting a mouse to its master.

"And what of the Southern Fleet?"

General Chen was the only one still referring to the fleet that way. Everyone else was calling it the Jiaolong Battle Group, because the Jiaolong-class battleship had become such a heroic symbol of Chinese victory. While Admiral Song still maintained the aircraft carrier *Liaoning* as his flagship, the Jiaolong had quickly become the pride and joy of the Chinese military.

But General Chen despised the thought. The idea that a navy ship would steal from his glory irked him to no end. This war would eventually be fought and won with his *armies*, or at least his strategic vision. He thought of himself as a brilliant tactician.

As several of his peers in the leadership team reminded him, he had not seen the importance of the Jiaolong-class technology. After Guam had fallen, he had suggested that the two newest carriers, which were still in the Sea of Japan, should be dispatched to Hawaii immediately. Their firepower, in combination with their support ships and submarines, would surely be enough to take on the single American carrier that guarded the island state, even with the air support from the island. But Jinshan had opted to wait for the beloved Jiaolong. It was humiliating to be the head of the Chinese military and get overruled by a man who hadn't spent a day in the uniform.

"The *Liaoning* Carrier Battle Group has begun their journey north, sir."

Headed for Hawaii. The prize of the Pacific. Once they had Hawaii, it was only a matter of time before Chinese troop transports landed in the Americas. It would be fierce fighting, but they would prevail.

Still, Hawaii needed to be taken. And the general needed to save face, lest one of those spineless fools on the leadership team try to dethrone him by getting in Jinshan's good graces. General Chen had sacrificed his only daughter for the cause. Surely Jinshan would always remember that. And he had been loyal. Well, that had mostly been paid back with promotions and other contributions to the general's well-being. His bank account certainly hadn't suffered. But that was how things were done. As long as Chen continued to be of value to Jinshan, both men would prosper. But if General Chen fell out of favor...

"General?" His chief of staff was softly calling his name, pulling him from his thoughts.

He glowered at the colonel. "What is it?"

"Did you want to include this slide? We redid it from this morning."

General Chen had lit into his staffers for not having updated positions on the carrier group outside Japan. Now it showed the two newest Chinese aircraft carriers, a few hundred kilometers to the east of Tokyo.

"What are they still doing there?"

"Sir?"

"The Northern Fleet. What are their orders right now? What are they doing?"

"Sir, they are headed toward Hawaii."

"Well, why aren't they farther along?"

The colonel turned to the slide, and then to the other staff officers sitting behind him. One of them shook his head. "I believe that their orders are to arrive at the same time as the Southern Fleet, sir. Because the distance is much shorter for the Northern Fleet, they are traveling at a slower speed."

The colonel looked back at his superior, bracing for another storm of spittle and screams.

"How far is Hawaii? How many days' travel?"

"About two weeks, sir. Ten days if they exceed their fuel consumption limitations," said one of the staff members.

"You said that the USS *Ford* was spotted near Midway Atoll?"

"Yes sir. Our reconnaissance satellite sent imagery this morning, before it was destroyed by American antisatellite weapons."

The satellites were being shot down as quickly as they went up. It was a wonder that it had sent anything at all.

"And what of Midway? Do they have reinforcements there yet?" The Americans were reportedly sending reinforcements to several of the small Pacific islands. Some type of special defensive perimeter was being set up.

The colonel again looked back at his staffers. The TV screen changed to an image of Midway Atoll. The tiny island barely surrounded the perpendicular runways. Construction vehicles sat on one of the runways. A scattering of vegetation and buildings covered the rest of the island, red circles with simplified Chinese inscriptions next to them, reading "Surface-to-Air Missiles" and "Air Defense Radar." One large construction site said, "Unknown Tower Antennae."

"It appears that the defenses have been set up, sir. But we still expect many more reinforcements to be brought in, as only a few aircraft are currently stationed there."

"How far is Midway from the carrier positions?"

"Perhaps seven days, sir."

General Chen grunted. He took another sip of tea and let his eyes stare off into the distance. His staff officers looked at each other, wondering if he was still with them.

"Continue..."

His men went on, but the general wasn't really listening. His mind was turning over an idea.

That evening, Chairman Cheng Jinshan and the other leaders gathered for their nightly roundtable. Military intelligence experts updated them on the progress of the war. Then came the conversations between the leadership team and Jinshan. These were the moments where strategy was decided. Where decisions were made on which targets to attack, and how.

As chairman of the Central Military Commission, Cheng Jinshan was the de facto leader of the military. But each of the members at this table jockeyed for position and influence. Several were politicians, members of the Standing Committee—the most powerful members of the National People's Congress. These men were infatuated with the idea that the war would be won at sea, with a brand-new technology. They didn't see that it was actually General Chen's job to make many of these military decisions. He saw the way they looked at him. As if he was their intellectual inferior.

One of the military intelligence briefers said, "The Jiaolong Battle Group has been resupplied and is now headed north. In two weeks' time, she will reach Hawaii."

Jinshan said, "What is the level of military readiness at Hawaii and the lesser island installations?"

The minister of state security said, "We have conflicting reports, sir. It is possible that some of our sources inside America have been compromised. We are looking into this. But our best estimate is that the American military is strengthening there. Many of their aircraft were evacuated from Guam and now reside at those airfields."

"That concerns me."

The head of the MSS replied, "I assure you, sir, we are doing everything that we can do to verify the accuracy of our human intelligence."

Jinshan frowned. "We attempt to deceive them, and they

attempt to deceive us. But seeing for oneself is better than hearing from many others." Jinshan turned to the military intelligence officer who had been conducting the presentation. "Thank you for your report. Please allow us time to converse."

The briefers left the room and shut the door. Now it was time for General Chen to make his move. He leaned forward over the table, holding his head high. "Chairman Jinshan. I have evaluated the latest intelligence and find the current plans to be insufficient. Waiting for the Southern Fleet to arrive will take too long. During that time, Americans will continue to strengthen their military forces there. It also gives them time to find potential weaknesses in our Jiaolong-class ships..."

Admiral Zhang, head of the PLA Navy, frowned. "Weaknesses?"

General Chen ignored him. "I propose a preliminary strike on the American fleet before the Southern Fleet arrives."

Jinshan seemed unusually tired today, General Chen thought. Jinshan's eyes went to the side of the room. General Chen followed his gaze and saw *her* sitting there in the corner. What was she doing here?

Chen continued. "I recommend that we use our Northern Fleet and strike the Americans near Midway. We have two carriers to their one. We shall hit them with speed, surprise, and overwhelming force. It will be a decisive victory. Then our path to Hawaii will be clear."

Admiral Zhang said, "With respect, General, the Jiaolong-class ship is unrivaled, and its new technology gives us a clear advantage."

General Chen's face darkened. "And like any military hardware, its novelty decays by the day."

A lively argument commenced, with several passive-aggressive jabs thrown at General Chen. He would remember each offense, and strike back when the time was right.

Jinshan stood, holding himself up with the table. The arguments ceased. "Excuse me, gentlemen." Jinshan's eyes were closed, a grimace of discomfort on his face. One of his bodyguards was at his side, holding his arm.

Li rose from her chair. *Lena*, he corrected himself. She went to Jinshan's other side and took that arm, escorting him to the door.

A slow, silent march. Each of Jinshan's footfalls was inspected carefully by the leaders at the table, their eyes filled with worry and thought. Had Jinshan's health deteriorated this quickly? General Chen knew Jinshan was ill. Had Chen been so preoccupied with war planning and palace intrigue that he had overlooked just how bad Jinshan had gotten?

If there was a change at the top, it would be swift. Chen looked at the other faces around the table. Each of these men was a political predator. General Chen didn't see this as an undesirable trait. Men like him lived in the jungle. It was a way of life. Here they were, hungry cannibals on a desert island, studying each other for the first sign of weakness.

The door shut as Jinshan left the room. The members of the leadership team looked shocked.

His personal aide, looking nervous, said, "The chairman has retired for the evening. He requests that you continue without him."

It appeared that sign of weakness had come.

The arguing commenced immediately. Little was decided. After a while, the group adjourned and went their separate ways. Each leader meeting with his staff behind closed doors, plotting his next moves.

General Chen once again sat behind his desk. His plan to attack Midway was a very good idea, surely. Jinshan had heard the beginnings of the plan. And he hadn't verbally *disapproved*. Chen's men were silently waiting for him to speak. He licked his lips and cracked his knuckles. Winning this war, and seizing the ultimate leadership position, would require audacity.

Chen was normally more cautious, only moving when he was sure that he would win. But if he didn't establish himself as Jinshan's successor, someone else would. He couldn't have one of those politicians running his war machine into the ground. After all, *he* was the highest-ranking military officer in all of China. It was *his* prerogative whether he should move his forces. He didn't need permission. And his plan was brilliant.

General Chen looked up at his staff officers. "Draw up orders to direct the *Shangdong* Carrier Battle Group to steam towards Midway at best speed. Summon Admiral Zhang and have him come see me immediately. He will need to be made aware and design an effective strategy." Chen would need to make promises to Admiral Zhang. He too had seen Jinshan limping away. Perhaps Zhang could fill Chen's own shoes.

"Sir, what are your intentions?"

"I intend to take Midway before the *Liaoning* Battle Group arrives at Hawaii. Tell them that they have five days to reach Midway. The Americans will be surprised by the swiftness of this attack. This will ensure our victory in the Pacific." *And my part in it.*

"Yes, General."

"However, for operational security reasons, we must keep this plan to only a few members of the military circle. I don't even want these orders in our leadership team meetings. We have all heard the rumors about possible intelligence leaks."

The colonel fidgeted in his seat. "Sir...do you not think it wise to—"

"Do not argue, Colonel. *Execute.*"

* * *

Lena stood over Jinshan's bed. His personal doctor had just given him another dose of medication. It would help with the nausea and stomach pain.

Jinshan waved away the doctor and his assistant. They left the room, and Lena was alone with her mentor.

"Did you see their faces?"

"Yes." Jinshan was referring to the lean and hungry looks on the military officers and Politburo members as he hobbled out of the room unexpectedly. She thought about pretending not to notice, but that wouldn't serve him well. He needed an honest assessment, however cold it might be.

Her expression was stone. "They will be tempted now."

"I agree with you." He gestured to the bedside chair, and she took a seat.

"What would you have me do? Remove and replace any that show signs of disloyalty?"

He scoffed. "That will not solve my true problem. Nothing can do that. I am running out of time, Lena."

She was surprised to feel her eyes moisten. More uncharacteristic behavior. She noted it and moved on. "Then tell me how to help."

"Whatever you might think of General Chen"—she was grateful that Jinshan didn't refer to the man as her father—"he raises a good point about the Jiaolong-class technology. Eventually, the Americans will find a way to defeat it. Just like every weapon ever invented. War creates a renaissance of sorts. The greatest minds in the world suddenly become much more interested in weaponry when their survival depends on it. The subsequent technology race is focused on lethal innovations. Poison gas. Jet propulsion. Nuclear arms. Scientists that were busy with lesser things realize that they have the power to shape history, if they put their minds towards the destruction of rival militaries."

Lena said, "Do you really believe the Americans have a plan to defeat the Jiaolong technology already?"

"I am certain that they are working on it."

She realized that he was getting intelligence reports that no one else was.

Jinshan said, "We know there are weaknesses to the system. Will they discover them and come up with a counter before we take the Pacific? Or before we win the war? That I do not know."

"What do our spies say?"

"They say many things. But we cannot trust our overseas human assets as well as we could a few weeks ago. Before the war began, I was much more confident. Now…"

"What can I do?"

He grimaced again, holding his stomach as a spasm of pain wracked his body.

"Would you like me to get the doctor?"

His face was damp with sweat. "No. The pain is subsiding."

"I should get a medical attendant."

He took her elbow. "Lena, there is an operative in the United States. Only two people, including myself, know his identity. This operative is able to get us near-real-time military positions and readiness data in the Pacific. This information will be of the highest quality."

Lena raised one eyebrow.

"This operative just sent us information that shows how the Americans plan to defend Hawaii. We don't know if the American plans will work. But if we are able to get updated status on these plans prior to our attack…our conquest of the Pacific shall succeed."

"What must I do?"

"I need someone that I trust to travel to America and verify that the information is really coming from our agent, and that our agent is not under duress. I trust only you with this task, Lena."

"I am honored by this confidence, Chairman. I will go to America and fulfill my duty, as you request."

Jinshan nodded, a look of pride on his face. "The operative in question is a member of the US Navy's Office of Naval Intelligence. Their organization, like many of the US military and intelligence community, has been decentralized as part of a security procedure. We have a team of military special forces soldiers inside the US. The South Sword Team. After the war began, we had to change our procedure for getting his reports. The South Sword Team is able to recover the information, but they cannot make contact themselves. They will assist you in locating the operative and providing you with security. The minister of state security is the other who knows of this agent. He can tell you the procedures for making contact. He can also provide you with travel arrangements."

"I understand."

"We will conduct our attack on Hawaii based on the information this operative provides. If his information indicates that taking Hawaii is not possible, we will take an alternate course of action with our fleet. This is an essential mission, Lena. It may determine the course of the war."

A knock at the door, and then the minister of state security entered. Jinshan explained his orders while Lena stood in wait. When Jinshan was finished, he dismissed them both, saying, "I must rest now. Good luck, Lena."

* * *

The head of the MSS left the meeting with Jinshan and was escorted out of the bunker to an awaiting helicopter. From there, he was ferried back to Beijing, where he was driven to the MSS headquarters.

As he usually did after high-level meetings, he met with his secretary to document everything. She took handwritten notes as he recounted each and every discussion. The notes were then locked up in his personal safe, where he could refer to them later if needed. The senior intelligence officer was, at this level, a politician. He needed to cover himself if the knives ever came out. In such a case, he could have his secretary turn his notes into memos that documented the past interactions.

What the head of the MSS was not aware of was that his secretary's eyeglasses contained an audio and video recording device. Every word of the conversation—both written and spoken—was stored within the temples of the glasses. Later that night, she uploaded the data into her communications device and sent a burst transmission towards a receiver on the roof of a nearby apartment building.

That device logged the receipt and sent an alert message via a short-range omnidirectional beacon to the CIA officer who had recently entered the country, posing as a Japanese national.

Tetsuo downloaded the message and fired it off through his own communications device a few hours later. This transmission was received by a very small and stealthy Air Force drone, one of several on a rotating schedule. These drones had been preprogrammed to fly over Beijing at exactly the same time each day. In order to protect itself from electronic attack, the drone wasn't able to receive or transmit information in flight except for precisely timed windows, designed for operators to send their data.

So it wasn't until it landed at Elmendorf Air Force Base ten hours later that Susan Collinsworth and David Manning learned that Lena Chou was headed to meet with a highly placed mole inside the US command center at Raven Rock.

26

USS Ford

Admiral Manning sat on a metal folding chair among hundreds of the ship's crew in the anchor windlass space. The room was oddly shaped. The forward-most bulkhead was sharply angled because it was so close to the bow. Bright white daylight shone in from portholes spaced throughout the room. Giant white metal beams ran along the ceiling. The flooring was a blue-and-gray perforated mat. It reminded the admiral of a gym floor, except for the bare sections where thick white bollards sprouted up from the deck. On either side of the space were two colossal black anchor chains that ran down the length of the room and disappeared into separate holes in the floor. Each link of the fourteen-hundred-foot-long chain weighed over 130 pounds. It connected to a thirty-thousand-pound anchor.

On a ship at sea, most rooms had multiple uses, and this one was no exception. Sunday morning Catholic service was being held. The faces of the churchgoers were solemn. Most of the crew had just learned that Guam had fallen to the Chinese. The American forces there, including the surface action group, had been defeated, and the remaining forces on Guam were ordered to surrender. Tens of thousands of servicemembers would become prisoners of war. Chinese military aircraft were now flying in reinforcements to the island.

The misplaced exuberance that many of the *Ford*'s youthful warriors had displayed in previous days had given way to what Admiral Manning had learned from history books: victory was never guaranteed.

American military superiority, however much it had been ingrained in our minds as an unwavering fact and a great source of national pride, was no more assured than the dominance of the empires of old—all of which, at one time or another, had fallen.

The chaplain had just finished reading the gospel and was now giving his sermon. Admiral Manning tried to pay attention but found himself thinking of all the things he needed to do. His eyes wandered as he thought. He could see the sunlit blue ocean through one of the nearby portholes. The carrier was making way, and welcome breeze flowed over his face. Before he knew it, the gospel was over, and they were standing and praying and sitting and praying and shaking hands and then communion and then a few parting words from the priest.

"We pray for our brothers and sisters on Guam. That they continue to show bravery and grace in the face of..." The chaplain paused, and the admiral looked up. "Adversity. Amen."

He had almost said *defeat*, Admiral Manning realized. *Don't use that language, Chaps.* The chaplains were getting used to this new world of war. Church service attendance had quadrupled since combat operations had begun.

"Amen," repeated a chorus of voices.

Soon the men and women in attendance were rising from their chairs. Their eclectic mix of uniforms denoted their job and community. The aviators wore flight suits. Those in blue coveralls were ship's company. The Shooters wore yellow turtle-neck shirts, the EOD detachment utilities. Everyone was rushing off after the service, heading off to breakfast or work.

On Sunday mornings, the ship tried to adhere to quiet hours. The galley cooks spruced up the cafeteria-style meals. The routine of cleaning and work was a little bit more relaxed, if only for a short while. Drumbeat meetings like the admiral's daily brief were on a modified schedule.

Admiral Manning would take advantage of that. He headed to one of the few places on the ship where he could find solace. Nine stories up, on the admiral's bridge, he'd had an elliptical machine installed. He felt old as dirt when he'd given up running. But time, tide, and formation wait for no man. Bad knees forced him to use this silly machine that made him feel like a cross-country skier. Still, he worked up quite a sweat. Whatever did the trick, he supposed.

He had the admiral's bridge to himself, except for two Marines that had been assigned as his personal bodyguards. He adjusted the settings on the elliptical machine and started his workout. From his perch in the far-right corner of the bridge, he could see the flight deck below, and a wide view of at least a dozen ships in his strike group. Flight ops had not yet begun. It was a bright, sunny, peaceful morning.

"Good morning, sir."

Goddammit.

"Good morning, Commodore."

The commodore was the sea combat commander for the *Ford* Strike Group. The admiral bobbed up and down with the elliptical machine, a bead of sweat running down his face. The commodore had one of his staffers standing next to him, a tired-looking lieutenant wearing a green flight suit.

"Something I can help you with, Commodore?"

"Sir, frankly, we need more SSC flights."

"We have two pages of SSC flights on the air plan. What's the problem, Commodore?"

The commodore turned to his lieutenant. The kid needed a shave and looked like he didn't want to be there. "Sir, I'm the commodore's air operations officer. I manage the surface surveillance flight schedule. You're right, we do have a lot of helicopters flying. Right now, we have twenty-five ships in company. At any given time, there are five helicopters flying."

"That's a hell of a lot of helicopters in the air. What's your point?"

"The helicopters in the strike group are needed close in to the ships to prevent against possible submarine attack, sir. We also need to use them for the constant logistics flights our ships need to move people and parts around the strike group. Both of these requirements affect the armament and fuel capacity of the helos, and the steal-away capacity to conduct surveillance missions."

"Alright...so let's fly more helicopters."

"It's not that simple, sir. We're near our limit as is, due to the number of helicopters and pilots available. But the real issue is range. We're worried about finding two Chinese fleets. The Southern Fleet with the Jiaolong-class and *Liaoning* aircraft carrier, and the Northern Fleet with the two other Chinese carriers. If we use helicopters to locate them, it'll be too late. As you know, our drones are susceptible to electronic attack, and I worry that we don't have good enough control over those resources anyway. We need organic, long-range surveillance aircraft, sir. That will alleviate the stress on the helicopters in the strike group. It will allow them to handle the closer-in missions."

"What are you asking for?"

"Sir, we need to ask for more maritime patrol aircraft and..." He hesitated. "Sir, we need our fighters to start flying medium- and long-range surveillance flights around the carrier. We need to extend our surveillance area greatly. This will give us enough lead time to detect the enemy fleets and react appropriately."

The admiral read the name on his chest patch.

"Plug? Is that your call sign?"

"Yes, sir."

"What ship were you on?"

"The *Farragut*, sir."

The admiral's wheels were turning. Now he remembered what was significant about this kid. He had been one of Victoria's pilots.

Plug said, "I served under your daughter, Lieutenant Commander Manning, there. Best boss I've ever had, sir."

Admiral Manning arched an eyebrow and glanced at the commodore.

Plug's eyes widened in horror. "Commodore...sir, I mean besides you, of course."

The commodore just shook his head. Plug often got that reaction from senior officers.

The admiral turned forward and continued exercising. He allowed himself a moment of pride in his daughter, and then a moment of worry. Then he put her out of his mind and turned back to the two officers who were interrupting his peaceful Sunday morning workout.

"Plug?"

"Yes, sir?"

"Are you familiar with the term *drive-by*?"

"Sir?"

"The commodore might not be your favorite boss, but I advise you to learn from his technique. The commodore and his minion—you—are executing what's known as a *drive-by*. The term has two meanings. One is used to describe criminal gangs shooting up a house as they drive by in a car. The other is used when a subordinate finds his superior at an unplanned and opportunistic moment with the intent of pitching an idea."

Plug's face reddened. The commodore looked amused.

Admiral Manning continued, "Both situations are ambushes. Tactics used to defeat an unprepared opponent." The admiral looked at the commodore. "Or in this case, an opponent that isn't present." The commodore's smile vanished.

The admiral stopped midcycle and got off the exercise machine. He walked to the front of the bridge and picked up a phone.

"CAG. I apologize for the climb, but we're having a conversation that you should be a part of. Mind joining us on my bridge? Yes, now. Thanks." He hung up the phone.

A few moments later, a Navy captain in a flight suit appeared through the door, huffing and puffing from climbing the nine ladderways to this deck.

Admiral Manning gave Plug the floor, and the four men spoke about the surveillance requirements. In the end, the CAG made concessions to provide more of his fighters for dedicated surveillance flights.

"Thank you, CAG. I think this will be a big help. Sooner or later, one of those Chinese fleets is going to reach us. When it happens, we want to find them before they find us."

An hour later, the admiral had finished working out and showering. He was brought a breakfast of eggs, corned beef hash, and toast, with a pot of coffee dark as night. The admiral read through his unclassified emails. One popped up that especially caught his interest. A drone must have flown over the *Farragut*, allowing the data transfer.

He read his daughter's email and grew sad. She was rarely emotional, but it sounded as if the war was taking its toll on her. There was nothing specific in the email. Like everyone in the military, specifics were left out. But Admiral Manning could read between the lines. She had seen combat and suffered loss. She was a changed person. He closed his eyes, praying for her safe passage.

He wrote her back, not knowing if or when she would get the message, but feeling more like a father than he had in a long time.

27

Chase and the prisoners were ferried to Wright Patterson Air Force Base near Dayton via Chinook helicopter and then flown to Eglin AFB in the back of an Air Force C-130. At Eglin, the prisoners were taken into specially made holding cells in a large hangar.

Chase was greeted by his brother just outside of the facility. They embraced and patted each other hard on the back. David looked tired.

"Lindsay here with you?"

"Yeah, we're in base housing, if you can believe it."

Chase smiled. "They gonna make you put the uniform back on? They gave *me* one. No rank insignia, though."

"Sorry to hear that. I'm sure you still make everyone salute, though. I know how important that was to you."

"Damn right I do." Both men knew the opposite was true.

David chuckled. It was good to laugh, considering that the world was falling apart around them.

"You heard from Dad or Victoria?" Chase asked.

"I've been monitoring our daily intel reports for their ships or names. Dad should be fine." David looked around the parking lot of the converted hangar. "Come on inside. We'll talk there."

They walked through a double layer of security checks. Chase was struck by how big the hangar was on the inside. Several football fields easy, with a sheet-metal ceiling over one hundred feet high. Rows and rows of what looked like shipping containers were lined up as far as the eye could see.

"Those are the holding cells?"

David said, "Yeah. One for each prisoner. Military interrogators are working round the clock on them." He waved. "Come on, this way."

Chase and David continued walking along the central corridor between the shipping containers.

Armed security personnel were escorting prisoners in and out of several of the holding cells. The prisoners wore black cloths over their heads as blindfolds and had their wrists handcuffed behind their backs. The scene was tense, but quiet.

David led his brother into an empty room on the far end of the hangar. Susan and several of the SILVERSMITH personnel were observing one of the interrogations on a nearby monitor. They wore over-the-ear headsets through which English-language translations were being piped in. Susan greeted Chase with a nod, then resumed listening to the interrogation.

David and Chase sat in the back of the room. David whispered, "Like I was saying before, I read the intel reports daily and pay close attention to the *Ford* and the *Farragut*. Dad's strike group has been placed near Midway Island and hasn't come into contact with Chinese ships since the day the war began."

"And Victoria?" Chase asked.

David's face grew dark. "Her ship took hits from Chinese antiship missiles near Guam. They had multiple killed and wounded, although I didn't see her name on the list."

Chase turned away, not saying anything.

David said, "I've emailed her. Just innocuous stuff, obviously. Just asking how her day was. But I haven't heard anything back. Which could mean anything at this point. The Navy's data transfer has shifted from satellite to a network of drones that they've got positioned over the Pacific as relays and surveillance. But the Chinese cyberoperations are sophisticated enough that we can't be sure the information we're getting hasn't been tampered with. And the drones that were in the Philippine Sea and around the Mariana Islands have been shot down. So..."

Chase faced his brother. "Where is her ship headed?"

"They're moving them to join the *Ford* Strike Group."

"Are there other carriers over there?"

"One is supposed to leave San Diego in a few days. Another is having maintenance problems and still isn't underway. The others are—well, not in this part of the world."

"Yet."

David shrugged. "That's above my pay grade."

The interrogation of the Chinese prisoner ended, and Chase could see on the TV monitor that he was being led out of the room. Susan and the others removed their headsets and turned to Chase.

"Chase, how has the progress been?"

Chase said, "Solid results. Good improvements. The JSOC teams have been very effective. At first, it was rough. We'd get reports from local law enforcement or surveillance drones about a Chinese troop movement or attack. Data on Chinese strength and capabilities was unreliable. The Chinese were moving quick, attacking utilities or infrastructure and then leaving before we could respond. But as we implemented tactics learned from the sandbox, things got progressively better. We set up forward operating bases with small teams, each with their own organic air support detachments. This allowed us to react faster. Every night—sometimes multiple times per night—we would conduct raids on suspected Chinese locations. Most of the ops were kill-and-capture. JSOC has its own interrogators. We would get information as soon as the raids ended and used that to uncover new targets. Every night the same thing. Hunt. Kill and capture, interrogate, learn new information, orient, get new targets, and do it again."

David could hear the intensity in his brother's voice. Chase's eyes darted around as he spoke, remembering what he'd done, thinking as he spoke.

"The big breakthrough came the night before last. Two companies of Chinese infantry. Most of them surrendered. We think the total strength in the US is now less than one hundred personnel."

"Excellent work. Those prisoners that you captured are providing us with a treasure trove of information."

Susan fidgeted with her pen as she studied Chase's face. She seemed to be deciding something. "How much has your brother told you about this place?"

Chase looked at David, whose face was impassive.

"He just told me it was the prison...where you're holding some of the Chinese soldiers that we captured."

Susan turned back to the TV screen as another prisoner entered the interrogation room. His mask was removed, and Chase saw that he was just a kid. Probably no more than eighteen or nineteen years old. The overhead speaker broadcast the conversation from the room. It began in Chinese.

Then the prisoner said, "We may speak in English, if you want. I speak English good."

The interrogator looked up at the camera.

Susan reached for a microphone device on the shelf and tapped the transmit button. "That's fine. English, please."

She turned to Chase and said, "We'll continue after this is over."

Chase recognized the kid. He was one of the prisoners they had taken from the highway raid a week earlier.

The interrogator was a young white woman. Chase found himself wondering whether she'd had to learn Chinese in Defense Language School. It was probably pretty tough to interrogate someone in Chinese if you had just learned the language a few years ago. She was probably pretty happy to be conducting the interview in English. "Lin Yu, we appreciate how much help you have been thus far. Your show of good faith will greatly improve your situation when China and the United States make peace."

"I only want peace. I want no more war," the kid mumbled. He looked shell-shocked.

"Of course. Listen, I have some paperwork that my superiors need us to get through. Would you mind signing this statement here? It's just some administrative stuff. Making it official that you'll agree to help us however you can. After all, we want the same thing, right? Peace."

The Chinese kid looked at his interrogator and gave a weak smile. "Sure. Yes. Okay." He took the pen and signed the paper, which the interrogator quickly placed into an envelope and moved away.

She asked a series of questions about what he had been doing over the past few weeks. Then she said, "The last time we spoke, you mentioned that your platoon had come into contact with a—how did you put it?—an elite special team. These were Chinese special operations soldiers, is that correct?"

"Yes, that is correct."

"And your team was not special operations?"

"They were a different type."

"What made this elite team different?"

"They have more training. Better training. They are the best of our region. Guangzhou. I believe this is where they were from. I heard them speak, and the dialect and accents were from the south."

The interrogator glanced at her notes. "That's where you are from as well, is it not?"

"Yes."

"So did this team have a name?"

"I know the Chinese name." He said something in Chinese. "I think you call this South Sword."

"Yes. South Blade or South Sword. Okay. So what was the South Sword Team doing?"

"They receive special instructions. They meet with my commander and use our radios. Then they get special instructions and leave quickly."

"Do you know where they were headed?"

"I do not know."

"What were their special instructions?"

Lin Yu shifted in his seat. His interrogator waited patiently.

Lin Yu said, "They were to meet with a Chinese woman. She enter United States soon. I hear this when they speak to my commander. I was not supposed to hear. I think this is important."

"Do you know the name of the woman they were to meet with?"

"No."

"But you are sure she is Chinese? And that she is entering the US soon?"

"Yes. She very important, I think. She have to send radio communication back to China. This is why they take radio communicator device from my commander."

The interrogation went on for another fifteen minutes, and then the prisoner was led away.

Susan turned back to the others.

The technical expert said, "If the Chinese team transmits

every day around the same time, and we have the rough time and location of their transmission from a few days ago, I can run a cross-check through our database. I'll look for similar metadata tied to the transmission. We might get lucky."

Susan said, "Do it."

The tech expert rose from his seat and left the room.

Susan turned to Chase. "The men and women in these cells aren't just prisoners you've captured. They include anyone that we suspect may have been providing intelligence to the Chinese. Whenever we can, we're obtaining the exact communications procedures that they use. If the prisoners cooperate, we're turning them into double agents. They will continue to provide the Chinese with regular updates, but we control the new content of their updates."

Chase said, "Didn't the Brits do that during World War Two?"

David nodded. "She made me look it up. You're right. The British Security Service had done something similar with Nazi spies. The idea was to keep the Nazi intelligence analysts' desks filled with disinformation."

Susan smiled. "Exactly."

Chase said, "Have many have cooperated?"

"Enough. But you can bet the Chinese are playing the same game. We've already seen signs that many of our China-based assets have been rolled up. Yet I'm afraid several of those same persons are continuing to communicate with us. You can draw your own conclusions."

Chase looked at his brother again. David said, "This isn't the first we've heard of this South Sword Team. It's an elite naval special warfare team from southern China. We think they were involved in several other special operations inside the US over the past few weeks. They're one of the last units that remain unlocated."

"So you want me to help find them?"

David glanced at Susan.

Susan said, "Sort of."

Chase looked between them, sensing a problem. "What's the problem?"

Susan said, "That interview we just listened to? It corroborates other intelligence we've recently received. Chase, we think Lena Chou is headed to the US, if she isn't here already."

Chase didn't say anything for a moment. His eyes darted among the three others in the room: David, Susan, and the other CIA officer.

"You want me to hunt down Lena Chou? Is that why I'm here?"

"Who better?"

Chase looked at his brother, annoyed.

Susan continued. "You know her, and you won't underestimate her."

"Do you have any leads?"

"She was spotted getting on a plane from Beijing to Russia twelve hours ago. Our SIGINT tracked that plane to Helsinki. We lost her at that point. But the expectation is that she's going to be connecting with one of this South Sword Team." Susan gestured to the monitor that showed where the Chinese prisoner sat. "We think she's going to meet with an American mole. Chase, tell me, why would Cheng Jinshan risk sending Lena Chou back into the United States to meet with one person?"

"Because he wants it done right. He trusts her. And rightfully so. She's very good at what she does."

"Exactly."

Chase said, "Where do I go from here?"

"You'll be back and forth between the JSOC base for now. We're not ready for you yet. But when we say go, you'll need to move fast."

28

USS Ford
50 nautical miles south of Midway

Admiral Manning evaluated the imagery. Dozens of white wakes in a vast blue ocean. The picture had been taken from an Air Force Global Hawk, the data transfer complete shortly before it had been shot down by Chinese fighters. The two Chinese carriers of the Chinese Northern Fleet were surrounded by over forty escorts and support vessels. Where the Southern Fleet contained a sizable contingent of troop transports, the Northern Fleet did not. More teeth and claws. Less soft underbelly.

"When was it taken?"

"We just got it, sir. The IWC told me to show you immediately," the young intelligence officer answered.

The call to GQ sounded over the 1MC, and Admiral Manning walked out of the secure compartment and into another.

"Battle Watch Captain, why are we going to GQ?"

"Sir, the *Ford* CO ordered it. One of our F-18s flying surveillance was just lit up by an air defense radar, sir."

Admiral Manning looked up at the movie-theater-sized screen at the front of the darkened room. The screen was carved into several sections, each showing important tactical information. Dozens of men and women were typing and talking at the rows of duty stations just in front of the screen. The battle watch captain and his assistants sat on an elevated row of terminals in the rear of the space. The BWC was the admiral's senior watch stander. This one was a Navy lieutenant commander and wore the double-anchored wings of a naval flight officer.

"Both the CAG and the commodore are looking for you, sir."

Admiral Manning nodded. The sound of afterburner igniting above them filled the room as the admiral walked out. The sound continued for a number of seconds, followed by a WHOOSH, and then another. The admiral walked into the air wing's secure compartment, where their own duty officers were yelling into phones and headsets, moving pieces on a magnetic whiteboard, and typing on computers.

"CAG, everyone good?"

The CAG was looking between one of the computer screens and the flight schedule with one of the lieutenants on his staff. "Everything's good, sir. We're launching our strike package now."

"Coordination with Air Force assets going smoothly?"

"Most Air Force assets are on deck. And they're over a thousand miles away with limited tankers. But we expect their alerts to be airborne within the next few minutes. So far so good, sir."

"The Chinese fleet looks like it's out of range of the ships. Is—"

The CAG looked slightly impatient. "They are. Our attack aircraft and Air Force assets are going to be first. The commodore expects his destroyers to be in range within the next two hours. We'll coordinate with him and update you, Admiral."

If not for the seriousness of the situation, the admiral would have smiled. Decades of training for this moment, and now it was here. He felt like a parent with his adult children. The kids didn't need him to tell them what to do; he had trained them well.

"Keep me informed."

"Yes, sir."

Admiral Manning went down to the Zulu cell next. The commodore stood menacingly over the same young lieutenant who had convinced him to have the CAG add more surveillance flights.

"Commodore, everything going well?"

The commodore ran down a laundry list of status reports, mostly ship degradations, and finally finished with, "But yes, sir. Everything is going well. We'll work with CAG and Strike Group to coordinate."

"Very well."

The commodore then stepped over to the side of the room to add a bit more about submarine movements. When they were finished, Admiral Manning headed back to sit with his battle watch captain. Real-time updates on the second battle of Midway began coming in fast and furious.

* * *

On board one of the Chinese carriers, the Chinese fleet commander received word that American fighters were inbound. He gave the order to launch Chinese fighters and was soon notified that his ships had turned on their air defense radars and begun launching their surface-to-air missiles.

The Chinese fleet commander knew the battle would be fast. With aircraft and missiles all supersonic, the time of flight for each wave was mere minutes. This would be the climax of his life, he realized. Of many lives. Scientists had been working on these technologies, working on improvements to various characteristics like the effectiveness of radar target acquisition and the range of each missile. Testing and training. Entire lives of military service dedicated to the expertise of each specific aspect of war. Yet it would be decided in mere seconds, with any number of variables contributing to the ultimate victory. The wind could be the deciding factor. Or the water temperature. Or how quickly one of the pilots pressed a series of buttons.

"Surface-to-air missiles are hitting their targets, Admiral. Combat Officer estimates that at least ten enemy aircraft have been shot down." Ten. Out of how many? They would be in range to let loose their strike packages soon.

"Send in the fighters."

"Yes, sir."

Above the Chinese carriers, stacks of Chinese fighter aircraft were flying circles at their maximum endurance airspeed, trying to conserve fuel for when they were given the okay to head into battle. The radio call came quick and terse. The squadron commander gave orders to his pilots and they separated into several formations at different altitudes. Jammers were on, radars off on all but a few. Shortly after they pointed their headings east, the aircraft with radars on communicated the targeting information to the others over their network.

* * *

Lieutenant Suggs had once again been given permission to get on the flight schedule. Everyone wanted to fly this mission, and he was no exception. But slipping a bottle of scotch to the scheduler in the air wing had helped his case.

Suggs shot down two aircraft within the first few minutes of combat. His eyes and mind were hitting sensory overload. The sheer number of hostile air contacts was overwhelming.

His weapons system officer said, "Hey, Suggs, come right to zero-eight-zero. I think I've got one of the carriers."

Suggs banked the Superhornet sharply and lined up on his attack profile. Moments later, the aircraft fired an antiship missile, which dropped low over the ocean and sped towards its targets.

* * *

The Chinese admiral tried to keep apprised of the battle's status, but the volume of information was overwhelming.

"Sir, our air defense systems are being jammed."

"Admiral, very few of the American air-to-surface missiles scored hits. But now the Americans have confirmed targeting coordinates—they know where we are."

"Sir, our fighters are engaged in aerial combat operations."

The ship-to-ship missile volley would be next. Sure enough, "Enemy missiles inbound..."

"How many?"

"Sir, our escort destroyer is reporting the acoustic signature of an American attack submarine. The torpedo doors have been opened, Admiral."

A rumbling thunder rocked the room. Alarm bells and whistles sounded, and he could hear screams in the distance.

* * *

The ship-launched missiles were numerous and lethal. Multiple hits on surface ships, including two on the other carrier. Lieutenant Suggs's antiship missile scored a hit to one of the carriers, and a *Los Angeles*–class submarine finished it off with a torpedo.

It was only forty minutes into the battle, but the fuel the fighters had burned in dogfights and expended in evasive maneuvers was requiring many of them to land. The *Ford* was recovering at the same time as the lone remaining Chinese carrier. But now the Chinese carrier had to attempt to recover aircraft from its sinking sister ship. That was less of a problem, as many of the Chinese fighters had been shot down.

In the end, it became an operations management problem. Which nation's fleet could go through a cycle of launch and recovery, of refuel and rearm, faster and without critical errors that would slow down the entire process? This was where the American training and decades of experience came into play, and where the electromagnetic catapult helped. The Chinese were still recovering aircraft when the next American wave hit.

Twenty more F-18s and F-35s flew in, now with the assistance of US Air Force assets. The Americans jammed Chinese air defense radar, divided up the targets, and fired their weapons. They scored over twenty more hits on ships, and two on the other carrier.

"Admiral Manning, the E-2 just updated the course and speed of the Chinese fleet. They're moving west now, sir. And both carriers have been sunk."

A few cheers in the room at that. Then one of the personnel at a computer terminal shouted to the battle watch captain, "Sir, we have an ESM hit. A Chinese periscope radar. It's close, sir..."

USS Farragut

Some things on a ship at sea seemed to move slow. Like the journey across an ocean. Waking up to the same blue water every day. The endless waves rocking the ship. The mindless routine.

These long periods could lull you to sleep or complacency, if you weren't disciplined and strong in spirit.

Victoria Manning was both.

She was in the empty hangar that the ship had converted into a gym. Her arm muscles were burning as she finished a set of pull-ups. Sweat covered her body.

She had faced war on the sea. The loss of shipmates. The guilt that she hadn't done enough to protect them. The feelings had nearly broken her. She allowed herself to internalize that despair and anguish. She had accepted it and grown stronger.

The pressure to protect her shipmates still weighed heavy on her heart, but she also allowed herself to believe in a peaceful future. She would see her family again soon. The war would come to a peaceful end, eventually. Life would be beautiful once again.

In a few days, they would be in Hawaii. She wondered if her father's aircraft carrier would be in port. He had written her a kind email, saying how much he looked forward to seeing her, and how proud he was of her. He never spoke like that. The war was causing everyone to do and say things that they never would have otherwise.

She stood at the open hangar door, the sea breeze drying off the sweat from her body.

Then the 1MC announced, "Flight quarters, flight quarters. Now launch, the alert ASW aircraft."

The hangars and flight deck came alive with people running. The gym hangar door shut quickly, and the other hangar door opened. The aircraft was brought out as Victoria got briefed by the TAO on the phone.

"We just got datalink connected. Still getting updates, but it looks like the *Ford* Strike Group has been fighting the Chinese near Midway for the past few hours."

"Why are we launching? They must have dozens of helicopters."

"Strike Group told us to. I think they have a lot of submarines that they're hunting."

Victoria realized that he was probably right. They had been hearing for days how the Chinese Northern Fleet was missing from the waters near Japan and thought to be headed towards Hawaii. If they sent the surface fleet, why wouldn't they send their submarines to support it? There could well be dozens of them.

The TAO continued, "We're about two hundred miles away, but the *Ford* Strike Group is headed south now, so we're closing."

She looked at the helicopter. They were unfolding the blades, and a torpedo was being rolled out onto the flight deck.

"We'll be airborne as soon as possible."

Later, she watched as the light on the back of the hangar went green.

"Beams open. Green Deck. Lift," came the call from the landing signals officer, who was standing behind a thick glass window in front of her.

Victoria was squatting forward in her seat. She looked from side to side, checked her instruments, and pulled up on the collective lever. "Coming up."

"Roger," said her copilot. "Clear right."

She watched the torque level on her instrument panel grow precipitously high. "Getting a few red cubes." That was the problem with carrying this much weight.

"Should we burn fuel first?"

Victoria's MH-60R helicopter was filled to the brim with antisubmarine warfare equipment. A dipping sonar, sonobuoys, and torpedoes. Radar, ESM, and FLIR. All the extra weight was pushing her engines to their limits. If she pulled too high on her collective lever, the power required to hover would exceed the power available. Something would have to give, and she knew what it would be. Her rotor would start slowing down as the aircraft's power supply failed to turn it fast enough. When that happened, they would start sinking back down to the deck. And the harder she pulled up on the collective, demanding more power, the more she would exacerbate the situation. This was a problem because her landing spot was moving forward at fifteen knots, and the tail rotor also would slow down, meaning that her helicopter would likely begin spinning.

But World War III had begun, and she needed every bit of equipment they had on board the helicopter.

"Okay. Let's just watch the rpms. Once I get up into the perch, we'll have more airflow over the rotor disk. That'll help."

With her right hand, she eased the cyclic backward. The ten-ton metal beast inched aft. Her peripheral vision caught white-caps on the deep blue ocean, and the imposing outline of the USS *Michael Monsoor*, the Zumwalt-class destroyer that was the flagship of their surface action group.

The green digital lines that represented her torque began to tick down as the helicopter crept further backward on the flight deck. The wind, which had been blocked by the ship's super-structure when they were close to the hangar, was now whip-ping around the ship and flowing directly towards them. The ship was traveling at fifteen knots, and the wind was blowing at ten knots. Since the ship was headed directly into the wind, this effectively gave them twenty-five knots of speed over the rotor disk. For a helicopter, twenty-five knots made all the difference in the world.

With a flutter of the rotors, Victoria felt the helicopter go through its transitional lift—that critical speed where the aircraft transitioned from a hover to forward flight. She pulled up further on the collective, and the aircraft responded graciously by providing her more power, increasing altitude to a spot fifty feet above the flight deck, and just aft of it.

"Nose coming right."

"Roger."

Victoria pushed in her right pedal and the aircraft yawed to the right. Then she centered the pedals when the nose was aimed forty-five degrees off the ship's course.

"Instruments normal, pulling power. One...two...three posi-tive rates of climb. Radalt on."

"Roger, radalt on." Her copilot depressed the radar altimeter button.

"Your controls."

"I have the controls."

"You have the controls. Take her up to five hundred feet."

"Roger, coming up to five hundred."

"Fetternut, let's get the radar up."

"Bringing the radar right now, Boss."

Victoria began speaking with the aircraft controller on the ship.

"ATO ASTAC."

"Go ASTAC."

"We have a P8 approximately one hundred and forty miles to your northwest laying a buoy field. It sounds like they got a sniff, ma'am."

"Roger, we'll be heading that way. Do you have a frequency for us?"

The ASTAC passed her the UHF radio frequency that the P8 would be listening on. Victoria dialed in the frequency and made sure she was transmitting on the appropriate channel. She climbed up in altitude and began racing towards them. After getting closer, she made her call.

"Penguin 123, this is Cutlass 471 forty miles to your southeast, inbound for ASW."

Antisubmarine warfare, or ASW, was the bread and butter of her helicopter community and of the maritime aircraft known as the P8 Poseidon. While her helicopter had three on board and was limited in the number of sonobuoys and torpedoes that it could hold, the P8 had a crew of nine and could hold many more sonobuoys, torpedoes, and other equipment. It was also much faster and had a longer on-station time, both of which could prove crucial in prosecuting an enemy submarine.

"Cutlass, Penguin, we've got you. Stand by for our report." The naval flight officer on board the P8 passed information about the situation and enemy submarine they were tracking.

Victoria quickly copied down the coordinates on a pad of paper that was strapped to her knee.

"Copy all, Penguin. Our ETA is twenty mikes."

Two clicks on the radio confirmed that he'd heard her.

Victoria typed on her multipurpose display.

"Cutlass, *Ford* Control, come up our datalink."

"Roger."

Victoria was out of range of her own ship now, so she didn't bother telling them that she was switching. They made the adjustments to start having the aircraft carrier *Ford* begin controlling her. The datalink connection made, her helicopter immediately began filling with real-time data from all the other ships and aircraft in the link.

"Shit. The *Ford* is only ten miles away from that submarine track." She checked her fuel, altitude, and navigational data. They would be there soon. She began rattling off checklist items, to which her crew responded appropriately, getting ready for antisubmarine warfare operations.

The voice from the P8 said, "Cutlass, Penguin. We're going to pass you a lat-long. Can you dip there?"

"Affirm." The language was nonstandard, and whoever was speaking sounded junior. But as long as it got the job done, Victoria didn't care. She glanced at her display again and realized that there were hostile submarine symbols all over the place, each with friendly air tracks above them. Now she knew why she had launched. They were pairing off two friendly aircraft to each enemy submarine. The fact that the *Ford* was headed in this direction probably meant that they didn't expect this particular track to be here. She and this P-8 were probably the last ones to get an assignment. Yet based on the locations, it appeared to be the biggest threat.

A few minutes later, they were parked in a hover roughly one hundred feet above the ocean surface, lowering their multimillion-dollar dipping sonar into the water.

AWR1 Fetternut, her sensor operator in the back of the helicopter, said, "Okay, ma'am, we're ready to ping."

Victoria contacted the *Ford* controller and informed them of what they were doing, then she heard the high-pitched noise of the ping in her headset.

Her sensor operator said, "We've got good contact. Up Doppler, two thousand yards."

Victoria typed a series of commands into her display while relaying the information to the P8.

The P8 naval flight officer said, "Roger, Cutlass. Penguin will be coming in for weapons run."

Victoria's copilot said, "I've got Penguin in sight at two o'clock."

On the horizon, Victoria could see the large dark shape of the P-8 making a steep turn and then leveling off on a heading that would take it right next to the helicopter. Lessons about wingtip vortices fluttered through her mind.

"Gonna be a little close." She watched as a torpedo dropped from the P-8, and then the aircraft again banked sharply, turning away from her aircraft.

"There it goes. Good chute." From the rear of the helicopter, her sensor operator said, "Torpedo's in the water, up and running."

"Roger," said Victoria. She had switched up her comms to listen to one of the closer passive buoys' acoustic transmission. She could hear the high-pitched tones of the MK-50 lightweight torpedo as it searched for the Chinese submarine in the depths below.

Victoria watched the updates of the sonar track on her display screen. "Looks like they're turning and picking up speed."

Whether it was Chinese or not, it was probably a nuke as opposed to a diesel-electric boat, based on the speed. The contact was now going over thirty knots through the water—so fast that their current dipping position was now useless.

"Let's reel up the dome."

"Roger," AWR1 Fetternut said and began procedures to bring the dipping sonar back up into the helicopter.

She scanned the instruments, checking her gauges to make sure their fuel was at a healthy level and her engines performing normally. Her copilot was supposed to be monitoring those things, but it was always smart to double-check.

"Sounds like the torp's gone silent."

"Roger." She switched up her UHF to the channel they had been using to speak with the P-8. "Penguin, Cutlass, we're available for a reattack if you need us."

"Roger, stand by."

"Dipping sonar is secure, ready for forward flight."

"Coming forward," her copilot said as he inched the cyclic ahead. The airspeed ticked up and the crew felt a flutter as they got past translational lift and into forward flight.

"Cutlass, Penguin, come to zero-nine-zero and prepare for weapon drop."

"Zero-nine-zero, wilco."

Victoria ran her finger down her torpedo launching checklist, saying each step aloud, her free hand physically verifying that each switch, knob, and digital readout was in the correct position. "Checklist complete."

"Boss, the P-8 just pinged with that buoy closest the target and got a good hit. If we can get there soon, it'll be a good drop."

"My controls," Victoria said, taking the cyclic and collective in her hands.

"Roger, your controls," said her copilot.

"Cutlass, Penguin, come left zero-two-five."

"Zero-two-five." She banked the aircraft to the left until she saw her heading approach the magnetic compass heading of zero-two-five and leveled off.

"Stand by for weapon release on my mark. Ready...now, now, now."

With her right hand, she pressed the weapons release button and felt a shudder as the aircraft let go of a six-hundred-pound torpedo.

"Good chute. It's in the water," came the voice of her sensor operator.

A moment later, they could once again hear the pinging of the torpedo as it began searching for the enemy submarine.

"Sounds like it's acquired the target," Victoria said as the pinging grew faster.

Then came a crunching mechanical noise that she recognized from the first day of the war, near Guam.

"Hit! It's a hit!"

Victoria checked her position and then banked left to see if she could see the surface of the water where she expected the submarine to have been located. Sure enough, she saw a large area of whitewater and debris coming to the top of the ocean.

"Cutlass, Penguin, we have a detonation and noises of breakup."

Her crew inside the helicopter cheered over the internal communications system. Victoria felt slightly ill. That submarine had contained men with families, she thought to herself, looking down at the floating debris. Now it was twisted steel and oil and bits of flesh. But it wasn't the first time for her. And the sensation of guilt was duller than before.

Victoria readjusted her lip mike to her mouth. "Roger, Penguin. Our fuel state is one plus zero-zero. Going to see if *Ford* can take us."

"Roger. Bravo Zulu, Cutlass."

Soon she was in the holding pattern on the starboard side of the USS *Ford*. The aircraft carrier was recovering jets. Presumably ones that had just returned from attacking the Chinese fleet.

"Cutlass, Tower, expect another ten minutes in starboard-D."

"Roger, Tower."

Victoria was guiding her copilot to make sure they stayed in the right spot. Two fighters zoomed by overhead. F-35s. The first one broke left over the carrier, circling to land. The second kept on going for another beat, gaining separation, then followed the first.

As her helicopter's racetrack pattern neared the carrier once again, she saw a tall gray-haired man standing on the uppermost bridge wing. He wore a khaki uniform and gripped the railings as he watched her aircraft fly by.

She couldn't contain her smile as she realized who she was looking at. After all that had happened, she was finally seeing her father again, if only for a moment.

"Boss, are you listening up on the ASW freq still?"

She looked down at her radios and saw that she wasn't. She had switched to tower and turned off the other channel so she could hear better.

She adjusted her switches so that she was listening to both frequencies.

"...strong contact. Classified as a Chinese submarine now bearing three-zero-zero at five miles."

Victoria frowned. "Fetternut, who's talking? Five miles from what?"

"Two Romeos to our north."

Then she noticed the pair of black specks just above the northern horizon. The carrier had turned back into the wind to recover its jets and was heading to the northwest. Whereas before, they had been headed away from all other submarines, it appeared this one had just popped up much closer than the others.

"Five miles from what?"

"From *Ford*, I think..."

Victoria's heart beat faster. She turned towards the *Ford*. The last of the F-35s had just touched down on the flight deck. She could see her father on the bridge wing, still looking up at her helicopter as she made her closest point of approach. He knew it was her, she realized. That was why he'd come out here.

Then she saw the smoke on the horizon.

"...missile launch! Missile—"

Victoria followed the smoke trail from the area where the helicopters were located. It disappeared in the sun for a moment. Then the missile's smoke trail reappeared as it gained speed and approached the carrier, rocketing into the superstructure of the USS *Ford* and exploding in a haze of fire and shrapnel, and then her father was gone forever.

30

Day 29

Victoria walked out of the dark hangar, holding her thermos of tea and squinting in the bright Hawaii sunlight. From the flight deck, she watched as the USS *Farragut* sailors worked to fasten the lines to the pier at Pearl Harbor.

A whistle sounded over the 1MC. "Moored! Shift colors!" A pair of sailors near the ship's stern raised the American flag. Simultaneously, the American flag was lowered from the ship's mast. A modern US Navy Jack, with its thirteen red and white stripes, rattlesnake, and the motto "Don't Tread on Me," was raised on the bow.

"Morning, Boss." A delicate tone.

Victoria turned to see her helicopter detachment's maintenance officer, Spike, standing at the hangar's entrance.

"Good morning." Her voice was subdued.

She walked slowly towards the flight deck nets as her maintenance officer updated her on the plan of the day. The USS *Farragut* would be taking on fuel, food, and stores. Gunner's mates were already gathered pierside, ready to start replenishing the vertical launch system's empty missile cells. A part of her wondered what good that would do, considering the Chinese antiair technology. The ship would also undergo expedited repairs to the hull and engineering spaces, and any other areas that had been damaged by the Chinese antiship missile.

She said, "Have we started the phase maintenance?"

"Yes, ma'am. Senior got 'em started on the night shift. So far we're only missing two parts, which we should get today. I've told OPS that we will need to do rotor turns while in port, if we're here more than two days."

"We will be."

"Okay. Well, I'm trying to get as much done as possible so that when we get underway, we'll just have a quick maintenance flight and be good to go."

Victoria nodded, looking at the dozens of workers waiting on the pier. Two gangways were being set up forward. Some of the contractors were pointing at the hole in the hull where the missile had struck, shaking their heads, their eyes full of incredulity.

"There's going to be a liberty call, the XO told me. Probably won't be until tonight, but they're going to let everyone blow off some steam. Once they call liberty, I'm going to let the guys off in shifts. Everyone could use a break, but the maintenance still needs to get done. And honestly, there's less risk of any horseplay if we send them off in smaller groups."

Victoria said, "On-base liberty only, right?"

"Yes, ma'am. That's from PACFLEET. Nobody's allowed off base. No overnights. The guys will have to get drunk at the E-club."

She looked up at that. "Make sure we're being smart and looking out for each other. I know everyone needs to let off steam, but I don't want someone in jail or injured. This isn't just about some readiness score anymore. We need each and every one of our men. Somebody goes down, that hurts our ability to fight."

"Yes, Boss." Spike scribbled something on his clipboard and departed back into the hangar.

She walked to the other side of the flight deck and looked out over the marina. Across the water, the USS *Ford* towered over the pier it was tied up to. Cranes moved supplies and parts from shore to the flight deck. Most of the jets and helicopters had been stuffed in the hangar. Hundreds of repairmen worked feverishly to get the carrier back into shape. Scaffolding and tarps had been set up around the superstructure. A floating city under repair.

The whole harbor was under repair, Victoria realized. Dozens of other ships with welders and hammers and needle guns and cleaning, rearming, resupplying. C-5 and C-17 transport aircraft flew in overhead, bringing in more people and parts crucial to the endeavor. Commercial aircraft flew in the opposite direction, taking civilians back to the continental US.

Everyone knew an attack was coming. The scales had been tipped. While the US Navy had defeated the Chinese Northern Fleet at Midway, they had suffered heavy casualties. Multiple ships and aircraft had been lost, and the *Ford* was temporarily out of commission. The Southern Fleet had been spotted leaving the waters near Guam. Its transit time was a mystery, but everyone expected them to attack Pearl Harbor eventually.

Victoria's eyes kept straying back to the USS *Ford*. To the superstructure where her father had been standing when a Chinese missile had evaporated his body.

"Victoria, there you are." The ship's captain, Commander Boyle, was wearing his summer whites. "You and I have been called to PACFLEET headquarters." His eyes went to the *Ford* and then back to her, studying her face. The captain was quite aware of the magnitude of her loss. He was a good man, but she didn't like the attention.

Victoria cleared any remaining emotion from her mind. "Now, sir?"

"Afraid so. A car will pick us up on the pier. If you can change in the next two minutes, please do so. If not, just come as you are. I'll meet you at the quarterdeck."

Victoria checked her watch. "Will do, sir." She let her maintenance officer and senior chief know that she was departing the ship and then hurried to her stateroom.

Two minutes later, she was on the quarterdeck with Commander Boyle, double-checking that her shoulder boards were actually clipped into place on her uniform. One of her flight school roommates had forgotten to wear her shoulder boards when she'd checked into her fleet squadron. The first person to point this oversight out to her was her commanding officer. The young pilot's mistake had been immortalized by her fellow junior pilots, who had given her the call sign "Salty," because Navy chief uniforms didn't have shoulder boards, and chiefs were salty, or experienced, sailors.

Victoria followed the captain down the gangway, pausing to salute the flag, and then got in the waiting blue government sedan. During the drive, she said, "Any idea what this is about?"

"Either we're being debriefed or fired. I'd say it's fifty-fifty."

Victoria glanced at him. He looked like he was only partly serious. When they arrived at the PACFLEET headquarters, Commander Boyle was led in one direction and Victoria in another.

She was escorted into an office with four stars on the door and asked to sit in the waiting area. The secretary gave her a sympathetic look and offered her coffee.

Of course. That's why I'm here. The admiral must have known my father. A part of her resented being treated differently once again. Even now, following his death, in what should have been a private moment to grieve.

Victoria shook off the sentiment. She was being stupid. These people were just trying to be kind in paying their respects, and she needed to get over herself. Just say thank you and move on.

"The admiral will see you now, Commander."

"Thank you." Victoria stood and gave three quick knocks on the door. "Sir, Lieutenant Commander Manning..."

"Come in."

She entered the office and found herself shaking hands with a four-star admiral in summer whites, with two other officers standing next to him. One was a one-star admiral, the other an Army general. The four-star made introductions, but Victoria didn't recognize the names. She noticed that the one-star admiral wore the gold trident insignia of the Navy SEALs. She figured that the fact these men were here meant that the admiral was busy, and her visit would last only a few moments. *Just grit your teeth and get back to the boat, Victoria.*

The admiral said, "First, let me just say how sorry I am for the loss of your father, Commander. I spoke with him a few weeks ago—after your temporary *command* of the *Farragut*." The admiral said it as if the event was humorous. Maybe to him it was.

"Your father was a friend of mine, and he was enormously proud of his three children, but he had a special place in his heart for you, I think."

"Thank you, sir." She forced herself to continue breathing in a slow rhythm. She was still numb from the loss and just wanted this talk to be over.

"There will be a memorial service for the fallen tomorrow. At the waterfront memorial. It will be a short service, but it is important, even in such times as these, to remember our brothers and sisters in arms with dignity and respect."

"Yes, sir. Thank you, sir. I'll make sure to attend, assuming my ship is still in port." Victoria pressed her lips into a tight line, nodding respectfully.

The admiral and general exchanged an odd look. Had she said something wrong?

"You'll be in port, Commander. But you won't be with your ship."

"I'm sorry?"

The four-star said, "No, Miss Manning, it is I who am sorry. I'm sorry to ask you to take on this assignment in the wake of your father's passing. But I recognize talent when I see it, and this mission requires someone of both your skill set and your considerable ability."

Victoria frowned, looking among the faces of the flag officers.

"Please, have a seat." He gestured to the Army general. "General Schwartz here has just flown in from the East Coast of the US. He is now going to tell us how we're going to win the war."

* * *

Victoria thought that the memorial service was well done. Short and sweet. White wooden folding chairs on a green lawn. The attendees wore their dress uniforms and were almost all active-duty military from the ships in the harbor. A way for the sailors, marines, and airmen who had just come into port to say goodbye to their fallen comrades—before they were called out to battle once again.

Victoria sat with her air detachment from the *Farragut*, and the other members of the ship's crew. They had all noticed something different about her.

She had been promoted.

After General Schwartz had outlined the operation, the PACFLEET admiral had informed Victoria that she was to lead the air portion of the mission. The billet was deemed appropriate for an O-5. Victoria didn't complain, but she also felt funny about skipping her place in line. It would be at least a year before she was supposed to have been eligible for that promotion, and she wasn't sure what this would mean for her career. The Navy was notorious for its backwards HR system. She wouldn't be surprised if this "honor" came back to bite her someday during a command selection board, with someone on the panel penalizing her because the assignment didn't fit into the normal list. Or maybe now that she'd put on commander early, she would have to compete for assignments with men who'd been in rank longer and, as a result, had several more checks in the required boxes. There were all sorts of ridiculous land mines to watch out for in the military promotion system.

But she kept coming back to the same thought.

She didn't care.

Not anymore.

Her father was the one person she would have wanted to see her get any more promotions or accolades. Her father was the one she had wanted to someday witness her first change of command ceremony. Without him, it wasn't the same. As she looked around the rows of uniformed men and women and heard the first cracks of ceremonial rifle fire, she searched her soul for a reason to keep on going. Had her own ambition always been about her father?

She dipped her head, willing herself not to cry. Anger welled up inside her, rage at an unseen enemy for taking her father, for killing her shipmates. The anger felt good. It reminded her that it wasn't just ambition that drove her. Maybe she didn't care about rank or making command as much anymore, but Victoria still felt a very strong sense of duty. A need to serve a higher purpose. To defend her country and stand up for a freedom-loving society.

She felt the three stripes on her shoulder boards that signi-fied her recent promotion. She should be grateful as hell for this assignment. It was a chance to make a difference.

She looked at the men and women of her air detachment and the USS *Farragut* who sat in the chairs surrounding her. She had a duty to them, too. God had given her many gifts. Her skill as a naval aviator was as good as anyone's. Her ability to lead under pressure, she knew, was exceptional. And with those gifts came a responsibility to use them when called.

The chaplain leading the ceremony said a final blessing, and then the group was called to attention and dismissed.

Her men, knowing that she was leaving, came up to her after the dismissal.

"Sorry for your loss, ma'am."

"Yeah, sorry, Boss." One after another, they all paid their respects.

She nodded and thanked them, eyes moist, barely holding it together.

"So are you coming back to the ship at all, Boss?" They had all heard about her reassignment. They didn't know what she would be doing. That was top-secret compartmentalized infor-mation. But they knew she would no longer be with them, and they were disappointed as hell.

"Just to clean out my stateroom. They said someone else will be replacing me later today."

"They know who yet?"

"Sorry, I don't know."

The senior chief said, "Alright, leave the commander alone. She's got to get out of here." He shook her hand. "Best of luck, ma'am. It's been a privilege."

"Thank you, Senior. Same here."

Victoria walked on the lawn towards the parking lot when a familiar face made her smile.

Plug, her old maintenance officer, currently embarked on the USS *Ford*, stood in wrinkly summer whites and a cover that was slightly cocked on his head.

Plug said, "Holy shit-balls. *Boss*. What's up with *these*?" He pointed to her shoulders. "Er...ma'am?"

"It's a long story." She smiled.

"I got time. Wanna grab lunch?"

Victoria turned in the direction of the warship masts, then checked her watch.

"Come on, Boss...we all gotta eat."

"Alright, but I may have to cut out early."

"Nice." Plug turned to walk in the direction of the vans, but Victoria said, "Actually, I have a car waiting."

He whistled. "Moving on up in the world, I see. RHIP." *Rank has its privileges.*

"RHIR," she responded. *Rank has its responsibilities.*

"Touché, Boss."

Victoria's driver was a petty officer stationed on the base. He recommended eating at the Lanai at Mamala Bay, also known as Sam Choy's. It didn't disappoint.

There were no windows or walls in the dining area. Just a magnificent open-air room only feet away from the calm turquoise water of the Pacific. Decorative chairs with wooden pineapples carved into their backs. High ceilings with running fans. Polished wooden floors and walls, with tropical plants decorating the area. Palm trees sprouted up along a well-trimmed green lawn.

It was Hawaii life at its finest. It could almost make someone forget that a war was still going on.

"You hear the latest about Korea?" Plug asked.

"I read the newspaper this morning if that's what you're referring to." Reports were circulating that the North Koreans had relaunched poison gas attacks. The death toll in that country was now over two million. "It made me sick."

Plug, normally not one to be serious for more than a moment, sighed, looking out over the water. "My old roommate from flight school was stationed there."

Victoria didn't bother offering an "I'm sure they'll be okay." Because they probably wouldn't be.

They ordered iced teas and sandwiches, which came quickly. A smiling woman who looked to have native Hawaiian heritage served them and then left.

"How's life on the *Ford*?" she asked.

Plug said, "Life on a carrier's not bad."

"And the job?"

"Oh, it's been good. I mean, as long as you don't care about flying. Or need sleep. Or dignity." He paused. "Every day I wake up and I feel like the guy in the movie *Aliens*. You know, the one who's about to have one of the baby aliens crawl out of his chest? And I'm looking at my friends saying, 'Kill me. Kill me now.' But then it pops out and I wake up and go to my seventh meeting of the day and poop out my third PowerPoint brief of the day." He stuffed his mouth with a handful of fries, and said, "It's fucking great. But it's better when nobody's shooting at us."

Victoria sipped her iced tea and crunched ice between her teeth. "Sounds like you could use a change."

He said, "Boss, I know that I wasn't always the easiest to deal with...but if you have any pull, I will sacrifice my firstborn child to get off that damn carrier, or at least get back into one of the squadrons. I'm trying to work it with the HSM guys on board to let me fly. I think I'm wearing them down. But I've been doing *PowerPoint*, Boss. *PowerPoint*. Me. It's truly awful."

She gave a wry smile. "Any word when *Ford* will put out to sea again?"

Plug shrugged. "I've heard everything from a few days to a few months. That hit to the superstructure really screwed up a lot of systems." He realized what he was saying. "Sorry, Boss..."

"It's fine."

Neither said anything for a moment. Then Plug offered, "I met your dad. Everybody liked him. They respected him a lot. I'm really sorry."

She placed her glass down on the table. "Thank you."

Plug squirmed in his seat. "So, are you going to tell me how the promotion happened?"

"The Bureau of Personnel has been updating a lot of their processes. Now that we're in wartime, recruiting and retention needs are changing. One of the changes will be more promotions, faster. It needs approval by an O-7 or above, but I won't be the last. At least, that's what I was told."

"But why? I mean, why you? Sorry. That came out wrong."

Victoria chuckled. "No offense taken. They're removing me from *Farragut* and reassigning me to a special project."

Plug looked shocked. "What the hell does that mean?"

Victoria studied him. "Are all of your quals still current?"

"Sure."

"I need one more Romeo-qualified pilot, Plug. You may have found your ticket out of PowerPoint land after all."

31

Khingan Mountain HQ
China
Day 30

Jinshan sat quietly, listening to the after-action report on the battle near Midway. He could have General Chen executed for issuing the order. But doing so would give the impression that he hadn't been aware the attack was going to take place. That would draw attention to the fact that he had been in bed for treatments for four days and make him look weak.

Jinshan stared at General Chen, who refused to meet his gaze. Jinshan was once again reminded of the penalty for picking loyalty over competence.

Jinshan said quietly, "We have lost two carriers that we might have used when the Southern Fleet arrives. This is most disappointing."

Admiral Zhang, head of the PLA Navy, must have made a pact with General Chen. Otherwise, this never would have occurred. Now Admiral Zhang was trying to refocus the conversation. "The Jiaolong-class ships are invincible. We will still be able to take Hawaii with the Southern Fleet. We can direct many of the Northern Fleet's support ships to join them."

Jinshan waved off the comment in disgust. "The Americans have now seen the technology firsthand. They already are developing a plan to defeat it."

The admiral in charge of the PLA Navy said, "Nothing short of nuclear weapons will destroy it, Chairman Jinshan."

General Chen looked up, his eyes brightening. "And if they do that, the Russians will attack them with their ICBMs. Either way, we will be victorious."

Jinshan frowned. He looked at the head of the Ministry of State Security. "Show them."

The head of the MSS snapped his fingers and one of his underlings came over, connecting a computer to a monitor next to the conference table. The monitor began flipping through a series of reconnaissance images. Some were taken from submarines, others from drones.

The minister of state security said, "The Americans are preparing a defensive perimeter around the Hawaiian Islands. Our sources tell us that within a few days, they will begin deploying enormous minefields in the Pacific Ocean, in the areas between French Frigate Shoals and Johnston Atoll. These minefield perimeters will extend around the Hawaiian Islands. At both the French Frigate Shoals location and Johnston Atoll, the Americans are setting up these antennae."

The image showed very large metal antenna towers being constructed on sandy islands, small transport aircraft on runways in the background.

"They had been attempting to use Midway Island as one of their gateways, but apparently the distance was too great. Not enough mines."

Admiral Zhang said, "What is this? What gates?"

Jinshan said, "It seems that the Americans have identified a way to defeat the Jiaolong-class ship's technology. These antennae are part of their own directed-energy weapon."

The head of the MSS explained the American strategy of using a perimeter of mines and gateways to let friendly ships in and out.

General Chen said, "But...but..." He looked around the table, frantically searching for an answer. "Does this mean the Jiaolong is no longer useful?"

Jinshan said, "A week ago, General, you were telling us all that it was not important to our Pacific strategy. Now that we have lost two of our carriers to one American carrier in open sea combat, I see that you have changed your mind. A pity that you needed to see evidence for yourself."

After a moment of silence, General Chen said, "Chairman Jinshan, what would you have us do?"

This constant question was Jinshan's penalty for being in complete control. Even his generals couldn't think for themselves. This one in particular.

Jinshan said, "The Hawaiian Islands need a constant influx of commercial shipping to bring in food and supplies. The Americans plan to surround themselves with mines. Fine. Let them. But they must leave open a gateway to allow commercial shipping and their warships to pass. And we cannot let them control a gateway in and out of the island chain. We must take one or both of those gateway islands before their directed-energy weapons are operational."

One of the Central Committee members said, "How will we know the progress?"

The head of the MSS said, "We have an intelligence source. We will know before the Southern Fleet arrives."

When the meeting was over, Jinshan left and went into his private quarters, allowing the other military leaders in the room to ponder the details of this secretive operation. They needn't know that Lena Chou was inside the United States, and that she would confirm the American plans. And the head of the MSS would revel in keeping it from them. Jinshan knew that each of the men around the table was studying him, watching for the tiniest misstep. Hoping that his health would continue to decline so that they could steal his throne.

A part of him wondered if his efforts were justified. None of the fools at his leadership meeting were worthy of this undertaking. Only Lena was, he thought. Lena more than anyone else would be responsible for China winning the war. The Americans knew Jinshan's fleet was moving towards Hawaii. It would take them another ten days, perhaps, but the melee would come. The whole world knew there was to be a battle. The exact timing and the victor were the only questions. Within a few days, Lena would send him a message, telling him how to best attack Hawaii.

32

Hawaii

The aircraft and equipment had been priority-transported to Dillingham Airfield, on the northern side of Oahu. The military units that were part of Victoria's program had completely taken over the airfield, and roadblocks kept civilians out of camera range. They ate, slept, and trained in a series of trailers and old buildings at the foot of Oahu's majestic green mountains. Maintenance crews worked on the aircraft in the warm sun. The sound of waves crashing against the shore a few hundred yards away. On either end of the airstrip, Army SAM crews had set up their Patriot missile batteries, large rectangular box shapes sitting on the back of trucks, angled towards the sky.

It was day one of training, and Victoria took her seat in a classroom filled with helicopter pilots, aircrewmen, and members of the Navy's DEVGRU, also known as SEAL Team Six.

She knew most of the aviators by name. There were eight pilots, including her. Each was a top-rated pilot from the two helicopter squadrons embarked on the USS *Ford*. Four were from the Helicopter Sea Combat (HSC) squadrons and flew the MH-60S. The other four were from Victoria's Helicopter Maritime Strike (HSM) community and flew the MH-60R. The latter group included her and Plug. Choosing them from separate communities had been intentional, as they would have different roles in this mission. The aircrewmen were also the pick of the litter. A few of the pilots saw Victoria as they entered the classroom and gave her the standard "sorry for your loss" condolence. No doubt the entire Navy had heard of her father's passing.

Plug arrived last, as expected. She hoped that she hadn't made a mistake in recruiting him for this. She'd had to put in a word with the helicopter squadron CO, who was still adjusting to her newfound rank. But while Plug had many shortcomings, his skill as an aviator wasn't one of them. Even the skipper had agreed with that assessment.

The sixteen tier-one special operators from DEVGRU sat along one side of the room, the Navy aircrews on the other. Quiet conversations, all covering the same topic. What the hell were they doing here? Victoria was the only one who knew, and she kept her mouth shut.

The door to the trailer classroom opened, and General Schwartz, wearing green digital camouflage utilities, walked towards the front of the room, two civilians in tow.

"Ladies and gentlemen, good morning. I have good news and bad. The bad news is, the Chinese have a new technology embedded in one of their warships. This ship is the central unit in the largest modern armada ever to put to sea. And our intelligence reports say they're headed this way, to attack Hawaii."

The general looked around the room. "The good news...is that you all get to do something about that."

Between the general and the two intelligence officers he had with him, they covered all aspects of the mission. He introduced Victoria and the DEVGRU commander.

"Commander Manning will have tactical control of the mission until the assault team puts boots on deck. At that point, it's DEVGRU's show. We'll be bringing in some special equipment today that will be installed in the aircraft. Tonight we'll have a team-building mandatory-fun-ex for you at the local tiki bar. I'm buying. Training begins tomorrow at zero eight hundred. Does anyone have any questions? No? Then let me begin."

The general and the two civilian aides went over the strategy, which had been developed by some joint CIA-military team he kept calling SILVERSMITH. Whatever the hell that was. The basic idea was that the US was now developing a new type of electronic attack weapon. A directed-energy technology that would enable them to use both Johnston Atoll and the French Frigate Shoals island as gateways. These gates would allow friendly ships in and out of a giant perimeter of mines that would surround Hawaii.

The helicopters were needed because the vital final parts of the American technology were going to arrive late, brought in from labs in the United States. By the time that happened, they expected the Jiaolong and its fleet to be within range of Johnston Atoll. It would be a race for the Americans to reach Johnston Atoll and install the equipment before the Chinese could get there. The special forces troops would ensure that even if they met resistance, they could still succeed. Well, within reason.

When they finished describing the plan, Victoria looked around the room. Stunned silence. She understood why. The plan was audacious at best, a suicide mission at worst.

"Questions?"

One of the aviators said, "Why helicopters? Why not use a C-130 transport or something?"

General Schwartz looked at Victoria, then back at the pilot who had asked the question. "By the time the Jiaolong is in range, anything that's airborne may be shot down. We have a jamming technology, if you could call it that, that will allow your four aircraft to remain off their radar. But you'll be very low over the ocean. We went over aircraft capabilities, and this was our best option."

The pilot frowned and started to ask a follow-up question, but Victoria interjected. "That's all we will discuss on that topic." He caught her eye. While he didn't understand, he knew enough to shut up.

Plug spoke from the back of the classroom. "Sir, okay...let me get this straight. I think what you guys are saying is that this Jiaolong-class ship is like the Death Star. And you guys think you have a way to find the air vent with your special equipment, which may or may not work. And the air vent isn't really like the Death Star, it's more like an inverse radar cone or something. So we fly like...*forever*...over water with these ultra-tough special forces guys." He looked at the operator sitting next to him. "'Sup." Then he turned back to the general. "And they're going to install our new American secret weapon, which will neutralize the Chinese super-weapon. Am I mostly getting it right?"

General Schwartz blinked. "So, anyone else have any questions or comments?"

Plug's hand shot up again. Victoria shook her head.

"One more thing, sir. You did say that you had the tab when we go to the tiki bar tonight, correct?"

* * *

The mission planning and aircrew brief took the entirety of the morning. Lunch was brought to them in the classrooms, and the first training flight was scheduled for that afternoon.

Like a coach training his team for the Super Bowl, General Schwartz oversaw each evolution.

That afternoon, the pilots, aircrew, and special forces soldiers stood in a gaggle on the flight line. General Schwartz and one of the civilians he had with him were speaking to someone on the radio and checking their watches.

Victoria saw the maintenance chief waiting over by a push cart. Two computers waiting atop the cart. He gestured for her and Plug to come over while they were waiting.

The chief said, "Alright, ma'am, sir, it took us all night, but we installed the new equipment in place of the APS-153."

Plug said, "Wait, what?"

Victoria said, "It's part of the special equipment package. Our radar has been replaced by the electronic attack package General Schwartz mentioned. It'll use the same power source and console as the radar. That's pretty much why the Romeo helicopters are involved."

Plug said, "So they just take off the APS-153 and throw on some new gadget down there? Doesn't it need to go through like five years of testing first? Is it even safe for flight? Wait. So now I won't have radar?"

Victoria shot him a look. "Correct. If they remove the radar, we no longer have radar."

"Safe for flight in the literal sense, yes. By regulation, no. But this is a special circumstance. Relax, Plug, we can't use our radar anyway. We can't emit anything that might be detected."

The chief said, "Sir, the internal switches are all the same. The contractor guy said you're supposed to have it on the whole time you're over water. There he is."

The equipment expert who had installed the electronic

jamming equipment came over and explained to the four Romeo pilots how it worked.

When he was finished, Plug shrugged. "Okay." He looked at the chief. "Replace anything else?"

"No, sir."

The chief smiled. "Now if you could just sign the book here." Plug rolled his eyes and then signed the maintenance forms.

A few minutes later, General Schwartz squeezed off an air horn. "Clock's running. That's our simulated alert. Let's go!"

The aircrews and special forces men ran into the helicopters. Victoria and Plug flew together. Their hands raced through the start-up procedure, verbalizing it as they went. All four helicopters' engines began whining, rotors turning over the pavement. Within minutes, the four helicopters had taken off and flew low over the water in a tight formation.

Twenty miles out to sea, a US Navy supply ship was in position. The four helicopters arrived overhead, and the DEVGRU team began fast-roping from the cabins of the MH-60S Seahawks. Then the aircraft flew racetrack patterns while the SEALs conducted a practice assault of the ship. An hour later, they were back on the beach.

General Schwartz was waiting for them there. The helicopters conducted a hot refuel, their rotors still turning. Everyone took turns using the head during those few minutes. Victoria met with General Schwartz. He yelled into her ear over the sound of the rotors.

"It didn't go well. Our test radars could still see you. You'll need to fly lower. And they're making tweaks on the jamming device now. The engineers want you to make another run."

Victoria nodded and gave a thumbs-up, then got back in the aircraft. They flew the training mission three more times, switching to night vision goggles after sunset.

It was two a.m. by the time they finished the day's training.

Victoria's flight suit was drenched, her muscles cramping from more than ten hours in the air, much of it spent traveling at twenty-five feet above the surface of the water at the aircraft's maximum speed. Her eyes stung from sweat and oil.

The next day's training didn't begin until sunset. The practice boat had been moved farther out to sea, to simulate the longer ride. On the way, Plug asked, "Why are we practicing on a boat anyway?"

Victoria said, "Because we can't let anyone see what we're doing on land. The operator's job is pretty simple. Secure an area and get the tech expert to the right spot to install the final piece of equipment."

Plug looked at her like the explanation didn't make any sense, but he let it go. Victoria was grateful for that.

Each training mission became a little more challenging. They added more weight and equipment. Auxiliary fuel tanks full of fuel to give them better range. Hellfire missiles on all aircraft, and even rocket pods on the Sierras. On day three, they began training with each weapon fired from the helicopters. Hellfire missile shoots. Sniper training from the cabin of her aircraft. Every possible contingency was planned for. But as Victoria flew back during one of the flights, she looked over her notes.

Plug saw her with her lip light on, scribbling something on her kneeboard in the dark. "What's a matter?"

"We wouldn't have enough fuel."

"We'll have a couple of LCSs to get gas on, right?"

"Right." She wasn't sure if she sounded convincing or not.

The flying and training were nonstop. Every bit of nighttime was used for training, and they slept during the day. Their tier-one special operations team members weren't too happy with the way the Navy crews were performing at first. They kept saying things like, "Well, the SOAR guys do it like this...".

By day five, things had smoothed out. After the aircraft had shut down, Victoria walked with the DEVGRU commander towards General Schwartz's trailer. "I think your guys are getting the hang of it."

She nodded. "Yours too."

He laughed.

"Think this'll work?"

"I certainly hope so."

Inside the trailer, the general said, "Our radar experts and engineers are following your flight over water. They still aren't completely satisfied with the radar signature, but it's gotten much better. They'll make some final tweaks to the equipment overnight. Tomorrow you won't be doing any training."

Victoria said, "Why not?"

"Based on the latest position of the Chinese fleet, we need you to start on a twenty-four-hour alert. Be ready to go at any time now."

33

Chase arrived at the JSOC base to find most of the units had packed up and shipped out. He had been traveling back and forth between here and Eglin every other day for almost two weeks. It had been frustrating. He'd been shut out of many of the SILVERSMITH meetings that his brother, David, attended. They had a whole other level of secrecy that they were operating on now. They fed him bits and pieces of information, but all he wanted to hear was that it was time to go after Lena.

That day had finally arrived.

The only remaining unit was the SEAL team he had operated with. He met with them in one of the briefing rooms and asked for an update.

"The Rangers got sent to the West Coast. Delta left this morning. The other SEALs too. Intel says we've killed or captured just about all of the Chinese that were INCONUS. That what you're hearing?"

Chase said, "Almost all of them." Until now, Chase hadn't been able to tell them anything about Lena Chou.

The SEALs waited patiently. Attack dogs licking their chops. Chase brought in two men from the SILVERSMITH team, including the NSA signals intelligence expert. They explained the new mission requirement, and why it was so important. Chase noted that they left out his relationship with Lena Chou. He was thankful for that.

The NSA man said, "The Chinese SOF unit is known as the South Sword Team. They're the Chinese equivalent of naval special warfare and should be considered a top-tier unit. They're using state-of-the-art communications equipment and following good COMSEC procedures, so we've had trouble tracking them."

Chase said, "But we know where they are headed. We've identified the American whom Miss Chou is set to meet with. There is now a counterespionage team assigned to that individual twenty-four-seven."

The NSA man continued, "Based on communications intercepts, we believe they'll try to meet face-to-face at one of several locations. Once that happens, she'll have information that's vital to Chinese war plans, which she will then attempt to transmit back to Chinese HQ."

One of the SEALs said, "How long has she been in-country?"

"For over a week, we think."

"Why hasn't she met with this guy yet?"

The intelligence briefer said, "You ever try to infiltrate a foreign country under martial law, after an EMP strike, and travel a thousand miles without being detected, then meet with a highly placed spy inside one of the foreign military's most secure facilities? The highways aren't really an option. It takes a while."

"Well, when you put it like that..."

The SEAL team leader said, "What's our objective?"

Chase said, "The South Sword Team has the communications equipment. Based on the communications procedures needed to operate this equipment, Lena Chou will have to physically be with the South Sword Team when she transmits her newly acquired information back to China. The counterespionage team is going to make sure that Lena gets information *we* want her to send instead."

"Did they turn Lena's spy into a double agent?"

"No."

The SEAL team leader and senior enlisted looked at each other, frowning. "Then how the hell are you going to get her to send the information that you want her to send, instead of what she gets from the mole?"

"We're going to swap out the mole with one of ours. A lookalike who will feed Lena Chou bad information."

The SEAL team leader said, "So Lena has never met this person?"

Chase looked at the intelligence experts, then back at the SEALs. "That's what we believe."

A few of the SEALs laughed. "Wonderful." One of them swore.

Chase smiled. "Look, I know, fellas. You're thinking this is FUBAR. But operationally, this is our best play. There's no way to feed the mole bad intel or take him too early. Both of those scenarios could tip off Lena Chou or the Chinese handlers. The best way to do this is to take the mole right as they're about to meet with Lena and replace them with someone else. If Lena buys it, she brings back the false information and sends it to the Chinese. Then they act on it the way we want."

"What is it you want them to do?"

"I can't go into that."

The SEAL team leader said, "So where do we fit in?"

"If something goes wrong—"

"Which it will," the SEAL team leader said.

"—then you'll need to neutralize the South Sword Team before they can transmit."

The SEAL team leader said, "Well, at least now you're making sense."

* * *

Two hours later, they were flying east over the Appalachian Mountains in a pair of Chinooks. They landed at a prestaged landing zone near Gettysburg, Pennsylvania, just a short flight away from the Raven Rock Mountain Complex where the mole was located.

The SEALs were wearing civilian clothes now and packed into a group of four inconspicuous-looking pickup trucks that were waiting for them at the landing site. Well, they were about as inconspicuous as two dozen extremely hard-core-looking men traveling together can be. At least the heavy weaponry was hidden in the truck beds, Chase thought. The plan was for them to split up into groups of four and look like hunters as they searched for signs of the Chinese South Sword Team. It was a little risky. Special operations air support was minutes away, standing by for their call. And in order to remain covert, they had to accept risk.

Chase spoke with the SEAL team leader through the passenger window of one of the trucks. "I'll be going back and forth between you and the counterespionage team."

"Understood. We'll be scouting out a few of the areas the signals intel folks want us to explore."

"Be safe. Good luck."

The SEAL tipped his ball cap, and the vehicles drove off.

Chase drove to meet up with the counterespionage unit. They were holed up in a detached townhome ten minutes from the Raven Rock Mountain Complex. His brother, David, and Susan Collinsworth were both there waiting for him.

She looked nervous. "The mole is a civilian employee at the

Office of Naval Intelligence. A GS-15. Name is Edward Luntz."

For OPSEC reasons, this was the first time Chase had been given these details.

"How do we know it's him?"

"Intel from China allowed us to uncover his handler. The handler is now in our interrogation center at Eglin and provided information that led us to Luntz. We've been closely monitoring him since. Luntz's communications and activities have matched up to Lena Chou's assignment.

"Does Luntz know that we have his handler?"

David said, "There's no indication that he does. The handler was supposed to break off contact and go underground, to avoid Luntz getting found out. The last thing he did was give him a new list of dead drops and meeting locations near Raven Rock, which we now have."

They spent the next thirty minutes going over the possible meeting locations, and how they would take down Luntz.

"Our lookalike agent will be standing by to go meet with Lena. The agent has strict instructions on what to do and say. Then they'll make an excuse and leave, so as to limit the potential for saying the wrong thing and tipping Lena off."

Chase shook his head. "Look, you're the one with the field experience here, but this just seems..."

Susan said, "We know, Chase. There's a good chance that Lena will realize something is amiss. That's why you're here. You'll attempt to take her down if she flees. And she'll probably have backup from the South Sword Team. Your friends from SEAL Team Two will be there to assist you if things go..."

"Tits up?"

"Colorful. But yes, exactly."

Chase said, "So let's say she buys it. We get the lookalike agent to Lena, she hears what he has to say and transmits it back to China. How does that help us?"

David said, "General Schwartz has been working with an assault team on Hawaii. The whole point of this operation is to give them the best chance possible of defeating the Chinese fleet."

"An assault team? As in guys with guns? I may not have had much sea time, but I was still in the Navy long enough to know that's not how you win a sea battle. How the hell is an assault team going to take down the Chinese fleet?"

David's face was stern. "That information is compartmentalized from this op. We don't need to discuss it here."

Chase shot him a look.

His brother shrugged. "Sorry."

Chase could see that something was bothering Susan. "What is it?"

Susan said, "The Chinese fleet is moving faster than expected. They're only another few days from Hawaii. And they'll be in range of Johnston Atoll within twenty-four hours."

"Will we be ready?"

"I don't know. But Luntz knows about our defense plans. We believe that's the exact information Lena Chou is attempting to get. Control of the Pacific depends on this one decisive battle."

Chase saw something else was bothering his brother. "What aren't you telling me?"

David looked at the floor.

Susan said, "Your sister, Victoria, is leading the mission to attack the Chinese."

Chase's mouth dropped open, the air gone from his lungs.

Susan said, "We'll do a few dry runs with all of the players tonight."

Chase, regaining his composure, said, "When is the meeting with Lena supposed to be?"

"A few hours from now."

34

Lena Chou was driven by one of the South Sword soldiers. They rode in a sedan, traveling through winding mountain roads near the border of Maryland and Pennsylvania.

They parked in the underground garage of an apartment complex. The troops wore American winter clothing, their weapons hidden under the jackets. And they were never in teams of more than three.

Once in the apartment, Lena met with the old Chinese man who maintained the safe house. It was owned by one of his LLCs, and he was the only one who ever went there. He had been living in America for many years. He owned two car washes in the county. The MSS paid him in cash, and he laundered the money through those businesses. He wouldn't have had a business if not for that extra influx of cash. Times had been tough, and his English wasn't so good. He owed everything to his Chinese benefactors and was loyal to his birth country.

The man's children had all been put through college with those funds, and one of his sons ran the business now. Lately, the old Chinese man spent more of his time reading on his phone in the parks and public spaces within driving distance of the Raven Rock Mountain Complex.

Lena knew that it was too risky to have the old man meet with their agent. He wasn't trained for it. But he had taken many pictures of the potential meeting locations and observed the patterns of life. It was these descriptions that he passed on to Lena now.

When she was done listening, she went into the guest bedroom. Three of the soldiers were in there, including Lieutenant Ping, their commander.

"I have selected my location. I will need you to transmit the meeting time and place in one hour."

"Just give us the coded transmission, Miss Chou, and we will send the communication."

An hour later, the transmission was sent. As soon as it was, Lena said, "Tell your men to be ready to move. And give me the keys to your vehicle."

"Do you want us to go with you?"

"No. I will go alone."

She could tell he disapproved, but the young officer remained obediently quiet. She liked him, she realized. He reminded her of someone else. Chase Manning. A man she wished she had met in a different life.

"Have your men waiting in their vehicles. If our agent is compromised, I will signal you, and you will need to move quickly. But if that occurs, make sure you send at least one of your men back here to transmit what happened."

"And if things go well?"

"If the meeting goes smoothly, I will return within the hour and send the transmission myself. No one can leave this apartment before that happens, lest they give away the location of our transmitter."

"I understand."

Lena nodded approvingly. A few miles away, two teams of three were parked in a crowded Walmart parking lot, their presence hidden by tinted windows. A few miles in the other direction, more teams waited in two other safe houses. Remote cabins in heavily wooded areas. At their lieutenant's signal, they would converge on a dozen different locations within minutes, ready for combat. But for operational security, she had kept the exact location to herself, until now.

"I have set the meeting location at checkpoint four."

Lieutenant Ping nodded. "Good luck."

She drove out of the garage and down the street. She passed a police cruiser on her journey, which made her feel more secure. If the Americans knew where she was going, they would likely have kept local police away. *Or if the true professionals were handling it, they wouldn't have said a word.*

She parked her car on the town's quaint-looking main street and began walking along the sidewalk. She kept her cotton winter hat snug over her head, and a maroon scarf tight around her neck. A tight-fitting down winter jacket kept her warm. She spent twenty minutes conducting her surveillance detection route. An infinitesimally short period, but she didn't have the luxury of time.

For the first time in quite a while, Lena Chou felt nervous. Preparation had always been one of her strengths. Over the years, her importance to Jinshan had given her the ability to say no to operations that could get her caught by the FBI's counterintelligence division. It was her duty to say no. So meticulous planning had to be done before Lena was brought in.

But now all cards had to be played. Even she was expendable today.

Only two restaurants were still open, and they both looked almost empty. One had an outdoor seating area, covered with a black tarp. An outdoor heating lamp in the corner of the space.

Lena walked into the restaurant and a chime alerted the hostess. She requested the seat in the far corner of the outdoor space. From there she would be able to see everyone coming and going from the street. She could hop the three-foot-tall wrought-iron fence around the sitting area and make it to the alley around the corner in under five seconds. The alleyway opened into several egress options.

Lena sat down. The waitress brought her a water.

"I'd offer you a lemon, but we don't carry them anymore, what with the war and all."

"It's no problem at all," replied Lena. Polite, but not overly so. She didn't want to make conversation.

"The menu's limited too. I'm sorry. We've crossed out everything we don't have. Some people wonder why we're still open. But the owner keeps paying us. So we keep showing up. You know how it is." The waitress's voice was distant.

"I'll wait to order. I'm meeting someone. Thank you."

The waitress seemed to notice the way Lena looked for the first time. Asian. The waitress's eyes narrowed slightly. She frowned and left Lena to herself.

* * *

A few miles away, the mole drove out of the gate at the recently reestablished military base at Fort Ritchie, Maryland. He drove into town and parked in a drugstore parking lot one mile from the restaurant where Lena sat waiting, although his followers weren't aware of where she was.

Chase sat in the rear of a government-owned undercover vehicle, a Honda Odyssey, along with two CIA special operations group men. Behind their van was another, which held the FBI team.

"Luntz is on foot," came the voice in Chase's earpiece.

"Headed north, into town." The CIA and FBI counterintel folks were working hand-in-hand on this. Each had brought in a very small team, and they were working surprisingly well together. But this was the high-stakes moment. Game time.

"We have eyes on her yet?"

"Negative."

"Van One, start canvassing the town."

"On the go." Chase's vehicle accelerated down the street, turning through the town. Everyone's eyes looking through the tinted windows. Two more civilian vehicles were doing the same thing. The routes had been preplanned to cover every possible meeting location and still ensure that the vehicles didn't hit any of the spots more than once. Now they had to figure out which one she was at.

Then Chase saw her, sitting at a restaurant patio, winter clothing on.

Heart beating through his chest, a surge of adrenaline hitting him. Her eyes were dark, and alluring.

He said, "Got her. Restaurant number two. Corner table." Their van casually continued on down the street, then turned and made its way back behind the FBI's minivan.

In the FBI's minivan sat a special agent of similar build and facial features to Luntz. The lookalike. The doppelganger who would swap places with Luntz and go to meet with Lena. He was an immensely talented officer of the CIA's clandestine services, and one that Susan made sure Lena had never met. The man had been studying everything about Luntz, interviewing his handler for hours on end. Practicing exactly what to say and how to say it to Lena, when the meet took place.

The operations team had even identified Luntz's exact clothing and ordered a matching outfit. Now that they had Lena's location, they could bag him and send in their lookalike.

"What color jacket is Luntz wearing?" asked the lookalike from the back seat. "The gray one or the beige?"

"The beige."

The lookalike swore and reached into a bag to switch jackets. The agent had guessed wrong. "He usually wears the gray."

"Who cares about the jacket? Just pick one."

There were a million things that could still go wrong.

Chase's pulse kicked it up another notch.

"Okay, let's take him," came the voice of the FBI SAC in the now-lead van. The vans began driving through the streets.

"Local police vehicle just pulled up near him."

Chase looked at the other operatives in his van. They shrugged as they readied their weapons.

* * *

Luntz walked at a steady pace, keeping his scan going as he made his way towards the meeting spot, just like his handler had trained him to do. It was a cold day, and very few people were outside.

A police cruiser parked along the curb twenty yards ahead of him. The cruiser's lights weren't on, and only one officer got out. No one else was in the vehicle. The policeman seemed more interested in a vacant car that was parked in a metered spot.

Luntz was well trained for a recruited agent. He kept his cool, not wanting to do anything to draw attention to himself. The policeman didn't appear to be a threat, so he kept walking.

It wasn't until he was a few feet away that the man wearing the police uniform turned towards him.

"Excuse me, sir, you live around here? You don't know whose vehicle this is, do you?"

Luntz slowed slightly but kept walking. "Sure don't."

The sound of vehicles speeding down the street alerted both

men, and Luntz jerked his neck in their direction, away from the cop.

The two vans peeled right and came to an abrupt stop on either side of the police cruiser, locking both men in. The side and passenger doors from the vans opened, and a total of six men wearing black tactical gear leapt onto the curb, their weapons drawn. The addition of the police cruiser made for an awkward takedown, adding a few more steps than the team would have liked.

Their weapons trained on Luntz, the FBI agents all yelled some version of "FBI, show us your hands!" The lookalike Luntz stood behind them, wearing the same clothes.

Chase saw Luntz's eyes go wide.

The local cop took out his weapon, holding it aimed towards the ground, trying to figure out what was going on. The dynamic was dangerous and unplanned. Six armed men approaching. The local police officer was standing right next to the mole, giving Luntz an extra few seconds to appraise the situation. Luntz moved a step closer to the cop.

Chase noticed that Luntz's eyes remained fixed on his doppelganger.

"Officer, please holster your weapon and step aside."

The police officer didn't holster his weapon but did change his posture so that it was aimed towards Luntz.

"Hands, please!"

Luntz's face reminded Chase of a suicide bomber he had witnessed in Iraq. A man who knew he was near his end.

"Watch him! Watch him!"

The FBI men stepped closer, their firearms still trained on Luntz. They had been instructed to refrain from discharging their weapons, lest any gunfire alert Lena Chou.

Luntz seemed to sense their apprehension. His hands never went up. They remained in his coat pocket.

Which popped in a puff of cloth and smoke.

A single muffled gunshot rang out, and the FBI agents dove on Luntz, wrestling him into submission.

"Oh shit, are you alright?" The local cop was looking towards the FBI minivan. "Hey, this guy is hurt..."

Chase turned to see the lookalike agent now on the ground, leaning back on the rear tire and whimpering. At first Chase couldn't see what was wrong. Then the agent frantically clutched at his neck. From between his fingers, dark crimson blood spewed forth in spurts, covering his beige jacket.

* * *

Lena checked her watch. *Five minutes overdue.* She hadn't worked with this man Luntz before, but his tardiness, combined with the sound she'd heard a few minutes ago, put her on the edge of her limit. On any other assignment, she would have been gone, she told herself. She opened her purse to check the radio transmitter she was using to signal the South Sword Team.

When she'd heard the noise, she'd reminded herself that she was in the countryside. It might have been a hunter, shooting a deer on his property. It wasn't like her to be optimistic. But the need for this information was so great, she had to give him every chance.

But if Luntz had been killed or captured, was waiting here another few minutes worth anything? With each passing second, the probability that Lena's life—no, not her life, her capacity to fight for Jinshan—was in jeopardy.

Footsteps on the sidewalk behind her. She craned her neck to see a man in a hooded sweatshirt headed her way. He was alone. Six feet tall, a lean, athletic build. Hands in the pockets of his sweatshirt. Wearing sunglasses, his gaze toward the ground. He carried himself with a military swagger.

It almost reminded her of Chase Manning...

A hollow feeling formed in the pit of her stomach. The queasiness was returning. What the hell was wrong with her? She never felt this way.

Sitting inside the fence of the restaurant's outdoor patio, she was separated from the man, but turned away so that he wouldn't see her face. She looked at him in the reflection of her water glass, ready to move if he turned towards her. He kept walking past her and then...opened the door of the restaurant. The door chime going off again. The waitress smiling and pointing towards the patio.

Lena placed her hand in her coat pocket, feeling the cold metal of her pistol grip. They wouldn't do it this way, she told herself. They would send a team. This was something different.

Chase Manning removed his hood and looked her in the eye. "May I join you?"

Her mind raced through a dozen scenarios. None of them had a desirable ending.

Her pulse racing, she said, "Be my guest."

Chase sat down at the table. His face was stone, but his eyes were filled with emotion.

"How long do we have?" she asked.

Chase just shrugged. "Are you going to run?"

"Why just you?"

"Because I didn't want anyone to hurt you. And if we did it any other way, they would have."

Did that mean that he cared for her? After everything she had said and done? She silently admonished herself. Of course he didn't. He couldn't possibly love a monster.

She noticed that they both kept one hand hidden from view. There. That was her proof. He would shoot her if he had to. *Only to protect himself. Only if there was no other way*, said the look in his eyes.

"What's the plan?" she said.

"You agree to come with me quietly, without signaling your men."

"You know I can't agree to that. And you'll eventually kill them."

"You could order them to surrender."

"You know better, Chase." Lena gave a soft smile. "You wouldn't obey that order. Neither would they."

Chase smiled. "Maybe."

She held her chin up. "This must be pretty important for you to go to all this trouble."

"I wouldn't know."

"Don't you? You don't know what information I came to get?"

"No."

"Hawaii? Johnston Atoll? Your country is developing a counter to our Jiaolong-class ship's new technology. Tell me, is it ready? That's all I want to know."

"Lena, put your gun on the table."

A minivan pulled up to the curb down the street. Then another, right behind it.

"Looks like your team is getting nervous. Don't they have faith in you?"

Lena heard the chime of her cell phone. Cellular service was not available in the US yet, but this phone had been specially calibrated by the MSS. The receiver had finished uploading all of the data from Luntz's transmitter. She smiled, realizing that he must have been in one of the minivans. They probably didn't even realize that they had just delivered to her what she had come to take. Luntz was never going to sit down and speak with her. He would just walk by, and his transmitter would do the rest. She just needed to read his face to make sure he wasn't under duress. But this was going to have to do.

Chase said, "Let's resolve this as peacefully as possible. Lena, I really don't want you to get hurt."

She felt invigorated, knowing something that he didn't. Her eyes glowed with realization. She could still win.

She stood.

Chase stood, removing his pistol. "Lena. *Please.*"

The waitress screamed. It took all of Chase's discipline not to take his eyes off Lena, the gun still aimed at her chest.

"Hey!" An angry male voice, coming from the restaurant's kitchen. Then the distinct sound of a pump-action shotgun sending a round into the chamber. Even Chase's years of experience and training couldn't fight the human instinct of preservation of life.

His head turned towards the sound. Only for a split second. But it was all Lena needed.

Her hand rose from her purse and she shoved a Taser into the flesh near Chase's collarbone. He convulsed, and Lena let go of the device, letting it clatter on the floor. The restaurant owner with the shotgun called out, but she had already hopped the small iron fence and made her way to the sidewalk. As she walked, Lena reached into her purse and thumbed her radio transmitter.

* * *

Susan was livid. "He went *alone*? Why the hell did Chase go in alone?"

David sat on the couch of a nearby safe house that was operating as the command center for this op. He was new to this type of clandestine work but was still pretty sure that this was not how things were meant to go.

"There's a team a block away ready to...stand by..."

Susan practically screamed into the radio. "What is going on?"

"Man down at restaurant number two. Subject is on foot. Just headed into the alleyway west of the restaurant."

Susan was furious. "Notify local law enforcement and SEAL Team Two. Tell them what to look for. And make sure they know that there's a Chinese SOF unit nearby that might try to assist her. God help us, this is a clusterfuck."

* * *

Lena had entered the building adjacent to the restaurant via a fire escape and unlatched second-story window. She could hear the squeal of tires and rush of engines as government vehicles approached the entrance of the restaurant. She shut the window, blocking out the sound of running footsteps on the pavement below.

The townhouse she was in was a residence, and she could hear people speaking on the floor below. She walked into the carpeted hallway and crept down the stairs. An elderly woman sat on the couch in front of a TV, mouth gaping as she saw Lena coming down the stairs.

"Martha, there must be ten men out there. They got guns and everything. Honey, I think it's the FBI! Must be a murder or something. Maybe it's them Chinese?"

The elderly woman who was gaping at Lena looked like she was about to scream, so Lena put a bullet in her forehead.

"Martha, what was that?" The elderly man came in from the kitchen and Lena fired a single shot into his chest. He collapsed to the floor, writhing in pain. Lena walked over to him and fired another shot down into his left eye.

The home had street access from the front and rear. The old man had been looking out his kitchen window, to the street that ran by the restaurant. It would only be a moment before some of the FBI agents ran through the door. She began walking to the opposite side of the house, to the back street, where she expected to find her South Sword support team coming to her rescue. Her internal clock told her it had been approximately one minute since she had tased Chase.

A sedan pulled up ten feet in front of the home, three Chinese men inside, each scanning the streets. Lena was about to open the door when a wave of nausea hit her. Overcome, she leaned over and retched behind the door for a full five seconds, then spat a few times and wiped her mouth with her sleeve.

What is wrong with me? She looked back at the two corpses on the floor. Images of others that she had killed over the past few months flashed through her mind. Especially the teenage girl. The Chinese president's daughter, standing on the penthouse outdoor terrace. That was it. That was the one that had changed her. She used to get a rush when she killed. A kick of endorphins similar to sex. It was something that she could never tell anyone about, but she knew it existed in her. But that had faded. Seeing these corpses here—two innocent civilians—was it *guilt* that had made her sick? Lena wanted to scream. She hated feeling weak.

Instead she turned back to the street, looking out the window, seeing the Chinese soldiers sitting in the sedan through the thin curtain. Lena gritted her teeth and pushed the door open, making her way out to the waiting car.

* * *

Chase was helped up by one of the CIA special operations group men. His collarbone stung, and he felt dizzy and tingly.

"I thought you said you could take her?" asked one of the FBI agents.

"Homeboy here pointed a shotgun at me."

The cook had been disarmed and was now explaining his story to the local police officer, who had been called to the scene.

"Are we following her?"

"Yes."

Two pickup trucks pulled up on the street outside. Chase recognized some of the passengers as members of SEAL Team Two. Everyone began leaving the restaurant, heading back out to the vehicles on the street.

One of the CIA men said, "You hear that?"

Chase frowned. "Hear what?"

The guy looked at Chase funny, then pointed at his ear.

"Damn. No. I think my earpiece got fried when she tased me."

One of the men snorted. "Collinsworth says we have eyes on a suspected Chinese vehicle. They're headed west to…"

The man jerked to the side, and then fell to the ground, the snap of a bullet whizzing by Chase's head and then a distant crack echoing through the street. Chase ducked and ran for cover as all the men on the street scattered to their vehicles. Two blocks away, the yellow flashes of gunfire appeared from two darkened windows of a residential building.

The cabin door of the nearest SEAL pickup truck opened, and Chase dove in. It accelerated and peeled around the corner just as he shut his door.

"Contact one block east," came the voice of the driver. He drove up on the empty sidewalk and brought the truck to a halt. "Spotter said there were gunshots coming from that second-story window." Chase could see a green attached home with two second-story windows opened, a white shade flapping in the wind.

"More gunfire coming from the south side of town, hitting Delta squad."

One of the SEALs in the back seat handed Chase a helmet and flipped on the comms. Chase snapped the chinstrap and could immediately hear the chatter from the SEALs and on-scene commander.

Susan's voice came through in a frantic tone. "Air support is on the way. Maintain pursuit. But whatever you do, we do not want her killed. Don't move in on her until I say so. Our best way to salvage this is to—"

Chase saw a flash of yellow from the open window across the street and then a spiderweb of cracked glass on the windscreen.

The driver slammed on the gas and turned down the street. Gunfire erupted from several of the windows, firing into Chase's truck.

The SEAL in the passenger seat was firing through the moonroof while another fired from the left rear window, laying down covering fire as the pickup truck raced through what must have been set up as an ambush alleyway.

Susan's voice came over Chase's headset. "White pickup. Take your next left."

She was directing Chase's vehicle from overhead drone footage. The pickup swerved left onto the next street, and more gunfire rained down on the vehicle. Pops on the metal and shattered glass. The SEAL in the passenger seat let out a curse and a howl of pain. Chase grabbed an M4 from the man on his left and began firing towards the Chinese out of the rear right window. The buildings and flashes of gunfire blurring together as they sped through the streets.

"Coming up. Two more blocks. You'll see a parking garage."

The gunfire had ceased.

"I recommend you park there by the streetlights and proceed on foot."

"Fuck that," replied the driver. He pulled right up to the townhome.

"Team Bravo, you guys will have air support in two minutes. Team Charlie will be to you in one. You can wait—"

Susan's voice. "Negative. Go in now. Don't kill the woman, for God's sake, but don't let her transmit, either. We don't know what she'll send."

The driver was checking on the SEAL in the passenger seat, who had taken two rounds, one in the arm and one in the shoulder. "Go. I'm good."

The driver hesitated, then nodded and got out of the vehicle. Chase and the other SEAL followed. Weapons trained forward.

"I'll breach."

"Copy."

The driver fixed an explosive charge to the front door and ignited it while all three men took cover to the side. After the explosion, they ran through the front door and began clearing rooms. Chase was the third man in but entered just as a Chinese soldier headed down the stairs with a rifle aimed his way.

Chase fired two rounds, both into the man's chest, and he dropped, falling down the stairs.

The other two SEALs paused, realizing that if one had come from upstairs, the others were likely there as well. Chase let the driver lead the way. At the top of the stairs, he chucked a flash-bang around the corner and down the hallway.

It burst, and Chase could hear the ringing in his ears as they raced forward and down the hallway. More gunfire. One of the SEALs was hit.

Someone screamed something in Mandarin.

Another burst of gunfire rang out.

Then Chase found himself through the entrance of one of

the second-story rooms, staring at her. Lena stood next to a black electronic device that reminded him of a small TV satellite dish. It rested on a nightstand table next to an open window and was angled upward towards the horizon. A dead Chinese soldier lay on the floor at her feet. Next to Chase, one of the SEALs aimed a rifle at her head. Lena held a black 9mm pistol in her hand, but it was aimed toward the floor.

Chase looked at the SEAL. His knuckles were white. The man's face was flushed. He had just witnessed two members of his team get shot. The one in the corridor might be dead.

Chase needed to defuse the situation. He stepped forward, placing his weapon on the floor. He held his hands out, palms facing the ground. "Put down the gun, Lena."

He half expected her to raise it to her own head. But she surprised him and quickly placed it on the table. There was a mix of emotion in her eyes. She looked tired, too, which he didn't think he'd ever seen in her before.

Chase stepped closer to her. She stared at him as they grew close. He removed a zip tie from his pocket and held it up, saying, "It's over now, Lena. I need to do this."

She nodded, holding her arms behind her back.

He could hear helicopters overhead now. Out the window, a half dozen vehicles filled with support team members parked in the street. Chase should have felt relieved, but he didn't. Something didn't fit. He couldn't understand Lena's transformation. She was a warrior. Why would she give up?

Chase fastened the zip tie and then began to march her out of the room when the satellite dish machine began making noises. A series of beeps and vibrations, and then the machine went quiet. On the digital display, a series of Chinese characters appeared.

She had sent her transmission.

Lena leaned in close to him. "Now it's over."

35

Chinese aircraft carrier Liaoning

Admiral Song toured the hangar deck of his aircraft carrier. He liked to walk about the ship now and then. It was good to let the men know that he might spot-check their work at any time. This improved quality.

"Admiral!"

An aide was running through the hangar, waiving his hand. They had a no-radio policy now that the carrier group was getting closer to the American islands, and messengers were being used to communicate among the higher-ranking officers.

The admiral and his entourage stopped next to a J-15 fighter jet as the messenger reached them.

"Sir, from the ship's communications room. A priority message from Beijing."

The admiral opened the folder and removed the printed message. He waved over his chief of staff to read over his shoulder. The admiral squinted at the faded print. He had admonished the supply officer for not planning to bring enough ink for the trip. They were now stretching out every ink cartridge to the last drop. This resulted in the admiral's increasingly blurred reading and slow loss of sanity.

His chief of staff beat him to the crucial part of the message, cursing under his breath as he read.

The admiral saw the passage.

AMERICAN MILITARY IS DEVELOPING DEFENSIVE WEAPONRY INTENDED TO NEUTRALIZE JIAOLONG-CLASS WARSHIP ON JOHNSTON ATOLL AND FRENCH FRIGATE SHOALS. MINEFIELDS WILL BE DEPLOYED SURROUNDING THESE ISLANDS AND HAWAIIAN ISLAND CHAIN WITHIN NEXT 24 HOURS. THE AMERICAN WEAPON SYSTEM AT JOHNSTON ATOLL IS NOT YET OPERATIONAL BUT MAY BECOME OPERATIONAL WITHIN NEXT 24-48 HOURS. LIAONING CARRIER BATTLE GROUP SHALL IMMEDIATELY PROCEED TOWARD JOHN-STON ATOLL WITH THE INTENT OF ATTACK AND OCCU-PATION. UPON COMPLETION LIAONING CARRIER BATTLE GROUP SHALL ADJUST COURSE TO TAKE STATION WITHIN STRIKE RANGE OF HAWAII. EXPECT TO PROCEED WITH ATTACK OF HAWAII ONCE ON STATION.

The admiral looked up. "Tell the navigator and the captain to meet us in the combat operations center."

A few moments later, the admiral stood over a digital chart table that had been adjusted to show Johnston Atoll and Hawaii.

"The minefields between Johnston Atoll and French Frigate Shoals will be enormous. Hundreds of miles apart." He furrowed his brow.

"And hundreds of miles west of Pearl Harbor."

"How many additional hours will the course change add to our track towards Hawaii?"

"Only two to three hours, Admiral. But we could just change the location where we launch the strike on Hawaii."

"Hawaii is our real target. We cannot lose sight of that. But we now have a serious obstacle. We must increase our speed and ensure that the Americans are not able to set up their new weapon there."

"Yes, sir."

"How much longer until we are in strike range of Hawaii?"

"Approximately eight hours until we are in range with our fighters. Our land-attack cruise missiles will be in range several hours after that."

"We will hold off our attack until both are in range in order to maximize the effectiveness."

"Yes, sir."

"Make the change. Send out the orders to our ships in company."

"Yes, Admiral."

Within an hour, all seventy-four ships in the fleet had adjusted their headings.

36

Victoria awoke to the sound of doors slamming shut, vehicle engines starting up, and boots hitting the pavement outside her trailer barracks. She went to the door and opened it. One of the DEVGRU men was in full tactical gear, throwing a bag into the back of a jeep.

"What's happened?"

"We've been moved up. Meeting in ten minutes on the flight line, ma'am."

Moved up? Victoria checked her watch. Zero one thirty. As always, Victoria was meticulously prepared. She'd filled her Camelbak before going to bed and laid out her clothing and gear. She threw on her flight suit and gargled some mouthwash while tying her boots. She was out the door in sixty seconds, helmet bag in hand, boots crunching on the gravel as she made her way to the flight line.

She could see dim green and red lights flickering over different parts of the helicopters. The flashlights of maintenance men and aircrews doing last minute checks. One of the green lights hopped down from the tail section of her MH-60R and headed her way.

"Morning, Boss."

"Plug. You been out here long?"

"Just a few minutes. Schwartz is in the OPS tent, but he's supposed to be here any moment. The SEALs are all ready to go."

"Are the aircrews?"

"Yes, ma'am."

Plug seemed more serious than normal. He was focused. It was game time, she realized.

"The bird is ready?"

"Good to go."

The four helicopters were parked twenty yards away from each other, lined up in a row. Auxiliary power carts and maintenance men were positioned in front of each aircraft. Ordnancemen had just finished their preflight weapons checks. A tense silence hung in the air. The other pilots and aircrews now stood in a group next to the special operations men, directly in front of the helicopters. Whispers and nervous laughter. Triple checks of gear and plans.

Plug asked one of the other pilots, "What time is sunrise?"

"Late. After zero seven. We'll be on goggles until we reach our target."

Plug nodded.

A golf cart drove from the OPS tent to the gathering on the flight line. The general's aide indicated for Victoria and the DEVGRU commander to get in. They were driven to the OPS tent and led into a room with a large paper chart spread out over a central table. Lining the edge of the tent were computers and communications equipment. Several men wearing headphones frantically spoke and typed, funneling information to the group.

General Schwartz saw them enter. He said, "The Chinese fleet was spotted by one of our Triton drones an hour ago.

Before it was shot down, we were able to intercept communications between the Chinese aircraft carrier and the Jiaolong-class ship." The general paused and looked up. "They changed course and now are headed straight towards Johnston Atoll. Our intelligence tells us that we can expect an attack on Johnston Atoll at any time over the next few hours, with an attack on Hawaii following that."

Victoria was eager. "We can launch anytime."

"It's time to tell the team what our plan really is," General Schwartz said.

Victoria and the DEVGRU commander nodded in agreement.

A few minutes later, General Schwartz spoke to the aircrews and special operations team in front of the waiting helicopters. The group was quiet, standing in the dark on the flight line. The sound of waves on the distant Hawaiian shoreline.

General Schwartz said, "Men, for the past week you've been training to land at Johnston Atoll. Well, there's been a change of plans. Your mission will be very similar to the training we've done. But you aren't flying to Johnston Atoll."

Stunned silence. Someone rolled out a cart and shined a red flashlight on it. It was filled with large white cylinders. Victoria recognized them as signal underwater sound (SUS) buoys.

"Each aircrew needs to have two of these on their aircraft."

Then the general and some of the civilian staff explained the change in the mission. Victoria and the DEVGRU commander were already aware. They had been sworn to secrecy until now.

At last Victoria said, "There's one more thing. With this change, we may not have enough fuel to make it back to a landing spot." She looked over the crews. "Anyone have a problem with that?"

No one spoke.

"General, we're ready."

Thirty minutes later, the four helicopters taxied to the runway and took off. They flew south over the Pacific, taking turns refueling on a pair of littoral combat ships. Then they continued on, the red sun rising in the east, and the Chinese fleet ahead of them.

37

Admiral Song watched the battle unfold from his bridge, several stories above the bustling flight deck. He wasn't thrilled about the night operations. His carriers weren't as well versed in night ops as their American counterparts. But they would manage. Below him, the J-15 jets were being positioned for launch, missiles and fuel tanks filling them to capacity.

He held up night vision binoculars, looking out over the ocean. As far as the eye could see, the masts of Chinese warships peppered the horizon. The radars on each ship searched the sky for any sign of trouble, the ships communicating with each other in short-range encrypted bursts of data as they sailed north towards Hawaii. The ASW drone dirigibles led the way, their sonar searching the strike group's path for any American submarines.

But no submarines had interfered with their journey. The Americans feared and respected the dirigibles now. They knew better than to waste their billion-dollar weapons and hundreds of lives on a fool's errand.

"We are ready to launch, Admiral."

"Any further word from Beijing?"

"No, Admiral."

They had spent the last few hours transiting east of their original course so that they could pass as close to Johnston Atoll as possible. They would capture the island, and with it whatever defensive mechanism the Americans were building there, which could supposedly render the Jiaolong technology less lethal. He was more worried about the minefields that the Americans were laying in the surrounding waters. His minesweepers were positioned toward the front of his fleet, but their transit speed was much too fast for them to be effective. The intelligence Chinese headquarters had sent was gold. They needed to act on it quickly.

"Then you may launch now, Captain."

The admiral's command was relayed around the fleet. Soon the carrier's jets were lighting off their afterburners and shooting up the ski ramp on the bow. The jets circled overhead in stacks for a few minutes until enough of them had gathered. Then they headed north in two separate squadrons.

Two junior officers sat behind computer terminals on the forward part of the admiral's bridge. They typed to their fellow staffers in the combat operations center below decks. These officers were here to relay to the admiral all the information the warfighters were seeing.

One of them now turned and said, "Admiral, we have inbound hostile air contacts! Over fifty headed towards the strike group from Hawaii."

"Classification?" the admiral asked.

"Unknown, sir."

"Are they in range of our air defense system?"

"They will be shortly, sir."

"Very well. Keep me informed."

Admiral Song nodded. He was confident, but not overly so. He looked through his night vision binoculars at the Jiaolong-class ship a few miles off the starboard side. During each encounter with the Americans, she had performed beautifully. With luck, she would again.

Several squadrons of US Air Force B-52s and B-1Bs had taken off in rapid succession. Another squadron of F-22s was already flying combat air patrol overhead.

Flying in command of one of the B-1s was Major Chuck "Hightower" Mason. He had flown his B-1 from Guam during the first attack on the Jiaolong, a few weeks ago. From his aircraft, he had launched nearly a dozen antiship missiles. But each of his missiles had been vaporized by this new directed-energy weapon the Chinese had. They had also shot down many of the American aircraft.

It had been humbling.

Even more humbling was accepting the orders to fly his aircraft from Guam to Hawaii, in anticipation of the American surrender there. But US commanders had evacuated all of its flyable aircraft before the Chinese destroyed them. At the time, the major had felt angry as hell about leaving Guam. But dozens of those aircraft were now flying this mission. *Live to fight another day.*

"Here we go. Just got the prep command," came the voice of the weapons systems officer in the rear of the aircraft.

"Bomb bay doors coming open."

They went through the sequence of commands to fire the weapons and then waited for the final signal from their flight lead.

Moments later, the sky was filled with streaking miniature air-launched decoys (MALD). The gray missiles traveled at hundreds of knots, flying towards the Chinese fleet.

Major Mason looked out his window. Below them was the US aircraft carrier *Ford*. In the darkness, he could see the afterburners of their jets taking off from the flight deck.

"They fixed that thing quick."

"Not sure if they fixed it or just put enough duct tape on the flight deck to let her launch jets."

"That where the Growlers are launching from?"

"They already launched. They'll be doing the jamming for the MALDs."

* * *

Admiral Song frowned. "What do you mean there are *five hundred* air contacts? That number is preposterous."

"Sir, that's what the air defense officer is saying."

"That is impossible."

"The air defense officer says that the..."

The officer had stopped midsentence and was holding his headset to his ear.

Admiral Song snorted. "What? Finish your sentence."

"Sir, there are now over *one thousand* inbound air tracks."

Admiral Song went pale. He looked out to his starboard side. The Jiaolong technology was about to be tested. Its artificial intelligence computers and rapid processing power should theoretically be able to shoot down that many contacts. But there were many nodes in the network. All that information would be flowing through the many ships in the battlegroup. The higher the number of air contacts, the more complex the problem. If...

"Sir..." The young officer looked scared now. "Sir, the air defense officer says that there are now over one thousand, five hundred inbound air tracks. The first wave is within range of the Jiaolong system. He has commenced firing."

Admiral Song shook his head. What was this trickery? The

Americans didn't have the capability to fire so many missiles at once. The admiral looked back out at the metallic monoliths fore and aft of the Jiaolong ship. He imagined the invisible beams of energy shooting upward toward the sky.

Relax. It will work, he told himself.

"Sir, the air defense officer has told me to inform you that—"

The admiral's head snapped to the port side as the yellow flame and white smoke of missiles began firing upward from the destroyer next to his aircraft carrier, illuminating the night sky. Then other streaks of bright flame and smoke came from the other ships in company, each one shooting into the air, arcing into the distance.

The admiral smiled. "The cruise missiles have begun firing."

"No, sir. I apologize. The air defense commander has begun firing our surface-to-air missiles. He says that the Jiaolong system is oversaturated with air tracks, and he is not sure if they are destroying..."

The admiral didn't wait for the officer to finish. He rose from his seat and practically ran towards the ladderway. His instincts told him that something was drastically wrong. He headed to the combat operations center to see for himself.

38

Victoria watched in awe as numerous bright green missile ignitions momentarily bloomed out her night vision goggles. Fired from ships over a dozen miles away, the missiles streaked upward, passing thousands of feet overhead, traveling in the direction she'd come.

Plug whispered into his lip microphone. "Jesus. Would you look at that."

As they flew closer, masts rose like spires throughout the horizon. Then the full silhouettes of countless Chinese warships appeared, backlit by the intermittent missile launches. The warships sat menacingly on the water, like graveyard wraiths, moving slowly through a hellish lightning storm. Every few seconds, more bright glows bloomed in their goggles as additional missiles were launched.

Plug said, "Right into the lion's den..." He had the forward-looking infrared (FLIR) camera aimed at the nearest ships. Frigates, by the look of them, now only a few miles away.

"No kidding." The hair on the back of Victoria's neck began to rise.

"The entire fleet is all bunched up by the look of it. Why are all of their ships so close together?"

"It's the way their new air defense system works. Instead of spreading out and separating the targets, they keep them packed in close to the high-value-unit. That way the Jiaolong's energy weapon can play zone defense for their entire fleet."

The flight of aircraft was now entering the forest of enemy warships, weaving in and out of the Chinese fleet, trying to keep them all far enough away that they might be confused for friendlies. Victoria knew they were bound to be seen any moment. But the Chinese had helicopters flying around as well. If the American aircraft weren't showing up on radar, most Chinese lookouts would just report the contacts and move on. With any luck, the controllers would assume that the American aircraft were Chinese helicopters. After all, no one would be stupid enough to do this...

Victoria said, "At least we know the jamming is working. No one's firing at us yet."

Plug said, "Or vaporizing us with a laser. If I have a pick, I choose that one."

"I don't think that's how it would work, but okay." She wiped sweat from her eyes. Her body ached from the hours of flying they'd already done, including a refueling stop on a pair of littoral combat ships. Flying close formation was challenging. Flying it for over six hours, on night vision goggles, only twenty-five feet above the waves, was excruciating. The concentration and discipline it took was monumental. Plug and Victoria took turns at the controls, switching every hour. Now he was flying again, and she was sucking back water from the thick Camelbak straw at her shoulder.

Victoria looked down at the digital map displayed on the center console. It was being fed information via a secure datalink, specially installed for this mission. Overhead, one of the Air Force's ultrasecret space-based reconnaissance assets had just sent updated locations of the Chinese fleet. The resolution of the imagery was so good that even her helicopter was visible. Military supercomputers on Hawaii processed the visual information and cross-referenced it with electronic signals intelligence, updating Victoria on her target's location, along with information tags next to every ship in the Chinese fleet. All displayed in front of her to help her make decisions. It had been part of her training over the past week. This allowed her to get passive navigation and targeting data without alerting the enemy to her position, like she would have if she had turned on her radar.

"Five minutes until target. Signal the other aircraft."

"Roger."

In the back of the aircraft, her aircrewman signaled the helicopter next to them with an infrared flashlight.

"Plug, see if you can get us down another five feet or so."

The four aircraft tightened up the formation and flew lower to the water. The waves were a good six feet, with occasional whitewater splashing upward. The ocean was a blur of dark green in her night vision goggles. The two MH-60S helicopters both had high-mounted winglets, carrying rocket pods and AGM-114 Hellfire missiles. The two MH-60R helicopters, carrying the weight of the custom electronic attack device mounted under the nose, carried only a left-hand extended pylon of Hellfire.

"Come a little right, Plug. Try to stay away from—"

"I am. But if I get farther from one destroyer, I get closer to another."

The feeling was surreal. The four US Navy helicopters were now flying within the Chinese fleet's surface screen. Snaking their way in between the Chinese warships. They were now flying at one hundred and fifty knots, which seemed incredibly fast at this low altitude.

The closest Chinese warship thus far had been two thousand yards away. Which certainly placed their aircraft within range of its heavier antiaircraft weapons. But anyone who had spotted them had to be incredibly confused. Their low altitude and close proximity meant that surface-ship watch standers actually had to look down to see them. Most of the Chinese sailors were busy looking at radar and digital readouts. They were launching missiles, after all. The attack would come from above.

The helicopter assault plan was so audacious, so unexpected, Victoria was beginning to think they might get all the way to their destination without taking fire. They only needed a few more minutes.

"Contact three o'clock level."

"*Break left*." Plug used the external UHF radio for this transmission. The jig was up now, so radio silence was pointless.

Victoria felt the helicopter bank sharply left and held her breath at the thought of the tight formation colliding in the night. They didn't. But a stream of yellow tracer fire emanated from one of the Chinese ships to their right.

Then they were beyond it, and out of range of the Chinese guns. Victoria said, "One minute to target. There it is."

Ahead of them were two behemoth ships, both captured on the FLIR camera and displayed on the monitor in front of Plug. The nearest looked like a Frankenstein mashup of a commercial supertanker and a *San Antonio*–class amphibious ship. But the metallic spires fore and aft went up much higher, she realized. Elevated flight deck platforms jutted out from each side of the hull. Four of them altogether. One was servicing a giant dirigible aircraft. These were the killer ASW drones she had heard so much about, the ones that were wreaking havoc on the US submarine fleet.

This was the Jiaolong-class ship.

Behind it by at least a mile was the Chinese aircraft carrier, the *Liaoning*, its curved ski ramp forward on the flight deck. No jets were launching or recovering at the moment, but she did see a small helicopter just above the horizon. That would be the SAR aircraft. Which meant that they were most likely conducting flight operations. God help her if a Chinese fighter got them in their sights. She realized how silly the thought was. There must have been thousands of surface-to-air missiles surrounding them. What did it matter how they got shot down?

"How much time?" Plug's voice was strained. He was now turning the formation of aircraft so low to the water that the rotor disk was only feet from the wavetops. The ocean's surface was easier to see. The eastern horizon was brightening on the goggles, giving them more light. Dawn was coming within the hour, and when it did, her helicopters would no longer have one of their chief cloaks.

Victoria looked at the timer in the top left corner of the datalink digital display. "Thirty seconds until the attack time."

"Roger. And what's our ETA?"

"Just over that."

"Nice. Well, if we live, I'm sure the SEAL Team Six guys will complain that we were a few seconds off, but I'm rather impressed. That's got to be an above-average grade for this flight."

"Let's start slowing it down."

"Roger. Bringing the speed back."

Plug pulled back on the stick and lowered the collective power lever. Their airspeed began to bleed off from one hundred and fifty knots.

One forty.

The profile of the Jiaolong-class ship grew in front of them. Now they could see Chinese sailors on the aft bridge wing, pointing at them. But no gunfire yet. They were in for one hell of a surprise.

One twenty-five knots. Fifteen seconds.

Advanced precision kill weapon system rockets began firing from the MH-60S helicopters' cylindrical launchers. Skinny white rockets were guided into the ship, targeting the bridge and the two antiaircraft guns.

One hundred knots. Ten seconds.

"I'm going to circle the ship and keep them on our right side," said Plug.

"Roger." Victoria was craning her neck to get a visual on the other aircraft in the formation. Everything looked good. They were loosening up the formation as they slowed, and the Sierras, which housed the majority of the special operations team, were now separated from the Romeos by a good three rotor diameters.

"Here it comes," said Victoria. She was looking out the cockpit window. "Let's hope they got the coordinates right."

Suddenly more surface-to-air missiles began firing from the Chinese fleet, upward into the sky, along with the tracers of anti-aircraft guns. All over the horizon, white trails of smoke shot up and then began streaking off to the north. There must have been fifty separate lines of tracer fire, all aiming up at the sky in a brilliant fireworks display, attempting to defend against the American attack.

* * *

Admiral Song was red-faced, spittle flying from his mouth, his arms flailing wildly as he screamed at his air defense officer.

The air defense officer tried to explain, "The Jiaolong system was overwhelmed with inbound air contacts, sir. We fired at some of them, and our computers told us that there was a better than ninety-five percent chance that those tracks were destroyed. But..."

"But what?"

"But then the tracks reappeared..."

That only made the admiral more incensed. He looked at the screen. There were still almost one thousand inbound American air contacts, now perilously close. Many of them were classified as fighters and bomber aircraft. But many more were thought to be enemy missiles. Cruise missiles headed towards his fleet.

The air defense officer had admittedly done the right thing. Once he saw that the Jiaolong air defense system was not working properly, he had begun to use the conventional systems. Thus, the surface-to-air missiles had begun launching from the Chinese fleet.

One of the junior air defense officers looked at his display, saying, "This still doesn't make sense. Some of the air contacts are just disappearing, and some are..."

"Are what?"

"They appear to be multiplying, sir. Where there was one, now there are twelve or more."

"What is the time until impact?"

"Sir, the first wave of our surface-to-air missiles should be reaching their targets any moment now."

* * *

One hundred miles to the north, three hundred cruise missiles and a dozen American fighters were putting a new spin on an age-old warfighting tactic: the feint. Together with the F-18G Growlers, the Air Force's MALD-N and MALD-X decoy cruise missiles were confusing the Chinese air-defense systems in several ways. Some of the decoys had electronic packages installed that made it look like they were in locations nearly ten miles from their actual position.

Other decoy cruise missiles, along with the Growlers, used jamming to "hide" some of the inbound missiles. Others created ghost images: fake radar signatures that made it appear as if there were multiple contacts when in reality, there was only one. But which one was real? That was the problem the Chinese were having as they decided which tracks to target.

The B-2 Spirits, the giant black wing-shaped stealth bombers, also launched a third type of cruise missile. The technology behind these cruise missiles had derived from projects like the Perdix program, out of the Pentagon's Strategic Capabilities Office.

These Perdix cruise missiles were quite large, and they themselves housed twenty other small drones. After fifty miles of flight, as part of their preprogrammed mission, the larger cruise missiles opened up a bay door and out dropped the drones. The mini-drones transformed shape, their wings expanding, and began heading towards the Chinese fleet, their small engines and antennae designed to simulate a normal American subsonic cruise missile.

The effect on the Chinese was a multiplication of air tracks. Hundreds of decoy drones, swarming towards the Chinese battlegroup on a preplanned flight path. These swarms of miniature decoys were fully autonomous yet communicated with each other to update their flight path and profile as they closed in on their target.

From the initial wave of one hundred or so American aircraft was born a deceptive wave of nearly two thousand inbound missiles, decoys, and faux radar signatures. It was nearly impossible for the Chinese to separate fact from fiction.

As the Chinese surface-to-air missiles reached these

inbound American weapons, the American missiles began to take losses. First by the dozens, then by the hundreds. As some of the MALD missiles and the F-18G Growlers took hits, the number of American missiles headed towards the Chinese fleet fell greatly as the faux tracks were no longer being projected.

While the Chinese fleet had been forced to use a great portion of its surface-to-air missile inventory, now the number of inbound American missiles was much more manageable for Admiral Song and his air defense team. Below the oversaturation point once again, the Chinese could use the Jiaolong technology, completely confident in the results they would achieve.

"Jiaolong air defense is coming back up, sir. We will begin shifting over any moment."

Admiral Song nodded at the air defense team. "Good. Much better."

He should be hearing from the commander of the strike fighters they had just sent toward Hawaii. And his strike commander must resume launching their cruise missiles. This American attack had slowed them down. The fighters would be running out of fuel and must proceed with their attack. Still, these were only minor delays.

Admiral Song watched the number of inbound missile tracks start to dwindle on the digital display in the combat operations center. He let out a breath. Now he could go back up to the bridge and return to his periodic updates.

"Sir, we have an alert message from the bridge."

"What is it?"

"They say that the Jiaolong ship is being attacked."

The admiral frowned. Had one of the cruise missiles gotten through? If they had, it seemed unlikely that it could have pinpointed the high-value unit so precisely.

"What is the nature of the attack?"

"Sir...it appears that...the Americans have sent an assault team to raid the ship."

The admiral didn't reply for a moment. They were hundreds of miles away from the nearest American ship or land base, and there were nearly one hundred Chinese warships surrounding them, each with its own high-tech air defense radar.

His mouth hung open in confusion and disbelief. Yet the hairs on the back of his neck began to rise.

* * *

Victoria flew in a slow circle around the Jiaolong-class ship. She stayed at fifty feet while the other Romeo flew one hundred feet above them, on the opposite side. The two MH-60 Sierra helicopters, after expending their rockets and destroying the dirigible that had been resting on the starboard aft flight deck, had positioned themselves right over the two forward side-mounted flight deck platforms. The DEVGRU SEALs fast-roped onto the platforms within seconds and raced down onto the ship's main deck.

The assault teams had been training for this mission for over a week now, and while their intelligence had been light on details, they had planned out every possible contingency.

Victoria felt and heard the pop of a .50-caliber sniper rifle from her own helicopter's rear cabin. One of the SEAL snipers was there, providing cover for his fellow operators below. Another pop. She could feel the burst of the large-caliber weapon as it went off, even under her helmet.

Victoria looked down at the ship as they circled. She watched the quick, methodical movements of DEVGRU assault teams moving from section to section of the modular compartments. There were three separate teams, each headed for different targets on the ship. Two explosive experts per team, for redundancy.

"Time check."

"They have two more minutes."

She looked out at the aircraft carrier. This was the most dangerous part. They were flying very low and close to the Jiao-long-class ship. The aircraft carrier was a few miles away, but surely the Chinese sailors aboard the *Liaoning* would realize what was happening when they saw four American helicopters circling the ship off their starboard beam. The Chinese on nearby ships would have seen the rockets slam into the bridge and antiaircraft weapon. The Jiaolong would have sent out a distress signal. They might have seen the American assault team fast-roping onto the deck, perhaps witnessing gunfire and explosions, if they were using binoculars or magnification on their external cameras.

But would they be able to do anything about it?

The American mission planners had calculated that the Jiaolong-class ship was so critical to the success of the Chinese fleet, they would not order their antiaircraft weapons to fire at the American helicopters while they were close to the vessel, as they would be too afraid of damaging the Jiaolong technology. So, Victoria and the others kept *damn* close to the ship. But the Chinese wouldn't just sit on their thumbs.

Plug said, "Contact nine o'clock. Level. Factor. That Chinese helicopter is headed over here. Shit. Another one just took off from the carrier and is turning this way."

"Both aircraft in sight."

The SEAL team commander's voice came over the radio. "Magnum One, mission complete, ready for extraction."

Victoria gave clicks of her UHF trigger switch in reply.

The MH-60 Sierra helicopters, which had been circling the other Romeo one hundred feet below Victoria's holding pattern, now repositioned themselves onto the flight decks. The assault teams were sprinting up the steps and piling into the helicopter cabins. They were almost ready...

"Hey, Boss, the sniper wants you to get him a shot at one of those helicopters headed this way."

She realized what he was trying to do. The sniper was on her side, and it would be easier if she was flying. Victoria said, "Roger, I have the controls."

"You have the controls."

She took the stick and turned sharply to the left. She looked first off to her left side to make sure she had all three friendly helicopters in sight. One was orbiting the Jiaolong ship low and slow. The other two were still on the flight decks, taking the special operations team into their cabins.

"Those helicopters are pretty far away," Plug said, looking at the two Chinese helicopters that were now bearing down on them.

"Yes, they are." But they were closing fast.

The aircrewman said, "He says to just keep the bearing straight."

Victoria checked her fuel and then quickly looked away. The numbers made her want to puke. They were going to be out of fuel or get shot down here in a few minutes. What the hell, they would go out in style.

She yanked back on the cyclic with her right hand and lowered the collective power lever with her left. The nose of her helicopter pitched up, and they slowed rapidly. The aircraft started shaking, a ferocious rattle that grew worse as she lifted in power and pulled them into a hover one hundred and fifty feet over the water. This was going to destroy her fuel consumption rate. But as she leveled off and smoothed out...it would give the sniper a good shot.

The sniper didn't wait for her permission.

Crack. Crack.

Crack. Crack.

The closest Chinese helicopter was about a quarter mile away. If Victoria had been closer, she would have seen that the Chinese pilots had both been killed by .50-caliber bullets. The nose of the Chinese aircraft pitched down and it flew itself into the water. The second helicopter was a few hundred yards behind the first. It circled the downed aircraft when her door gunner began firing his own .50-caliber. This one was a GAU-16 machine gun. Hundreds of rounds fired at the remaining Chinese helicopter, tracers tearing through the cockpit and airframe. Victoria watched out her window as the Chinese aircraft began yawing rapidly out of control. One of the .50-caliber sniper rounds had torn through the tail rotor control line. It was in the water within seconds.

"Magnum one, three and four are off deck, outbound heading zero-four-five."

Victoria nosed over her aircraft to pick up speed and began following the two Sierras. The other Romeo helicopter formed up on her left wing as she dropped to twenty-five feet of altitude.

"Magnum one, the SEAL commander wants to confirm that you are clear of the ship."

"Affirm."

"Detonating."

On board the Jiaolong-class ship, three separate explosive charges detonated simultaneously. Two were located at the base of the radar towers. The giant metallic monolith structures collapsed under their own weight in a haze of gray smoke and fire.

The third explosion was near the ship's main fuel tank. The explosive used had been specially chosen to ignite the hundreds of thousands of gallons of fuel on board.

The resulting explosion was catastrophic. The fireball rose

over five hundred feet into the air, sending containers and metallic fragments in all directions. The shockwave from the explosion cracked some of the glass windows on the aircraft carrier one mile away.

The Jiaolong had been destroyed.

* * *

David and Chase Manning sat in forward seating of the CIA's Gulfstream aircraft as it flew towards Eglin Air Force Base. Lena was under guard, handcuffed and sitting in the rear of the cabin.

Susan was reading over reports, out of earshot of the two brothers.

From his seat, Chase could see Lena's face. She wore a look of satisfaction. Of someone who knew that their sacrifice was a worthy one.

Chase shook his head as he whispered to his brother, "She did what she came here to do."

David turned to look back at Lena. She had turned to look out the window. "No, she didn't," he whispered. They hadn't been flying long, and this was the first real chance the brothers had to speak in private.

Chase said, "What are you talking about?"

"She came here to send information back to Jinshan."

"Right."

David said, "Information that was crucial to their war effort."

"Yeah. Exactly. And she transmitted it out to them."

Susan let out a yelp of delight from the front of the cabin. The brothers turned towards her. She waved them over.

Chase and David left their seats and went to sit next to her. Other than Lena and the guards in the rear, the plane was empty, but Susan still spoke in hushed tones.

"General Schwartz just sent word. The Jiaolong-class ship has been sunk."

Chase's head spun. He looked at Susan and David. "What happened?"

David ignored him. "Any word on the assault team?"

"No. We won't know about that for a while, I think. The battle is still in progress."

David said, "What course did they take?"

Susan gave him a knowing grin. "They shifted east. The Chinese fleet will be passing within sight of the Johnston Atoll."

Chase shook his head. "I don't understand. I thought this black hole weapon we were developing wasn't ready yet?"

David clasped his hands together, speaking rapidly. "That puts them right at..."

Susan nodded. "*Exactly.*"

Chase said, "Could somebody tell me what the hell you two are talking about?"

David said, "Can I tell him?"

Susan looked at her watch. She paused in thought and then nodded. "Sure."

David turned to his brother. "When we met to go over ways to counter the Chinese Jiaolong technology, we got an idea—"

Susan said, "David got an idea. A beautiful, brilliant idea."

"There never was an American technology being developed on Johnston Atoll."

Chase said, "What are you talking about?"

David said, "As part of a deception plan, this information was put out to the Chinese. Susan's network of Chinese agents put lots of information out. Some true, some not true. But the whopper was about the American plan to defend Hawaii. At first, our scientists thought we might have a way to counter the Jiaolong air defense by developing our own directed-energy weapon. That's the black hole system you heard us talking about. It was this plan that the Chinese mole, Luntz, was briefed on at Raven Rock."

Chase said, "And you're saying that wasn't true?"

"After a few days of working on it, we realized that even under the best-case scenario, a weapons system like that was years away from development. We never would have had it up in the time that it took the Chinese to bring the Jiaolong warship from Guam to Hawaii. But we *did* have some new jamming equipment that could cloak a small group of aircraft from Chinese radar. We mounted this jamming equipment on a pair of Navy helicopters and designed an air assault on the Jiaolong. We came up with a plan to overwhelm the Chinese while this air assault was going on. It worked. And now the Jiaolong has been sunk..."

"So you guys were briefing all the military and intelligence leaders at Raven Rock with a bullshit plan about this black hole system?"

"We had to. We didn't know Luntz was the mole until recently. We only knew that Lena was headed to the US to meet with *a* mole, and that the mole was most likely at Raven Rock. It took us a while to narrow down the list of suspects, and we couldn't risk that the mole would find out we knew about him. Once we knew Lena was coming here, we saw an additional opportunity. She's one of the few that Jinshan really trusts, right? So if we're going to deceive Jinshan, we have to deceive her. We have to make her think that she's sending good information back to Jinshan. That's why we needed to keep you and everyone but a select few on the counterespionage team members in the dark on the real plan."

Chase was starting to understand. "You were feeding Luntz bad information. You were telling him that this black hole system was going to be operational. You basically had a backup in case your lookalike agent didn't...wait a minute. *Why the hell did you need to swap Luntz with a lookalike agent?* If you were already feeding him bad information, why not just let him pass that on to Lena?"

Susan said, "It would have been too risky. We couldn't be certain that Luntz didn't know we were on to him. If he or Lena suspected that he was being misled, then they would no longer trust the information. We were pretty confident that our deception was working on Luntz, but we didn't want to take the chance."

Chase was floored. "That could have gone so many different ways. What if...?"

Susan said, "It didn't go as expected. We didn't expect you to go in there, for example."

"So what information got transmitted?"

"Luntz's original transmission."

"Was that intentional?"

"It wasn't our first choice, no. But it appears our deception worked. It corroborated the story that some of our captured Chinese spies at Eglin were sending back to Beijing. And the Chinese bit. Luntz must have sent Lena the information that the minefields were being laid, and that the Johnston Atoll project was still not operational. Lena then must have transmitted the message, because their fleet changed course over the past several hours. They maneuvered where we wanted them to be. And this allowed us to attack their precious new ship."

Chase leaned back in the leather seat of the jet cabin. "Holy shit. You did it."

David smiled. "Not quite yet. But we took a big step."

Chase glanced at the back of the aircraft. Lena was looking at him again. She saw that Chase's expression had changed. And then slowly, so did hers. Concern on her face now. Then horror, as she realized what Chase's look of triumph must have meant.

She was an amazing talent, Chase had to admit. She could read him like a book.

Chase turned back to his brother, frowning. "I still don't understand something. You could have sent the helicopter assault team in like that no matter where the Chinese fleet was sailing. I mean...from any direction. But Lena's message transmission..."

David nodded. "When we saw what the Jiaolong technology was capable of at Guam, we knew that we would have one shot to defeat their fleet. Now that they know how we destroyed the Jiaolong, they won't make that mistake again. They will be able to make more of those ships. It's replaceable. But the entire Southern Fleet...now that is not replaceable. If they knew that we could defeat the Jiaolong-class ship, they wouldn't risk blue ocean combat against our submarines. But they didn't expect their Southern Fleet to be exposed without the Jiaolong."

Chase frowned. "What are you saying?"

"When Lena sent that transmission, she gave the Chinese a reason to direct their fleet over a certain stretch of ocean, near Johnston Atoll. It would still take them towards Hawaii, but it would move them through an area that we wanted them to transit through."

"But why?"

Susan was smiling. "Your brother is a genius, Chase."

David reddened. "It wasn't all my idea," he said. "One of the things we learned about the new Chinese ASW capability was that it didn't do as well in detecting submarines that were bottomed. And our plan really does use a lot of mines. Just not the way we described."

Chase said, "I still don't understand."

David said, "Brother, they've sailed right into our trap."

* * *

"Magnum one, two and three are forming up on your right side."

"One," Plug said into his helmet's lip microphone. Victoria had handed him the controls again, and together they were doing their best to navigate through the maze of hostile Chinese warships.

"I'm taking off my goggles."

"Roger, me too," said Plug. The sun would be up over the horizon any moment now, which meant the Chinese ships could see them clearly. They had only been flying for a few minutes after the Jiaolong explosion, but she was honestly surprised they had survived this long. Victoria expected surface-to-air missiles or antiaircraft gunfire to end their lives any second now. She only had one remaining part of her mission.

"Is the buoy ready?"

"Yes, ma'am."

"Send it! And signal the others to do the same!"

Inside each of the helicopters, an aircrewman threw a heavy white cylinder out the open cabin door. The SUS buoys hit the surface of the ocean and were activated upon contact with the seawater. Each of the buoys exploded a few seconds later, emitting a distinctive-sounding noise.

The noises were detected by US Navy submariners in sonar rooms scattered throughout the shallow ocean floor that surrounded Johnston Atoll.

It was time for the hunt to begin.

* * *

USS Columbia

"There's the signal, Captain."

Commander Wallace said, "Conn, get us off the bottom as fast as you can."

"Aye, sir."

The USS *Columbia* had been thought destroyed before the battle of Guam, several weeks earlier. But in reality, *Columbia* had only been slightly damaged. In the confusion, and after suffering several casualties from a near-miss torpedo, Commander Wallace had ordered his crew to bottom the submarine. It was a last-ditch effort, and his only option.

Miraculously, the Chinese had not reattacked the *Columbia*. And they hadn't redetected it either, even though the sonar techs had picked up multiple sonobuoys and dippers being deployed above them for the hours after bottoming.

After waiting a full eighteen hours for the Chinese fleet to pass by, and another few hours of repairs, the *Columbia* had surfaced and communicated with COMSUBPAC. They were given new orders to head towards Pearl Harbor and had relayed their experience.

Apparently, the new Chinese ASW equipment had a hard time detecting submarines that were bottomed. This information could be useful. But in the Pacific, there were few places with depths shallow enough to perform the maneuver.

Johnston Atoll was one of them.

Quick commands, barely above a whisper, were issued and echoed throughout the submarine's bridge. The vessel began vibrating and then went still, free from the friction of the ocean's surface. They had been preparing for this moment for days. There were eight fast-attack submarines bottomed on the underwater terrain surrounding Johnston Atoll. A combination of *Virginia*-, *Los Angeles*–, and *Seawolf*-class submarines.

They had been there for days, waiting for this moment.

Over the past few hours, watching the sonar returns with excruciating concentration, Commander Wallace observed dozens of lethal Chinese warships steaming overhead. Surrounding them. With each dipping sonar ping, with each sonobuoy splash, the submarine crews winced in pained silence.

Yet they waited.

They waited for the sounds of more pings, closer in, followed shortly by the high-pitched noise of a torpedo's propeller and range-finding system that they had borne witness to near Guam.

But that moment never came.

The submarines blended into the ocean floor and remained undetected as the Chinese fleet steamed by, hundreds of feet above.

Then, at last, the sign had come. SUS buoy explosions. Their signal to begin. The submarine crews sprang to life as their commanders began issuing orders. Each submarine had a certain section of water assigned to it.

As the submarines rose silently off the ocean floor, their screws turned and propelled them forward. Slowly. Barely a few knots. But each of the hunter-killers made their way towards their assigned waterspace. Torpedo doors opened. Eager captains gave the final attack orders.

Within a two-minute period, thirty Mark 48 Advanced Capability torpedoes began racing through the sea, each headed towards separate targets.

The US Navy submarine force was about to have its revenge.

* * *

Victoria heard a warning tone coming through the earpieces in her helmet. She saw the flashing master caution lights blinking in front of her and then felt a shudder as her aircraft released chaff and flares. Countermeasures for the supersonic surface-to-air missiles that one of the Chinese ships must have just fired at them.

A blur of white zoomed by outside the cockpit. It exploded in a burst of gray and yellow a few hundred feet to their left. Victoria was rocked as the shockwave hit the airframe of the helicopter. The sound was muffled, but still sickening.

"*Shit*," muttered Plug. He was already maneuvering, his training kicking in, pulling the helicopter into a series of hard turns.

Victoria realized that air was coming in from a small crack in her window. Then she noticed a searing white-hot pain in her shoulder. She was bleeding through her flight suit.

"*Motherfucker*." She winced in pain as she examined the wound. "AW1, everyone okay back there?"

"Yes, ma'am. We're all good. That was pretty close."

Victoria ignored the pain in her shoulder and spoke over the external comms. "Magnum, flight, check in."

"Two."

"Three."

There was a pause, then one of the other helicopters' pilots radioed. "Dash Four was hit. No survivors."

Plug continued maneuvering the helicopter, expending more chaff and flares, the other two aircraft in close formation behind them. His voice was strained as he said, "What do you want us to do, Boss?"

Victoria closed her eyes, forcing away the feeling of dread and guilt that crept up inside her. She held down the external microphone switch. "Are you sure?"

"Affirm," replied the voice of the other helicopter's pilot. "They took a direct hit."

"Roger."

Victoria checked the digital map that was being beamed to them from above. They were almost at the outer ring of Chinese warships. Their fuel would run out soon, but they still had a chance to make it to the atoll, or ditch close enough that a SAR asset might spot them.

Victoria turned her head to look out the right-side window. Her shoulder lit up in white-hot pain as she moved it, dark blood flowing from the wound. She could see a destroyer a few miles away. Two contrails of smoke floated in the air, reaching out towards them from the Chinese ship like long fingers of death. The remnants of the surface-to-air missiles it had just launched. Why weren't they finishing the job? Maybe they would.

"Maintain this heading."

"Roger."

Victoria looked at the map again. If they were able to get out of range of that destroyer, they might have a chance. But it had fired at them once. It knew they were there. Surely it would strike again.

She had to do something.

"Magnum flight, prep for a right turn and engagement of the nearest Chinese destroyer."

Plug looked up at her in surprise, then went back to his outside-the-cockpit scan, the water only twenty-five feet below, zooming by at over one hundred and twenty knots. He put in a shallow right turn.

Victoria said, "I've got the controls. Set up for a Hellfire shot."

"Roger, your controls."

"Magnum flight, spread out."

"Two."

"Three."

Plug's hands danced over his keypad. He yelled out the checklist steps, Victoria and the aircrewman in the back of the helicopters responding immediately. Then Plug gripped the hand control unit and used the forward-looking infrared camera to target the Chinese ship.

Radar warning tones began whining in Victoria's headset again as the Chinese ship used its air defense radars to target them.

"Fire at will, Magnum…"

She hadn't even finished her call when Plug said, "Bruiser away!" A tongue of yellow flame shot out from their left side and rose up into the sky. The laser designator from the FLIR was aimed right at the Chinese destroyer.

Another missile left the rails. Then two more as Plug emptied their stores. More Hellfire missiles fired from the other two helicopters.

Twelve AGM-114 missiles popped up into the sky and then rocketed down into their target, the shaped charges, which had been designed as antitank weapons, exploding right before impact, turning themselves into a small stream of molten-hot metal and shooting through various parts of the warship.

One of the missiles missed. Each of the others hit the target, in various locations. Multiple yellow-orange explosions, in rapid succession. The bridge, the centrally located combat information center, the engines, and the fuel cells were all hit. One of the missiles ignited a torpedo in the ship's storage locker. Secondary explosions detonated in the center of the ship. A gray-white tower of wreckage and seawater flew up into the sky.

"Magnum flight, form back up. Continue outbound."

"Two."

"Three. And, Lead, FYI, we're getting pretty low on fuel. Might have another twenty mikes."

"Copy."

Plug leveled out the wings on an outbound heading.

And that was when she saw the other ship. Victoria's eyes went wide. She looked down at the map, and there it was. How had she missed that on the digital map? And they had just fired all of their weapons…

Plug saw what she was looking at. "You want me to take a different heading?"

"No, that'll just put us closer to the rest of the fleet. We need to keep heading this direction. Otherwise, we won't have enough fuel to make it."

She stared at the ship. It was just on the horizon. They probably weren't on radar yet. But the other warship must have told them they were there. And…

As she watched the Chinese warship on the horizon, its midsection lifted in a giant geyser of gray-and-white water and then fell rapidly, the hull snapping in two. The two separate pieces of ship angled upward at an impossible angle, sinking lower and lower into the water.

Plug's mouth was open. "What the hell?"

Victoria felt a surge of relief wash through her. "The American submarines are here."

* * *

Admiral Song watched in horror as he received word of the American submarines' surprise attack.

"Admiral, the *Changchun* and the *Jinan* have both been hit."

"Casualties?"

The young officer shook his head. "Both destroyers have been sunk, Admiral."

Admiral Song gripped the table in front of him. Two more destroyers, sunk within moments. Hundreds of sailors dead, and with them, the ability to defend against further attacks.

The Chinese fleet was now surrounding the waters around Johnston Atoll, still heading north towards Hawaii. But at this rate, they could not continue.

"We must consider all of our options."

"Yes, Admiral."

Out of the one hundred and two ships they had had when the battle had begun, a third had been destroyed, including the Jiaolong-class ship. If they kept heading north, they would come closer to the range at which American surface-based antiship missiles could reach them. And closer to the American air bases on Hawaii from which they could launch further attacks.

The old Chinese naval officer felt sick at the thought, but they needed to turn around. To regroup out of harm's way. He studied the battlespace. With the destruction of the Jiaolong, their overwhelming advantage was gone. While the Americans had kept their surface ships far away, his fleet was now quite susceptible to attacks from both the air and subsurface.

Still, their fleet was formidable in size and capability. If he proceeded with the attack now, they could do much damage to Hawaii's military bases and finish the job that the Chinese had started a few weeks earlier. Perhaps he could land his forces here at Johnston Atoll and fortify his position.

He calculated his chances of success. With the American submarines here, that would be suicide.

He wiped sweat from his brow. "Why is it so hot in here?"

"Sir, we have lost control of some of our systems. The heater has been put on."

"The heater? Why? What...?" He paused. "What do you mean, we have lost control of our systems. Which systems?"

"We have been under some sort of cyberattack over the past hour, sir. The cyberwarfare officer is saying that they are doing the best they can, but..."

The digital display that the admiral had been studying went dark.

"What just happened?"

"I will find out, sir."

The minion scurried off as another ran up to the admiral.

"Admiral, I regret to inform you that the *Kunlun Shan* has been sunk."

Admiral Song felt weak at that. The *Kunlun Shan* was an amphibious ship. A troop transport, with over one thousand soldiers and sailors aboard. He closed his eyes, sighing.

"We must turn south. We must turn around."

"Admiral?"

"Give the order."

"Yes, sir."

"Regroup two hundred kilometers to the south. We can—"

His head of air operations approached. "Sir, our fighters are ready to attack, but the strike officer has not yet fired his cruise missiles. Your orders were to accomplish a simultaneous strike, sir."

Admiral Song did all he could to control his rage. Everything was failing at once. No one was offering solutions or good news. Everything was a problem. A failure. A catastrophe.

He screamed at the strike officer to approach. "Why have we not fired our cruise missiles at Hawaii yet?"

"There is no excuse, sir. I...I..."

Admiral Song was dripping with sweat now. It was sweltering in the combat operations center. "Say what the reason is!"

"Sir, we have come under cyberattack. We have not been able to fire our cruise missiles."

Admiral Song's mouth hung open. This was total and utter failure to fight. Jinshan and the others would have him shot, if he lived through the next few hours. He tried to think. They had to do *something*.

"Tell the fighters to proceed with the attack."

One of the junior officers said, "Sir, the air defense officer is reporting that another wave of enemy air contacts is approaching."

Admiral Song looked up at air defense screen. "Show me."

"They are staying two hundred kilometers away, sir. They have been identified as American B-52 bombers. They are remaining just out of our air defense range."

"They are not firing?"

"No, Admiral."

"Why are they just circling us that far out?" one of the officers asked.

Then the admiral realized what they were doing. It made him want to vomit.

Thirty B-52s flew the mission, supported by JSTARS and F-15 fighter escorts. Inside each B-52 were eighteen Quickstrike ER weapons. The Quickstrikes were essentially mines with winglets. The bombers dropped their ordnance, which "flew" almost forty miles towards the Chinese fleet. This allowed the bombers to keep out of range of many of the surface-to-air missiles, which—now that the Jiaolong had been slain—were running in short supply.

The bombers laid minefields along huge swaths of ocean on either side of the Chinese fleet, forming a giant V. The minefields were cutting off the Chinese escape route, effectively sealing them in. The US attack submarines were inside the minefield perimeter, hunting and killing everything in range of their torpedoes.

Frigates that were positioned on the edge of the fleet's surface screen were the first to get a taste of the American mine warfare. Three Chinese frigates, on the southern side of the formation, were destroyed as they obeyed Admiral Song's ordered retreat.

This confirmed the admiral's worst fear. As the Chinese warships maneuvered to avoid the newly activated submarine threat, they ran into this wall of mines. They found that a minefield of unknown size and shape had cropped up all around their fleet.

Like someone had planned it that way. They had sailed into a trap.

"Recall our fighters," Admiral Song said. "We must continue to retreat."

"Through the minefields?"

"What choice do we have?"

The flight of six F-22s flew at super cruise. Supersonic airspeed without lighting off their fuel-guzzling afterburner. The AWACS command-and-control aircraft had already fed in the targeting information.

Twenty-two Chinese carrier-launched J-15 attack aircraft were flying towards Hawaii, and the F-22s engaged them before they were recalled.

The fight was short-lived.

A flight of F-18G Growlers jammed the Chinese aircraft as they approached. The Chinese threat warning was nonexistent. The F-22s each fired four AIM-120 missiles. The missiles streaked towards their targets at Mach 4.

All but one of the Chinese fighters was hit, the fifty-pound blast fragmentation warheads detonating only a few meters away from their targets. The lone remaining Chinese fighter's pilot realized he was in peril. He jettisoned his air-to-ground weapons and attempted to engage his yet-unseen attackers. He could just barely make out the silhouette of one of the American fighters when his aircraft was destroyed by gunfire from one of the F-22s. He hadn't known it was there.

* * *

Victoria had flown her helicopter back from the ship on every one of her deployments. After six to nine months at sea, it was always a joy to see American land on the horizon and know that you were going to return to it.

But she had never been so happy to see land as she was now. Johnston Atoll lay ahead of them. The only problem was that she wasn't one hundred percent sure they were going to make it.

"Fuel low light's steady now, Boss," Plug said with worry in his voice.

"I know..."

The island wasn't much more than a flat rectangular patch of white sand that surrounded a long blacktop runway. There were a few charred buildings and hunks of twisted metal—the remains of the American air defense team that had been positioned on the island. Smoldering ash and several destroyed aircraft. The Chinese must have hit them recently. Victoria wondered if they had been sacrificed by the American war planners as part of the ruse.

The second helicopter in the formation called over the radio, "Dash Two is on fumes. Not sure we'll get there, but we can see the beach."

Victoria replied, "Just another minute. Single up engines if you have to."

"We *did*."

Plug looked out the window and depressed his transmit switch. He said, "Try going like this." He began bobbing his body forward in rapid movements, pretending that it would make the helicopter move faster.

The pilot from Dash Two gave him the bird. "Some guys have no sense of humor."

"Lead, Dash Two, we might need to ditch."

"Roger," was all Victoria said. It was their call. She was going for land.

Just a little closer. They were *so close*. The aquamarine ocean reflected bright sunlight below. The water was getting shallower. Dark patches of seaweed and coral reef. She felt a burning angst in her chest, an urge to get this damned aircraft on deck before it ran out of fuel. She winced in pain as she made a control input that caused her shoulder muscle to twitch. Plug still hadn't realized she'd been hit—the blood was all down her right arm, out of his view—and she hadn't bothered to say anything. A part of her knew that it was wrong to keep this information from him, but another part of her said, *Suck it up, Victoria. We're almost home*.

A fireball of orange-yellow caught her eye in the distance. It was thousands of feet up in the sky. An air battle. Now several more fireballs were appearing near the first. Black smoke trailed pieces of aircraft as they fell to the earth. She didn't know whose they were. She didn't care. All she cared about was this island straight in front of her.

"Almost there, Boss. You good or you want me to take it?"

Plug had a suspicious tone in his voice now. The smart-ass tone was gone. He was leaning forward, trying to peer at her shoulder.

He said, "My controls."

"I'm fine."

"*No, Boss*. My controls. You're hurt."

He grabbed his cyclic and collective, and she could feel his inputs transferred to her own. She let go. "You've got it." Her voice was tired and so was the rest of her.

"Fifty feet." Plug switched his radio and made a call to the other helicopters. "I'm lining us up for the taxiway. Going for a running landing to keep some speed on in case we flame out."

"Two."

"Three."

Victoria watched as the paved taxiway grew larger and larger in the glass chin bubble window at her feet.

"Parking brake."

"Off."

They touched down and slowed down, palm trees and unkept island brush on either side of the runway. Within a few minutes, all three helicopters had taxied to a flight line and shut down. Victoria got out of the aircraft and looked around. She was dizzy, and her muscles were cramped.

"Holy shit, Boss! You're bleeding bad! Fetternut, you got a first aid kit?"

The rescue swimmer sat her down on the cabin floor of their parked aircraft. She had removed her helmet and taken her arm out of her flight suit—gingerly. A large gash was in her shoulder. Dark red blood and pus emanated from the center.

AWR1 Fetternut said, "I'm gonna fix you up, Boss. You just relax."

She nodded, looking off into the distance. Her hair was a wet mess of tangles and oil. Her ears were ringing, as they always did after a long mission. She removed her leather flight gloves and wiped her eyes with her left hand. Her right was still as her aircrewman cleaned and bandaged her wounded shoulder.

The SEALs and aircrews were in a circle in the center of the three shut-down helicopters. Plug was dragging something over there. She wasn't sure what it was, but it looked heavy. A few of them laughed when they saw it. Then she realized what he'd done. Plug had stored a Yeti cooler on her bird. He removed several bottles of liquor, plastic cups, and a few bottles of soda.

The SEAL team commander approached her. "What's your boy doing?"

She rolled her eyes, feeling like a mother who could never take her eyes off the problem child. "I don't know."

They motioned Plug to come over.

"You brought alcohol on the mission? I mean...how does something like that even enter your mind?"

He said, "What? I...I just figured if we lived, we'd want to celebrate."

Victoria said, "What if we need to fly again?"

"Boss, look at this place. We're *done* flying. The only thing that's gonna happen now is we either get rescued or starve here."

"They could take us back to Hawaii and ask us to fly again."

Plug smirked. "Well, not right away. That would violate my precious crew rest." He pointed at the beach, which was only fifty yards away. "Or if the Chinese show up...wouldn't it be better to be a little buzzed?"

The SEAL commander said, "Kid's got a point." He looked out over the waves. The island was deathly quiet, save for the crash of waves and the distant roar of fighter jets. "I tell you what. Get everyone a drink and round them up over here."

Victoria shot the SEAL commander a questioning look. He shrugged.

AWR1 finished patching up Victoria's shoulder. "There you go, Boss. That's the best I can do. You should see a doctor when we get back. I think they'll need to pick some more pieces out of there, unfortunately."

"Thanks."

The DEVGRU SEALs and helicopter crews gathered around. Everyone raised their plastic cups as he said, "In memory of the warriors who perished beside us today."

Cups were raised in front of tired faces. Plug and a few others were in a celebratory mood, but most were somber. Some refrained from partaking in the toast, but most took sips of Plug's whiskey in respectful silence.

Victoria felt the warmth of the liquor hit her belly and was instantly light-headed. Her stomach was empty, which didn't help.

She announced to the group, "Stay close. We should expect a SAR attempt within the next few hours."

Nods and smiles. Somber eyes. A group mourning the loss of their brothers but elated to be alive, all at once.

Victoria said, "Screw it." She walked over to the cooler and filled her cup, then headed over to the beach with a few of the other aviators. They drank and relived the mission, watching the waves and distant air battle. Wondering what would come next in the day. And in the world.

39

Jinshan stood on a wooden deck overlooking the mountains. His security chief had strenuously objected to the outdoor excursion, but Jinshan had overruled him. It was only a thirty-minute walk, and unplanned. He needed to clear his mind.

He took deep breaths, looking out over the distant rolling green hills, remnants of cloud filling the valley. There was nothing out here for hundreds of miles but this network of military bunkers. It had taken thousands of men years to make this structure. It had been sold as a doomsday bunker, but Jinshan had earmarked the project for a more planned scenario.

Running this war.

He had made sure that the builders had installed the best communications and computing equipment. Redundant systems. Adequate quarters not for just surviving, but for living and working over a prolonged period. Still, one needed to see daylight every once in a while.

He sighed. Was this all for naught?

"You wanted to see me, Chairman."

Jinshan didn't bother to turn. General Chen's voice was distinct. At once arrogant and ignorant. Not a good combination.

Jinshan didn't often make mistakes in choosing personnel, but he hadn't thought of General Chen's position as one that needed anything more than a figurehead. A warm body to serve as his puppet. One that he could control.

But Jinshan hadn't counted on his cancer and treatments lowering his strength so much. His weakness had left him out of commission just long enough for this oaf to stumble into making a real decision. And that decision had cost them. If the carriers of their Northern Fleet had remained in play, they might have been able to overcome the American air attack on the Southern Fleet. But now...

General Chen said, "The *Liaoning* has made it through the minefield with minimal damage."

"And the ships that were escorting her?"

"A quarter of them have made it through."

A quarter. Seventy-five percent losses. Unthinkable only a few days ago.

"The fleet is heading to Dinghai for replenishment and repairs."

Now Jinshan turned. "You say this as if it is good news."

"It is better than the alternative." He looked as if he regretted saying it as soon as it came out.

"*What* alternative?"

The old general was wide-eyed, but he continued. "It is better than if the carrier had been *sunk*." He still actually thought himself faultless, Jinshan realized.

Jinshan's face contorted in disgust. "If you had not ordered our other carrier fleet to attack Hawaii early, this battle could have turned out differently."

Even General Chen knew to be quiet now. The look in Jinshan's eyes was the last vision of many men.

Jinshan waved him away. "Get out of my sight."

Jinshan thought he heard a whimper as the general walked

away. He almost had relieved Chen on the spot, but he would need to find a replacement first. Someone trustworthy and competent. A truly rare combination.

"Mr. Chairman, it has been thirty minutes, sir. We should go." His security detail waited on the footpath to escort him back into his subterranean hell.

"Very well." As he hobbled along the rocky path, he thought of Lena Chou.

Jinshan hated losing the battle, but a battle was not a war. He still had cards to play. His mind was already thinking up ways to overcome the loss.

But the thought of losing *her*. That hurt just as much. And to think that her ignorant father had had a part in it. She was Jinshan's special creation. His prima ballerina. It was such a shame to lose her.

* * *

Lena sat in a small rectangular room, resting her elbows on a bare white table. Concrete floors. One long mirror taking up a full wall. She knew what was on the other side of that mirror. She used to sit in one of those seats.

God help her, Lena felt awful. Maybe she had caught something. Some kind of stomach bug. Or maybe it was this same feeling of anxiousness that she had been dealing with for the past few weeks. Whatever it was, she wanted to puke.

The door opened and in came a middle-aged white woman. Lena recognized her. She knew her by reputation, though not personally. Susan Collinsworth was a career operations officer within the Agency. She was hard-nosed and detailed.

And the look on her face told Lena that Collinsworth had information.

"What is it?" Lena asked. Her hands were cuffed, so she blew away the errant strand of long black hair that flowed down her face.

Susan's expression changed slightly as the move exposed more of Lena's facial burn scars.

Susan said, "The Chinese think you're dead."

Lena stared unblinking. "So?"

Susan placed a manila folder on the table. She tapped it. "There's something in here you'll want to know about."

"So then tell me."

"It may come as a shock."

"Nothing shocks me anymore."

Susan said, "We can help you."

Lena let out a short laugh. "Unlikely."

Susan turned the folder around and opened it to reveal two black pictures. Lena stared at the images, her mind trying to fit them into place. At first, she thought they were satellite images or some type of acoustic signature, but that wasn't it. What the hell was she looking at? They almost looked like...

Lena's face went pale. "I think I'm going to throw up."

Susan said, "That's to be expected, in your condition."

This couldn't be possible. She shook her head, staring at the images, then looking up at Susan's face. The woman was calm. Lena knew that she was telling the truth. Because...because Lena herself had known it, deep inside.

"How..." Her voice faltered. She took a deep breath, then said, "Is it healthy?"

"Our doctor says that it is a healthy boy. So you really didn't know?"

She shook her head, anger and shame rising up within her.

Lena was looking at the sonogram, breathing heavier. Then she stopped breathing as the thought occurred to her. She looked up at Susan. *Does she know who the father is?*

Susan said, "This changes things for you, Lena."

Lena stared back across the table, a new set of emotions forming. A desire to protect this being inside her womb. And a most unfamiliar sensation: fear.

Susan said, "Now let's talk about ways that we can work together."

40

San Diego, California
Two weeks later

Chase sipped through the froth of his IPA and then guzzled down big gulps of cold beer.

Victoria watched him with one eyebrow arched. "Easy there, tiger."

They sat in an open-air beer garden. Green trees and curated lawns, flagstone flooring, white-cloth table umbrellas and finished wooden lawn chairs. The place was full. Probably one of the first weekends that business was coming back, now that electricity and utilities had been restored.

It had been two weeks since the Battle of Johnston Atoll, as it was now known. The Chinese attack had been repelled, and the United States was on the mend. The patrons of the brewery looked happy. You could almost forget there was a war going on. But everyone was talking about some aspect of it.

David arrived at the table holding two more full glasses and placing one in front of his sister.

"What's this place called again?" David asked. "It's pretty great."

"Stone Brewery. It's good stuff," Chase said.

Victoria raised her glass. "To Dad."

The other two followed suit. "To Dad," they said in unison and clinked glasses.

They ordered plates of hot appetizers and burgers. They spent most of the evening recounting tales of the past few weeks and remembering their father. It felt good to be together, even if it was only temporary.

"Where will you go now?" Victoria asked.

David said, "We're both headed back to Florida tomorrow morning. I'll be staying there, working on the same team I've been with."

She punched his arm. "Pretty vague."

David smiled. "You know the saying. Loose lips..."

"Yeah, yeah."

Chase said, "What about you?"

Victoria shrugged. "Your guess is as good as mine. I report to the Wing tomorrow." The Wing was the unit that commanded multiple squadrons of aircraft based in a given region. "I guess they'll give me my next set of orders when I check in."

David stared out into the distance. After a moment of silence, he turned back to his siblings. "Whatever happens, let's enjoy the time we have together."

* * *

Sign up for the Reader List and be the first to know about new releases and special offers from Andrew Watts.

Join Andrew Watts' Reader List at AndrewWattsAuthor.com

ALSO BY ANDREW WATTS

The War Planners Series

The War Planners

The War Stage

Pawns of the Pacific

The Elephant Game

Overwhelming Force

Max Fend Series

Glidepath

The Oshkosh Connection

Books available for Kindle, print, and audiobook. To find out more about the books or Andrew Watts, go to andrewwattsauthor.com.

GLIDEPATH: MAX FEND #1

Charles Fend, the billionaire CEO of Fend Aerospace, is only days away from launching the world's first autonomous commercial airliner when a mysterious cyber attack threatens to cripple the project. But who is responsible?

Is it the wealthy ex-KGB agent, Pavel Morozov, who has shown up from a past Charles had long-forgotten?

Or was it Charles' own son Max—now on the run from the FBI after he was accused of sending corporate secrets to a criminal enterprise?

And just what is hiding inside the top secret CIA file on Max Fend? The one that even his FBI investigator isn't allowed to see?

GLIDEPATH is a pulse-pounding race to uncover the truth, before it comes crashing down from above...

Get your copy today at AndrewWattsAuthor.com

ABOUT THE AUTHOR

Andrew Watts graduated from the US Naval Academy in 2003 and served as a naval officer and helicopter pilot until 2013. During that time, he flew counter-narcotic missions in the Eastern Pacific and counter-piracy missions off the Horn of Africa. He was a flight instructor in Pensacola, FL, and helped to run ship and flight operations while embarked on a nuclear aircraft carrier deployed in the Middle East.

Today, he lives with his family in Ohio.

SIGN UP FOR NEW BOOK ALERTS AT ANDREWWATTSAUTHOR.COM

From Andrew: Thanks so much for reading my books. Be sure to join my Reader List. You'll be the first to know when I release a new book.

You can follow me or find out more here:
andrewwattsauthor.com

35683316R00253

Made in the USA
San Bernardino, CA
13 May 2019